I0719424

For Dad, yet another of a handful of early readers who
provided me with the feedback I cherished most

ORDER'S TRIALS

BOOK TWO

A DANCE WITH DEATH

AUSTIN WINDSOR

ORDER'S TRIALS

BOOK TWO

A DANCE
WITH DEATH

AUSTIN WINDSOR

CHAPTER 1

"Hey! Guard!"

The guard, half-asleep until that point, stood up and walked to Elaeínn in her cell. She was hunched over, clutching her midriff.

"I need more medicine. Can you please get me some?" she pleaded.

"Who do you think you are, wretch?" the guard spoke. "Now shut up and behave."

"I'm not going to shut up until I get something to kill this fucking pain!" she snapped. "Have you ever been hit with a crossbow bolt? Probably not, given your job is to stare at us for twelve hours a day. Let me tell you—not a pleasant experience! Not one I would happily relive! And given that the medics only barely healed me up with their magic, rather than waste precious energy on a full procedure, it still feels like I've got the bloody thing lodged in me! So, if you want me to shut up, get me some fucking drugs!"

"If these bars weren't between us your face would be getting a new bruise," the guard retorted.

"If these bars weren't between us, I'd be out of here. I'd run so far and so fast and hopefully that'll be a reality if my good-for-nothing dragon friend finally turns up. It's happening soon, I'm telling you."

"If I get you some medicine, you'll not utter a word for at least twenty-four hours. Got it?"

"Yes sir, absolutely sir."

"Fine. Don't go anywhere."

The guard turned and left the dungeon, sighing. As his armoured footsteps faded into the distance, Elaeínn sprang into action.

"Velrin!" she whispered in a hushed tone. "Give me your hands!"

Accompanying her in her cell was a man—dark bronze hair, typically High Elven olive skin, grey eyes. A former professor of destructive magic, he had joined the FTA before the battle for Fallía and was captured with the rest of the castle's surrendered inhabitants who hadn't been able to escape through a portal in time.

Velrin stirred as Elaeínn resorted to shaking him awake.

"What are you trying now?" he asked resignedly.

"To get us out, obviously. Hurry up, we don't have much time. Give me your hands."

Velrin extended his hands. He, unlike Elaeínn, was wearing shackles entwined with hevula, the magical inhibitor.

Elaeínn reached down for the one of the tankards they had been given by the guards and snapped the handle from it. A particular nail in one of the door's hinges could be pulled out effortlessly and with these makeshift lockpicks she attempted to free Velrin from the shackles.

The keyhole in the shackles was much smaller than she remembered, but the implements could just barely fit. And with more effort than she was used to, having been out of practice for three months, she was able to produce a click and the shackles fell from Velrin's wrists.

"Nice work," he mused, a grin crossing his face.

"Can you unlock the cell now?"

"Not quite unlock. This will take a few minutes."

"Be quick about it!"

Velrin moved over to the mechanism barring access to their freedom and placed his hands against the side facing into the cell. He closed his eyes and began to mutter a spell under his breath.

Elaeínn couldn't quite understand what he was doing, but she looked around at the other prisoners, who had grown very interested in the escape attempt. Many of those locked up were also from Fallía.

As the agonisingly long minutes passed, Elaeínn began to understand Velrin's spell, judging by the sweltering heat emanating from the lock. The door finally swung open, just as the sound of footsteps and jangling armour returned.

"Hurry, let's go!" Elaeínn whispered, rushing from the cell, staying light on her feet. The small dungeon had one exit – the stairs from which they could hear the guard returning. Elaeínn took one last sorrowful glance at her allies and mouthed, "I'll come back for you!" before pressing Velrin up the stairs.

The stairs were steep, yet they raced up. Each bound sent a jolt of pain through Elaeínn's torso, but she fought through it.

Velrin was quick to utter a spell as they careened into the guard. Lightning bolts shot from his fingers and the guard collapsed, convulsing, before he could even shout for help. They continued promptly upwards, but not before Elaeínn collected the dropped container of medicine from the floor and shoved it into her undergarments.

Before long, the stairs gave way to an exit into a dingy, run-down room. Velrin motioned for them both to stop, and Elaeínn squeezed past him to be able to peek for herself.

The room in which they had arrived was occupied by a pair of unenthusiastic soldiers, both of which appeared to be dozing off, and a maid. It wasn't an excessively large space, but there were doorways leading away on their left and right.

"What now?" Velrin asked.

"Can you, I don't know, pacify them or something?"

"No, not really."

"I guess we're running then. Come on!"

Elaeínn gave up on stealth and fled through the doorway on the right, spending no longer than a second in the room. Velrin followed, somewhat dazed, but kept pace.

"Excuse me!" the maid shouted. "Hey!"

It wasn't the escapees' footsteps which woke the guards but the maid's shouting as they rose, blinking, and gave chase.

The doorway Elaeínn had chosen led outside, but to a bridge between two towers, overlooking the castle's courtyard.

"Where the hell are we, Velrin?" Elaeínn called.

"I would say the North, if I had to guess!" Velrin stated, glancing around for the brief time they spent on the bridge before reaching the other tower.

"Halt, in the name of Vanad and the King!" one of the pursuing guards cried.

"Vanad?" Elaeínn questioned.

"No idea," Velrin said.

In the tower was another set of steep stairs and they flew down them. Instead of leading to an underground dungeon, however, these stairs stopped at an exit into the courtyard.

There were now more soldiers milling around and the escapees' profile was growing rapidly. Their pursuers were not being quiet, and soon they had more than two guards on their tail. They raced for the gate to find it on its way down—but not yet closed.

"Close the gate!" one of their pursuers called.

"We are closing the bloody gate!" one of the gatekeepers replied.

Elaeínn reached it before Velrin and slipped beneath the portcullis with ease, turning back to face her companion. Soldiers grabbed at his shoulders as he collapsed to the floor and rolled underneath, moments away from the spikes of the portcullis slicing him in two.

They glanced at each other before subsequently deciding to run.

"Open the gate! Open the gate!" the soldiers cried, staring angrily at the escaping prisoners.

"We are opening the bloody gate!"

"I can't keep this up forever, Elle," Velrin gasped, his pace slowing as they took off towards the forests ahead.

"We just need to reach the treeline and then we can steal some horses and find our way home."

"Home? What home? Fallía is gone. Berri is dead. The FTA is broken. Who is there left to put it back together?"

"Maybe you're right, Fallía is gone. But we can reclaim it. And we can reclaim more than that. But we're going to need the dwarves' help."

"The dwarves didn't help last time. We were slaughtered."

"Because the King is a spy. That's what Jaelaar implied, anyways."

They had placed at least two hundred metres between themselves and the soldiers before the gate finally opened enough to allow the chase to resume. The forest was nearing—nothing as thick or foreboding as the southern Darklight, but it would be enough to disappear.

The soldiers cried as they thundered after the pair, while other soldiers kept some distance and began to launch arrows in their direction, most of which sailed straight over their heads.

"Do they not have... any mages?" Elaeínn huffed, grasping her bandaged wound.

"That's why I was sure it was the North," Velrin responded. "These soldiers are far too lax for a warzone."

They breached the oak forest's treeline as an arrow thudded into a branch and continued to run, the terrain steepening. They were forced to slow as they ran downhill, dodging various natural obstacles and fighting to maintain their balance.

"There! A cave!" Elaeínn exclaimed, gesticulating towards a rocky hillside with a slim opening at its base, a stream flowing into it.

The soldiers had not managed to match the pace at which Elaeínn and Velrin had traversed into the gully and as such did not notice as they slipped through the crack in the stone wall and disappeared.

It was pitch-black inside the cave and Elaeínn stepped carefully forwards, feeling along the moist walls as she went. The sounds of the forest had dulled—the rustling of the trees and the singing of birds replaced with the steady trickle of the stream at their feet feeding into a larger opening ahead. The soldiers' clamouring fell quiet as they finally made their way into the gully but lost sight of the escapees.

"Can you give us some light or something?" Elaeínn whispered.

Velrin responded by pressing ahead and producing a small flame in his hand, giving off light similar in brightness to a candle. It illuminated the smooth walls, showing how they slowly widened as the cave burrowed further into the ground.

Continuing to tiptoe through the cave, the pair eventually emerged into a larger chamber with signs of further openings back into the forest. Sun shafts streamed through gaps in the roof and small patches of plant life decorated the otherwise bare clearing.

"Don't you know how to open portals? Why haven't we done that already?"

"I don't, actually. I'm a professor of destructive magic, not transportational."

"Former professor," Elaeínn quipped. "And who cares what you used to teach? Every mage I've ever known has been able to make portals! It's the most useful thing you can know!"

"Well, I never got around to it. So, we'll have to do things the old-fashioned way."

Elaeínn hopped down from the slightly elevated platform from which they had emerged, followed shortly thereafter by Velrin. After glancing quickly at their surroundings, they padded warily across the cavern towards an opening, the ground beneath it awash with golden sunlight.

Each step, although soft, sounded much louder than she knew it really was. Their every movement was made with exact precision, avoiding the stray pebbles and rotting branches strewn across the floor.

The soldiers' cries became faintly audible once again as they reached the cave's exit, but Elaeínn concluded there was no danger as she continued into the forest.

No longer fuelled by adrenaline, she keeled over and grabbed her abdomen, pain rippling through her body. She retrieved the stolen medicine and unclipped its lid, revealing a pasty grey substance with a particularly repulsive smell. She didn't think twice before scooping the paste out of the small container with her fingers and into her mouth. The taste was enough to prompt vomiting, but she covered her mouth and fought to keep it down. It was worth it—the pain immediately began to drain away.

Velrin had taken a position sitting atop a nearby rock. They had ended up in a small clearing at the precipice of another hill, overlooking much of the forest. From their position, they could see what they thought was the hill containing the cave, as well as the castle from which they had fled in the distance.

"I don't know what we're going to do," he concluded. "I have no idea where we are. I have no idea where the nearest town is. We're dressed in rags, we have no money, we have no contacts. If we go anywhere, we'll be arrested."

"Nonsense, we'll just go to some small village and steal some clothes and horses," Elaeínn decided.

"And what then?"

"We'll go to Hamatnar," she began. "We'll request an audience with someone powerful and we can let them know that the King is a spy. And then when the dwarves root him out, they'll win the war with ease. I'd be surprised if they weren't already."

"We just don't know anything, Elle," Velrin muttered. "We've been away for too long. Any number of things could have happened. Jaelaar will have been succeeded. Who by? We don't even know for sure if war will have started. What we do know is that we are fugitives who probably won't get thrown in prison the next time we get caught."

"Then we won't get caught. We fought for a noble cause. Sure, we suffered a terrible defeat. Maybe that was the nail in our coffin. But who doesn't admire an underdog?

"We can rebuild, Vel. We can return to the people and give them back the cause they so desperately need. We can rebuild, and this time, we'll be victorious."

Velrin pondered Elaeínn's words for a few moments before standing up.

"Alright," he exclaimed. "To Hamatnar, then."

CHAPTER 2

VIRILIA, SANSKAR

2 months before

"She's in here! Up the stairs! Quickly, kill the witch!"

The Virilian guards tore through the entrance to the house, one staying behind to bar the troubadour's access.

"She stole my sword and I'd very much like to retrieve it," Ferris protested.

"We will retrieve your sword. You must stay in safety. If there is a witch, she will be very dangerous," the guard blocking the door explained.

"Of course, sir," the bard seethed.

The guards weren't quiet about ransacking the house and numerous muffled comments could be heard about its contents. Equally audible were their disgruntled remarks about the lack of witches.

Some time passed and the guards returned, carrying tomes, alchemy reagents, potions, and Ferris's rapier.

"Excuse me, that one's mine," the bard said, clamouring to claim his sword.

"There was no witch inside," the leading guard spoke gruffly as the others handed over the rapier. "But certainly evidence of one."

"She must have teleported away, I reckon," Ferris deduced. "Probably to report back to her Miradosi overlords. A witch in the heart of Virilia! Who could have thought?"

"It is a grave discovery. I will be reporting to my superiors at once."

"Of course. I applaud your work, good sirs, you truly are the backbone of society."

The guards snorted and walked away in the direction of the palace.

A fine situation you've got yourself into here, Ferris, the troubadour thought, walking away from the house and back towards the port. *A fine one indeed. You'll only be able to speak to these people for how long? A couple days, did she say?*

Ferris had no intention of staying in Virilia and wasted no time in reaching the harbour, where he began to search for ships headed to Mirados. He spent an hour without success before he realised he was unlikely to ever find such passage.

"Well, shit," he muttered to himself, eyeing up a fish vendor's stall. He had no Sanskari money, so instead quickly swiped a smoked cod fillet while the vendor was distracted with another customer.

"Back to Kelmar, I suppose. But then what?"

A ship to Kelmar was a much more manageable objective and not long passed before he found a merchant offering passage aboard his cog, a sizeable single-masted ship.

"Good morning, sir." Ferris approached the merchant, who was standing at the gangplank, scribbling in a notebook. He looked up as the bard planted himself at the base of the plank.

"Can I help you?"

"Passage to Kelmar, correct? How much?"

"To Kalsefar, yes. Although I am running a little bit low on space so a further weight fee will apply on top of the normal rate—"

"Just how much is it?"

"Thirty-five pestas normal rate... plus the surcharge for extra weight at ten pestas... bringing the total to forty-five pestas."

"Yes, I can count, thank you. When are you leaving?"

"Within the hour. Will you be joining us?"

"Probably—give me some time, I'll be back."

Forty-five pestas. Where am I going to get forty-five pestas? Then again, do I need to pay?

Ferris retreated from the merchant's cog but didn't stay far away. And it didn't take him long to hatch a plan.

He walked back off the jetty and approached an aged beggar sitting out of the way of the dock's thoroughfare and revealed a small bag of Miradosi rions from his pocket.

"Excuse me, sir, would you like to help me with something?" Ferris asked, jingling the coins.

"What is it?" the beggar replied, eyes trained on the pouch of coins.

Ferris turned and gestured subtly to the merchant, who was now engaged in conversation with another man. "I need you to distract him."

"Why's that?"

"Am I paying you to ask questions?"

The beggar reached to grab the pouch and Ferris quickly pulled it away. "Oh, no. Payment comes after the job."

The beggar huffed and rose to his feet, joints audibly creaking. He then set off slowly towards the merchant, assuming an off-balance demeanour. Ferris stayed close behind.

"Oi, 'scuse me, mate!" the beggar said, addressing the merchant. His voice sounded entirely foreign to that which Ferris had heard only moments ago. The merchant shook his head and ignored the beggar.

"Oi, 'scuse me!" he pestered, walking even closer, at which point the merchant could no longer ignore him.

"Get back or I'm calling the guard, scum. Get away from me."

"No, you don't understand! I need to tell you something!"

"Get back or my guards will put you down themselves, blasted tramp!"

A pair of guards brandishing swords appeared on the gangplank, walking apprehensively towards the beggar. It was then that the beggar abruptly rushed towards the merchant and pushed him backwards into the sea.

The guards stormed forwards as the beggar turned tail and ran with surprising speed. Ferris used the moment to slip up the gangplank while the merchant struggled in the waters below, the beggar disappearing into the backstreets of Virilia.

He reached the deck to find a few paying passengers standing amongst a meagre arrangement of crates. The passengers didn't object as he began to untie and hoist the sail.

The guards returned from the back alleys as the merchant rescued himself from the water, climbing back onto the jetty. Ferris interrupted his hoisting of the sail and rushed over to the gangplank, the guards having nearly reached it. He kicked it off the ship's side and allowed it to clatter onto the jetty and then into the water below.

The merchant refused to give up and ordered his guards to jump onto the ship. They attempted as much, leaping remarkably far and managing to grasp the edge of the ship's deck. Ferris stamped on their exposed fingers and let them fall into the harbour. Blubbering, the merchant at last ran away in search of further help while Ferris finally unleashed the sail and then used his rapier to slice through the rope connecting the ship to the jetty. A sudden gust of wind ballooned the sail and Ferris assumed a position behind the wheel as they moved off from the harbour and into the Redwater Bay.

"Let's hope I pick this up quick," he muttered, sheathing his rapier and gazing into the open water. "To Mirados!"

CHAPTER 3

LETHAM DEREGOR

1 month before

The vampire's head did not resist as the scimitar's oiled blade split it in two. It was barely able to produce a scream—though as brief as it was, it was still mind-wrenchingly shrill.

"They didn't put up much of a fight," Nendar Varanus exclaimed. "Hopefully the rest won't either."

"This is your plan?" Lynn seethed. "You'll be fine, father, but you seem to forget I am without a crystal."

"Oh, I don't forget. But I don't change my plans to accommodate it, either."

They traipsed through the pitch-black halls of the vampire stronghold of Letham Deregor, pupils wide under the effect of a night vision spell. Neither Nendar nor Lynn had travelled to the stronghold before, and neither knew of its layout. They were relying purely on Nendar's ability to track Tregor's faint magical signature, a signature which had grown weaker and weaker over the duration of their journey.

Letham Deregor was like nothing either of them had ever seen. Its majesty, looming over the forest, rivalled that of castles and palaces of human civilisation—yet it was empty. And, Nendar thought, pointless.

"This corridor," Nendar said suddenly, turning to the right. "I think..."

His sword met the attacker before it could make contact and the vampire was slain in moments. Nendar stopped to inspect the body, turning it over with his boot and examining its teeth, which did not, as he had expected, end in points. It also carried a sword.

"These are nothing like Kalahar," Lynn remarked.

"They are lesser. They don't possess strength even close to rivalling his. Which is why we cannot let our guard down, because he is probably already here."

Nendar continued to lead Lynn towards Tregor's magical signature, moving ever further through the labyrinth and searching for what felt like hours. The scenery never changed—just stone walls, doors leading to empty rooms, ancient furniture. The air was musky and cold. They encountered a few other vampires and dispatched them with ease. Despite the ambushes, they felt no danger as they paved slowly towards what they assumed to be Tregor, feeling often as if they were going in circles. But eventually, after countless identical corridors, abandoned rooms, and fruitless explorations, their efforts paid off.

"There! That looks different!"

Nendar stepped into an open room. It was more like a hall than a room, given its size, and was open to many floors above, floors which Nendar and Lynn were certain they had already scoured. The hall's crowning feature was a chalk-etched pentagram in its centre. And levitating above the pentagram, silent, motionless, and kneeling, was the figure of Tregor Lopan.

"Tregor!" Nendar called thoughtlessly.

The sorcerer did not respond, and it was then that Nendar noticed the hevula shackles binding his hands together. He waved a hand in an attempt to release the shackles, but his spell had no effect. Bewildered, he tried again, to the same result.

"What in the world?" he mused, attempting once more to release the shackles. And he was once more presented with the same predictable outcome.

"It's devious, isn't it?" the voice said. The guttural, baritone, immediately recognisable voice. "Your spell would have definitely worked, had I not placed him in the pentagram."

Kalahar appeared a level above and looked down upon the magicians. He then leapt over the railing and landed before them with a flourish.

"What have you done with him, Kalahar?" Nendar seethed, brandishing his sword.

Kalahar said nothing, only assuming a quizzical expression and staring at the motionless Tregor, and then back at Nendar, repeating this a few times.

"Let him go," Nendar hissed.

"Why would I do that?" Kalahar retorted innocently. "He intruded upon my territory. It is only my right to defend it. You would do much the same with your empire, no? But while I am only defending my territory, you actively expand yours. At least I am not practicing the same."

"I didn't come for a lecture, vampire." Nendar scowled. "How did you defeat him?"

"With relative ease. He was overconfident. He was unprepared. I hardly even touched him, because I knew he would draw you here if I left him alive."

Nendar stepped apprehensively forwards, maintaining eye contact with the unmoving Kalahar.

"What even are your motives?" he asked, shaking his head. "None of your actions make a scrap of sense. What is the point of this place? It's empty! What use do vampires have of a stronghold? You aren't coming under attack any time soon!"

"It is majestic, though, isn't it?" Kalahar remarked. "Even just as a feat of architecture I think it a terribly wonderful creation."

"What about this, vampire," Lynn finally broke her silence. "We stop behaving like enemies. You work with us again. We can help each other achieve our mutual goals. We would be much stronger together than divided as we are now."

Kalahar chuckled. "Tried and tested, dear Lynn. I won't be going back. It also wouldn't help that our mutual goals are somewhat... at odds with each other, would that be reasonable to say? Hell, even your own ideals are at odds with one another. It's no wonder the Council has fallen apart in recent years. There is nothing to unite you."

Lynn stepped forwards to join her father, Kalahar glancing casually between them.

"Are we done here?" Kalahar asked.

"We will be done once you free Tregor," Nendar asserted.

"And then you will attempt to kill me as a trio? Futilely, of course, because it's impossible. No, Nendar. Tregor will be staying here for the time being."

Nendar gritted his teeth and eyed the elder Tregor Lopan. The way his eyes were shut so tight as if he was pressing them, the way his chest didn't rise or fall with each breath, the wrinkles he allowed to exist.

"I've grown tired of our conversation now, Varanus. Now, would you like to choose your exit destination, or shall it be random?"

Nendar acted with a movement so swift he appeared as a blur. His arms traced a portal as he spiralled through the air and grabbed the sorcerer from within the pentagram, launching him through the portal with a quick burst of might. And then he, just as quickly, leapt through it as well.

*

The portal disappeared almost as quickly as it had been opened and Lynn was left alone with the vampire in the lonely stronghold of Letham Deregor.

"Well, would you look at that," Kalahar mused. "A trade."

Lynn exasperatedly attempted to trace a portal of her own, but the rift she was able to create was immediately closed. The vampire's hand was raised as he walked towards her, grinning deviously.

"No, I don't think you understand," he said, quashing another attempt, more strained than the first, to open a portal. "This is your new place of residence. What has just happened is a transaction. And given your weakness without your crystal, you'd best not waste your energy. Especially as I won't be tiring anytime soon."

"Bastard!" she shouted, attempting one last futile time to open a portal. Kalahar's expression remained unchanged, nonchalant.

"I will let you go, eventually," he claimed. "But some events must first run their courses."

He clenched his fist and Lynn lost control of her limbs as she rose into the air, her neck snapping back, her arms and legs extending. She levitated to the centre of the room and was restrained with another pair of hevula shackles appearing from what seemed like thin air.

15

The vampire released her and she attempted to free herself, but her attempts at magic were killed by the shackles and her attempts at movement were killed by the pentagram.

"Welcome, dear Lynn," the vampire spoke, "to Letham Deregor."

CHAPTER 4

MERANA, MIRADOS

1 month before
Richard trudged along the dreary harbour in search of the largest ship he could find. The country had broken down following the King's assassination, and Richard had Tregor Lopan's blood on his mind. But that was only secondary to his main objective.

"Passage to Santeros?" he asked one sailor busy loading crates onto a galleon.

"Nope," they replied bluntly.

Richard continued looking, though none of the other ships quite matched his expectations for one intending to sail across the Great Sea. Eventually, he resigned his search following a smattering of rejections from other ships, all of which had been heading north. He wasn't surprised—most Miradosi people probably didn't know Santeros existed. Even he had been unaware until the day he had met Elton Redwinter.

Resigning from the harbour, the bounty hunter searched for a new tavern in which to drown his sorrows. Upon entering the high street, the yellow façade of the Canary immediately stole his attention, as it did most days—he had been in a few times, hoping to find Ferris. Though with each passing day, the bard failed to appear, and Richard grew less and less hopeful that he had survived Virilia. Regardless, he thought he would try his luck once more.

The tavern was lit with candles atop sconces on the yellow walls as well as braziers hanging from the ceiling. Richard thought it a veritable miracle that the tavern hadn't been ransacked by thieves, though Ferris employed security to patrol the surrounding area.

"An ale, please," Richard mused, absentmindedly staring out the window and placing three rions on the counter.

The tavern was mostly empty, so Richard had plenty of choice for seating. He opted for a place by the window and solemnly sipped his ale.

"Is that who I think it is?"

A jubilant voice shattered the monotony and Richard turned to see him, dressed not in his signature outfit but in more hushed blues and blacks.

"Master Ordowyn!" Ferris boomed, disturbing the few day drinkers settled in various corners of the tavern.

"Ferris!" Richard exclaimed in bewilderment. "Where have you been?"

"Quite the journey, my friend, quite the journey!" he continued loudly, before settling into a seat next to Richard with a drink of his own. "I'm sure you remember our parting back in the Sanskari capital," he then said quietly. "Well, first I hijacked a ship at the port. It's actually hitched up down at the harbour—you might have seen it. There were some passengers aboard who I took with me who were... dissatisfied, to say the least. I dropped them off at Kalsefar, as was the ship's original destination, then headed for here. Some bad weather, a near miss with a Sanskari patrol, and a touch of scurvy later, here I am! But what about you, my friend? Tell me what happened to you!"

Richard's account was much longer than Ferris's, and the bard indulged in several tankards throughout, though the bounty hunter omitted information about what happened after the cataclysm.

"And now I need to find Kalahar, because..." he faltered.

"Because?"

"I never finished learning. And he's the only viable teacher for what I need."

Ferris cast a suspicious gaze over Richard as he downed the remainder of a tankard and stood up. "You're not telling me something, Ordowyn."

"You won't understand."

"On the contrary," Ferris rebuked. "There were plenty of things you just told me now which I would have plenty of reason not to understand, or to outright deny took place. But I'm very much interested in your story, Richard, so I'm willing to listen in a way which is very much reserved for those for whom I have a great deal of respect. So please, tell me the full story."

"Someone very dear to me passed away," he confided sharply. "And I need Kalahar to show me how to bring them back to life."

"That wasn't so hard, see?" Ferris said, grabbing Richard's empty tankard and beckoning for a barmaid, who came over and replaced their drinks once more as he returned to his seat. "So you think Kalahar is in Santeros? That's quite the way."

"I don't know. But I visited Letham Deregor before coming here, and he wasn't there. Only some others, permanent residents. The man who had frequent contact with him, though, lives there. You said you hijacked a ship. How big is it?"

"Well," Ferris said, uneasily putting a hand behind his head. "She's sizeable. But if you're insinuating using my ship to travel across the Great Sea…"

"Show me it," Richard cut him off. "Even if it isn't too big, it can work. I can guide us. And I thought you had never sailed before."

"Adaptation in the face of adversity is an incredible thing, isn't it? Though the sickness is still a thorn in my side I hope to pluck. Are you paying me for the use of my ship?"

"Come with me," Richard asserted. "I don't have money to pay you, but I could use your skills. And, I have a further plan after we find Kalahar. What would you say to putting down the Emperor of Sanskar?"

A mischievous glint appeared in Ferris's eyes as he stopped sipping his ale.

"I like the sound of this."

Ferris downed the rest of his ale and slammed the tankard on the table before woozily rising from his seat and clambering onto a nearby table. "You hear that, folks?" The bard raised his voice, once again disturbing the tavern's other patrons. "Richard and I are going to kill the Emperor!"

"Pipe down, you fool!" Richard scolded as Ferris received some light cheers. "Spies could be anywhere!"

"There are no spies here, my friend, just patriots!" he continued. "Just good-hearted fighters of the King!"

"The King is dead!" one of the patrons spat. "Killed by the Emperor in his own court. He was betrayed!"

"The King's memory lives on!" Ferris responded, undeterred. "As does the spirit of Mirados! I won't back down until the day the Emperor's head rolls and the people are free from tyranny!"

The door to the tavern swung open and produced a man and a woman, both dressed in dark brigandines over whiter doublets and black breeches, and also sharing the same darker skin tone and black hair. They were also both equipped with longswords at their waists, sheathed in decorated leather scabbards.

"You're some way from home!" Ferris blurted out as the man approached the bar.

"And how do you know where our home is?" the woman retorted.

"Don't play us for fools, it's evident where your home is," Ferris growled. "You're even dressed the part."

The woman ignored Ferris and pulled a folded piece of paper from her satchel, unfolding it and studying its contents. She then looked at her companion, who had paid for two drinks and placed them on a nearby table. His face looked expectant, and she nodded as if in confirmation.

They slowly drew their swords from their scabbards and walked towards the bard with predetermined steps.

"Oh, actually, we have a no weapons policy in the Canary," Ferris slurred. "You're going to have to put them away."

Richard sighed and rose from his seat, retrieving his bow from his back and nocking two arrows.

"Don't move any closer," he warned, drawing the bowstring back.

"We're not here for you," the woman hissed, holding her sword across her body. "The bounty rests on this man's head."

"This man is under my protection," Richard stated calmly. "If it's bounties you're after, there will be plenty at the board in the harbour."

"Tell you what," the man chimed in. "You let us take him and you can have twenty percent."

"Twenty percent?" Ferris ridiculed. "Don't take any less than thirty-three, Richard."

"Shut up," Richard snapped, holding his gaze on the two bounty hunters. "Get out of the tavern."

"The problem is with the bounties at the harbour," the woman began, "is that they don't pay quite as much as bounties in the North. The difference is astonishing, actually. Now move out the way and let us claim our reward."

She took one step forwards and Richard drew his bowstring back as far as it would allow.

"One more step and these arrows find themselves in your skulls."

"What do you think you are, some kind of circus performer?" she ridiculed. "Two arrows at once? It's already bold enough to use a bow in close quarters. And now you're telling me that you could seriously hit both those shots?"

"That's exactly right," he confirmed, unwavering. "Now leave."

"No," the woman retorted. "I don't think we shall."

Both Sanskari bounty hunters leapt forwards and reached Richard's feet face-first. Blood pooled on the floor as most of the remaining patrons filed quietly from the tavern, though some stayed and continued to watch.

Richard bent down and retrieved the slip of paper from the woman's satchel. On it was a startlingly accurate illustration of Ferris alongside some writing in a foreign language he assumed to be Sanskari.

"I don't think the previous owner of your ship is very happy with you," Richard said, pressing the paper into Ferris's chest. He then grabbed both bounty hunters' satchels and slung them over his shoulder.

"I can't possibly see why not..."

"Come on, Ferris." Richard pressed the inebriated bard towards the exit. "We're leaving."

"We'll need supplies, if we're to travel across the ocean."

"Of course we'll need supplies. Let's go get some."

They turned and left the tavern. Richard tossed a pouch of coins to the nearest guard he found, informing them of the situation in the Canary.

"We'll need food... lots of food," Ferris mused, bumbling after the determined bounty hunter. "Fruits, mainly. That scurvy was not a pleasant experience."

"Pipe down, would you? You were lucky it was only bounty hunters after you. I wouldn't be surprised if the Emperor sends someone more specialised to shut you up. You have more influence than you think."

"Oh, I don't know about that. I just sing a few songs! Incite a few rumours! Nobody takes them that seriously."

They reached the dockyard, and it was at that point that Richard realised he had no idea what he was looking for.

"Where's your ship?"

"That one, just there," Ferris exclaimed, pointing at the cog he had stolen from Virilia.

"You weren't kidding about it not being much," Richard said softly, considering the ship's single sail unsurely. "But no, it will be enough. Now split up, grab some supplies and meet me there in an hour."

Richard spent his hour gathering a crate of various salted foods and a barrel of ale. When he arrived at the ship, Ferris had several bottles of wine, his lute, extra outfits, and a crate of oranges.

"What are we going to do with a crate of oranges?" Richard ridiculed, climbing the gangplank.

"Oh, I don't know, Richard. Eat them?"

"They'll rot, for Lanthanis's sake. I hope you're ready to eat a lot of them in one go."

"Gladly," Ferris said, untying the rope from the jetty and then hoisting the sail. "Now, Santeros is what, due west?"

"Yes, but Dannos is in the country's north. Whatever, we'll find a port city on the eastern coast and travel by carriage the rest of the way."

"And my ship?"

"I don't know how long we'll be gone, so perhaps you might want to sell it. How often would you use it, anyways? And what do you mean, sell it? It's stolen!"

They drifted away from the harbour and Ferris gazed longingly at dry land as the inevitable rocking began.

"Get cosy, Ferris," Richard said, kneeling on the ship's deck.
"It's going to be quite the journey."

CHAPTER 5

1 month before

It was several hours before Tregor awoke. Nendar could have roused him sooner with the use of magic, but he wasn't confident as to the nature of the spell the vampire had used to bind him.

He was dazed at first, seemingly unaware of his surroundings. Even after he regained full control of his consciousness, the sorcerer's countenance reflected confusion as he cast his eyes upon the room in the unassuming tavern to which Nendar had taken him.

"Nendar?" Tregor spoke. "Where are we?"

Nendar looked up and out of the window to view a tavern across the street awash with garish yellow paint, the brightest front in the entire city. "We're hunting."

Tregor squinted scrutinisingly as he looked upon the tavern. "Hunting what?"

"Vampires, of course. Or rather, vampire. And what better way to hunt vampire than to hunt the Fateborn he so desperately wants for himself? If we couldn't defeat him head-on, then we will have to try another way."

"Why don't we just take the Fateborn ourselves? Use him to protect us against the vampire?"

"How would we then find the vampire to kill him? He conceals his signature. If we find the Fateborn, we can follow him to the vampire. And once we have neutralised the vampire—this time with better preparation—we can then attempt once more to convert him."

Nendar had tracked Richard's signature generally to the Miradosi port city of Merana and it didn't take long to find him. He and Tregor chose to lay low, keeping to the concealment offered by the room in the tavern and leaving only for essentials. They took turns watching the street outside, scouring it for a familiar face and, with the aid of magic, soon recognising one.

They watched on several occasions as he entered the garish tavern across the way. Some days, he only passed by, and some days, he stayed inside for up to an hour. Every single time they spotted him, Nendar donned a hooded cloak and went out to follow him, and every single time he came back to report exactly the same thing. He went to the harbour, he asked around for passage to Santeros, and then he gave up for the day.

One day brought an interruption to the routine. It was an occasion on which Richard has chosen to enter the tavern, entitled the Canary, and promptly reappeared at its window clutching a mug of drink. Nothing appeared to be amiss and that remained the case until Richard was at one point joined by another individual whose voice boomed with such volume that Nendar and Tregor could almost make out his words through the general bustle. At first they thought nothing of him, assuming him just to be a random drunk, and that preconception remained in place until two armed individuals of distinctly northern appearance entered the tavern with shared expressions of determination.

Nendar looked expectantly at Tregor, who nodded affirmation. The Emperor stood up and donned his cloak, leaving the room and arriving at the tavern across the street just as Richard's bow twanged with the release of two arrows. Richard and the drunk were too preoccupied with the ensuing mess to notice Nendar's entrance as he took a seat at the bar, lowering his head and listening intently to their conversation.

"I don't think the previous owner of your ship is very happy with you," Richard said.

"I can't possibly see why not..." the drunk replied.

"Come on, Ferris. We're leaving."

"We'll need supplies, if we're to travel across the ocean."

"Of course we'll need supplies. Let's go get some."

Ten seconds passed after their departure before Nendar emerged into the street. He made eye contact with Tregor and sent a message telepathically as he set sight upon Richard and the drunk now known to him as Ferris. Tregor responded in acknowledgement and then disappeared from the window, donning a cloak of his own and joining Nendar in pursuit of the pair.

Each of the sorcerers chose a target of their own to follow and in the hustle of the port city it was easy for them to keep their distance and avoid detection. That was especially true for Tregor as he followed after Ferris, the bard staying continuously inebriated for the entire time he spent meandering around the city in search of random commodities. Nendar endured the overpowering stench of fish in trailing Richard through the seaside marketplace.

They found themselves reunited in an hour's time, as did Richard and Ferris on the deck of a cog in the harbour. An invisibility spell enabled them to board unnoticed and search for a hiding place while the pair squabbled.

Have you ever been to Santeros? Nendar asked as he nestled into the cramped space behind several crates in the cargo hold.

I can't say that I have, Tregor responded, joining him. *But I've been to Lazeria for the academies and I made it as far as pre-division Benetia.*

The ship jerked with its departure from the jetty and the sorcerers shared a sigh.

"Get comfortable, then. And let's try not to get caught."

CHAPTER 6

Hortensio surveyed the visitor with his usual suspicion. The visitor had brought a gift, and the young King had learned some time ago not to trust a visitor who brought gifts. One of his pages accepted the gold while the King kept his eyes trained on the visitor and his hand trained on the hilt of his sword.

He wasn't a threatening man—he was weedy, seemingly unarmed, and dressed only in what looked like thin linen. He was elderly, even. But Hortensio had thought similarly little of Rosa Feranimor.

"Introduce yourself, then," he sighed.

"My name is Villius Abranor," the man croaked. "I represent the Fencing Academy of Altercant. As you are quite probably aware, Altercant is known for producing swordsmen of the highest standards."

Hortensio chuckled, glancing dramatically over the old man's frail body. His stance did not falter, and he waited patiently for the King to respond.

"Go on, then," Hortensio said exasperatedly after a lengthy period of silence.

"The Free City of Altercant remains stable after the vampire crisis. As such, we are still able to provide swordsmen to bolster armies such as those under your control. I come seeking to establish a prosperous relationship between our academy and your court, Your Majesty."

"How much are you trying to charge us for your mercenaries?" Hortensio asked, rolling his eyes impatiently.

"Not a copper," Villius said sharply. "Instead, we only request a place on your court. In return, the Academy will provide two hundred skilled fighters free of charge."

"Where were you born?"

"I'm sorry?"

"You heard the question," Hortensio repeated. "Where were you born?"

"I do apologise, Your Majesty, but I do not see the relevance of such a question."

"Fuck me. I don't really care what you think, just answer it," the King swore, running a hand through his hair.

"I was born in Thorne, originally, though—"

"Who's this, Your Exaltedness?" Jannis, appearing from a side entryway, interrupted. He was clad in a full suit of armour, bar a helmet, as usual.

"An instructor at some fighting school," Hortensio snorted.

"Is that right?" Jannis ridiculed. "Are you having us on? Have you seen those arms of yours?"

"With all due respect, I am not an instructor, but a representative," Villius corrected, maintaining his composure. "And it is not just some fighting school, but an academy for the finest swordsmen of not just Altercant but the east of Temerios and beyond. Our fighters are favoured by the Kings of Thorne and South Benetia as well as countless private enterprises and noble houses across the continent. You would do well to join them."

Hortensio rose from his throne, finally letting down his guard.

"When I conquered Dannos, I heard about how the man in charge there, Elton Redwinter, sacked a bank employed by fighters very similar in description to those you describe to me. Do you know what happened when they were confronted?"

"No, I—"

"They laid down their arms and took a bribe before dispersing. And they weren't even foreign mercenaries – they were homegrown Santerosi. If soldiers of their own homeland can't be trusted to loyalty, why could yours possibly be?"

"Because—"

"That was a rhetorical question." The King stepped closer, slowly descending down the stairs from his throne. "You were born in Thorne. I am the King of Salyria. My armies are made up of Salyrian soldiers trained by Salyrians. Not the dogs of some foreign man who comes to my court and asks for a place in return for a couple hundred slaves. I'm afraid your journey has been made in vain, because my answer to your offer is no."

Villius nodded and huffed, "Very well," before turning and leaving the throne room.

"I have never heard of Altercant," Hortensio confided to Jannis as the man left earshot.

"Some free city in the East. Wealthy, apparently, but they don't have any real power. Now, I have something to show you."

"Oh?"

"Or rather, our court mage does. Come with me."

Jannis led the way back through the corridor from which he had originally appeared with Hortensio following in eager pursuit.

They arrived shortly at a room retrofitted for the use of their new court mage. Shortly after the eclipse, both having witnessed Rosa's abilities in Dannos, Hortensio and Jannis had mutually decided that despite tradition, they wanted the assistance of a mage in their own court. And, miraculously, one had appeared.

It was the day they had arrived back at the Blue Palace. Their strategy of ignoring the crisis had worked for them, isolated out on the roads. But it had not worked for those at the palace. The scene that greeted them was carnage—decomposing, mutilated bodies strewn like litter, buildings of thatch, wood, and stone reduced to rubble, and, strangely, the treasury raided of all its precious gemstones.

Yet amongst the chaos they found a man. A man with neatly brushed flame-red hair and a face swarmed by freckles. A man dressed elegantly in ornamental robes and a thick leather belt. A man who stood amid the wreckage and greeted the King with the calmness of a lake on a windless day.

"Hablar Arcaea," he began. Neither Hortensio nor Jannis knew what this meant, but they allowed it not to possess their thoughts.

The man introduced himself as Kasimir, and only Kasimir. He told the King that he was a sorcerer, and an adept one at that. He explained to the King that he had defended the palace to the height of his abilities, and he explained that he was wandering, searching a place to settle permanently. It was too perfect, and Hortensio didn't waste a second in recruiting him to the Salyrian court.

Hortensio and Jannis observed Kasimir looking into a mirror as they arrived at his room. They thought they could hear him quietly speaking to it—but the moment the mage noticed their arrival, he set the mirror down and turned to face them.

"My king," he began, rising from his seat.

"What have you got for me?" Hortensio inquired, clasping his hands together.

Kasimir gestured to the left side of the room, where a linen sheet concealed a large object nearly as tall as the wall. The sorcerer made a show of walking over to it slowly and grasping the sheet with one hand before yanking it off.

Occupying the slight indent in the wall was an ovular frame carved from stone, with slight incisions at its centre. Hortensio's excitement faded and his expression was replaced by one of confusion.

"What... what is it?"

Kasimir did not respond, and instead spoke something in a language neither Hortensio nor Jannis recognised. But it had an effect, as a shimmering image of the throne room engulfed the frame's empty space.

"Go on, step through," Kasimir encouraged. "You can come straight back."

Hortensio's excitement returned as he practically dived through the portal, arriving, as expected, in the throne room. He then returned without quite the spectacle.

"At the moment, I'm concentrating the spell. However"—the sorcerer fished a small, jagged crystal the colour of amethyst from his pocket—"I can use my crystal here to sustain the portal without expending my own stamina."

He then demonstrated by placing the crystal into one of the incisions and uttering another spell. The portals did not close, but any strain which could be seen on Kasimir's face, as slight as it was, disappeared.

"And this can go where I want?" Hortensio asked, his jaw remaining dropped.

"Well, I would have to activate the portal, and it would have to be somewhere of which you have knowledge, but yes, in theory," Kasimir confirmed. "However, I cannot simply always leave the crystal. I need it on my person to practice my own magic. So, I would like to ask for something. It would be for mutual benefit."

"Which is?"

"I would like more crystals. I know of their vague location, but I am unable to collect them on my own. I would like to take some of your soldiers on an expedition with me to mine them together."

"My soldiers?" Hortensio's eyes shimmered. "Forget my soldiers, I'm going! I wouldn't bloody miss this!"

"Excellent, then," the sorcerer affirmed. "I would like to leave soon. Would you be ready in, say, two days' time?"

Hortensio glanced at Jannis, who, though not quite sharing the King's excitement, looked thoroughly enthused himself.

"Yes," the King stated. "I'll be more than ready."

CHAPTER 7

Elton surveyed the pile of grey bodies lying in the alley with a grimace.

"He's been here."

He reached down to lift one of the arms of the slain vampires and it fell from its socket. He quickly threw it back to the ground in disgust.

"Rosa," he said, turning to the small group he had brought with him. "It's been three months. Still no progress?"

"Afraid not, boss," Rosa confirmed. "He's... elusive."

"Well." Elton kicked one of the motionless bodies. "Each day passes, and more vampires are slain. Either by vigilantes or Kalahar himself. We are, quite frankly, running out of time."

"On the bright side, boss, I've got some news from Salyria," Felix chimed in. He had swapped his usual red jerkin for a black one, still outfitted with his collection of knives. "News about their new court mage."

"Oh, do tell," Elton said, turning and leading the group back out of the alley.

"His name, or at least the one he's going by, is Kasimir. No last name, and they reckon he's Benetian or even Lazerian. Apparently even Hortensio doesn't know."

"If he's Benetian, what's he doing working for Hortensio?"

"Your guess is as good as mine."

They returned to the Redhouse with surprisingly minimal obstruction. Elton's new regime had experienced growing pains, with many of those who had previously served him under the Syndicate unhappy with the new state of affairs. That had led to a handful of confrontations in the street, only solidifying Elton's belief that he needed an escort to travel.

The Redhouse had undergone a transformation in the past three months. The symbol hanging above the entrance had been replaced—what had previously been a bleeding snowflake was now a pair of crossed swords behind a shield bearing the symbol of the snowflake, though without the blood.

"I've got some things to do, boss, so I'll be back in a bit," Rosa declared as they arrived, before promptly turning and walking away.

"She's been acting weird recently," Felix said in a hushed tone, as soon as Rosa was out of earshot. "Have you seen her in public at all? Or even in the Redhouse?"

"Admittedly not," Elton conceded. "And I am concerned with the fact that she has been unable to locate Kalahar. In fact, I have a new job for us. We need to find a new mage."

"You're ready to replace her just like that?" Felix asked, bewildered. "I wasn't insinuating that, I just thought it was worth mentioning. At least give her some time."

"There's nothing wrong with expanding our workforce. We employ one mage for the entire city. That's frankly insufficient. I would like to see at least three working for us. And I would also like to find out why Rosa has, as you point out, been acting weird recently."

They continued through the Redhouse, greeting the various bustling workers. The messy fray which existed during the lifetime of the Syndicate had become a relic of the past—there were no more card games played in the lobby, no more spars in the corridors, and a much more temperate use of language. Even Elton found himself struggling to set an example.

"Excuse me, Count," a woman, employed as a receptionist, said as Elton walked past. The Count stopped and turned to look at her, raising an eyebrow.

"I apologise, Count, but we have something of a situation. There is somebody waiting—we think for you, but we can't speak with him. He doesn't speak Santerosi."

"What does he look like? Black hair? Grey skin?" Elton interrogated, briskly approaching the desk where she was sitting.

"N-no," the woman, flustered, responded. "Just brown hair, about shoulder length… wearing a leather coat, if that helps? Oh, and he's with one other person."

"Show me to him," Elton ordered, beckoning the woman from her chair. She hastily rose and led them away at speed.

The receptionist brought them to a room out of the way of the main thoroughfare. Elton knew it to be a meeting room, one which saw frequent use. There were several people loitering outside who Elton assumed were waiting to use it.

"They've essentially taken the room hostage," the receptionist explained. "We've tried to have security remove them, but they've locked the door."

As she finished speaking, the door drifted open. Standing inside were, indeed, two people. Two men, one of which Elton recognised.

"All of you, clear off," Elton barked, gesturing to those who had been patiently waiting, as well as the receptionist. Disgruntled, they shuffled away, leaving Elton and Felix to slip quietly into the meeting room.

"Richard Ordowyn," Elton greeted, crossing his arms as Richard closed the door by magic with a flourish of his hand.

"Hablar Arcaea," Richard said, enabling the Santerosi men to understand him. "Hello again."

"Who's your friend?" Elton began, gesturing to the man at Richard's side.

"Ferris of Limara, more commonly known as Ferris of Arbeford," Ferris cheerily introduced himself, extending a hand across the table separating the two pairs. "Minstrel, patriot, explorer, and insurrectionist. A pleasure."

Elton wearily shook the bard's hand. He did not introduce himself back, gathering that Richard had already done so for him.

"And Felix." Richard nodded at Elton's companion. "It's good to see you again."

"All pleasantries aside, Richard, you have trespassed in my city," Elton said gravely. "I assume you have a reason for this."

"Yes. I need to know where Kalahar is. You were my best bet, seeing how close you were with him."

Elton and Felix glanced at each other, smirking, and they then chuckled in unison. Richard, unamused, lowered his hands onto the table and gazed at them while the smiles fell slowly from their faces.

"We want to know where he is just as much as you do," Elton asserted, his tone suddenly serious. "But we just don't know. Our resident mage has spent months trying to track him. And she said he was here, in the city. In this very building, even. But she cannot find him, no matter how hard she tries. We interrogated every single person that visits this building on a regular basis. And none of them reacted. Kalahar can change his form, as he demonstrated while we were together at Letham Deregor. But he still reacts to that concoction, even in the form of another."

Richard stared down at the table as an awkward silence fell over the room, interrupted only by Felix twirling a dagger on his finger. Ferris, devoid of his usual jubilation, shrugged as he met Elton's glance.

"You say he's in the city?" Richard finally asked.

"Rosa claims he's in the Redhouse."

"If he's here, I'll find him. Do you have any leads?"

"Just mutilated bodies of malevolent vampires. We've been trying to keep track of numbers—they tend to group together. But then they either get lynched by do-gooders or massacred by Kal himself. You know his handiwork when you see it. What do you need with him, anyways?"

"Something personal. And why do you need him?"

"Information. I want to find out why he's slaughtering all these docile vampires. I want to know the whole truth behind the eclipse. Because frankly, I'm convinced that most of what he told us was a lie."

Richard withdrew from the table and paced back and forth, face creased with contemplation. Ferris looked quizzically at him, a reaction mirrored by Felix. But Elton empathised entirely.

"I can feel him, that's for sure," Richard said suddenly. "Rosa is right." He stopped pacing and turned to face Elton dead in the eyes.

"You said you interrogated everyone?"

"Everyone who frequents this building, yes."

"Including Rosa?"

Elton and Felix looked at one another with uncertainty before Elton shook his head.

"Then we need to find her," Richard said with alarming urgency. "If it even is her. Because it sounds to me like Kalahar has been hiding under your noses this entire time."

The bounty hunter didn't wait for Elton to respond and burst from the room, Ferris pursuing. The eager crowd had returned and one person was unfortunate enough to have been standing just a little bit too close to the door as it flew open.

"Where would she be?" Richard shouted back as Elton clumsily followed.

"She said she had to do something and left to go somewhere as we arrived," Felix answered, doing a much better job of keeping pace, though without the bounty hunter's unnatural fluidity and grace.

Richard moved with determination and Elton was steadily left behind, ever lacking the physical fitness to keep up. But as he faltered, he was suddenly infused with an unnatural surge of energy, a sensation like adrenaline, only stronger.

As Richard reached the exit, he stopped, but only briefly to turn and ask Felix a question inaudible to Elton, deafened by his own deep breaths. Richard then immediately returned to a sprint, turning right and tearing into the streets of Dannos.

While Felix had kept pace with the bounty hunter, Ferris had fallen behind to almost meet Elton. But the bard didn't appear particularly exhausted—he seemed just to be relaxed with his pace.

"If he's not already learned that Kalahar is... far too smart... for a chase like this, then I don't know what hope he... he has to find him," Elton wheezed to the bard, who had purposefully fallen even further behind to his position.

"That man is one of the strangest I have ever met," Ferris said. "But he knows what he's doing."

As the race continued, Elton almost managed to catch up as Richard unexpectedly slowed down. And then, just as unexpectedly, he turned and lifted a sewer grate before leaping down. Felix followed without hesitation, followed shortly thereafter by Ferris and finally Elton.

It was dark. It wasn't Elton's first time in the sewers, but he would never get used to the total absence of light. That, and the unbearable stench.

The cacophony populating the streets above died almost as soon as the group entered the underground, replaced by the gentle rushing of water and the skittering of rats. And, further ahead, the sound of screaming.

Richard loudly uttered a spell and an orb of light appeared ahead of him, bright enough to illuminate the entirety of their surroundings. He rushed ahead, carefully but efficiently traversing the watery tunnels, a task not so easily attempted by the remaining three.

The screaming grew louder as Richard navigated like a bloodhound towards the source of the sounds. The freeing of his sword from its sheath further added to the discordant racket.

One more turn and the temperature of the air fell dramatically as Elton stumbled over an object half the width of the sewer, floating in the water. He looked down and was met with the mangled corpse of a vampire. It was the first of many, but they could see just ahead a collection of others standing together, not yet slain, hopelessly attempting to fight off an assault from an enemy moving so fast as to become a blur.

"Kalahar!" Richard called.

The assault on the vampires ceased, and the attacker, its back turned, allowed the remaining survivors to flee.

"Richard," Kalahar gurgled. "What a pleasant surprise."

"You owe me, vampire," Richard said, his voice shaking. "You owe me."

"What do I owe you, exactly?" the vampire asked nonchalantly. "Do I owe you for the fact that you were able to eliminate the woman you despised so much as a result of my teaching? Do I owe you because you were able to defend your own country from being razed by vampires? It isn't my fault you brought your king's own assassin before him. I owe you nothing for that."

"You know damned well why you owe me," he seethed, fists clenching and unclenching.

"I owe you nothing, boy," the vampire retorted. "Our relationship ended the moment you failed to continue to fulfil your end of the agreement. While malevolent vampires still walk the face of this planet, you, in fact, owe me."

Richard trudged slowly through the sludge towards the unmoving vampire. "Teach me," he pleaded. "Teach me how to bring her back to life."

Kalahar's countenance remained static, but Elton caught the subtle glint in his eye.

"Why are you slaughtering them, Kalahar?" Elton asked, pushing a floating body aside and moving to join Richard.

"To protect you, of course. You saw what they're capable of."

"I've seen what you are capable of. And I know what you really are. And believe me, within time, I will kill you, Kalahar. I will kill you."

"Oh, I doubt that. Now, Richard. You were interested to learn the secrets of resurrection?"

The bounty hunter's eyes lit up and he nodded, moving ever closer to the vampire.

"Don't do it, Richard. Don't fall for his lies," Elton said, trying to grab him and haul him back. But Richard resisted and continued forwards.

"I will do anything," Richard said resignedly. "Anything... just help me bring her back."

Kalahar met the bounty hunter and rested a hand on his shoulder, an action Richard accepted, hanging his head.

"If we are going to work together," Kalahar began, "then you must prove that you will be loyal to me."

"Anything," Richard repeated, his voice weaker than before.

Kalahar looked beyond the bounty hunter and stared straight into Elton's eyes, continuing to do so as he spoke. "I want you to kill Elton Redwinter."

Richard raised his head and turned slowly to face Elton and Felix, now bristling with anticipation. Felix had equipped each of his hands with a throwing knife, which he twirled idly in wait. Elton reached a hand for his dagger but did not unsheathe it. Ferris stood between them, unsure of what action to take.

Richard looked uncomfortably between the pair and Kalahar, who stood unmoving, eyes still locked with Elton's.

"I'm sorry," Richard choked. "I really don't want to do this."

Elton drew his dagger.

"Richard, don't do anything brash—" Ferris tried to say, but he was cut off.

Richard flew through the narrow space, past Ferris, and landed in front of the pair with a splash. Felix immediately launched a knife which, to their shock, he deflected. The bounty hunter took three swings, narrowly missing each. Felix launched the second knife, which Richard also deflected. Elton paced backwards, as quickly as the water would allow him. Passion burned in Richard's eyes as he fought onwards.

Felix liberated a further three throwing knives and launched them in quick succession at their assailant. Two clashed with his sword while the third nicked his wrist, sending a splatter of blood across the wall. Richard grimaced and clutched the wound with his hand, presenting Elton with an opportunity to counterattack.

He stepped forwards while the bounty hunter's focus was trained on Felix, grabbing the hilt of his sword and placing his dagger against his neck.

"One wrong move and you're done for."

Richard's eyes widened as Felix unveiled a further two knives. "I didn't want to kill you. I have no quarrel with you. But it was my only choice."

"It doesn't really matter, because you won't be killing us now, anyways," Felix spat.

"I've tried the honourable way. But now I have to cheat. I am sorry."

Before Elton or Felix could process his words, the bounty hunter lifted his arms and sent them flying backwards into opposite walls, crashing with such force as to crack the stone. Any attempt at movement was futile, as Richard kept his arms raised in concentration.

"You're making a big bloody mistake," Elton rasped, residual pain still pounding through his head from the impact.

Richard dropped his arms and allowed them to fall.

"Go on, Richard," Kalahar encouraged. "Finish them."

Two figures rounded the corner with speed rivalling that of a diving falcon. Richard immediately looked up and placed his sword across his body protectively while Elton and Felix moved back in the direction of the sewer's exit.

The figures stopped between Richard and Elton. One, a man with pale skin and raven-black hair, wielded a scimitar. The other, a dark-skinned man with similar short-cut dark hair, wielded a dark blade of magical conjuration.

"You," Richard hissed.

"We knew you would go looking for the vampire," the pale man said. "We've been following you."

"And why were you following me? You want to try and convert me again? It isn't happening. I'm free now."

"But not truly free, are you, Fateborn?" the dark-skinned man chimed in. "Not while that burden hangs on your shoulders so. That guilt."

Ferris rejoined Richard at his side and placed his hand on the hilt of his rapier.

"That's him, Ordowyn! That's the Emperor!"

"Yes," Richard seethed. "Yes, it is."

Richard stretched his arms out once more, this time not to his sides, but towards the Emperor. He was lifted from the water, but he hung in the air for only moments before the dark-skinned man sent his magical blade sailing towards the vulnerable bounty hunter.

The Emperor fell as Richard dropped him and sidestepped out of the way, the blade continuing onwards and striking Kalahar. The vampire allowed it to impale his torso and he showed no sign of pain. Instead, he merely clenched his fist and the sword evaporated.

"What lies has he fed you now?" the Emperor asked as his companion materialised a new sword. "Do you not remember the warnings I gave you?"

"I remember you telling me that Kalahar would convert me on the day of the eclipse," Richard said. "That didn't turn out to be true." He walked towards them, the dark-skinned man keeping a watchful eye. "I remember you telling me that I have much more potential than what he's showed me. But he has just agreed to show me more. Did you ever do that?"

Richard's sword arm tensed as Elton and Felix approached Ferris.

"We don't know you very well, bard, but your friend has gone batshit," Felix said.

"We aren't leaving until that man there lies dead on the ground. Or, more aptly, dead in the water."

"I will say this straight—all three of us are out of our league. I take it you aren't a magician?"

Ferris shook his head.

"I've seen what magic-wielders can do. And I don't want to be anywhere near a fight between them. Come with us, you'll be safe."

Elton, Felix, and Ferris turned and attempted to round the corner with the onset of the clashing of steel. But they couldn't, because their way was blocked.

"Elton, did you really think I would be letting you leave so easily? Before the main event has concluded?" Kalahar asked, having materialised in the gap between them and the route to the exit.

"Get out of our way," Elton growled. "This affair does not involve us. Any of us."

"You're staying until Richard has done his job. And then—"

Kalahar was unable to finish his sentence as the liquid splashed over his face. He let out a monstrous cry and was then flung backwards into the wall, crashing deeper into the stone than Elton and Felix had.

While the noises of battle continued, the dark-skinned man forced his way through them, extending one arm towards the restrained vampire while the other hung at his side, empty vial clutched firmly in his fingers. His face betrayed intense strain and his arm shook slightly as it remained extended.

"You three," he said harshly, not removing his gaze from the vampire. "Leave."

Elton glanced between the duel taking place on his left and the vampire screaming obscenities on his right and made the decision to follow the advice.

CHAPTER 8

NORTHERN TYEN'AEL

Elaeínn crept behind the thatched house at the edge of the village, her surroundings illuminated only by faint moonlight. Velrin stood watch on the path leading through the little settlement, looking nervously between Elaeínn and the point at which the path climbed over the hill on the northern side of the village.

The house around which she skulked was built from stone at its base with a wooden extension protruding from its front supported by sturdy beams. Elaeínn had chosen this particular house because she was confident she would be able to scale onto the small balcony overlooking the road leading south. A balcony on which she could see a door without a keyhole.

She quickly climbed an apple tree adjacent to the house and tiptoed precariously across one of the thinner branches before jumping onto the balcony. Her first mistake was made when the branch from which she had jumped snapped as she left it. Her second was when the snapping of the branch crippled her focus and she crashed into the balcony's guardrail, managing to catch herself on the deck. She hung freely over the ground as the sounds of life within the house began to stir.

Velrin stared in panic at her and Elaeínn shot him an instructive glance which he understood at once. The professor left his position and took refuge in a cluster of alders up a hill further from the village, but still within view of the house.

Elaeínn heard the door creak and she shuffled along to position herself flush with the wall, her arms outstretched to grasp both sides of the balcony so that she hung directly beneath it.

A heavy footstep sent a creak through the planks above her, followed by another, and then another. Fatigue crept through her arms as she waited patiently for the person to depart.

"Who's there?" a gruff, elderly voice called, shattering the night's silence. "You're not fooling anyone. I can see you've vandalised my garden, so come out!"

A thick pain engulfed the muscles in Elaeínn's arms and shoulders and a numbness snaked through her fingers as she continued to grip the edges of the deck.

Another footstep, this time back towards the door.

"You had better run, because I am coming to find you," the elderly man warned.

And then the footsteps withdrew into the house and the door creaked shut.

Elaeínn acted without delay. Using what little strength she had left, greatly assisted by adrenaline, she pulled herself onto the deck and gracefully vaulted the guardrail. She placed a hand onto the door's handle and twisted it slowly before using her other hand to pull the door open. It creaked, but only quietly.

She paced into the house and could hear noises downstairs, incentivising her to move quickly while the sound of her footsteps was muffled by the commotion.

The balcony led straight into a bedroom where one woman, also elderly, lay asleep in the bed. Elaeínn made a beeline for the wardrobe and opened it as she heard the front door to the house open and then shut with force. The subsequent reverberation was enough to cause the woman asleep in the bed to stir.

The woman groaned as she slowly sat up and Elaeínn promptly fell prone to the floor, hiding behind the footboard.

"Arlen?" she croaked, placing her feet into sandals at the bed's side.

Elaeínn, now sure that she would be spotted, tried cautiously to move to the side of the bed opposite to that from which the woman had risen. But the sound of her shuffling against the floorboards was far from silent.

The elderly woman rounded the corner and met eyes with the raggedy escapee and they both froze momentarily. It was Elaeínn who acted first.

"I'm grabbing some clothes. That's all I've come here for. You don't say a word, I take two sets of clothes, and I leave," she hissed, standing and approaching the woman slowly.

"I—"

"No. You never saw me."

"Arlen!"

Elaeínn grabbed a vase from a table adjacent to the wardrobe and smashed it over the woman's head. She fell to the ground amidst a sea of terracotta shards, blood streaming from her forehead. At the same time, she heard a call from the elderly man as he returned to the house.

She gave up on stealth and ripped open the doors to the wardrobe, finding several outfits, pairs of shoes, hats, and other assorted items of clothing. She grabbed a few folded robes, belts, and two pairs of shoes as the downstairs door crashed open.

Elaeínn burst out of the balcony door and jumped over the guardrail without a second thought as she heard the elderly man's cry behind her. She then sprinted for the alders in which Velrin had taken refuge.

"Okay, Vel," she said, handing him a robe, belt, and pair of shoes. "We need to get out of here."

"Are you alright? Did you get caught?"

"Doesn't matter. You see that building over there? I think it's a stable. Hopefully there will be saddles and all sorts inside. You've ridden a horse before, I hope?"

Velrin ignored her patronisation and looked worriedly over the whole village before focusing his attention on the stable. It was a long, barn-shaped building with a sloped wooden roof and an expansive doorway, the doors of which were closed and, Velrin assumed, locked.

"What's wrong? We can't afford to wait," Elaeínn pressed.

"There's someone coming out of the house you were in. Look." Velrin pointed at a man bearing a torch in one hand, a lone light in the darkness. He began to shout something, incomprehensible from their position atop the hill some distance away. Soon enough, his torch was joined by several others, and then several more. Before long, the entire village was lit up like the night sky.

"What are you waiting for? Come on," Elaeínn said.

"Are you joking? Look at the place! They're looking for you!"

"You think I haven't noticed? I've got a plan. I just need you on standby in case it goes wrong. Come on!"

Velrin sighed and placed his palm forcefully against his forehead. He followed Elaeínn along the ridge of the hill until they came in line with the stable, where she instructed him to wait as the number of torches lighting up the village only continued to increase.

Elaeínn ducked her head and sprinted for the side of the stable, flattening herself against its outer wall as she arrived. A quick peek around the corner revealed several villagers scouring the nearby area, moving closer to her with each passing moment.

She shuffled her way along the length of the barn, pressing against each of the closed shutters in every window, finding most to be locked tight. But one was loose—loose enough that with just enough pressure, she was able to force it open.

Unfortunately for her, that didn't come without its consequences. The faulty lock snapped as she pressed the shutter open and a loud crack resonated through the still air. Elaeínn froze, listening for the expected reaction. It occurred.

The villagers shouted to one another and stormed towards the stable. Elaeínn clambered through the window and landed in an empty horse stall, a layer of hay softening the impact. She scrambled to reclose the window, but it stubbornly refused to stay flush with its intact counterparts, drifting slightly open with each attempt to close it.

Elaeínn gave up and vaulted the gate to the central walkway through the stable. Several horses occupying other stalls stuck their heads over the gates and snorted contemptuously as Elaeínn, and in extension the villagers, ripped them from their slumber.

The clamouring outside the stable grew louder as Elaeínn found four saddles tucked neatly into a set of shelves next to the entrance amongst various other equestrian paraphernalia. She bounded across the walkway and lugged two of them from a shelf, grunting as they fell into her arms, before tottering back towards two of the horses in opposing stalls, a black mare and a grey gelding. The rest of the horses had begun to nervously whinny as the key to the stable was inserted into the lock, the volume of the crowd further increasing, and it gave Elaeínn an idea.

She abandoned the saddles, tossing them boisterously into the stall with the gelding, and ran down the length of the stable, unlatching the doors to all the other stalls and flinging them open. The horses first trotted out before breaking into a canter.

The door to the stable burst open as Elaeínn opened the last door and the horses stampeded, neighing with fear. The villagers' surprised cries only amplified the horses' angst and the crowd dispersed as the horses' hooves clopped against the hardened ground in their escape. Elaeínn swiftly saddled the two horses she had kept in their stalls in the rush, attaching a lead to the gelding and then releasing them, too, as she leapt onto the mare.

The villagers could do nothing as her horses joined the stampede, egged on by her whipping the reins as she cleared her way through the few who hadn't fled or been crushed. She leaned towards Velrin standing atop the hill and the two horses peeled away from the rest as the villagers fought to restrain them.

"Come on, Velrin, jump on!" she yelled, bringing the horses to an abrupt halt. Velrin climbed awkwardly into the saddle of the gelding, using the stirrups for support.

Several villagers, including the presumed husband of the woman Elaeínn had assaulted, had trudged their way up the hill and a select few were even brandishing weapons. Elaeínn didn't consider her options for very long.

"Hee-yah!" she hollered, whipping the reins and directing the horse straight down the hill, through the approaching villagers. It whinnied unsurely but complied, reaching a gallop as the ground levelled out. She then turned onto the path and continued on, Velrin in steady pursuit. As they galloped into the night, the villagers' cries became only distant memories as the sprawling plains of the South began to take shape.

"What's your plan, then?" Velrin asked, the excitement long since having subsided. "We just escaped a military prison and stole two horses from a nearby village. I don't even want to know what you had to do to get these clothes. People will be looking for us—I would be surprised if they weren't already."

"You're too paranoid, Vel," Elaeínn said nonchalantly. "How fast do you think news travels?"

"Pretty bloody fast in wartime. The moment we left that castle, hell, even before we had left. As soon as a commotion arose, the mages in that castle will have been opening communication to the Serenna Palace or at least some subordinate. You weren't exactly a low-profile prisoner. You were their prize."

"We have time. We just need to keep on the quiet side. Avoid large towns. If we can make it to the Darklight—"

"Then we'll be cut off by a military blockade. You don't think every mouth of the Darklight will be guarded around the clock? That forest is the most strategic landmass in this entire war."

"What if it's the dwarves that control it?"

"But what if it isn't? We can't take any more risks, because I don't think we'd get away with prison next time."

"We don't have much choice," Elaeínn asserted. "We either risk capture or we don't go anywhere at all. And if we don't go anywhere, we can't make a change. I'm not accepting that."

They carried on in silence, fatigue beginning to settle in as the moon crept across the night sky. The roads through grassy meadows and rustling wheat fields were empty, the occasional signs of civilisation appearing in the form of distant villages at the end of thin offshoots from the highway on which they travelled. They were passed periodically throughout the night by other travellers, exchanging nothing more than polite nods.

A village built around the highway came into view as the sun introduced itself over the horizon. Elaeínn decided it would be a good location to rest not just herself and Velrin, whose eyelids were visibly drooping, but also the horses, who had begun to slow down in a display of torpor as well.

Judging by the architectural style, the village's buildings being constructed from traditional stone, this new village was much more affluent than the previous and was large enough to verge on becoming a town. It had a guardhouse, a couple taverns, a butcher, an apothecary, even a blacksmith with a proper forge.

Elaeínn and Velrin rode up to the first tavern at the roadside, a sign hanging above the door designating it The Dusty Mandolin. They hitched their horses to a post outside and sauntered in.

The atmosphere was deader than the roads they had travelled to get there. Two people were present, and both had their heads facedown against their respective tables. The innkeeper was nowhere to be seen, so Elaeínn made the most of the opportunity.

"What are you doing?" Velrin seethed as she approached one of the unconscious men, his fingers still wrapped around the handle of his tankard.

"We need to pay for our accommodation somehow," she aggressively whispered back, reaching for the man's pockets.

"Oh, what, so we're stooping to common thievery?"

"What do you think we were doing when we stole these clothes and those horses? We aren't acting within the law! We're just trying to survive!"

She gingerly fished into the man's pockets and felt a small leather pouch. The gentle jingling of coin rang out as she withdrew her hand, clutching the coin-purse with a smirk.

"Think of it as our levy," Elaeínn suggested. "These people need to pay us somehow for the duty we do for them."

"Not all of them are on our side. Especially not northerners."

"So I'm stealing from the enemy. That suits me just fine."

She checked the other man's pockets and came up empty. Some sounds of life had begun to arise as the outdoors basked in morning light and the pair considered moving to another tavern to hide their tracks, but decided it would have looked too suspicious and instead chose a table and waited for the innkeeper to appear.

Within time, a woman in traditional dress with her hair tied into plaits materialised from a door behind the counter. Her face creased with perplexity when she spotted Elaeínn and Velrin as they eagerly locked eyes with her and rose from their seats.

"What's on the menu?" Elaeínn leaned over the counter.

"Bacon... Eggs... Tomatoes..." the woman groggily answered. "What are you two doing here so early? And who are you?"

"Just travellers. Bacon and eggs sounds lovely. How much?"

"For both of you? A half-naemmon."

"And do you have any horse feed? Oh, and a couple tankards of drink, please!"

"For another quarter."

Elaeínn fished out the necessary coins from the stolen purse, praying there would be enough. She was left with only a quarter-naemmon after paying.

The innkeeper served them both a mug of mead and then disappeared back through the door. She returned with a sack of oats before disappearing once again, the sounds of the kitchen penetrating the thin walls as she started to prepare their breakfast.

Elaeínn and Velrin slouched into their seats, thirstily slurping down the mead while the two drunkards stirred and then confusedly blinked at their surroundings before stumbling out of the tavern. It remained reasonably quiet as the escapees relished in the arrival of their breakfast.

"What now, then?" Velrin asked, popping the yolk of his egg.

"Sleep," Elaeínn replied unequivocally. "And then we carry on."

"And if someone has recognised us and informed the guards?"

"They haven't, Vel, they haven't done that. We've only just arrived and the only person to have seen us is the innkeep."

"That's all it takes."

"She won't have reported us. Do you think we'll be able to get a room for a quarter?"

Velrin nearly jumped out of his chair as the door swung open, the air resonating with the grating of steel plate as a detachment of soldiers filed in. They looked over the lone patrons sternly, Elaeínn bowing her head as she focused intensely on tearing apart her strips of streaky bacon.

"What can I get you boys?" The innkeeper, hearing their entry, appeared from the back room.

"Whatever's in your larder. We're bloody starved," one of them responded, turning their gaze from Elaeínn and Velrin.

Another soldier approached the pair while his cohorts crowded around the counter to speak with the innkeeper.

"Who do we have here at this hour?" he sneered.

"Travellers," Elaeínn said calmly, keeping her eyes down.

The soldier abruptly placed his hand under her chin and tilted her head to face him, an action immediately met with a swipe of her arm as she slid back, her chair scraping noisily against the floor.

"Get off me," Elaeínn growled, lowering her head again.

"Someone has a temper," the soldier snarled.

"We have no quarrel with you," Velrin interjected. "We just wish to be left in peace."

The soldier slowly turned to look at him, a mischievous smirk crossing his face.

"What'd you say?" he chortled, bearing down on the former professor.

"We have done nothing to provoke you, we would just like to eat our meal in peace. Is that so much to ask?"

"Oi! Boys! What do you think that we leave these two stragglers in peace?"

The other three soldiers joined their comrade, each with a tankard in hand. Their gazes mostly fell upon Elaeínn, each of them smirking like the first.

"He your dad, sweetheart?" one of them taunted.

"Hey, pops, what you say we take her for a little bit? You'll be, uh... contributing to the cause?"

Elaeínn tensed, reaching for her belt. But there was no sword to draw.

"You would bring dishonour to your countrymen," Velrin said, his voice remaining calm. "Not to mention you would be crossing the law."

"We are the law," one of them chuckled.

One of the soldiers placed their hand on Elaeínn's shoulder and she ripped his sword from its sheath in a flash, rising and sending her chair flying to the ground with a crash. The disarmed soldier backed away as Elaeínn brought her newfound sword to his chest while the other three drew their own weapons to confront her. One guarded Velrin as he, too, stood up.

"You've got some nerve, whore," one of the soldiers rasped, closing the distance between himself and Elaeínn as she backed away into the limited space. "Looks like we'll be gutting you before we have our fun."

"No!" a female voice cut across the air. The innkeeper burst through the door to the back room, gesticulating at the confrontation to little effect as the soldiers kept their gazes and weapons trained on Elaeínn and Velrin. "If you're going to do this, take it outside! I'll have no blood spilled in my tavern!"

"Shut up and pour us another drink, wench," the disarmed guard barked, slamming his fist against the counter.

"I beg your pardon?" she snapped.

"Pour us a drink or we'll report you as an FTA delinquent to the commander," he growled.

The innkeeper scowled and reached below the counter. The bolt had left her crossbow before the soldier had even registered its appearance.

Elaeínn lashed out at her opponent as steel crunched through bone, using surprise to her advantage as she stabbed clean through his chest before he had time to block her strike. She brought up her foot to launch the soldier backwards as Velrin exhaustedly uttered the words to a spell, lightning sparking from his fingertips and electrocuting his guard.

The one remaining soldier looked frantically to each side, considering each of his threats with a quick glance, before he tossed his sword to the ground where it rattled to rest at the feet of a fallen comrade.

"I surrender," he whimpered.

Elaeínn withdrew her sword and plunged it through his neck. A gasp escaped his mouth, followed by a river of blood as Elaeínn tossed the dirtied sword to the ground.

"He was unarmed, Elle," Velrin said disapprovingly.

"He was a witness," she seethed.

An uneasy silence ensued as the innkeeper glared at them so coldly they thought the blood in their veins would freeze.

"You two," she finally said. "You were never here."

"No, ma'am," Elaeínn said. "No, we weren't."

CHAPTER 9

The Emperor flew towards him as they synchronously drew their swords from their sheaths.

Richard swung first in an arc in front of his body, an attack Nendar parried with ease. He then counterattacked with two quick jabs and a swing over his shoulder, which Richard deflected with equal ease. They continued to dance, their swords coming together in predetermined motions, not a single strike posing any tangible danger as the ringing of steel echoed through the sewer's empty tunnels.

"You can't defeat me, Nendar," Richard warned, bringing his sword back across his body. "You've left it too late."

"It's been left later than this before, boy."

Nendar clenched his fist and then released it, pressing forwards and sending a gale through the tunnel. The sludge beneath them flowed up onto the walls and splashed over Richard as his sword was forced from his grip and he was blown through the air like a ragdoll. He crashed into the water some distance away, face submerged in a city's worth of excrement.

He breached the water's surface as Nendar's scimitar was plunged into his shoulder. He roared through gritted teeth and grabbed the handle with his left hand while Nendar continued to drive the blade deeper and deeper until Richard felt its tip pierce his back. In a burst of adrenaline-fuelled strength, Richard drew the sword's handle further still until he felt its carved wooden surface rub against the wound.

Nendar still gripped the hilt, his face exuding controlled ferocity as he and Richard struggled for control. They were so close that Richard could feel the Emperor's sharp breaths against his cheek.

"What is your plan, Fateborn?" Nendar snarled. "Do you want to die?"

Richard's free hand flowed into his jacket and he clenched the hilt of his dagger tightly before ripping it from its sheath and slashing Nendar's wrist. The Emperor grunted as a volley of blood further decorated the sewer's walls and he withdrew his injured hand. Richard used the opportunity to raise his leg and kick his opponent squarely in the stomach.

Nendar exhaled sharply as the boot knocked him from his feet and expelled the air from his lungs. He lost his grip on the sword, which remained planted in Richard's shoulder, and toppled over into the mire.

Richard searched frantically for his fallen sword, but soon gave up and reached for his bow and an arrow. Excruciating pain shot through his chest as the bowstring caught on the sword protruding from his back and he doubled over as Tregor placed his hand against the bounty hunter's forehead.

"Sleep, Fateborn," the sorcerer said. "And by tomorrow you will not remember a thing."

The darkness crept over Richard's consciousness and he fought to stay awake through the pounding pain in his shoulder and the effects of the magic snaking through his skull.

"I'm not going..." Richard murmured, stumbling backwards. "I'm not going back..."

Tregor traced a portal and leaned down to embrace the bounty hunter. In his stupor, Richard could see only blurred images of a dingy room with barren stone walls.

"Stay away from me!" he shouted, aimlessly jabbing the air with his dagger. His threats did nothing to deter the sorcerer.

Tregor lifted him up and Richard sheathed his dagger as the sorcerer tried to throw him through the portal.

"El'kak favor!" Richard cried, a spell nullified by Tregor's muttering. "Vampire! Where are you?"

"You reject your abilities for so long," Tregor said through gritted teeth. "Embrace them! You have the ability to alter the world at the snap of your fingers, but you choose to reject your incredible gift until you absolutely cannot go on without it! Why?"

"I don't need a lecture from you," Richard grunted, resisting Tregor's attempts to throw him through the portal. But nothing could distract him from the fact that his energy was dwindling.

"It's not a lecture but an imploration! You have so much potential, but you do not use it! It is a waste, and there is nothing I despise so much as wasted potential!"

"Perhaps I will embrace my abilities just this once," Richard seethed. "Just for you."

He drew his hand up and ripped the sword from his shoulder, crying in pain. Tregor, stunned, was not prepared as he dropped the bounty hunter, who attacked ferociously with the bloodied scimitar. He nicked the sorcerer in the chest, tearing his robe and leaving a shallow gash. Richard then fell to his knees and channelled his anger. Not into any spell, but into his uncontrollable potential.

He began to lift slowly into the air as blood poured from his shoulder, Tregor standing back as Nendar joined him. Richard's eyes glowed a faint blue as he held himself stationary in the air, crying with rage, still battling to stay conscious.

The two sorcerers slowly backed away as Richard poured his remaining energy into his rage. He drew one hand back, opened his mouth to scream, and pressed it forwards again.

A gust rustled the hair of both sorcerers as the bounty hunter, spent, fell into the water. He did not get back up.

*

"Grab him, quickly, before the vampire escapes," Tregor instructed.

Nendar dragged the bounty hunter's body through the portal, tossing him carelessly onto the barren table on the other side.

*

Richard awoke to chains dragging his limbs in each direction. He looked around for his belongings and found nothing. He had been stripped naked and left in a chamber devoid of all contents, even furniture—apart from the structure on which

54

had been chained up, and a wooden door directly opposite him.

He then remembered the events of the sewer and looked to his shoulder, expecting to see the gaping wound left by the scimitar. Instead, there was nothing—the skin was flawless.

"Nendar!" he called. "Get me down, you bastard!"

He attempted to mutter one of the few spells he knew that he thought could have helped him in the moment, but it had no effect. He looked again at the chains holding him prisoner and noticed the roots wound through them. He remembered seeing similarly modified shackles at Letham Deregor but had never asked what they were.

The door creaked open and Nendar Varanus slipped through, ensuring it did not open entirely. He closed it softly and stood, stone-faced, observing the defenceless bounty hunter.

"What are you waiting for?" Richard spat. "Convert me. Isn't that your goal?"

"Indeed it is," Nendar confirmed. "The only problem is that we have tried it twice before. And it has failed both times."

"Twice?"

"Yes. But you naturally only remember the second time."

"You're going to have to explain, because I'm just not following."

Nendar exited the room, again only allowing the door to open a crack, and then quickly returned with a chair. He sat, hunching over and using his arm to support his head.

"You have been a project of ours, Richard," Nendar began. "A project spanning some years now. The Council spent a long time searching for you, and it was actually Lynn who first discovered you, interacted with you. But you have no memory of that, correct?"

Richard thought long and hard, trying to remember a time before meeting Lynn Varanus in the operating theatre of the Virilian Palace. But the only thing he could find was the memory of her and the other members of the Council relieving him of his senses in the besieged city.

That was a new detail. It had been a while since Richard had been visited by his fragmented memories, but he had never realised the identities of the faceless mages. Now he recognised them all.

"The only memory I have of meeting any of you before Valerie is that city you were attacking," he hissed.

"Ah, yes, we'll get to that," Nendar said nonchalantly. "But yes, it was Lynn who you first met. In much a similar scenario to Valerie. Much the same setup. In fact, she didn't even tell us that she had found you, at first. She made it something of a pet project. One made significantly easier by your recent departure from that woman you loved so… what was her name? Linelle, was it?"

Richard scowled.

"Yes, you fell right into her arms. You ate up everything she had to say. And you made tremendous progress learning from her. Such limitless magical potential. That potential which you have again, despite Tregor's insistences, so excellently harnessed. A shame we will have to reset the progress once again."

"Why don't I remember any of this?" Richard growled, tugging futilely on his chains.

"Lynn kept a detailed log of her progress, one which we eventually discovered," Nendar continued, ignoring Richard's question. "She made sure to write about how you were wrapped around her finger. But, unfortunately, her success led to arrogance. She became cocky. And she attempted to convert you herself. In the city of Lana Rel."

The name rang a bell in Richard's head, but when he focused, he could think of nothing associated with it.

"Lana Rel was the site of Lynn's base of operations," Nendar explained. "The site of your training. Lynn finally told us how she had found you, trained you, and was in a position to convert you. It was quite a surprise, to hear that she had been concealing something we had dedicated our existences to. And to convert someone so powerful—it wasn't something any of us had ever done before. We weren't sure how stable you would be if we moved too quickly. Which is exactly what Lynn did.

"You were asleep and we were en route to visit for the first time. My foolish daughter decided she would try to impress us by attempting a conversion herself. A procedure which should only ever be carried out by an entire team on the weakest of wills. As you can imagine, things went wrong."

Nendar looked back at the door behind him before continuing.

"She wasn't strong enough. Nor was she deceptive enough to fool you once you awoke. The procedure triggered something in you, something we were very lucky not to trigger again back in the operating theatre of the Virilian Palace. You say you remember us attacking Lana Rel?"

"With hordes of Corrupted at your beck and call."

"Fascinating. That memory evidently is missing parts. The most significant of which being that the city was not destroyed by us, but by you. You destroyed Lana Rel."

"Liar!" Richard seethed, again struggling against his chains. "I've never even heard of the city! How could I have destroyed it?"

"You're hard to control, Richard. Very hard to control, which is why we have come so close to giving up. But the reward we could reap—it simply nullifies the risk.

"It was at that point that Lynn knew she had lost you. So she either killed you, and prevented anyone else from controlling you, or tried again. And you can see how that has gone."

"Well you've failed again," Richard mulled. "And this doesn't explain my memories."

"We arrived to the city to find it utterly decimated. After summoning nearby Corrupted to assist us in your capture, we wiped—or rather attempted to wipe—your memory, and implanted fabricated ones to fill the gap. But it was clearly a failure, as you are indeed beginning to remember things. Just as Valerie warned. And—"

"Just how long was she grooming me before I found out?"

"Two years," Nendar said bluntly. "Two long, arduous years ruined by arrogance. Two years of learning undone."

The door opened and Tregor entered, carrying a set of uninspiring beige clothes.

"And what was your role in this conspiracy?" Richard asked, his face still disfigured by a scowl.

"I would have liked to have been the one that recaptured you after your escape," Tregor said, placing the clothes on the floor and producing a chain ring from his robe, also laced with hevula root. "But we can't have everything we wish for."

He approached Richard and attached it to his bicep before fishing a small lock from his pocket and further securing the bracelet with it. He then undid the chains holding Richard spread-eagled in the air, allowing him to fall roughly to the ground as physical sensation snaked back into his limbs.

"Get dressed," Tregor said, gesturing to the bundle on the floor.

Richard eyed both sorcerers with suspicion as he donned the linen shirt and shorts, which were uncomfortably tight.

"Here's what we're going to do," Tregor continued. "We are going to attempt to wipe your memory once more. It is our only option, quite frankly. It was a risk the first time—it's an even bigger risk this time. And if you resist, you will almost certainly kill yourself. Do you want to kill yourself?"

Richard didn't respond, instead backing away, towards the door.

"Do not try to escape, because there is nowhere for you to go," Tregor warned. "We are not at the Retreat. We are not at Letham Deregor. We are nowhere that you would recognise. Nowhere that the vampire would recognise. There is no hope for you other than us."

Richard's suspicious grimace still refused to leave his face as he stepped further still towards the door.

"I want to go on a walk," he announced.

"Then go," Tregor said. "But be back soon."

The bounty hunter didn't know what to think. But he didn't argue, leaving the room without a moment's hesitation.

As soon as the door closed behind him, he took off. He had entered a semi-circular room, occupied by a staircase spiralling down. He flew down the stairs and found the bottom, a circular, carpeted room almost as empty as the room in which he had been chained up. Across from the bottom of the stairs was a solid oak door with a rusted handle. He raced towards it and tore it open.

The fresh air was invigorating and Richard slowed his pace, comfortably certain that he wasn't being chased, and also acutely aware of the fact that he would likely break an ankle if he continued to run barefoot. Instead, he allowed himself to admire the scenery.

The location of his new prison was another forest, this time deciduous, the semblance of a path leading into the brush. He looked behind him and took in the scale of the prison—an old tower constructed from stone bricks, it loomed over the surrounding landscape, having been built on the highest point for miles around. In one direction, he could see cliffs rising from the ground in the far distance. In the other, the land seemed just to fall away.

Richard picked up a rock and laid his arm against the ground before bashing the lock separating him from magic. Though he quickly came to realise that he was making no progress and frustratedly launched the rock into the brush as he walked into the forest. A slight breeze from the direction of the cliffs rustled his hair and sent a chill down his spine as he appreciated the smell of fresh dew and flowers.

The path eventually led to a lake, but one small enough that Richard could see easily to the other side. A jetty protruded from the lake's edge, where a rundown wooden shack stood beneath an oak. He walked over to the shack, opened the door, and was surprised to find what he thought would have been debris—instead, the shack was occupied by fishing poles and nets which appeared to be in good condition.

He withdrew and walked to the end of the jetty, sitting down and dipping his feet into the water. It was cold, but he remained there until they became numb, lying back and gazing into the cloudy sky.

Not long later, the cold became too much, and he drew his feet from the water, but stayed on the jetty. Overcome by an encompassing calm, he allowed his eyes to droop and fell to sleep, soothed by the rustling of the leaves and the gentle whistling of the breeze.

*

"He isn't returning, Tregor."

"He will," the sorcerer assured, removing the boiling pot from the flames. He poured two cups and then sprinkled the ground camomile into both before stirring with a silver teaspoon.

"And if he doesn't?"

"Then he'll live out his days in the Florian wilderness. Not a bad way to go, if you ask me."

"I thought our goal was to convert him. So we could use him to safeguard the future of the Council."

"I'm no fool, Varanus. Your objective has been to use him as a tool of the Empire from the very beginning. I have played along thus far, and I will continue to play along out of simple gratitude for your rescuing me from Letham Deregor. But I have no intention of converting the Fateborn so that you may use him for conquest."

"You're a bastard," Nendar said, slamming his fist on the table. "I left my daughter in the clutches of the vampire so that I could save you instead. Lynn would not have resisted in this way. Not at all. I saved you, Tregor. You owe me."

"I owe you nothing," he said calmly, raising one of the cups of tea to his lips and sipping carefully. "The Council is dead. Look at us, Nendar. We're all that's left. Us and Kasimir, hiding out on the other side of the world."

"Lynn could still be alive."

"But what are the odds? I could waste my energy searching for her signal, but I simply do not care."

"That's it, then? You're just going to give up on centuries of work, centuries of preparation and anticipation, just like that?"

Tregor sipped the tea again. "The project was a failure the moment it began. We were out of our leagues, Nendar. Trying to control the most powerful source of magic known in this world. A direct product of the Heart. I thought perhaps I could give it one more try. One last attempt to salvage the wreckage of the Council. But I can see quite clearly now that you did not come to me with the security of magic on your mind, and equally clearly see that that boy is never going to succumb. His will is too strong. Even before you consider his magical strength."

"He will fall into the open arms of the vampire if we do nothing," Nendar admitted, relaxing in his chair and taking the first sip of his own tea.

"The vampire cannot find him out here," Tregor assured. "Nobody can. Perhaps the safest thing for magic is for him to realise his own role in the years to come. I do not want to kill him, because there are still grave threats which he could easily put down. The dragon, for example."

"The dragon and the elf girl who rides it," Nendar added. "Lynn was easily wooed by the dragon's proposition that our crystals are 'corrupting' magic. It's a dangerous creature. We really ought to find it."

"We would have to travel to Fenalia."

"It's not such a terrible journey. We would look rather out of place, though."

Nendar rose from his seat, turning back towards the tower's entrance. "And what do you suggest if the Fateborn breaks the lock on the band and escapes?"

"He won't," Tregor affirmed. "Not by himself. He would need the assistance of a magician to break that lock. And there certainly aren't any out here. No, the Fateborn isn't going any-where."

Nendar was silent for a while before responding. "Alright then. Shall we go?"

Tregor finished his tea and set the cup back onto the table before rising himself.

"Yes," he said. "We'll sail from the Isles." The sorcerer then traced a portal to a wooden dockyard nested between two skerries.

"After you."

*

When Richard finally awoke, he found that he wasn't alone.

61

CHAPTER 10

FREE CITY OF DANNOS, SANTEROS

Elton, Felix, and Ferris stood above the sewer grate for no more than five minutes after the sorcerer had told them to leave.

"We should probably go have a look," Elton decreed, having obtained a torch from a passing trader.

"I don't know if either of you have considered this," Ferris said as they scaled the ladder back down into the dark. "But the spell Richard used to let us conversate is not an endless one. And unless the native language here is Miradosi, I don't speak it."

"Good thing we're going back to find them, then, isn't it?" Elton patronised, grimacing as he set foot into the grimy water.

It didn't take long for them to reach the site of the battle and its sole remaining combatant.

"Vampire," Elton said in bewilderment, staring at the chained-up, oil-stained body buried into the cracked bricks of the sewer wall. He raised his arms to prevent his companions from moving any further before taking a closer look himself.

Kalahar was not moving—his ruby eyes were closed and his body was constricted by silver chains woven around his limbs. Laced through these silver chains were what looked to be withered roots.

Elton prodded the vampire's body with a finger before jumping back. Felix let out a chuckle when he saw the fright plastered across Elton's face.

"He's not dead. He can't be," Elton enunciated. "He has wittered about his immortality to me too many times. There is

"

no way that one man can kill him. And in the same way I already tried."

"I doubt he's dead," Felix commented, joining him and running a finger along the chains. "Just neutralised."

Felix's suspicion was confirmed when the vampire groaned, a sound which came out as more of a guttural rumbling. He strained against the chains, hissing with pain.

"How's this happened, then?" Elton asked, raising his voice.

"Get me out of these chains, Elton," Kalahar rasped. "Get me out or I will raze this city to the ground, saving you for last."

"You ordered my death anyways. I don't really see the benefit for me of either choice."

"You were never going to die, you fool. I knew the bounty hunter would not kill you; he's too pure. He doesn't kill those he deems innocent. Despite the fact that he thought he could recover his lover out of it."

There was a period of silent contemplation before Elton finally said, "I'll release you," to the shock of Felix and the confusion of Ferris. He silenced them before they could voice any protest. "On two conditions."

"You think you can make demands?" the vampire laughed.

"I'm not the one bound by silver chains," Elton retorted. "And you claimed to be impervious to the likes of this. I have a lot of questions."

"None of which I'm going to answer. What are the conditions?"

"One. You tell us where Rosa is and return her unharmed."

"Ha! Is that it?" the vampire laughed. "She is at Letham Deregor. I will quite happily return her, for she is of no use to me anymore. Now, break these chains and I will have her with you almost instantaneously."

"And two, you will stop feeding me nightmares every single night. They will stop, forever."

"But of course, that can be arranged," Kalahar smirked.

Elton glanced at his companions for reassurance and was met with nods, though Ferris still looked more confused than assured. He then sent Felix to retrieve an axe while he and the bard stood guard.

"I'd like to add one more condition, while we're here, vampire," Elton exclaimed.

"You don't get any more conditions."

"Do you want to be freed?"

Kalahar scowled.

"I want you to teach the minstrel our language," Elton continued. "Not temporarily, permanently."

"Do the schools of Dannos have any spare classrooms I may use? Or are we to begin lessons here?"

"You know what I meant."

"I cannot teach a language. It is not so simple. I can cast a spell to extend the length of your mutual understanding of Archaeish, but nothing more."

"For how long?"

"A week."

Felix returned shortly, hatchet in hand. He handed it to Elton, who cast a weary glare over the vampire, a look met only with indifference.

"You had better stay true to your word."

"When have I not?"

Elton drove the hatchet onto one of the chains dragged taut across the vampire's torso, narrowly missing the vampire himself. The chain snapped and Kalahar burst instantly free, diving into the water in a flurry of motion before rising again, cleansed of any remnants of the oil left from the attack.

"Thank you, Elton," he said, his voice deep and echoing off the walls of the sewer.

He vanished without a word and Elton swore successively to himself. Felix just sighed. Both were then surprised when a portal opened itself moments later, through which the vampire appeared with Rosa's unconscious body in his arms.

"I keep my word," the vampire said, turning to Ferris and resting a hand on his forehead. "Hablar Arcaea ek'stezzar."

Ferris's pupils briefly dilated before returning to a normal size and he dazedly blinked several times.

"My side of the deal is done," Kalahar said. "And now I depart."

The vampire subsequently dropped Rosa's body into the sludge and disappeared.

"Grab her, Felix, for fuck's sake," Elton swore, turning and running a hand through his hair. Felix trudged up to the sorceress, whose head had landed in a pile of refuse and narrowly avoided submersion. He picked her up, carrying her over his shoulder.

Elton inspected the chains lying broken in the indent in the wall. They appeared to be freshly forged, bearing no signs of age or wear. He didn't recognise the root woven through them. Collecting the chains into a pile, he slung them over his shoulders before marching for the exit.

A few hours later, they reconvened in the Redhouse, bathed and changed—apart from Rosa, who had failed to wake from her slumber. She had been taken to her office and left there, though Elton had periodically checked to see if she had stirred, each time with the same conclusion.

Elton, Felix, and Ferris sat around the table in the director's office in the section of the Redhouse dedicated to the Dannosi Intelligence Service, joined this time by Ant and Fez. They had been recruited to the agency upon its foundation, having spent years running the Redwinter Syndicate's operations in Santhion and Thorne respectively. The two men had been informed of the day's events, and both were rendered mostly speechless.

"And remind us who he is?" Ant asked Elton after a lengthy silence, directing his apprehensive gaze to Ferris.

"You don't need to worry about him. He's no foreign agent, he just came here with Richard. And then we were separated."

"What does he want to know? I'll tell him," Ferris exclaimed.

"Nothing of importance," Elton dismissed. "He's just suspicious. Especially considering you two can't bloody converse."

"What's our next move, boss?" Felix cut in. "We had him at our fingertips and now he's gone. Gone probably for good."

"I'm not going to rest until that vampire is dead. Actually dead," Elton stated. "That will involve finding him again. And now that we have Rosa back, hopefully she will find him a lot faster than before. And"—he jostled the chains resting on the table—"she will hopefully be able to tell us what these are."

As if on cue, the door swung slowly open and produced a bedraggled Rosa, still soaked and reeking of sewage.

"Rosa," Elton exclaimed, rising from his seat and moving to greet her. "Are you alright?"

"I have been better," she rasped, her face bearing only disgust. "I will recount my story after a bath or several. Good day, gentlemen."

One bath later and Rosa returned, hair still wet, but the stench of sewage thoroughly eradicated.

"Alright, then," she began, slouching lazily in one of the chairs and resting her legs on the table. "You know, it's occurred to me that I have no idea how I ended up in that state. Would anyone care to explain?"

"Kalahar happened," Elton mused.

"Sounds about right," the sorceress said distastefully. "Okay, then. What happened beforehand? It wasn't so long after the eclipse. I was tracking Kalahar, as you know. What I didn't know was that he was also tracking me. Because one night, my room got awful bloody cold. I woke up, and there he was, red eyes and all. He did his little monologue, opened a portal, and I wasn't really left a choice. He took me back to Letham Deregor. Made me his prisoner, shackled me up in some side room."

"Why couldn't you just teleport back?"

"He wove hevula through the shackles. Stopped any attempt at magic in its tracks. In fact, I notice that's the same thing you have here, whatever this is," she said, reaching to grab the chain and dragging it towards her.

"We found Kalahar in the sewers. Do you remember Richard?"

"The man from Letham Deregor?"

"Yes. He was also searching for Kalahar. But apparently, some wizards were searching for him. They found him, and with him, Kalahar. They managed to restrain Kalahar with those chains. After dousing him in the oil we brewed to fight off the eclipse."

"Interesting," Rosa remarked. "Hevula root is a magical inhibitor. Has completely mystical properties. I didn't think it could work against someone as powerful as Kalahar, but you say it restrained him?"

"Utterly immobilised him. He had to beg us to free him."

"Incredible." Rosa stood up and swept her eyes across the room's occupants.

"I have a theory," she announced. "I think Kalahar is a malevolent vampire. Just like those we slaughtered. That part isn't hard to deduce, we figured it out on pretty much the day of the eclipse. But for some reason, he has always been invulnerable to the same weakness shared by all other malevolents. And I think that's down to magic. I think he magically protects himself, and that's why we've been unable to kill him. I think if we could trap him, restrain him again with hevula chains, I think he would become vulnerable. Truly vulnerable. And then we could finally put an end to him."

A content silence engulfed the room as the theory was considered with nods of approval.

"We'll need a plan, then," Elton decided. "We don't know where he is, but we do know where the one place in the world is that he seems to care about. We threaten that, I'm sure he would come running to save it."

"And how do you propose we 'threaten' it?" Fez asked.

Elton smirked. "Explosives," he chuckled. "A lot of fucking explosives."

"If only Paul were here," Felix said. "Sounds like just his sort of job."

"This isn't an intelligence mission, so I might just invite him," Elton said. "Ant, Fez, I know it isn't your usual line of work, but I'd like you to find out about sourcing enough black powder to take down a fortress the size of five Redhouses. When you're ready, us five and Paul will go to Letham Deregor and prepare a trap. Then we'll place the explosives, and hopefully the vampire will show up. We'll spring him with the chains, douse him in oil, and finish him off for good."

"Excellent plan, Count," Ant concluded. "We'll get right on it."

"And you, bard, I haven't forgotten about you," Elton added, turning his focus to Ferris.

"I have skills that might help you in such a fight," Ferris claimed. "I can wield a sword to the same proficiency as I can strum a lute. A rapier, ideally—I'm not such a fan of clunkier weapons."

"If you want to come to Letham Deregor, I'm all for it," Elton said. "But what do you get out of it?"

"I get one step closer to the Emperor of Sanskar. If they're hunting Kalahar, then I bet my breeches they'll be coming to this Letham Deregor as well. I'll help you kill the vampire – and if the opportunity arises to put down the Emperor, I would very much appreciate your help in doing so."

"I can agree to that. Let's call this meeting done. Ant, Fez, get to work."

They all rose from the table in unison and Elton filed out alongside Felix, Rosa, and Ferris.

"Apologies if I am stepping out of line here, but I think we really should act as soon as possible," Ferris said. "I don't know where Richard has gone but you saw how he tried to attack you. That vampire is using him and the longer we wait to kill him, the more likely it is that he finds Richard again. I don't particularly want that to happen, because I need him."

"If I may be frank, I don't give a shit about what happens to Richard," Elton said. "That man obeyed the order of a devil-spawned monster without hesitation. It was pure luck that those other sorcerers appeared, because we would have died, otherwise."

"You don't understand. He lost someone very dear to him and he seems to think Kalahar will be able to teach him how to bring them back."

"I don't really care for his motives, I care for his actions. And his actions involved swinging his sword at me with intent to kill."

Elton led the group back towards the exit, thoroughly exhausted. The only things on his mind were a bottle of Knight's Relief and his bed. Unfortunately for him, he couldn't have either, as he was interrupted by the receptionist once again.

"I'm sorry to be a bother, Count, but there's someone else here to see you. A Villius Abranor."

"Never heard of him," Elton said. "Who is he?"

"He said he represents some academy in Altercant. I don't exactly know where that is. I had him go sit down, just over there."

Elton sighed and approached the frail, uninspiring man occupying one of the seats in the lobby. Though he quickly banished any appearance-based prejudice from his mind when he realised that he must have come across as much the same, only fatter.

The man stood up proudly and brushed down his clothes, keenly extending a hand. Elton shook it wearily.

"Count Redwinter, it is my honour," he said, bowing slightly. "It is truly noble what you have done with the Syndicate."

"What brings you here? And who are you?"

"Villius Abranor of the Fencing Academy of Altercant. The governor sends his warmest regards. If it is possible, I would like a meeting in private."

Elton looked at his companions and they agreed without words to depart.

Villius followed the Count into the bowels of the Redhouse in search of an empty room and, eventually finding one, Elton gestured him inside. It was then Villius who insisted on locking the door, which Elton did.

"You never know who's listening," Villius said, taking a seat. "Now, Count, I'm sure that you're aware of developments in King Hortensio's court. Namely the appointment of a court mage."

"Yes, we are quite aware. We don't see the implications as of yet."

"We in Altercant unfortunately do. Hortensio has demonstrated himself to be irresponsible at best and outright dangerous at worst. He is not fit to rule, and he endangers the order of the entire continent with every minute he spends upon that throne. We are acutely aware that Dannos has an existing grudge against him. Am I correct?"

Elton nodded, stroking his chin.

"A meeting with the King resulted in only belittlement from both him and his general. Quite simply put, there is no room for polite discussion with him. He must be replaced."

"You mean—"

"Yes, I do. This would not be the first time we have involved ourselves in foreign affairs for the benefit of the continent. It will certainly not be the last."

Elton took a deep breath and stared at the table. "And what would our role be in this?"

"It is our understanding that your court mage has been inside the Blue Palace already and possesses the ability to open portals. We would like to use this to get inside. We have an informant on his court, who has been feeding us a steady stream of information. The King is preparing for an expedition – part of this preparation apparently involves a banquet at which he will be personally present.

"This will be our opportunity—we will sneak in before the event begins, disguise ourselves, and attend the banquet as normal guests. One of us will have, however, visited the kitchen. Namely the vats, with a bottle of poison. When the King calls a toast, it will be his last."

Villius looked expectantly at Elton, whose eyes were still trained on the table.

"Well, Count? Do we have an agreement?"

"You're going to kill everyone in that hall," Elton said coldly.

"That is a risk, but everyone can be replaced. In fact, the more of his associates we eliminate, the better, quite frankly. I'm surprised by your hesitation, Count. You act as if you haven't spent your life a ruthless criminal. You have killed hundreds—what difference is a few more?"

"Is there not another way?" Elton protested. "Is there not a way where we just take out Hortensio—and maybe Jannis— and leave the innocents alive?"

"That would be much riskier," Villius said sharply. "And Altercant would not be willing to deal the final blow in such a way. If that is the method you wish to pursue, then it would have to be someone on your side to do it."

"Fine," Elton said. "One of *my* men kills him and we will help you."

"Wonderful. I will send a report back to the governor at once. While I am doing that, I will require accommodation here—is that possible?"

"I'll sort something out. Come find me in a couple hours."

Villius bowed once more and turned to leave.

"One more thing," Elton said as Villius caressed the door's handle. "When exactly is this banquet?"

"Oh, did I not say? The banquet is a leaving celebration—and it's taking place tomorrow evening."

"Tomorrow evening?" Elton repeated in shock.

"That is correct. You do not need longer, do you?"

"No... No," Elton confirmed, shaking his head. "Tomorrow is fine."

*

Rosa and Felix reached the Leaky Tankard with Ferris as the sky took on a deep shade of orange.

"We used to just drink in the Redhouse," Felix explained, batting off an invitation to play cards as he passed through the busy outdoor dining area. "But Regi cracked down on that when he reorganised the place. Now we have to go here. And you know what? I prefer it."

The music exploded in their ears as they pressed open the freely swinging door to the tavern. Ferris beamed at the assembly of musicians gathered on the tavern's sizeable stage next to the bar, playing a host of instruments from lutes to horns to fiddles to drums. Torches bathed the room in warm yellow light and drinks were poured by the gallon to the many revellers settling in for the evening.

"Drinks?" Felix asked, beckoning Ferris and Rosa to the bar. Both accepted the offer with enthusiastic nods.

They found a free table on the mezzanine floor above and claimed it as their own while more and more guests arrived in droves. Ferris sniffed the ale Felix had provided with excitement before raising the tankard to his lips and drawing a long swig.

"This is better than anything they brew in Mirados!" he exclaimed, wiping his lip before taking another gulp.

"It's the one thing they can do right in Santeros," Rosa chuckled.

Ferris downed the rest of his drink and stood up, looking over the banister. Specifically, he focused on the musicians.

"Do you think I'd be able to perform?" he turned to his companions and asked.

Felix rolled his eyes and rose from his seat to follow the bard down the stairs. He approached the barkeeper, a burly

71

man with an extravagant moustache, and leaned casually onto the counter.

"He wants a go on the stage," Felix said.

"He'll have to wait his turn," the barkeeper said. "They booked the space earlier."

"You hear that, Ferris?" Felix asked, turning back to face the bard. Except the bard wasn't there.

"Ferris?" Felix asked again, this time quieter and more confusedly as he surveyed the tavern. It was then that he spotted him.

Ferris strode proudly onto the stage, interrupting the performance and brandishing the lute that had until that point only been slung over his back.

"Ladies and gentlemen of Dannos!" Ferris called. "I know you can't understand a word of what I'm saying, but I'm about to play you a new song—*The Final Flight of the Phoenix*, a work of my own!"

The crowd responded in confusion with a few boos ringing out from further back as the performers whose show Ferris had interrupted muttered angrily to one another. But then Ferris began to strum, and the negativity in the room evaporated.

Felix stared in bewilderment as the bard strummed a song with a melody completely foreign to him. He had never heard anything of the like. The tempo was rapid, the playing energetic, the lyrics—he didn't understand the meaning behind them, but they sounded meaningful. The crowd reacted similarly, despite the fact that they couldn't understand a word the bard was saying as he danced around the stage.

He's pretty good, Rosa thought to herself as she emptied her tankard and stood up to search for another. But as she moved towards the stairs, she found her passage blocked.

"Where do you fink you're goin', miss?" one of the men blocking the stairs asked. He was missing several teeth and wore an eyepatch.

"Down the stairs, for a drink, as it happens," Rosa said defiantly, attempting to manoeuvre around them. But they remained planted in their position.

"You don't recognise us, do ya?" a second man, much skinnier than the first, asked.

"Why would she?" a third, brutish and deep-voiced, spoke. "She's a suck-up for new King Regi."

"I'd rather you just told me who you were rather than fucking around like this," Rosa said, backing away almost unnoticeably slowly.

"We worked for the Syndicate," the skinny one said, closing the distance between himself and Rosa. "That is, until Regi went soft and kicked us out. Now we've got nothin'."

"There are plenty of opportunities for former associates of the Syndicate," Rosa supplied. "Many still work for the Count."

"Fuck the Count," the eyepatch-wearer exclaimed, baring his remaining teeth. Rosa felt a fleck of spittle fall upon her face and disgustedly wiped it off.

"You're 'is favourite, aren't you?" the brutish one said, backing her towards the corner. "You were probably the one who told him to destroy our lives."

"I think there's been quite a misunderstanding—"

Rosa couldn't finish her sentence as the shiv entered her gut. She produced a fireball the size of her palm and released it as the shiv was retracted, sending the eyepatch-wearer through the air, where he crashed against the banister and fell, alight, over the mezzanine.

The shiv was retracted and she was stabbed again, this time in the chest. She gasped and coughed violently, decorating her assailant's face with blood as he stabbed her a third time before she sent him, too, sailing over the banister.

The sole remaining attacker was the skinny man, who drew his own shiv and raised it. It fell, and he fell with it as the throwing knife pierced the back of his skull.

Rosa coughed and showered the floor in blood, wheezing for breath. Felix and Ferris bolted towards her as she laid her head against the ground, blood continuing to pour from her wounds, saturating her tunic.

I never noticed the music stopping, she thought to herself as she began to lose consciousness.

Felix reached her first and used one of his knives to slice through her tunic without hesitation. He saw the three wounds and began to apply pressure to each in turn, shouting something Rosa couldn't hear.

Why did I stop carrying a sword? That would really have helped...

A vignette appeared around her vision as Ferris dashed down the stairs on Felix's command. The affair had attracted a sizeable crowd, though the bystanders did nothing but watch.

Well, Regi, I hope you can find someone else to take you to Letham Deregor. I don't think I'll be able to do it. Not soon, anyways.

She placed her hand over her body and deliriously uttered a spell, one she had learned from the Lazerian sorceresses. As she spoke the last word of it, the vignette engulfed her vision and she fell into darkness.

CHAPTER 11

CAMELION, SALYRIA

Hortensio, pouting, allowed the maid to finish buttoning up the navy jerkin. It was tight, and, combined with the collar of his doublet being so close-fitting that he felt on the verge of choking, he was almost convinced she was trying to kill him.

"I look bloody ridiculous," he complained, trying vainly to pull the collar away from his neck to give him room to breathe.

"Nonsense, Your Majesty," the maid beamed. "You look positively dashing."

"You're just trying to impress me," he muttered. "As long as the rest of the guests are dressed in outfits just as embarrassing."

"There's nothing embarrassing about dressing to impress, Your Majesty," she giggled. "The other guests will of course be dressed up. I don't know how many balls you have attended but typically the only people who wear armour to them are the ones guarding the entrance."

"And what happens if someone comes at me with a knife? Fat lot of good this will do against a sharp edge."

"That's what the guards are for, Your Majesty. You need to relax."

"Relax? There are enemies everywhere. I can't trust any-one."

"You can trust me."

Hortensio rolled his eyes and allowed her to affix a golden brooch over his heart, bearing the Salyrian coat of arms—two white lions on a navy field.

"Perfect," she said, lightly clapping her hands together.

"Ridiculous," Hortensio retorted. "Where's Jannis?"

"I will show you to him, Your Majesty."

The maid opened the door from the King's wardrobe, a room large enough to house a family—a room which went largely unused under Hortensio's rule.

Jannis's room was located just across from Hortensio's, and the maid knocked rhythmically before backing away and standing close to the King's side. He felt the urge to step away.

"I can't breathe in this bloody thing," Jannis could be heard shouting in the background as the door swung open, another maid having come to greet them. Jannis stepped out of his own wardrobe, much smaller than Hortensio's, yet still extravagant.

"We look ridiculous," he exclaimed, gesticulating.

"Agreed," Hortensio said, briskly entering the room. "What time did we say the banquet was?"

"Seven o'clock tomorrow, Your Royalness."

"Tomorrow! Then what is the meaning of being forced into this today?"

"I'm as clueless as you. But it was your idea to host the banquet."

"I didn't know I'd have to put up with this!" he again yanked the collar of his doublet, drawing exaggerated breaths.

It was at this point that they were joined by Kasimir, who was dressed entirely in black, though just as formally.

"You make it look easy," Hortensio rasped.

"I've been to my fair share of feasts," the sorcerer smiled.

"I can't wait for it to be over. I've not stopped thinking about this expedition."

"I hope you're good with sailing, Your Majesty, because there's a lot of it involved."

"Oh." The King frowned. "Is that right?"

"The Heart of magic is located on an island in the middle of the Great Sea. Legend places it at the precise centre of the known world."

"Nothing I can't conquer," Hortensio claimed, resuming his usual confidence.

Kasimir nodded and clasped his hands, turning to face the door. "Was there anything I could do for you before I depart, Your Majesty?"

"Yes, actually, there is."

Hortensio strode to the doorway and pushed his way through the maids, beckoning Kasimir and Jannis to follow. He barged through courtiers, servants, guards, and barons, feeling their stares penetrating his back as he went.

It didn't take long to reach Kasimir's room and Hortensio made a beeline for the portal frame. He had a single destination in mind.

"I want to go to the Redhouse," he announced.

The room was silent for a moment before Jannis was the first to speak. "Are you crazy?"

"It's a banquet. I would like to invite Count Redwinter."

"For what purpose?"

"To kill him, of course."

"You'd be killed the moment you set foot on those streets," Jannis asserted. "I won't let you. I know we could get away with a lot before, but they aren't bandits anymore. They've an actual government."

"They'll always be bandits at heart. Besides, I won't be the one inviting. You will." He fixed his gaze upon Kasimir.

"Me?" the sorcerer laughed. "I am but your court mage."

"Precisely why you are the only applicable candidate for the job. You need to be able to open a portal back here to let him and his posse through. I feel that leaving this one open constantly would pose a security risk. And they don't know who you are—you wouldn't have a bolt placed between your eyes the moment you stepped onto those forsaken streets."

"And say the Count refuses?"

"I will write him a letter personally. Bring it with you, and hopefully it will tug at whatever heartstrings he has left. He won't refuse."

CHAPTER 12

TYEN'AELI HIGHWAY

Elaeínn and Velrin spent the following week travelling south, avoiding confrontation by any measure. They wore hoods to hide their faces. They travelled at night, under cover of darkness. And they did not speak to anyone, except to ask innkeepers along the way for meals and rooms. The closest they came to danger was when a group of rowdy drinkers attempted to coax the pair into a brawl one evening, when the tavern was mostly clear. But the innkeeper cleared them out just as fists were raised.

Their muscles numb with fatigue, their horses slow with exhaustion, and their bellies hollow with hunger, the foreboding sprawl of the Darklight Forest rose before them at last. The closer they had moved towards the region, the greater the presence of the Tyen'Aeli military had become—and so they were forced to be more careful than ever as their horses trotted steadily through the night.

"I never thought we'd make it," Velrin exclaimed. "But now we've got a new problem."

"What is it now, Vel?" Elaeínn's eyes drooped as she spat the question.

"You really want to march us through the Darklight unarmed? It's dangerous enough with weapons. We go in as we are, in our condition, with no weapons—we'll be eaten alive. Have you ever seen a crawler?"

"Not in person. I've seen illustrations."

"You don't want to see one in person. Because chances are, if you don't have a means to defend yourself, it'll be the last thing you do ever see."

They brought their horses to a walk as they approached the treeline, a military camp lit by enormous bonfires visible in the near distance. In the dim light of the moon, the mouth to the enigmatic forest appeared only as a void, not even a sliver of light penetrating the thick canopy. And not even a whisper of sound escaped the entangling brush.

"No, Elle," Velrin asserted, bringing his horse to a halt. "I'm putting my foot down. I'm not going in defenceless."

"What do you want us to do, then?" she hissed, yanking the reins. "Go ask that camp over there if they have any spare swords? Or maybe ask for an escort?"

"Don't be banal, you know it would be suicide to go in there unprotected! We need a plan!"

"You have your magic. Is that not enough?"

"I haven't the energy to conjure so much as a candleflame let alone anything significant enough to strike down a spider the size of an antelope! You've never cast a spell in your life! You don't understand that it isn't as simple as knowing a few words!"

Elaeínn's horse snorted, echoing her own thoughts perfectly.

"We can't afford to be impatient," Velrin urged.

"Well, then." Elaeínn smirked. "I guess you know what we have to do."

She yanked the reins again to turn the horse around until they faced in the direction of the military encampment. White tents stretched along the border to the forest, but a sizeable gap had been left before the treeline. They basked in a constant orange glow, the bonfires situated periodically through the camp fed by meticulously kempt stacks of logs which allowed the flames to blaze high.

Velrin sighed and followed Elaeínn's lead. They traced the treeline towards the back of the camp, dismounting and hitching their horses as they neared.

The pair crept alongside the tent behind which they had stowed the horses, rounding the corner to come into view of one of the bonfires. It was mostly deserted apart from a pair of soldiers who they assumed were meant to have been on guard, but both were dozing.

"Awfully quiet for wartime," Elaeínn mused.

"You know what that means, right?" Velrin whispered agitatedly. "If they're so lax even here, then it means they've pushed beyond the Darklight. It means the elves are winning. And if they're winning so much that they can afford to sleep on the job, then we have a serious problem."

Elaeínn quickly mulled over her options as she glanced around the subsection of the camp through which they crept. Ramshackle fences had been erected to divide different areas housing various items and supplies. She spotted a pile of logs, just like those feeding the bonfire, next to a pen of horses—all of which were sheltered by white sheets of the same material as the tents. Creeping around to the other side of the tent, they could see opposing storage areas, one full of food, and another lined in its entirety with loaded weapon racks.

She looked at Velrin and they exchanged nods, tiptoeing around the barricades towards their newfound destination. They were just about to vault the fence into the horse pen when they heard a voice and stopped in their tracks.

"...and when we come back tonight, they'll all cry out in delight..." a soldier sang quietly out of tune as he passed through the storage area, leisurely dragging his feet. Elaeínn and Velrin did not tear their eyes from him, nor did they dare to move as he continued on towards the bonfire where the two guards lay asleep.

"We can't move til he's buggered off," Elaeínn whispered.

"Oi!" the soldier suddenly shouted, having stopped in front of the bonfire. "You two! What do you think you're doing?"

They froze, a shot of panic racing through Elaeínn's body before the soldier continued.

"Wake up, you useless layabouts! You're supposed to be on watch! What if a troop of midgets was to sneak up on you? You'd be dead!"

A subdued groaning resonated from the bonfire, mostly masked by the roaring of the fire as the two guards awoke and stood to attention.

"There are no midgets here, commander, and I rue the fact. Do you know how long we've been stuck here at this camp and not seen a lick of action?"

"Honestly, commander, there's no point us being on guard... there's nothing to guard against..."

"I don't want to hear it! You two nod off again and you'll have to guard yourselves against the scaffold! Now scout around and report when you've finished!"

The soldiers groaned and trudged noisily past the commander and through the storage area where they stopped to impertinently inspect the contents, dramatically turning over empty bowls and looking behind horses' ears. All the while they opened their mouths in feigned shock and stared with artificially wide eyes at the commander, who only shook his head.

The commander gave up and marched away, passing Elaeínn and Velrin in their meagre hiding place next to the white sheets of the tent. They flattened themselves to the ground, watching him intently as he entered a tent in an adjoining area of the camp and did not return.

The soldiers tasked with inspecting the storage area also took the commander's disappearance as a sign to return to their dozing. They hastily abandoned their search and settled back around the bonfire, snoring within moments.

Elaeínn pressed herself up from the ground and gestured for Velrin to stay behind, a suggestion he did not find difficult to refuse. She skulked around the edge of the tent storing the weapons, opting to squeeze between the boards holding the fence together rather than vaulting it, and came to stand before an arsenal of weapons enough to arm a platoon. There wasn't much in the way of diversity, the racks lining the tent's walls being occupied almost exclusively by swords. There were a handful of spears and pikes as well as a single axe, but she determined that it must have been plundered from the dwarves, based on its craftsmanship. A chest, the lid of which she lifted with immaculate care, was full of bows, and an adjacent barrel contained the corresponding arrows, hundreds of them.

She trod silently over the hardened ground and picked up a sword about the same length as the Dragonsteel Blade and stepped away, twirling it around to get a feel for its weight. It was heavier than what she was used to, but it would work.

A second identical sword found itself directly next to the first and she collected both, laying them flat along a table— one which resembled a desk, with only one open side between its legs—in the middle of the room. She then rummaged through another chest she found to be filled with leather scabbards. Acutely aware of the time she had spent in the open, she grabbed two which looked to be about the right size and tossed them over to the table—a little bit too hard.

The scabbards landed with enough force to thrust one of the swords over the table's edge, where it fell and landed with a metallic clatter. She didn't hesitate before diving under the table, allowing the lid of the chest containing the scabbards to slam shut.

The guards' snoring came to an abrupt halt and they leisurely made their way into the tent where Elaeínn kept her breathing shallow and rapid.

"Alright, commander, very good..." they called. "And now we're expected to clean up your mess, I presume?"

One of the soldiers approached the table with heavy, dragging footsteps before bending down to retrieve the fallen sword.

"Where even are you? You can't have got away that quickly..."

An armoured foot landed directly in front of Elaeínn, joined shortly thereafter by a second. She brought her shallow breathing to a halt.

"He's quick when he wants, isn't he?"

"Pedantic bastard. I bet this is his way of saying he wants a report."

"Oh, right, we never gave him one."

"What's all that noise about? Are you two finally doing some work?"

The two soldiers were joined noisily by the commander whose voice had travelled up the path from his tent. They looked confusedly at each other as he stepped into the storage area.

"Didn't you—"

"Didn't I what?" he interrupted. "Expect you to disregard my instructions? Yes. Which is why I'm in quite the state of shock to see you actually inspecting the place."

"We thought... didn't you make this mess on purpose?"

"What? Why would I ever do such a thing?"

"Wait, you didn't? We thought you made the mess to get us to have a look. But if you didn't make this mess…"

The scraping of steel whined lazily as the soldiers drew their swords, darting their eyes frantically around the shadowy surroundings.

"Are you telling me an intruder has slipped under your noses?" the commander bellowed. "Whoever they are, find them right bloody now! Or you'll be off to the scaffold not for idleness but negligence!"

The feet finally disappeared from in front of Elaeínn's face as the soldiers scurried away, allowing her to take a much-needed breath. She did so calmly, slowly, before cautiously peering out from under the table to find the path clear. The swords had been left unsheathed above her and she extended an arm to clutch one before bringing it silently back down, repeating this action for the other sword and the two scabbards. While the guards shouted commands, threats, and obscenities, she sheathed the swords while choosing her opportunity to withdraw from under the table. And then she ran.

Velrin was not where she had left him. She practically dived through the gap in the fence, rolling not-so-elegantly in the grass on the other side before returning to her feet and tiptoeing quickly around the outer edge of the adjacent tent. She found her companion, alarmed, at the rear end of the tent, out of view of the paths leading around the camp.

"For you." She thrust one of the swords, the one which didn't fit quite as snugly into its scabbard, into Velrin's hands.

"Whoever's there, show yourself!" one of the soldiers shouted. "You can't hide for long! Show yourself and you'll receive a swift trial!"

His demand was echoed by a soft chortling from his partner as they continually failed to find the pair of intruders, who traipsed closer and closer to the treeline.

"Elle," Velrin said quietly as Elaeínn tried to catch sight of the two soldiers. "Where have our horses gone?"

She turned slowly to face the place where they had previously tied their horses to a tree. Only the horses, as Velrin had suggested, were no longer there.

"They can't have found them. They weren't even looking for them!"

Velrin slowly kneeled down and ran his hand gingerly along the grass before passing his thumb over his fingers, grimacing.

"It wasn't the soldiers who took them."

Elaeínn shivered as she looked uneasily into the dark forest, seeing only blackness beyond the little foliage visible in the dim moonlight. She turned her ear to listen for any emanating sounds but heard only the shouts of the soldiers as they continued to look in all the wrong places.

"Well what do we do?" she asked in a frantic whisper.

"I'm not going through this forest at night. We wait until tomorrow."

"And where do you expect us to wait? Here? In the camp? In the middle of the surrounding fields? We've walked ourselves into an impasse!"

They both fell silent as the sound of a branch crashing to the forest floor rang out from the darkness. Their argument drew to a swift conclusion as they decided in unison to sprint back to the camp.

"Aha! I see you!" one of the soldiers exclaimed, having finally left the fence-enclosed areas and ventured into the open. "Surrender yourselves and I promise you won't be tortured! At least, not much!"

Elaeínn drew her sword and charged with a flourish towards the soldier, who was caught entirely off-guard as he clumsily readied his own sword, deflecting her strike in the nick of time. She used her momentum to strike again, this time swinging wide to leave an opening for a third, final blow.

The soldier could not scream as he sputtered blood over Elaeínn's face, his comrade in a state of shock as his eyes traced the length of Elaeínn's blade. She withdrew it swiftly and moved without hesitation to confront him, but he was eliminated by a sudden bolt of lightning before he could even raise his sword.

"We aren't staying here anymore," Velrin said emphatically, grabbing Elaeínn's wrist and dragging her around the back of the camp but refusing to step any closer than was necessary towards the treeline.

"You two! Drop your weapons, now!" the commander bellowed, his voice waking up any sleeping soldiers who hadn't already been roused by the clashing of steel.

Elaeínn and Velrin ignored his instructions as they pressed back towards the path, and the commander wasted no time in thundering towards them, weapon drawn.

Elaeínn's sword was the first to meet his. They came together with a sonorous clang, obliterating what little remained of the night's serenity. Soldiers began to file alarmedly and confusedly from their tents, some armoured, some unarmoured. Velrin's sword was the next to meet the commander's, a blow the skilled soldier easily parried. He attempted to counterattack, stepping forwards and aiming a jab at Velrin's unguarded thigh, but Elaeínn's sudden strike from below sent the sword out of the way just as it would have penetrated.

"Running out of time, Vel! Think of something!" Elaeínn called, sidestepping around the commander and attacking with three successive diagonal strikes, each blocked with relative ease.

The bolt of electrical energy tore a hole through the commander just as he raised his sword. He faltered, dropping his sword and looking down at his mangled torso, before his eyes glazed over and he fell.

"Run," Vel panted.

Elaeínn looked to her left, where she saw only the endless void of the Darklight. She looked to her right, where the soldiers had organised themselves and were approaching with rapid speed.

She sheathed her sword and took off at speed around the back of the camp, straying equal distance between the treeline and the outer tents. The pair were able to run faster than the soldiers, slowed by their heavy armour and general ineptitude, as well as a lack of direction as some lagged behind to observe their fallen commander.

Panting, wheezing, forehead slick with sweat, Elaeínn conquered the final hill between her and the mouth of the Darklight, the clamouring having grown quieter and quieter with each step. She felt herself on the verge of collapse, spurred only by adrenaline. Velrin was keeping up with her, but the strain on his face inferred a much deeper discomfort. They practically fell down the hill as they clambered over its peak and stumbled awkwardly onto the path leading into the darkness.

They looked at each other with nervous, exhausted, and desperate glances as the first National soldiers swarmed over the hill, their paces much quicker, their movements more organised. Elaeínn stared in every direction, considering the grasslands to the north, the empty, trodden path to the east, before finally settling her gaze upon the forest engulfing everything to the south. She and Velrin confirmed their choice with a gentle, reluctant nod.

Time seemed to slow as they took careful, measured steps into the forest, swallowed by the brush as light ceased to exist. The soldiers reached their location but did not press any further, shocked murmurs rippling throughout the growing troop as they lowered their weapons.

"Vel?" Elaeínn called softly. "Are you there?"

"Yes. Take my hand," he responded, somewhere to her right.

Elaeínn extended her hand towards the sound of his voice, though she could not see him and almost leapt into the air as she felt his hand encompass hers. And as they walked away from the moonlit entrance, further along the invisible path, Elaeínn felt genuine fear for the first time in a long while.

"Vel? What are we going to do?" she asked, her voice the only sound in the endless void.

A small flame burst into existence in the palm of Velrin's hand, and it was in the dim light, akin to candlelight, that the exhausted features adorning his face became so prominent. The heavy bags under his eyes; the rapidness with which he blinked.

"I don't know, Elle." He shook his head. "We try to stay alive. Because to put it simply, I'm surprised that's still the case."

They continued to traipse along the path, each step revealing more identical beaten road and sprawling brush. Branches descended like gangly limbs from the canopy. The occasional sliver of moonlight snaked its way through rare gaps in the leafage.

Although their delicate footsteps and breathing were the most frequent sounds to arise from the seemingly lifeless ecosystem, they were not alone. They could hear the occasional chittering of some unknown creature, the resonant, isolated crack of a fallen branch and the subsequent hurried scurrying—and at one point, sounding extraordinarily close, the pattering of heavier footsteps.

The dwarves were upon them before the debilitated pair had even registered they were there. Although their assailants bore weapons, it was not fury or determination occupying their half-concealed faces, but unadulterated confusion.

"What are ye two doing? Are ye trying to get yerselves killed?" one of them hissed, lowering his axe. "Who are ye? Identify yerselves!"

"Do the dwarves control the Darklight now?" Elaeínn tiredly asked. "We thought..."

"Identify yerselves," the dwarf growled.

"Elaeínn Tinaíd," she supplied. "FTA... what's going on?"

"Velrin Caliríen," Velrin added, cooling the dwarf's temper.

"Are ye suicidal? Do ye not appreciate the life yer gods have given yous?" he whispered aggressively. "What would drive ye to wander into the forest at night? And not just any forest, but this one?"

"We had no other choice," Elaeínn countered. "It was that or be hanged by the soldiers at the camp stationed just past the treeline."

"Ye said ye were FTA. Terrorists, right?"

"Freedom fighters."

"Yer friendly towards dwarves? Ye wish to bring down yer government?"

"Yes. You dwarves have a spy at the top of your chain of command and we need to let your commanders know about it. We're on our way to Hamatnar right now."

"No, yer bloody not. Yer on yer way to an early grave. Gah, gimme yer weapons and let us search yous. And quickly, gods, I never want to see another crawler for as long as I live."

Elaeínn and Velrin submissively dropped their newly acquired swords in their sheaths and allowed the dwarves to pat them down, having to physically lower themselves to allow the process to be completed in full.

"We will open a portal for yous. Darius here will go with yous. Ye will report to the castle, where someone will find a use for yous. Got it? And no funny business."

Elaeínn and Velrin nodded as enthusiastically as they could in their condition.

The thick smog of the dwarven capital city poured into their lungs and they both began to choke as they exited the portal. They had landed in a street surprisingly busy for the time of night.

Their arrival had quite rapidly prompted panic among the passing dwarves as they were subjected to penetrative gazes and foreign curses. But their escort shielded them, spitting back with such ferocity that each abusive passer-by retreated with a look of pure terror.

They were both thrust firmly through the night in the direction of Castle Rockfell, awestruck by the gargantuan fortress's majesty in the moonlight.

They were led by their guard through the industrious city and were not taken to the bridge Elaeínn had crossed when she had visited the city with Tynak. Instead, they were taken to a smaller—but still grand—crossing a short distance beyond the bridge to the Royal Quarter. The crossing was much busier than that into the Royal Quarter and had it not been the middle of the night, it would have been a struggle to get through, though the guard handling them had no qualms about forcing people out of the way.

They eventually reached the end of the bridge and were shown into the castle, this time without the winding tunnels and the drab corridors. Instead, they were met with a reasonably well-furnished reception, two further dwarves sitting behind a stone desk while guards streamed in and out of a stairwell.

"Ezketil, menne hezmar," their escort said, interrupting the receptionists' conversation. He initially received two stern gazes in return but those gazes softened as they realised to whom they were talking—something of which Elaeínn and Velrin weren't even sure themselves. They engaged in brief conversation before one of the dwarves behind the desk then stood up and barked an order to someone in the background.

"What's going on?"

"I think they need to confirm some things," Velrin explained. "From what I gathered. They didn't say what."

They were left to wait for no longer than fifteen minutes before a robed dwarven woman appeared from a doorway next to the stairs and whispered something to the guards. They withdrew, releasing their firm grasps, and exited back into the city.

"Welcome to Rockfell, and I apologise for the wait," the woman said, brushing a stray strand of umber hair from her face. "I understand this is not yer first time here. However, security has got a wee bit... tight." Her accent was thick and Elaeínn was only just able to piece together her High Elven.

"I was here once before," Elaeínn said. "With Captain Tynak of the Elite Division. Do you know what happened to him?"

The woman hung her head and remained silent for some time before placing a hand on Elaeínn's midriff, inspecting it. "Our clerics will heal yous up properly. For now, intelligence has a few questions for yous. But that can wait—ye are clearly exhausted. Come, ye can stay in the generals' quarters for the night."

The generals' quarters were attached to the same part of the castle in which the guards resided, but were much grander, even giving some leeway in terms of height. Elaeínn was too tired to take much notice of the typically drab dwarven surroundings as she was led there in a state of semi-delirium. Without anything in the way of consideration, she finally collapsed into the seemingly endless, enveloping sheets of the bed.

The next morning, she and Velrin were greeted by the same woman as the previous day, who proceeded to take them back towards the reception before continuing on to meet people she had only referred to as 'intelligence'. Elaeínn had never stopped expecting the endless, cramped corridors and she braced herself as they were led down the stairwell at the end of reception. To her surprise, they stopped soon after reaching the next floor down where the woman fished a key from her robe and unlocked what looked to be an ordinary wardrobe. She looked briefly to her left and right to confirm they were alone and then opened the wardrobe's doors, revealing a secret passageway.

"Tynak never showed me this," Elaeínn mused as she and Velrin were corralled into the narrow space, the woman closing and locking the door behind them.

"I would bloody hope he didn't show it yous. That would be quite the violation of national security. Now, this way, please. It gets a little bit cramped."

Elaeínn and Velrin were led down a further set of stairs, much less worn than those they had seen in other parts of the castle. The passage wasn't particularly well lit, with sconces placed every several metres. Continuing down into the earth, the air grew stale, still heavy with pollution. Both elves' coughing reverberated throughout the tunnel until they finally reached their destination.

At the bottom of the stairs was a hall stretching to beyond the size of the Common Chamber of the Tyen'Aíde. And it was abuzz with activity.

Dwarves of statures and in outfits not considered typically dwarven occupied desks arranged with typically dwarven efficiency on the right-hand side of the chamber. Others raced around with stacks of paper while others still pored over documents around tables on the left-hand side of the chamber.

"May I introduce yous to General Flint Korvald," the woman said theatrically, gesturing to a red-haired man bearing a striking resemblance to Tynak, though his features were slightly softer.

"Greetings." The man extended a hand to Elaeínn, which she met graciously. His grip was firm and predetermined.

"I take it you aren't an army general?" Elaeínn deduced as he repeated the same handshake with Velrin.

"That would be correct," Flint chuckled, though at what Elaeínn didn't quite understand.

Flint opened a door to a private office, almost identical to the war room adjacent to King Kagyan's throne room—complete with the sheet of slate hanging on the wall, the round table, and the map of the countries west of the Great Channel. He then quietly closed and locked it after Elaeínn and Velrin had both taken a seat.

"I've been told ye reckon we've a spy, then," he said sternly, the earlier softness completely eliminated from his expression. The general tried his best to tower over them, refraining from taking a seat, but could only meet their sitting height.

"I know you do," Elaeínn said, matching the dwarf's gaze. "Because the Prime Minister told me you do. I don't think he expected me to survive Fallía."

"The Prime Minister meaning Ferrilíen Vanad?"

"Is that who that is? Interesting. No, I meant Jaelaar, but of course, I killed him."

"And ye mention Fallía. Of course, we did not refer to it as such, nor did many have knowledge of it."

The dwarf paced across the small space and retrieved a bound document from a cabinet containing many similar-looking scrolls. "This is our information about the operation at Fallía," he explained, removing the binding and examining it. "It was due to be burned soon, so it's rather convenient timing, ye turning up."

"How many people, exactly, knew about Fallía?"

"Fewer than ten. There were logistical works associated, of course, but the project was referred to under a secret name, and details were hidden. It was kept secret; of that I am assured. The King demanded as such."

"My question is this," Velrin chimed in. "Who could be spying for the elves in a dwarven kingdom? I assume it won't be a dwarf, which leads me to believe that it could in fact be something magical. An experienced illusionist could disguise themself as a convincing dwarf, but still not for overly extended periods of time. And even then, it would still be an illusion—an accidental touch in close quarters would be enough to reveal them. So I have a different theory. Our spy could be a changeling."

"And that would explain why he's been able to pose as the King for so long," Elaeínn concluded. "This will sound like a heavy accusation, General, but King Kagyan—he isn't really King Kagyan. The Prime Minister admitted it to me himself. It's a spy."

"A changeling? The King?" Flint stroked his chin, staring into space. "Interesting. Not a theory I would have concocted."

"Because why would you? The creatures are exceedingly rare," Velrin commented. "And exceedingly intelligent. But also exceedingly arrogant. And if my theory is correct, we could exploit that."

Velrin's eyes sparkled as Elaeínn looked to both for a reaction.

"Ye look like ye have a plan, wizard," Flint said.

"That I do. But it would require some resources. Do you have anything I can write with?"

Flint handed over a sheet of paper and a quill, and Velrin set to work writing a list for his plan comprising both the necessary resources and the steps to implement it.

"I know we probably aren't allowed to view the document with the information about Fallía, but however many people there are, they would need to be rounded up. Would that be possible?"

"Aye, they should all be in the castle right now, in fact. Minus Captain Tynak, of course. I must make one comment, though. Are ye absolutely certain that our spy is a changeling? It would be quite the embarrassment for me to round up the most powerful dwarves in Hamatnar and accuse one of them of being a spy only for yer experiment to fail. I cannot afford to be made a fool of."

"I see no other possibility," Velrin concluded confidently. "Especially if Jaelaar himself said that King Kagyan was dead. Why would he do that if it wasn't a changeling in his place?"

"Ye had better be right."

Some hours later, Flint had assembled a collection of important-looking dwarves. They occupied yet another room in what Elaeínn had dubbed the Intelligence Quarter, this time larger and more circular. Each person stood around a sizable round table, and Velrin had been allowed to take charge of the experiment, to the evident annoyance of many of the room's occupants—annoyance largely expressed through body language, but occasionally through disgruntled muttering.

Notable characters included the King, who had stayed mostly silent whilst his companions bickered amongst themselves. Those standing nearest were a few army generals in full suits of armour, as if they had been ripped straight from the battlefield. Dressed more modestly were those introduced to Elaeínn as aides to the King, including the court mage.

Resting on the table were the materials Velrin had requested, and it was now that he picked up the first of them—a pair of shackles. Next to them were some wilted roots Elaeínn recognised as hevula which he proceeded to carefully weave through the shackles.

"Before we begin, I would like to ensure everyone in this room that this is for the good of the dwarven cause," Velrin announced, lifting the shackles into the air. "We are fighters of the FTA—please allay any suspicions you have of us. We want to see our government fall just as you do."

"What's yer plan, elf?" one of the generals spoke up. "Ye want to shackle us all? And then what? Whisper a charm? Administer snake oil?"

"Nothing of the sort. I will simply see how you react to contact with this," he responded coolly, raising a set of silver chains into the air alongside the shackles. "And this test is being carried out one at a time. You are not 'all being shackled' in any way."

He approached the first dwarf to his left, a woman in an ornate gold-trimmed green robe and wearing copious amounts of golden jewellery.

"No taste for silver?" Velrin asked, half-jokingly.

The woman smirked and revealed her wrists as Velrin attached the shackles.

"If you could just allow me to place this around your neck and beneath your collar, please," he continued, the chains jangling as he set them into place.

The woman graciously stretched her collar and allowed the chains to flow onto her skin. She did not react in any way other than a further exasperated smirk.

"Excellent," Velrin said. "It isn't you."

He moved on to the next person, another aide, and repeated the process, to the same result. And then again, and again.

He then came to one of the generals adjacent to the King and invited him to remove part of his armour, which he did begrudgingly. Velrin then shackled him and rested the chain around his neck. And once again, there was no visible reaction.

"Go on then, elf, chain up the King," the general antagonised. "I'm sure he can't wait to be bound by one of your kind."

King Kagyan eyed Velrin suspiciously as he approached, hevula shackles in hand. Elaeínn thought she noticed a shade of fear, too.

Velrin was flung away from the King by a sudden burst of energy as a portal tore open the wall. Several high-ranking dwarves were similarly thrown across the room with varying degrees of severity. Elaeínn managed to plant her feet but Velrin wasn't so lucky, his leg catching a chair as he flew. He landed squarely on the table and did not move.

From the portal, which was anonymised and occupied an entire strip of the room, streamed elves dressed in dark attire. Elaeínn was instantly reminded of Ríyael, and she reached to draw her sword out of instinct, but again found herself to be unarmed.

The dwarven generals, both armoured and unarmoured, leapt into battle, axes flying from their backs and into the skulls of the intruders. But the intruders kept coming.

"Everybody out! Out!" Flint shouted as the invading elves moved to cut off escape routes. Blood spurted over the table and the walls as swords screeched from scabbards and blitzed through the unguarded crowd.

Elaeínn leapt to grab the motionless body of Velrin and pulled him from the table, using all her strength to hoist him onto her shoulders. She struggled, making her way slowly to the door guarded by Flint, who had drawn a weapon of his own to fend off a stray attacker.

The King met her with several aides at the door, and she allowed them to pass first while she set Velrin down against the wall and turned to observe the massacre.

Many of the attackers were unidentifiable, masks covering the bottom halves of their faces. But one woman stood out to Elaeínn the moment she emerged from the portal, armoured lightly and more elegantly than the rest, bearing the Tyen'Aeli coat of arms. Her sprawling, wild hair; her defined jawline; her shadowed eyes.

Erría, Elaeínn thought, before Flint grabbed both her and Velrin. He thrust them violently from the room before exiting and locking the door. They accelerated into a run and were only metres away as a fireball exploded behind them, sending reverberations through the underground complex and incinerating whatever and whoever remained inside.

CHAPTER 13

FLORIAN WILDERNESS

The curious faces to which Richard awoke were unlike any he had seen before. They were humanlike in their shape and features, but their skin was a bright green, one which blended with the budding leaves of the trees. They were covered in plant matter—some had patches of moss growing across their bare skin, others wore woven vines like clothes, while others still were dressed only by patches of leaves sprawling across their waists. Most notably, they all appeared to be female.

He leapt up and backed away, stepping to the jetty's edge and catching his balance. Instinctively, he reached for his belt, where he would usually have found his sword, but grasped only air.

The creatures—Richard was not sure whether to refer to them as people—did not approach and were instead just as startled as he was. They jumped away, retreating to the lake's edge, continuing to observe him from a distance.

He counted five in total, all with matching bark-brown hair and hazel eyes. They stared at him with looks the bounty hunter commonly saw in prey, and he did not look away.

"Who are you?" he called. They visibly flinched and a few retreated further back.

Richard looked back to the path he had taken from the tower and then again towards the creatures.

"Are those your poles?" He indicated the hut next to the lake. Again, he received no response.

He sighed and trod slowly across the jetty, raising his hands and maintaining eye contact. "I need your help," he said, not convinced they could understand. "I need someone to help me get this off."

Richard rolled up his sleeve and pointed to the chain ring. The creatures squinted but still maintained their distance and their silence.

"What about this? Do you understand this?" he said, switching to Archaeish.

The creatures glanced at each other and then one of them pricked up its ears, looking back over its shoulder, past the treeline. Richard followed its gaze and almost had his innards torn out by the arrow that flew from the brush.

His first reaction was to drop, flattening himself against the jetty. They were upon him in moments, grabbing his arms while others held him down. He didn't fight back; he couldn't. Only seconds after the arrow had whizzed past, they had noiselessly traversed the entire jetty and bound his legs together and his arms behind his back.

Four of the creatures lifted him without so much as a grunt, carrying him on their shoulders, as the fifth sprinted silently into the forest.

"I take it you did understand, but now I'm a little bit confused," Richard said, turning his head to one of the creatures. It returned his glance and quickly flitted its eyes away, fixing them directly ahead.

They soldiered on, their pace not faltering as they delved deeper into the brush, unfazed by the winding roots and stray boulders, undeterred by the homogeneity of the scenery in every direction, and not even remotely unsure of the direction in which to travel through the pathless, untamed forest.

Richard watched in awe as a doe appeared from behind a hill and trotted past the group, unconcerned. The same was true of several rabbits, squirrels, even birds who landed on nearby branches easily within reach of the ground. The creatures carrying Richard did not seem to care for his enthrallment.

Their journey continued downhill for some time, Richard catching occasional glances of the tower through gaps in the canopy, growing ever smaller in the distance. They came upon a ravine, only able to be crossed by a fallen log bearing obvious signs of rot, and they traversed it without slowing their pace in the slightest.

Eventually, Richard began to take note of small abnormalities in the surroundings. Areas relatively clear of debris; small depressions which he could only describe as pathways. They were almost unnoticeable, but he didn't have much else to distract his mind.

As they then became increasingly obvious, a cloth was suddenly wrapped around his head, covering his eyes. He struggled initially, but soon gave up after one of his captors struck him in the face. It was only shortly thereafter that the cloth was then removed and he was set down onto a bed of lashed-together branches. The captors dispersed, leaving him to listen to the birdsong, distant animal cries, and the nearby running of water.

He turned his head to find the source of the running to be a river, flowing around a small cliff atop which stood a mighty oak with a trunk as thick as the tower from which he had fled, and a height which must have matched or even surpassed it. He wondered if he had simply missed it when surveying the landscape from the tower, or if they had travelled so far downhill as to make it seem of regular height from a distance.

Turning his head in the other direction, he could see a vast array of huts constructed from branches lashed together to form structures, like the platform on which he lay. They had not been constructed in a clearing of any variety, and instead blended directly into the trees, some being built around them. None of the buildings, Richard noticed, were built from logs. They were decorated with flowers in a multitude of colours, though they didn't look to have been placed on the buildings—instead, they looked to be growing from them.

Milling between these buildings were the creatures which had brought him here—many more than the five he had encountered. And they were all female.

He wasn't left long to rest before being hauled upright, sitting to face yet another of the creatures. Though this one looked older—her hair was wild, sprawling, caressing her entire person like a cloak and nearly touching the ground in length. She had the same hazel eyes but they reflected wisdom, as did the slight, almost invisible wrinkles lining her face.

"You trespass on our land, human," she spoke in fluent Archaeish. "What business do you have here?"

"None," Richard replied. "I was brought here against my will. I had no intention of trespassing on... whatever this is."

"You find yourself in the Eretria Forest. Everything you see is under our guard. We protect her from people like you who brazenly intrude and disturb her."

"I'm telling you, I didn't want to come here. I was brought here. And they—the people who brought me here, sorcerers—they must have been here before, because they opened a portal to that tower. I don't have any interest in harming you, or the forest. I just want to leave. But I can't because of this bloody contraption."

He nodded at his arm and the woman—Richard felt it was now appropriate to refer to her as such—rolled back the fabric of his shirt and inspected the ring, running her finger along its circumference before fondling the lock itself.

"It is enchanted," she claimed. "It will not be able to be broken off by force. Only a spellcaster can unlock it."

"Or you could torch this bloody root out. I'll put up with the burns."

"Fire is forbidden in Eretria," the woman said icily, Richard almost certain her eyes even shifted in colour.

"Fine, no fire. But I need to escape somehow. Surely one of you must be a sorceress. This place reeks of magic."

"It might be possible that we can help you," she alluded. "But we need help first. Help that only a humanoid can provide."

"How about you undo these binds first?"

The woman revealed a dagger and, in two blindingly fast strikes, severed the binds restraining his arms and his legs. Richard looked her scantily clad body up and down and was unable to discern where the dagger had come from, but he didn't allow his mind to wander.

"I'd like to know more about you. About this place. Who are you? What are you?"

"My name is Calliope. We are dryads, sworn protectors of Eretria and nature beyond. And this particular forest is my domain. I have lived for three thousand years and I will continue to live for thousands more as long as my domain remains safeguarded—and that is precisely what we need your help with."

"You need my help with protection? I wouldn't have thought so, given the arrow which nearly killed me at the lake."

"We are perfectly capable of defending ourselves. However, we are also frequently the targets of killings because of who we are. We're seen as violent, uncivilised monsters who only exist to disrupt the lives of humans who wish to tear down our home and replace it with their farms, their mills, their granaries. We will not hesitate to kill anyone who strays too close. But humans are not easily deterred—far from it. For each human we kill, with every intention of scaring off the rest, five more dedicate themselves to our hunting. Our numbers are dwindling, to put it plainly. We will not be able to defend ourselves for much longer, given that we rely on those very humans to procreate.

"We need a new approach—one which does not incite murder and further trespass. We need them to speak to one of their own kind so they will finally see reason instead of blind fury."

"And what do you expect me to do? I don't know where this place even is. It doesn't look like Mirados, so I doubt they speak any language I know. If they don't kill me for looking like an escaped prisoner then they'll kill me for casting spells to allow me to speak to them. And then, even if I manage to survive that, what am I supposed to say? 'Excuse me, the dryads want you out of this forest. Can you please pack up and go?' I don't see it working."

"We will be watching the entire time. If anyone makes one wrong move, they will die. And we have clothes you can wear. They might not be a perfect fit, but they will be better than your current attire."

"I'm not going to condemn a whole village to death for existing, either. I'm not a dryad—I don't care for nature in the way you do. I just want to leave this place."

"I know desperation when I see it." Calliope narrowed her eyes. "You more than want to leave this place, Richard Ordowyn. You ache to leave this place. You cannot think of anything other than how you are going to escape. Escape and bring her back to life."

Richard looked away, furrowing his brow. "What did you just do?"

"I read your mind. Take it as proof, if you will, that I can help you. But only if you help us."

Richard looked away, studying the colony of dryads with intense curiosity. Some carried weapons, most of which were crafted from materials found on the forest floor, but he also saw the occasional blade. He didn't, however, see any blacksmiths.

"Where is the settlement?" he finally asked.

"You don't need to feel so bitter," Calliope said. "It isn't murder to defend your territory. You seem to understand this quite well."

"Stop reading my mind. Please. Where is the settlement?"

Calliope gestured in the direction of the cliffs he had seen earlier, just visible through the breaks in the canopy allowing the soft sun shafts that illuminated the forest floor to filter through.

"A day's walk," she said. "They came through the pass a couple years ago and we've been unable to get rid of them ourselves. This will be our greatest effort yet."

"How many villagers are there?"

"We estimate two hundred. While we number only thirty, and that's all of us, not just those who are capable in combat."

"If this is going to work I'll need a bow."

"That can be arranged."

"And some food. I haven't eaten in days."

Calliope turned to a passing dryad and said something in a language Richard could only describe as melodious, with each word seeming to flow seamlessly onto the next. The dryad nodded and sprinted away, returning soon thereafter, hands cupped. She presented Richard with an assortment of berries and nuts, which he scooped voraciously into his mouth.

"You don't kill animals, do you?" he asked, wiping his hands, slick with berry juice, on his shorts.

"You are correct. Their lives are precious, just like ours. They feel emotion, just like us. We share our domain with them, and they in turn maintain it for us. We wouldn't dare to upset the balance mother set in place as humans do so brashly."

The dryad who had provided him with the food then departed and soon returned with a bow and quiver of arrows. It was shorter than that to which Richard was accustomed, but it was light and strong. He was given twelve arrows in total, each of varying quality. Some looked clean and new, while others were dirtied, the fletching worn.

"Are you going to come with me?" he turned his attention from his inspection of the ammunition to Calliope, who looked on patiently.

"We will all be coming. But this is your job, Richard Ordowyn. I will only free you if you rid us of the villagers without our involvement."

"Let's get this over with, then."

Calliope hosted Richard in her personal hut for the night. It was by no means luxurious—located atop the cliff under the giant oak, nestled at its base between roots protruding from the ground. There were two beds constructed, like everything else, from branches. But there were also sparse furnishings—linen blankets, worn cushions, and a chest containing the clothes Richard had been promised. He pulled on a pair of muddy brown breeches and a yellow tunic which fell to his knees. There was a rope girdle which he fastened around his waist and he had been provided with a pair of leather shoes, but he left these off as he lowered himself into bed.

The next morning he woke up ravenous, but the offerings were much the same as that which he had been given the previous day. Calliope allowed him a larger portion than the rest of the dryads, but his stomach still felt hollow as they began to trek towards the cliffs under the morning sun.

It was then that Richard began to realise Calliope's estimation of the journey's length was using a dryad's pace for reference—a pace which he completely failed to match. He was by no means unfit, but their fluid motion through the untamed brush was unnatural and Richard found himself stumbling and tripping with increasing frequency as he tried to keep up.

He was forced to slow so that he could focus on the ground after a root sent him tumbling to the floor.

They stopped only for two breaks before nightfall, the dryads foraging for food along the way. He was treated to walnuts and blackberries, though he couldn't help but crave the wildlife he could see darting around the forest.

Richard's sleep was occupied by dreams of Lana Rel. Not the usual dreams, either, but new, melancholy dreams of time spent with Lynn Varanus. He experienced his first magic lessons in a cosy, candlelit room. The sorceress smiled at him warmly as he levitated a book in the air above a desk. The desk was situated in front of a window providing a view of the quiet town streets. He smiled back. There was no danger, no strife. He would have even gone so far as to call the dreams pleasant.

The trek continued the following day and Richard noticed the dryads' relentless silence. The only conversation he had during the entire journey was with Calliope, when he asked her about it, and she said they were simply timid.

The cliffs loomed overhead as the forest began to give way, though evidently not for natural reasons. Richard's pace increased rapidly as the paths forged through the sparse trees made the ground even, and he observed piles of freshly chopped logs within fields of stumps, a sight which incited rage amongst the dryads.

It was as they approached the first sign of civilisation that the dryads dispersed, leaving Richard with only Calliope. A thatched farmhouse stood ahead of them, a single man visible in a garden at the front of the house.

"I have faith in you, Richard," Calliope whispered. "Now get rid of them if you ever want to see Linelle again. Hablar Aflorea."

She, too, then disappeared into the brush. He quickly glanced around and it was impossible to know that there had been a whole tribe of dryads walking with him only moments before.

"Excuse me," Richard said loudly, breaching the forest's edge and alerting the man in the garden. The man quickly raised a pitchfork, guarding himself with it as Richard approached.

"Who are you?" the man called, squinting and apprehensively raising his chin.

"I'm a bounty hunter, sir. I was looking to talk to the ealdorman of this village."

"For what purpose?"

"That's a private matter. Could you please direct me to him?"

"Listen, drifter, I don't think you understand how this village works," the villager pointed at Richard, lowering the pitchfork and holding it with one hand. "We don't just let outsiders walk in and do as they please. Especially not ones that appear out of nowhere. Where've you come from?"

"I've travelled through this forest from the South," Richard lied. "The road ended abruptly."

"Is that right?" the man hopped over the fence separating him and Richard, planting his pitchfork between them. "You managed to walk through the whole Forest of Death without being murdered by those savages? No, I don't think that's what happened. I..."

The man trailed off as his eyes traced Richard up and down.

"I know that's not what happened, actually," he then continued. "Because you're wearing my son's tunic. And they killed him last week."

Richard ducked out of the way as the villager drew back the pitchfork and thrust it forwards.

"You're with them, aren't you?" he seethed as a second villager, who Richard assumed to be the man's wife, appeared in the garden, face stricken with horror.

Richard leapt away and simultaneously grabbed the bow from his back, nocking an arrow.

"I don't want to kill you," he said, drawing the bowstring, the arrow aimed at the man's skull. "I just need to talk to the ealdorman."

The man dropped the pitchfork, raising his hands and taking a few weary steps back. "I'll... I'll take you to him. But he won't be very embracing of what you have to say."

Richard lowered his bow and returned the arrow to his quiver, kicking the pitchfork behind him. He noticed then that the woman had disappeared from the garden. "Where's your wife gone?"

"Probably to warn the village. What did you bloody expect?"

"You're going to defuse the situation. Or you won't be returning to this house. Understand?"

"Y-yes sir."

The man led Richard away from the house, along a worn path bedecked with hoofprints and ruts. On their left was an expansive maize field surrounded by trees at its edges, enough forest having been cleared to enable a view of the village ahead. It was situated along the same river which flowed from the cliffs, which Richard now realised turned into a canyon. Its size and position behind the village made the village itself look tiny.

"What have they offered you?" the man said at one point. "What could possibly make you work for them?"

"You wouldn't understand."

"Whatever it is, you shouldn't believe them. They're savages, they don't understand civilised people. They just kill for the sake of killing. They're monsters."

Richard remained silent as they arrived at the village, an arrangement of some thirty houses around the base of the cliffs forming the exterior of the canyon. Several villagers were tending to the maize field while others were at work in a wheat field across the river. The buildings were very much similar to the thatched house from which they had come. Mostly the same size, all built from logs, with one particular building standing taller than the rest.

"That's the ealdorman's house." The man pointed to the taller house as they made their way further into the village.

A small crowd had assembled from the villagers not busy at work in the fields, clear discontent common across their visages. They muttered incomprehensibly to each other as the man brought Richard to the door of the ealdorman's house.

"I hope you get what you want, sir," he trembled, before turning and walking away.

Richard knocked on the door and was met, after a brief wait, by a man he thought to be surprisingly young for the role of ealdorman, judging by his soft, wrinkleless face and long umber hair.

"Who are you?"

"Richard Ordowyn, a bounty hunter. Can we speak in private?"

"No, we can't," the man said, stepping out of the building and pressing Richard down the stairs. "We can talk out here, with everyone to listen. We have no secrets here, Richard Ordowyn."

"Okay, then. Quite bluntly, you need to leave this forest. All of you."

The ealdorman narrowed his eyes. "I'm sorry?"

"The dryads are planning to kill everyone here. You need to leave, or you will all die."

"We're not scared of those savages. We've killed them before. We'll kill more of them. We'll set fire to this forest just to spite them. They'll never drive us out of our territory."

"They would argue that this is their territory, and that you are the ones driving them out."

"What are you, their mouthpiece? I don't have to listen to this," the ealdorman said, turning back to the door.

"Yes, you do," Richard said, nocking an arrow and drawing back the bowstring.

The ealdorman turned slowly around, his fingers caressing the hilt of the blade sheathed at his belt. "You are playing a dangerous game, taking their side," he warned. "Look around you. You're outnumbered."

Richard did not lower his guard but could see the increased number of villagers in his peripheral vision, forming a circle around him on the path before the ealdorman's house.

"I don't know how much you've drunk to think you—a nobody—can walk in here and tell us to pack up and leave. On the tree-fuckers' orders, no less. We won't be leaving."

"Then I'm sorry," Richard mumbled. "But you leave me no choice."

His bowstring twanged as the ealdorman's blood brought colour to the brown façade. The villagers roared and ran at Richard as he discarded his bow and dashed forwards to grab the sword from the ealdorman's belt. He turned around, drawing the sword, just in time to watch a volley of arrows rain over the oncoming mob, felling at least a dozen of them.

The first villager to reach him at the steps leading to the door wielded a hatchet, and Richard ducked his first blow before planting his sword through his gut. The bounty hunter threw the body against the crowd as they reached the stairs and he backed slowly into the house, more arrows appearing from the trees and bushes dotted around the path.

Two more attackers burst through the door, sprinting at him with no restraint. Richard parried a blow from the first, lacerating his neck as he deflected a slash from the second. A third came through the door, leaping at Richard and being skewered on the bounty hunter's sword as he sailed through the air. Richard grabbed the axe from the impaled body's fingers and threw it with his left hand at the second attacker, splitting his skull as he charged.

Richard withdrew his sword from the body of the attacker and slashed the neck of yet another villager who had approached with only a pitchfork. Another entered the building with a sickle and was eliminated just as efficiently.

The clamouring of the mob grew quieter and quieter as Richard sliced his way through villager after villager, his face streaked with hot blood, his tunic stained crimson. He fought towards the doorway, his killing rhythmic, thoughtless.

The last few attackers fell quickly. Two were finished by arrows from the brush. The last had the bounty hunter's sword plunged through his heart.

Richard's breathing was heavy as he withdrew the blade, more red than silver, from the villager's chest. The bodies had to be shoved out of the way to allow him back onto the village path.

He dropped his sword, which clattered against the ground, and fell to his knees. A hollow feeling engulfed his throat and he swallowed, fighting the tears that welled in his eyes.

You're not finished, Richard, Calliope's voice sounded in his head. *All the villagers must go.*

He looked up and saw a terrified mother peering through the window of one of the houses, staring at the bounty hunter. She appeared to be shielding the eyes of someone else—a child.

Richard glanced at his sword, and then back at the woman. "Lanthanis forgive me," Richard said, his voice and breathing shaky. "I'm sorry, Lin. I'm truly sorry for what I'm about to do."

He stood up, retrieving the sword and traipsing towards the house. Their screams pierced the sky, ringing out over the cliffs. And they were only the first of many.

CHAPTER 14

"What the fuck happened?"

Elton dropped to his knees and pored over the sorceress's wounds. The bleeding had slowed, the wounds appearing to close up, but Rosa remained unconscious.

"They happened," Felix responded, gesturing to the corpses of the assailants, which had been left untouched. "If she was awake she would be able to tell you more. We were downstairs when it happened."

"This is no good. No good at all," Elton picked up her body with a grunt and laid it on a nearby table. "The wounds don't look so bad considering she was stabbed, what, three times? She did something to counteract it before she blacked out, it looks like. But at what cost?"

"She'll recover, boss, I don't doubt it."

"I'm equally sure. But we need her to transport us to Salyria tomorrow."

"What?"

"I will explain at the Redhouse. Quick, you two, carry her back."

Elton departed the tavern, tossing a pouch of coins to the innkeeper, and raced back to the Redhouse. Rosa was taken to her office, where Elton swept a table clear of various implements and alchemical paraphernalia to allow Felix and Ferris to set the sorceress down.

Elton lowered his ear to her nose, satisfied that she was still breathing. It was then that he explained Villius Abranor's plan to both Felix and Ferris.

"Well, shit," Felix said. "Might be a little bit too optimistic to hope we could travel by cart to Camelion in a day."

"If only we had more bloody mages," Elton muttered. "I'm going to find Villius and let him know of this... development."

It didn't take long to find Villius, because Villius happened to be looking for Elton. They collided with each other in the corridor leading away from the main hall, Elton nearly toppling the frail man.

"Ah, Count Redwinter," Villius began, smoothing down his shirt. "I was coming to talk to you about that accommodation."

"It's going to have to wait," Elton said sharply. "We've a problem."

"A problem?"

"It interrupts our plans, let's say. In fact, makes them completely undoable."

Elton returned to Rosa's office alongside the Altercantian, who cast a disappointed gaze over the sorceress's body as they arrived. He stepped closer to her to examine the wounds, cursing under his breath.

"This is not ideal, Count. Not ideal at all," he concluded. "Do you know anybody else that could take us there?"

"Richard could have," Ferris chimed in. "But he's obviously not here anymore."

"And Kalahar isn't going to do anything for us anymore, either," Felix added.

"You know no other magic wielders? None at all?" Villius questioned exasperatedly.

"If you have a roster at your disposal, please, give them to us," Elton patronised. "It's not your place to come in and criticise us for things that are far out of our control. Rosa will hopefully wake up before the banquet is due to take place. Otherwise, we must find another way to attend."

"It's pointless," Villius said dejectedly. "This plan was riding on her. There is no other way to travel such a distance in the time we have available."

There was a sudden knock at the door and Elton opened it to find a servant clutching a scroll in his hands.

"Pardon me for interrupting, Count, but you have a visitor waiting for you in reception. He brought this letter."

"Who is he?" Elton asked, grabbing and unfurling the scroll.

"He introduced himself only as Kasimir. Does that name mean anything to you?"

Elton looked perplexedly at Felix and Villius. "I'll be there in a moment," he mused, shooing the servant away.

The door closed and Elton began to read the letter aloud.

"Count Redwinter,

"Father, I know we haven't had the best of relationships but I was looking for an opportunity to make amends. You have done an excellent job in bringing honour to that city you call home. It really is inspiring to see it evolve from a hotbed of crime to a thriving metropolis. And it is because I believe you are turning yourself around that I would like to extend an invitation to you and your associates to join me at a celebratory banquet.

"We are celebrating my imminent departure on a mission my court mage says will help us to alter the course of history, forge a new path for humanity. We will unlock power to allow us to rival the elves and the dwarves, power that unlocks the unseen potential of magic among men. It would not be proper if I was not to invite the great leaders of the continent, so I extend this invitation to you just as I have already extended it to the kings of South Benetia, Thorne, Santeros, and Kina.

"This is our chance to forge a better future for the both of us. I have sent my court mage to you, and he will bring you in turn back to me. I hope you do not pass me up on this offer—it is an event not to be missed."

"Yours sincerely,

"King Hortensio of Heathervale, first of his name, Kingslayer and Saviour of Salyria."

Elton gingerly rolled the scroll back up and then tossed it onto Rosa's desk. "What a load of horseshit. But that there is our opportunity."

"It's a trap, boss," Felix cautioned. "I don't think he's had a sudden change of heart."

"Oh, I know."

"Then what are we going to do?"

"Spring the trap." Elton smirked.

"I will need to disguise myself, Count," Villius said. "He will recognise me otherwise."

"I'll get someone on that. Meanwhile, we must of course dress appropriately. Let's speak to this Kasimir and then we will have to visit the tailor, I think."

"You already wear fancy clothes as it is, boss," Felix said.

"I didn't mean for me."

They reached the lobby and spotted him immediately—his pale white skin and bright red hair made him a beacon among the rest of the hall's occupants.

"Hablar Arcaea," he said, moving to greet them.

"No need," Elton said, extending a hand and locking eyes with the mage. "Spell is already active."

"Is that so?" Kasimir raised his eyebrows. "Fascinating. Who might be the caster?"

"Our court mage, though she is currently indisposed," Elton lied.

"Why Archaeish? Does she not hail from here?"

"We had a run in with some foreigners."

"I see. Well, you know why I'm here. What did you think of the King's proposal?" He clasped his hands together.

"We would very much like to attend. But I'd like some details, before we do. How many people will be there?"

"Last I checked, thirty guests had responded. Plus the King's courtiers and associates, and whatever entourages the other rulers bring."

"And will we be allowed to carry weapons? I hope you can understand that my trust in the King is... shallow." Elton narrowed his eyes.

"I will request a personal exception. But know that there will be plenty of guards present."

"Of course. When do we leave?"

"Meet me here, tomorrow, just after dusk. The banquet begins at sunset in Camelion."

"We're looking forward to it."

Kasimir bowed before departing and the group peeled off back into the Redhouse. Elton provided Villius and Ferris with a room each before checking on Rosa, who he found still to be unconscious. Then Felix accompanied him to his house before they went their separate ways.

The next morning, Elton awoke to a faint knocking on the front door. The knocking continued as he took his time dressing, undoing the locks and latches, and sauntering downstairs. He unlocked the door, one hand on his dagger, and peered through the crack.

"Boss?"

Elton allowed Paul to step inside, too slow to reject his sudden embrace. He did not return it, but did not fight it away, either.

"It's been a while, bossman," Paul said.

"I saw you last week."

"Yeah, but I mean… since the good ol' days. 'Cause Felix is your right-hand man an' all. I like my new job, boss, but… I miss the Syndicate. I miss the rush of it all."

"You've got one of the most important jobs in the bloody Redhouse. And I haven't forced you to change your lifestyle, either. What is there to miss?"

"I dunno," Paul mused, rubbing his head.

"How about some breakfast?" Elton stepped into the kitchen.

"Fried egg?"

"On the one side, because you're a mental case."

He took the eggs and a pan outside, lighting a fire and taking a deep breath of the brisk air.

"What do you say about joining us on a mission today, Paul?" Elton called as he tossed a knob of butter into the pan.

"What mission?" Paul asked eagerly, appearing outside and taking a seat on the stone bench opposite Elton.

"You remember our dear friend, Hortensio?"

"Would be hard to forget."

"You'll have to dress up, I'm warning you now," Elton said, cracking the eggs into the pan.

"I've had to dress up loads recently," Paul mused. "What is it, then?"

"We were visited by a man from a free city in the East. One thing led to another, and now we're going to attempt to assassinate King Hortensio. What do you say to attending a royal banquet?"

Paul jumped out of his seat, a smile wide across his face. "Are you jokin'? Yes! It'd be just like one of our old missions!"

"Of somewhat more significance, but yes," Elton said, flipping one of the eggs. "Go get some bread."

"What's the plan? How we gonna kill him?" Paul asked as he ran back to the kitchen.

"A dagger to the heart, ideally. Villius—the man who came to us—wanted to poison everyone there, but I wouldn't agree. So now we need an assassin."

"Me?"

"No, of course not. Felix, most likely. You really think you could be the one to take out the King? In his own ballroom?"

"I think you'd be surprised by what I can do, boss." Paul reappeared with several slices of bread. "I've caught out lots of people who remembered me as the dumb idiot sidekick from the Syndicate. I'm not stupid like you always thought I were, boss. I've got smarter."

"I don't want you killed by a Salyrian blade," Elton said harshly. "I don't care if you do manage to kill him, you'd end up killed yourself. I'm not allowing it. I'm not losing another one of my partners—my friends."

Paul didn't carry on the conversation as Elton placed the egg fried only on one side between two slices of bread and handed it to him. Elton pressed it firmly, causing the yolk to burst so that it spilled out of the sides and onto the patio. Paul sat back down, chewing quietly as the Count more carefully prepared his own breakfast. They ate in silence as the sounds of the day rose into existence, Elton sipping a glass of wine.

"What are we gonna do after we kill Hortensio?" Paul asked, brushing the crumbs from his breeches.

"I think I'm leaving that to Villius to decide," Elton rose, draining the rest of his glass. "Come on, then, let's find Felix and go see the tailor. We're leaving for Salyria this evening."

Felix was found waiting in the intelligence office and reacted with glee at the sight of Paul, meeting his embrace with enthusiasm. They were joined by Ferris and Villius before the five set out for the tailor, where it was decided that only Paul, Villius, and Ferris needed new outfits. Paul decided on a crimson jerkin over a white doublet; Villius a dark grey tunic and matching cowl large enough to shroud his face in shadow; and Ferris a bright blue jerkin over a white doublet, and a navy cloak to finish.

"Lookin' sharp, fellas," Paul said, admiring himself in the mirror.

"Kasimir's going to have to cast the spell on him," Ferris said, nodding in Paul's direction. "I don't have a clue what he's saying."

"Nobody ever does, anyways," Elton mused.

The sun crept towards its climax as they left the tailor's, a small shop in the corner of Silverstone Square run by a woman Elton had known since moving to the city when it was still under the control of King Ramsey. It had always been his first choice for clothes, and she had always known special protection under the Syndicate. The same special protection continued to apply under his new government.

They split up and spent the day attending to regular duties before reconvening an hour after sundown, Kasimir found exactly where he had said to meet. He complimented them all on their attire and granted Ferris's request to cast a spell on Paul to enable his understanding of Archaeish before clasping his hands together and looking among them all expectantly.

"Shall we depart? His Majesty is waiting."

"Gladly," Elton said. "I wouldn't want to keep him waiting."

Kasimir stepped back and traced a portal, pressing forwards to reveal a room not unlike Rosa's office, complete with the same alchemy equipment and miscellany of magic-related items. The Santerosi nationals were immediately struck by the drop in temperature, but they soon adapted.

"We are a little bit early, but the sun will be setting soon," Kasimir said, closing the portal and leading them from the room as Elton curiously eyed up a large object concealed by a linen sheet at the side of the room.

"Where is the King, then?" Elton asked, rubbing his arms.

"Probably cosying up to the early arrivals. Would you care for a drink, Count?"

"I'll have a glass of wine."

Elton groaned quietly to himself as they entered the decorated great hall, a room with the same marble floor as seemed to be the case in the rest of the palace. Navy banners bearing two white lions hung from the pillars supporting the ceiling. The tables set out between these pillars were draped in white tablecloths, but the chairs placed on their outer edges all bore the same navy banners, only smaller. Several blue candles burned at various points across each table, and between each were bundles of wildflowers organised neatly into vases.

Some guests had already arrived, as Kasimir had alluded to, and they stood around the tables in conversation, none taking their seats. Of those present, Elton recognised nobody.

"I wonder if there's a theme," Paul muttered as they entered the kitchen, where a vast amalgamation of wondrous smells infiltrated their noses and forced salivation. A team of chefs worked tirelessly across multiple stations, tending so actively to the diverse arrangement of dishes to the point where they didn't seem to notice the visitors enter the kitchen.

"How do you feel about Knight's Relief?" Kasimir asked, gently retrieving a bottle from a small wine rack that seemed more ornamental than functional. "1328."

"I should hope that's not where it's normally stored," Elton commented, nodding as Kasimir opened the bottle and retrieved two glasses from a nearby cupboard.

"Of course not, of course not. They've just been brought out for the banquet. The King is sparing no expense."

"I don't suppose you have ale?" Villius asked, turning down a glass of wine.

"But of course. I'll show you to the vats."

A narrow set of stairs on the far end of the kitchen led down into the cellar, where the drop in temperature was dramatic. Even Ferris shivered as Elton, Felix, and Paul muttered to one another about their distaste for the underground.

"The vats of the Blue Palace," Kasimir raised his arms as they came into the main chamber of the cellar. Seemingly the only part of the palace not constructed from marble, eight oversized wooden vats lined the stone walls, four on each side of the room. They were so large that there were ladders nailed onto their sides to allow access to the lids.

"A tankard, anyone? I don't drink ale, myself, but I've been told by His Majesty that it's the finest around."

"And I bet the royal bog is the most comfortable on the continent," Felix mused.

Felix, Paul, and Villius accepted a tankard and drank slowly, careful not to show excess appreciation.

The population of the great hall had ballooned during their short excursion. Some twenty people crowded into the increasingly tight space, still refusing to take their seats. Elton recognised King Moltarov of Thorne, someone he knew personally from his days in the Syndicate. Their eyes met and they exchanged a curt nod, but nothing more.

Another notable individual was King Mateo of South Benetia. Elton had also run in with this king, but he hadn't embraced the Syndicate quite as graciously as Moltarov. As such, they did not acknowledge one another as Kasimir brought them back towards the entrance.

They had just found a quiet corner in which to wait when his voice finally cut through the fray, silencing the conversation of every noble, monarch, courtier, and waiter.

"Count Elton Redwinter! Oh, how I am surprised that you accepted my invitation." Hortensio beamed as he approached, raising his hands. His expression was then interrupted by a short curse as he fiddled with the collar of his doublet.

"You look uncomfortable," Elton noted, the chatter returning to the background.

"No shit, have you ever worn anything like this?" Hortensio seethed, pulling the collar away as he spoke. "I'm surprised we don't stock it in the torture chamber!"

"He's never had a problem," Elton gestured to Felix, who nodded.

"He's crazy, is what I think," Hortensio laughed. "And you of course remember Jannis?"

Jannis joined the group, equally uncomfortable in his outfit. His attempt to feign friendliness wasn't quite as convincing as Hortensio's.

"Would be hard to forget," Elton grunted, images of their duel in the Redhouse flashing through his mind.

"And I of course wouldn't forget your band of miscreants," Hortensio continued. "But who are these new faces?"

"Rhett van der Kelder," Villius quickly supplied, putting on an accent and extending a hand to the King. "A new appointment to the Count's court."

"Is that so, Count?" Hortensio shook Villius's hand firmly, almost harshly. "And you, my friend with good taste in colour. Who are you?"

"He doesn't speak Salyrian," Elton interjected. "He's a bard, if you couldn't tell from the lute. Not one from around here."

"Really? What's he doing in your band? Perhaps he can play us a song." Hortensio extended a hand to Ferris anyways, which the bard accepted. "And the witch? Rosa? She was by far the most interesting of your associates."

"She is indisposed," Elton said curtly. "Busy with more important things."

"Wouldn't be Elton Redwinter if he wasn't lying to my face, would it?" Hortensio smiled icily. "But I digress. We're here to celebrate, and celebrate we shall. Penelope! More wine for the exalted guests!"

A woman—or rather a girl, judging by the softness of her face—with mousey brown hair, dressed in a cream blouse and a long, faded green skirt, perked up at the mention of her name and nodded fervently at the King. She dashed away into the kitchen, seeming nearly to trip over her skirt.

"I thought you were too high and mighty to refer to the common folk by their names," Elton said.

"Father, you know I am one with the common folk. These people are my people—I am them. Therefore I treat them with the respect they rightfully deserve."

Penelope returned moments later carrying a platter of wine glasses. She grinned as Hortensio thanked her, subtly placing a hand on her lower back before shooing her away. It was not so subtle as to escape Elton's notice but he refrained from comment.

"Come, then, take a seat. I've reserved places at the head of the table for you." Hortensio beckoned them across the hall, cutting through groups of people still waiting to take their seats. "We'll be sat with the King of Thorne, too."

"Excuse me, Your Majesty," Villius suddenly interrupted. "But I require the use of the privy. Could you perhaps direct me to it?"

"Penelope!" he clapped. She appeared in moments, like an obedient dog. "Show this man to the lavatory."

"Right away, Your Majesty," she said enthusiastically. "Come, sir, just this way."

Penelope and Villius peeled away from the group in the opposite direction, towards the entrance on the other side of the room. The table at which they finally took their seats was nothing special, if only slightly larger than the other tables. Hortensio's seat in the centre was, of course, grander than the rest, but that was the only noticeable difference.

A quick gesture from the King indicated to the rest of the guests that they were then to take their own seats, which they did in a rapid fashion. Elton had been placed on the King's right, followed by Felix, Paul, an empty seat for Villius, and then Ferris. Jannis and Kasimir sat to his left, and then it was the Thornish aristocracy to follow.

Servants came around with a fresh round of drinks as the first course appeared from the kitchen, delightful scents infusing the air of the hall. Plates of vegetables—sliced pickles, roasted parsnips, potatoes, plums, boiled cabbage, garnished mushrooms, black and green olives—all were interspersed between an assortment of starters—creamed fish, leek and potato soup, lamb stew, grilled venison, and whole stuffed chickens.

The guests filled their plates but did not begin to eat as the King rose from his seat and called for silence, holding a glass of wine in his hand.

"Honourable guests of Houses Lorca, Tretamine, and Fennimore, and those from beyond our lands—King and Queen Moltarov of Thorne, King Mateo and Queen Priscilla of South Benetia, even noble representatives of the Lazerian and Kinan thrones—I welcome you, I welcome you all. This is the first such banquet I have held in my short time as King of Salyria and it will certainly not be the last.

"While this is a celebration of the great journey upon which we in Salyria are about to embark, it is also a time for us to reconcile any differences we may have had in our pasts. Salyria is experiencing the beginning of a golden age, and we want you to join us for it.

"There is only one obstacle to this golden age—the King of Santeros. You will have of course noticed his absence today, as he is too busy dragging his country and his people into despair, pursuing thoughtless wars against those with whom they have no grievances."

"Pot callin' the kettle fuckin' black," Paul mouthed.

"The Santerosi people must be freed," Hortensio continued. "It is why today that I announce we Salyrians will support the Kinans in their defence against the aggressors by launching a campaign into Santeros in the coming weeks. Santhion will soon fall, and any who join our cause will be entitled to a stake in the carving up of the land.

"So let me present this toast—a toast to the future of Temerios, a toast to the future of us, a future of freedom, progress, and prosperity!"

Hortensio raised his glass and was met with a discordant jumble of responses—some shouting "To us!" while others shouted "To Temerios!"—before everyone indulged in their drinks. It was only then that Villius returned, gingerly taking his seat at the table. He received a sharp glare from Hortensio, but nothing more.

"Ask him what took so long," Elton whispered urgently to Felix, who repeated the message.

"He says it was a big one. Don't know if that's Paul's words or his," Felix said as Paul murmured the response into his ear.

Elton cast a suspicious gaze over the expressionless Villius as he sipped the wine from earlier and began to fill his plate.

As the last of the dishes from the first course were finished, a band of brightly dressed bards entered the hall and began to play a jovial tune, the mixture of strings, wind, and percussion breathing further life into the already merry atmosphere. Elton remained ever cautious as the King engaged in conversation with the Thornish, largely ignoring the Dannosi presence.

It wasn't long before the second course arrived. Whole roast boar, ducks, partridges, and geese carried in on their own, separate tables, too large to fit on the existing tables. They were accompanied by another round of drinks and some smaller dishes—hard-boiled eggs, roasted nuts, caviar. Elton accepted a refill to his wine but turned down a tankard of ale.

"Your palate too refined for a proper drink, old man?" Hortensio turned suddenly to face the Count, nearly spilling his drink. "Our wine is fantastic, of course, but nothing beats a mug of ale."

"I've a sophisticated taste," Elton said drily. "But I would've thought these simpletons would enjoy it." He gestured to Paul and Ferris, who had accepted mugs, but both still appeared to be full. Villius and Felix both continued to sip wine, refusing the offer entirely.

"What's wrong with your friends?" Hortensio asked. "I never knew anyone from Dannos to be so abstinent."

"I'm not sure, myself," Elton said. "I'll ask them when the food's been finished."

Hortensio withdrew from Elton's side and returned to his conversation with the Thornish king and General Jannis.

"What's going on? Why aren't they drinking?" Elton hissed, turning to Felix.

"Villius told them not to drink the ale," Felix said through a mouthful of boar. "That's all I know."

The realisation hit Elton at once and he rose quickly from his chair, attracting a confused response from Hortensio as he made his way into the centre of the room where the band were situated.

"Stop drinking the ale!" Elton called, grabbing tankards from people mid-gulp. "It's poisoned!"

He received an assortment of reactions, from anger to confusion. Some ignored him, snatching their drinks back and continuing to imbibe. Others cautiously placed them at the edge of their tables.

"Count Redwinter, what are you talking about?" Hortensio's voice boomed across the hall, the band ceasing their song as concerned chatter grew louder and louder.

"Don't drink the bloody ale!" Elton repeated, continuing his excursion around the hall and relieving everyone of their drinks. Several people rose from their seats, including the entirety of Elton's company. Felix, Paul, and Ferris came to join him, but Villius was nowhere to be seen.

"Boss, this is our opportunity," Felix urged. "He's vulnerable. Nobody feels safe."

"Someone find me that scrawny little man," Elton seethed, ignoring Felix's imploration.

"Felix is right, boss," Paul added. "If we're gonna kill him, we need to do it now."

"And how would we escape?" Elton asked brashly. "He is likely on his way out thanks to the actions of our Altercantian friend. A few more minutes and we will have targets on our backs. We need to escape."

"You go, run," Ferris suddenly suggested. "I can create a distraction."

"Why would you do that?" Elton questioned.

"Because this king has nothing against me. They won't kill me, but I can tell he will kill you."

Hortensio was losing control of the situation as the unsettled chatter drowned out his attempts to restore order, many of the nobles organising themselves towards the exit.

"Guards!" he called. "Seize that man! Seize Elton Redwinter!"

"I don't think we'll need that distraction," Felix said.

Elton drew his dagger and held it out defensively as the guards stationed around the room closed in on him. There was danger in every direction and his options slimmed with each passing moment.

Felix and Paul ran together towards the King, who himself vaulted the table, scattering a plate of greens across the floor. Felix drew two knives from his jerkin in an imperceptible motion as Paul drew his sword from his belt. Hortensio was joined immediately by Jannis, each of them grabbing a sword from a nearby guard as they stepped closer to the Dannosi men. Ferris pre-emptively drew his own rapier and held it across his body, standing back-to-back with Elton as the guards closed off their escape routes.

Half the occupants of the room had disappeared by the time the first attack was made. Felix flung a knife in the direction of the King's head with a flick of his wrist. Hortensio sidestepped the attack, the blade whizzing past his ear.

One of the guards lunged at Elton, who parried the blow and stepped forwards with the momentum, slashing the guard's wrist. The guard grunted and stepped back, the space filled by another. Ferris lashed out with a quick series of jabs, each of which was blocked by the guard opposite him. He then feinted an overhead strike before bringing the blade back and jabbing again, aiming at the guard's throat and hitting the mark.

The guard collapsed, gurgling his own blood, as the rest of the guards counterattacked. Ferris deflected blows from three sides, sweat beading on his forehead. Elton breathed sharply, deeply, as swords danced through the space before him, a space which was fast becoming narrower and narrower.

Hortensio and Jannis advanced on Felix and Paul simultaneously, their swords moving as one in a predetermined set of strikes. Paul deflected each of the King's blows, forced backwards, while Felix had no option but to dodge, sidestepping and ducking out of the way of Jannis's swings and jabs.

Felix then launched a knife at the King, a move for which the King was not prepared. Hortensio stumbled out of the way and Paul used the opportunity to strike Jannis, who was preoccupied with Felix. He cut deeply through the general's shoulder, tearing his doublet and narrowly missing his ear. Jannis snarled, taking a step back as Felix readied another knife.

Paul raised his sword, this time aiming at the King. But it struck darkness as it fell.

"I'm afraid that won't be happening," Kasimir said calmly, clutching the magical blade that had intercepted the path of Paul's sword.

He drew his arm backwards and uttered a spell before pressing forwards again, propelling Felix and Paul through the air with a burst of energy. They crashed into the guards attacking Elton and Ferris, toppling one, which Elton did not hesitate to finish off.

The four came together, brandishing their weapons as the last of the banquet's guests and the band drained from the room. The guards left a space for the King, Jannis, and Kasimir, the former two of which approached with expressions of steely determination.

"Oh, Elton," Hortensio rasped, clutching his stomach. "That was clever of you. I'll admit, this was a trap. But I did not expect you to trap me first."

"I didn't want this," Elton grunted, wearily holding his dagger in front of him. "This wasn't my plan."

"But it's worked... hasn't it?" Hortensio said, coughing. "And how I didn't see it coming. You made it so obvious! Not a single one of your little gang touching the ale. Bandits that don't drink ale. And I suspected nothing!"

Hortensio gestured his guards to stand back, moving to stand at the fore of his trio.

"I had planned for this to be an event for the guests," he said, twirling his sword. "But I guess now it will just be my last satisfaction."

Hortensio raised his sword and was about to order his guards to converge. But his attention was wrenched out of his control.

"Stop!" Villius called, entering the hall, cowl removed. Every single guard turned to face the old man, Jannis and Kasimir keeping their attention trained on Elton. But Hortensio dropped his weapon and ran straight towards him.

In Villius's clutches, bound and gagged, was the maid. She did not resist as she was forced forwards. She did not make a sound. Instead, she only exhibited fear in her trembling and her widened eyes.

"Don't move one step closer," Villius growled, making a point of brandishing the dagger he held to her throat.

Hortensio obeyed, raising his hands and freezing in place.

"Lay down your weapons and free the Count and his associates," Villius continued. "Tell them to do it!"

Hortensio looked back to the group and indicated for them to follow the order. The guards glanced at one another before gently lowering their weapons to the ground. Kasimir whispered a spell, his sword dissolving. Jannis swore under his breath and launched his weapon across the hall in the other direction.

"Step away. All of you. Except the mage. Come here and stand with the King."

They did as Villius commanded, breaking their formation and retreating to the wall. The only exception was Jannis.

"Why the fuck are we listening to this old man over the life of some peasant?" He raised his voice. "We had them this close, Hortensio. This close. And you falter because of some throwaway girl from some rundown village in the middle of nowhere! Is that really going to be the obstacle to our dream? We've come so far! How can we stop now?"

Hortensio's face was engulfed by a deep red, accompanied by a fierce scowl.

"Tell him to keep quiet and stand against the wall," Villius growled.

"Get back, Jannis. And don't say another word," the King reiterated.

Jannis joined the rest of the guards standing against the wall, bashing his fists against it as he arrived. He breathed heavily, stifling his anger.

"You, mage," Villius continued. "You're going to open a portal to Dannos. The Redhouse. We are all going to walk through, and you are then going to close the portal. Understood?"

Kasimir looked to Hortensio for approval, which was granted with a slight nod. The anger decorating the King's face had become mixed with nausea as he placed a second hand on his stomach.

The sorcerer stepped forwards and opened the portal, the destination of the Redhouse's lobby clearly visible, as were the surprised expressions of the people within.

Villius indicated for his allies to step through it. Ferris was the first to leave, followed by Paul and then Felix.

"You can't do this!" Jannis called as Elton was about to cross into Dannos. "I'm not allowing it. I'm not allowing you to slip away again!"

He dashed forwards, grabbing one of the swords dropped by the guards, and leapt through the air.

"No!" Hortensio screamed, leaping up to step into the way of the blow.

Elton dived through the portal as Jannis's blade pierced Hortensio's chest, the King sputtering blood over the marble floor.

Villius thrust the bound girl from his grasp and stepped backwards, expecting to land in the sweltering heat of Dannos. But there was nothing.

Kasimir contorted his hand and forced the dagger from the old man's grip with another spell. It clattered across the floor and he turned to run, but couldn't.

The sorcerer raised his hand and dragged him through the air as Jannis let out a gut-wrenching cry, Hortensio coughing up more and more blood. The King drew pained, extended breaths, weakly removing the gag from Penelope's mouth as she broke down into sobs, collapsing onto the King's bloody chest as Jannis cut through her binds.

"Fucking idiot!" Jannis swore, throwing another sword across the room. "Mage! Heal him!"

Kasimir looked to the floor at the dying King and summoned a shadowy blade in his free hand. In a flick of the wrist, he flung it through the air as if it weighed as much as a dart. Villius could do nothing as it tore through his chest.

"Wizard! Do your job!"

Kasimir only shook his head as he kneeled, placing his hands against the side of Hortensio's chest not occupied by Penelope. He began to murmur an incantation as Hortensio's eyes glazed over, his breathing slowing, his heartbeat faltering. Jannis's angry questions became white noise as the sorcerer focused solely on the spell.

"Kan'ze van deth los," he whispered. "Vallan ze nav les nam'fanath."

The King's pupils steadily dilated until his eyes were only black. His breathing turned into wheezing as black streaks snaked through his veins. And then he began to convulse.

"What the hell are you doing?" Jannis questioned feverishly.

"A last resort," Kasimir said quietly.

The sorcerer produced a small, purple crystal as a grey mist evaporated from Hortensio's body, the convulsions slowing. He murmured a new incantation, drawing the mist closer and closer to the crystal until it made contact and bathed the entire hall in a sudden, intense burst of bright purple light.

The light in the crystal faded, and with it, any remaining signs of life in the King. He did not breathe, his heart did not beat. Penelope caressed his face, gingerly sliding his eyelids shut.

"I—"

"I captured the King's soul before it was lost forever," Kasimir cut Jannis off. "It will remain in this crystal until the end of time. Or until we return it to a host. I will begin to work to repair his body, but I am not versed in the art of resurrection. However, I know people who have done it before."

"What..." Jannis stammered. "What do you want us to do?"

"Bring his body to my laboratory. And clean up this mess."

CHAPTER 15

Elaeínn was unable to protest as the dwarves tossed her and Velrin into the cell.

"Obviously there's no concrete evidence of yer treachery," Flint said, dismissing the other guards who had accompanied him to the dungeon. "It will be the King who gets the final say in yer punishment."

"General, you know that the King is the changeling," Velrin said. "It seemed a little bit too convenient that the portal opened as I was about to test him, wouldn't you agree?"

Flint subtly indicated for them both to approach the bars of their cell as he glanced nervously around.

"I would agree," he said quietly. "We don't admit it, but we are losing this war on every front. The elves just seem to know our every move. It's why I was so hasty to let yous in without any rigorous background checks. We've lost our portion of the Darklight and much of the eastern coast. Our connections to the Eye have been mostly cut off. Meanwhile the Tayannans attack our backside despite having declared war on the high elves themselves. It's not a good situation."

"We would be a lot more use to you out of here," Elaeínn said. "We're not spies for the elves—we were locked up by them. We only just broke out after three months in a cell."

"I believe ye, girl, but I need to watch me own neck. Quite understandably, not many trust an elf round here, regardless of who they are. I'd risk the noose if I was to break yous out."

"Surely you must have the authority to speak with the King. Finish the experiment," Velrin urged. "You'd be a hero, and we could be let out."

"It's risky." Flint rubbed his palm against his forehead.

"You said yourself that you were losing the war. If you don't act, you will be destroyed."

The General sighed. "Yer right, elf, yer right. I will see what I can do. I pray for yer sakes that yer right."

*

Flint withdrew from the dungeon, taking his time as he traversed the halls of Castle Rockfell. His first destination was the site of the infiltration, with one particular goal in mind. When he arrived, however, he was out of luck.

Among the incinerated furniture and scorched stones were not a pair of shackles and a set of silver chains, as he had hoped to find. Either they had been melted, a theory he believed less and less as he scoured the ruins of the room, or they had been taken.

His next two visits were determined for him. First, he visited the castle's blacksmith, who sold him a pair of shackles and set to work smithing a new silver chain. While the chain was being forged, he visited the castle's apothecary and stocked up on hevula.

Supplies replenished and packed away, he opted to travel the official route to the Royal Quarter, rather than using the secret passages between the castle's segregated sections, extending his journey by at least half an hour. The normal bureaucracy was made much worse by his luggage, but he flashed his badge enough times to get him over the bridge. He trudged through the dingy, narrow corridors and wound up in the throne room, where he had his magical signature checked twice, instead of the usual once. The guards forced him to empty his bag, but they allowed him to pass, despite their suspicions.

"Where is the King?" Flint asked one of them as he returned the items to his bag, taking notice of the empty throne.

"He's locked himself in his chambers, for some reason," one of the guards provided. "Never told anyone here why."

"I have to see him."

The guards looked at each other and shrugged. "I'll take yous to him."

128

Flint had spent time in the halls behind the throne before, but never had he visited the King's personal chambers. It wasn't a long walk from the throne room, and the reinforced wooden door to which he was delivered looked typical of any other room in the castle. Nothing of the exterior betrayed the interior to be of any particular importance.

He knocked the door and waited patiently. By the time the door swung open, he had raised his fist to knock again. He and the King proceeded to share an awkward stare, the King raising his eyebrow and nodding at the bag slung over Flint's back.

"Greetings, Yer Highness," Flint finally spoke.

"Drop the formalities, Flint. What's in the bag?"

Flint pressed his way inside, closing the door and then lowering the bag with a metallic clattering.

"With yer consent, Yer Highness, I would like to finish the experiment the elves started. I know it's very unlikely that ye are the spy, but I need to check everyone. It's simply pro—"

"Ye can stop right where ye are, Flint. I am not allowing ye to pursue that bastard experiment that wound up with half me court murdered in yer offices. That entire affair is yer fault. It happened under yer watch and the elves nearly had me head as well. If anything, I ought to be locking yous up for incompetence."

Flint reached for the chains in his bag. "My king, I must object. The spy is responsible, and I was doing me job. It was unfortunate, tragic that they managed to infiltrate so deep. But that could only have happened as a result of one possibility."

The General launched the chains over the King and wrapped them tightly around his neck. He began to grunt and swear as Flint ran circles around him, binding his arms to his body.

The grunting quickly evolved into pained crying as the silver sizzled against the King's skin. He shouted something in a language unknown to Flint and a portal opened behind him.

Kagyan howled and threw Flint off him, charging towards the portal. Flint whipped his axe from his back and launched it at the stampeding King, his flesh still burning as he struggled to shake the chains off. It lodged in his arm and he let out a guttural roar, stumbling over the chain and landing on the floor mere centimetres away from the portal.

Flint stepped into the space between what had been the King and the portal. The majestic dwarf who had greeted him at the door was gone, replaced by a disfigured mess. Blackening burn marks crisscrossed his body while new ones continuously formed under the tangled chains. Its face was slightly warped as it continued to cry and convulse, baring teeth which elongated as its shouts grew louder and louder.

Flint withdrew his axe and found it covered not in a bright red layer of blood but an opaque yellow one. The creature, seeping a slug-like trail onto the floor, extended a desperate grasp, its fingers of different lengths. It attempted to crawl the little remaining distance but never made it as Flint brought the axe down.

He brought it down once more to sever the other hand and grabbed the creature by the scruff of what would have been its neck. What had been clothes felt instead like leathery flesh. He threw the changeling against the wall above a bench and looped the tangled chains around it as its screams distracted him from the frantic banging on the door.

The creature then uttered the beginnings of what sounded to Flint like another spell. He leapt to his bag, grabbed the bundle of hevula, and set about weaving it through the chains.

The door slammed open as a black-clothed elf stepped through the portal. Flint turned and rolled, narrowly avoiding her blow, the changeling using the opportunity to flop onto the floor and crawl towards the portal.

Flint's eyes darted between the elven agent, the two guards who had drawn axes and dashed into the fray, and the escaping changeling. He lowered his head and charged towards the agent, who stood defensively in front of the changeling, and then he sidestepped at the last moment. She missed her attack with her sword as the two guards stepped forwards to engage her and Flint barrelled into the changeling.

He struck twice more and relieved the changeling of its legs as the agent's sword lashed his backside. He growled and turned, swinging blindly, narrowly missing his assailant as she pirouetted out of harm's way.

The changeling, rendered immobile, moaned pathetically on the ground as it continued to burn under the chains. The commotion had attracted a crowd of new guards who streamed into the bedroom, and they all marched on the sole elven agent as one.

The elf recognised a losing battle and moved nimbly backwards, not wasting a step as she deflected a blow on her right, parried Flint's axe on her left, and fell gracefully through the portal. The portal closed no more than a second afterwards.

The attention of every dwarf in the room fell upon the charred mess of a creature whose screams and cries had progressed to numb moans and whimpers. Flint stood above it and saw only fear in its eyes.

"I hope yer not tired of the silver," he cackled. "Because we've got a lot to talk about."

*

Elaeínn stood up eagerly as a trio of men, dressed similarly to those she had seen in the Intelligence Quarter, approached the door to her cell. Velrin stood up too, but not with quite the same enthusiasm.

The men shooed away the guards sitting on the chairs in the small dungeon, who complied with content shrugs. They then retrieved a set of keys from a hook on the wall and freed the elves of both their cell and their binds.

"Yous are coming with us," they ordered, turning and marching from the dungeon.

The dwarves led them to the Intelligence Quarter, past the room they had fled during the attack. They came to an unassuming door through which they were pressed before Elaeínn had an opportunity to try to comprehend the aftermath of the attack. Inside the room were several dwarves, though it was Flint they noticed first. Elaeínn and Velrin were careful so as not to hit their heads on the low ceiling as the red-haired general greeted them amicably.

"Ye were right, elves," he said. "Ye will be glad to know that yer reputation has been solidified among us dwarves. And we thought we would let yous have the honour of interrogating our little friend with us."

131

Flint gestured towards a rack facing the back wall, surrounded by a gathering of intrigued dwarves inspecting its contents with magnifying glasses, rulers, and other implements. Elaeínn hadn't heard the moaning over the hubbub when she had initially entered the room, but now it was audible with complete clarity.

She covered her mouth and turned away when she saw the monstrosity occupying the rack. Velrin, however, was just as intrigued as the dwarves.

Flint had swapped the silver chains for a set of steel ones, lacing them with hevula for good measure. The changeling had begun to recover, having morphed partially into a normal form, but still patterned with black burn scars. Its wounds had sealed, and it had reshaped limbs from its remaining flesh, but its features were still warped and it was still largely unresponsive to the dwarves' questions.

"Out of the way." Flint barged through the crowd examining the changeling, whipping his axe from his back. He grabbed the changeling by its neck and stared into its eyes. Its breathing rapidly increased in pace and volume. "Who are ye?" he asked, lowering his voice to a growl. The chatter in the room immediately dried up.

"Not an elf," the changeling choked, speaking in a voice other than the King's for the first time since Flint had apprehended him.

Flint tightened his grip on the changeling's neck and repeated the question.

"Let... go..." it struggled to say.

Flint slightly loosened his grip.

"The elves... the elves have been paying me. A lot of money." Elaeínn thought that it sounded as if it was speaking with a snake's tongue.

"Yer not working out of pride? Just the money?"

"Of course, you blithering idiot. You see what I am. Nobody accepts me and nobody ever will. The least I can do for myself is accrue a meagre bit of wealth so I may at least live comfortably in my solitude."

"Spare me the sob story. How long have you been posing as the King? Where is the real King?"

"The real King is dead," the changeling spat. "I took his place three years ago. Prime Minister of Tyen'Ael put me here himself."

"Did ye kill him?"

"It wasn't particularly difficult. Bribe someone who works in the Royal Quarter into giving me their knowledge of it. Disguise myself as a guard, teleport in. 'Check in' on the King. No more King."

Flint clenched his fist and turned around, bristling. "And ye have been feeding information to the elves? About all our plans?"

"About all of them. Every single strategy, every single troop movement, every single target. Straight from the planning room to the Serenna Palace. The preparations made for the expiration of the Peace Treaty—I gave them straight to Jaelaar. The plan I gave Captain Tynak to sack the silver shipment to Teneth—given specifically because the elves requested it. And Fallía—Jaelaar was told about it the moment the FTA's leader was given a room for the night. You dwarves had no secrets, because I got very rich from selling them."

An irate murmur engulfed the room as many of the dwarves clamoured to spit insults at the changeling. Elaeínn herself felt overcome with a wave of exasperation as she thought back to the humiliation she had suffered at the battle for Fallía.

They knew, she thought. *They knew the whole time.*

Flint tempered his breathing and raised a fist in the air, an action the dwarves understood at once as the angry chattering stopped.

"Give me one reason why I shouldn't drive me axe through yer skull," he said, lowering his voice further to a growl-like whisper.

"Because I will work for you just as easily as I will work for the elves. Pay me well, and the elves will also cease to have any secrets. You want to know about their plan to track down and capture the dragon? Or how about their intention to annex Teneth? I will tell you anything you want to hear, and I will work without any qualms—I don't have any particular moral compass in this conflict."

Flint's arm twitched and he let out a long breath. "Unfortunately for yous, I do."

The General split the changeling's skull in two to an uproar of discordant cheers and jeers. The dwarves had now decided to speak exclusively in Dwarven, and though Elaeínn didn't speak the language, the expressions fighting for control of Velrin's face were enough to allow her to understand.

The ruckus continued for some time as Flint tried to wrestle authority, even drawing attention from the rest of the Intelligence Quarter when someone knocked on the door. It was Elaeínn and Velrin who had to answer, as the rest of the room was too preoccupied.

Velrin explained something to the people at the door while the commotion only continued to grow louder. Elaeínn watched as several dwarves surrounded Flint, ranting constantly without giving him a moment to speak up for himself. Others surrounded the changeling's mangled corpse, prodding it and peering inside its skull. Elaeínn had to stifle a laugh when one of the dwarves pressed the two halves of the skull together with an expectant look on their face.

"Enough!" Flint shouted, bellowing louder than any of the other combating voices. "We were not going to get any more information out of that abomination. He told us what we needed to know. He was the spy. And he won't be spying anymore."

"El larn hev ust terarben! Wir larnen hev el tenullen!" one dwarf, particularly scraggly, retorted.

"Vel, translate," Elaeínn whispered.

"He said he—the changeling—could have worked for them. They could have used him."

"The moment we let that monster free would have been the moment he started working for the elves again," Flint countered, shooting the scraggly dwarf a venomous glare. "There was nothing more to be done with him."

"Siril darva!"

"Speak Dwarven," Velrin translated.

"The next person to speak to me like a foot-soldier instead of their general I will court-martial meself! We're at war, gentlemen, and scrapping with one another over yer personal opinions on the way to approach a matter is not going to re-take any of our stolen land. Raising yer voice to challenge me will achieve quite the opposite, because the elves will then re-alise that we have got a serious breakdown in discipline. Re-member yer bloody places!"

The entire monologue had been given in Dwarven, as re-quested, and Velrin had done his best to translate it with the same emphasis. The dwarf who had shouted for Flint to speak Dwarven, as well as most of the others, grew sheepish under the fury burning in Flint's eyes, a fury Elaeínn had only ever seen so passionately in Captain Tynak Llavadi.

"Here's what's going to happen," Flint said, tempering his voice. "We are going to organise an attack. One they won't see coming. One which drives a wedge through their front line. We are going to retake Fallía for the FTA. And for us."

"And who do ye think ye are to be conjuring up battle plans?" the scraggly dwarf interjected.

"I'm General Flint Korvald of the Hamatnarian Army, and ye, Corporal Krillick, are in no position to question me! Cap-tain Tynak fell at Fallía. The King is dead. We have got some-thing of a power vacuum, and I am stepping up to make sure it does not swallow us. If we do not fall in line and organise ourselves, we will collapse and the whole damned country will fall to the enemy. Is that what ye want?"

The scraggly dwarf shook his head and pursed his lips.

"Elves." Flint turned his attention to Elaeínn and Velrin, who had been standing quietly by the door. "Yous ought to know Fallía best. What would it take?"

"It took a whole National army against our band of civilians and the Elites," Elaeínn said.

"And dwarven armies are worth five elven!" Flint ex-claimed, to many cheers. "We can take the path directly through the Darklight to Fallía. From there we can then work eastwards and cut off Teneth, encircle the lands they occupy, and reclaim them. Their focus is very much on pushing ahead, securing the entire eastern coast. They wouldn't expect an attack from their own territory."

"We would need help defending Fallía, General," Elaeínn cautioned. "When it fell last time they did a pretty good job of annihilating any influence the FTA had. It will take time to re-build not just our castle but our reputation. And our support."

"I have faith in yous," Flint said. "I have faith in us all. We have today defeated the only thing blocking us from turning this war in our favour. Captain Hralvor—ready the fifty-first army at the southern mouth of the Darklight! Captain Bornol—stage a counterattack at Molnor, a diversion! And I will get us inside, we will infiltrate the old castle in much the same way that they infiltrated us. These bastards are finally going to taste defeat. Sweet, sweet defeat."

The dwarves saluted in unison and hollered their support for Flint, any lingering animosity from only moments ago having completely vanished. The dwarves rapidly filed from the room, leaving Elaeínn and Velrin alone with Flint.

"Yous are going to work with me," the General declared, placing a hand on each of their backs. "I have a good feeling about this. A very good feeling. Come on, let's go."

Flint took them across the Intelligence Quarter to a small library. Attached to the library at one end was a laboratory operated by a grey-haired dwarf wearing oversized goggles, and at the other end a meditation chamber.

"I'd like to introduce yous to a few important people," Flint said, indicating the opening to the meditation chamber. An assortment of candles burned at the centre of a circle of straw mats, each mat occupied by a different robe-wearing dwarf. Though these dwarves weren't the typical workers milling around outside—they had an elegant look to them. When they stood, they held their heads high, their backs straight. They wore jewellery and the women makeup.

"Janria Tallinor," Flint began, gesturing to a woman of a stature short even for a dwarf.

"Isak Gravanas," he continued, introducing a grey-haired man wearing a monocle over his left eye.

"And Tora Verne." He placed his hands on the shoulders of a third dwarf, a woman with rosy cheeks but a permanent scowl.

"What are ye planning, Flint?" Isak asked, his tone laced with sarcasm.

"I'm planning our comeback," he said proudly. "And ye three are a vital part of it. Do ye think ye could teleport us to Fallía?"

"If I had been there before, yes," Janria mused.

"We have," Elaeínn chimed in. "You can... have our knowledge, do whatever it is that you do."

"And then what, General?" Tora joined in. "Do pardon my impertinence, but I don't often agree to plans without a full understanding of them."

"Gather intel. Eliminate key targets. We're going to soften the place up before our army arrives."

"And if we get caught?"

"We'll be bringing the Shadow Division. The Shadows don't get caught."

"It seems awful vague, General," Isak said. "Almost like ye have thought of it in the past few minutes."

Flint sighed and closed his eyes. "Isak," he enunciated. "We have one day to prepare. The fifty-first must march through the Darklight and Captain Bornol must plan a diversion. But we are the spark. I know it isn't as prepared as ye would like it. I know ye are fond of an exhaustive plan. But we are at war. We don't have any choice. And I am commanding yous to follow me orders."

The three magicians looked at each other apprehensively but eventually sighed, practically in unison, and bowed.

"Just one page, General," Isak rasped. "I would like to see just one page."

"And one page ye will have."

*

Elaeínn and Velrin had been taken back to stay in the generals' quarters overnight. Though their furnishing was luxurious, the time at which Flint came banging on their doors in the morning was not.

As they were dragged down into the Intelligence Quarter, Elaeínn peeked through a window and saw the moon in its entirety, though it looked to be on the way down.

"May I introduce yous to the leader of the Shadow Division, Captain Agria Fillock," Flint said, semi-hushed, as if to avoid waking anyone nearby.

A woman dressed in dark leathers nodded to the two elves. She was equipped with two daggers, one sheathed on either side of her body. Her belt held several vials of various substances, and she wore a utility belt over her shoulder complete with an array of tools from lockpicks to ball bearings.

"Who are the Shadows?" Elaeínn asked.

"Ye spent time with the Elite Division," Flint chuckled. "Imagine the Elite Division but a lot quieter."

They made their way to the meditation room where the mages rested. They had anticipated Flint's return and Isak was the first to greet them, extending a hand which Flint met with the expected document.

"Ye really do work to the letter." Isak shook his head, stuffing the piece of paper into his back pocket.

"The dwarven way."

It was then Janria who asked Elaeínn for permission to access her knowledge of Fallía, permission she granted as the mage pressed her fingers against Elaeínn's forehead. She felt the same tingling sensation as before and this time she found it oddly pleasant.

"Alright," Janria said, withdrawing her fingers. "We're ready when ye are, Flint."

"Captain Fillock?"

Agria whispered something under her breath and disappeared. Janria uttered a spell and traced a circle in the air, pressing forwards to reveal the lobby of Fallía's keep. It looked just the same as Elaeínn remembered leaving it.

She felt a sudden motion of bodies brushing past her, though she could not see anyone. The motion continued for some time as Flint chuckled to himself, amused by the confusion that had struck Elaeínn's face.

"The Shadows are all skilled illusionists." Flint lifted his axe and tapped its head against his hand a few times, turning to face the portal. "And they were the first part of the plan. Now"—he twirled his axe and tightened the straps of his armour—"it's our turn."

CHAPTER 16

FLORIAN WILDERNESS

The last villager's scream fell silent as Richard placed his sword through her chest, unable to look as he did so. His face was wet with tears, his eyes narrowed and facing the blank wall. His blade, as he withdrew it, was coated in blood.

He burst from the house, letting out an anguished roar as he launched his sword into an adjacent tree. It was the only sound left in the graveyard of a village.

Calliope appeared from the brush as Richard stood paralysed, staring at the ground, at his hands, wet with the blood of near every villager. He took deep, rapid breaths as she approached, seeming not to take notice of her presence.

"Richard," she said, touching his face. He felt the restraint on his arm fall away, the lock thudding to the ground, but Richard could barely hear her, a piercing ringing reverberating in both ears.

"Richard," she repeated, caressing his cheek with her other hand.

He grabbed the dryad's neck and slammed her into the tree. She attempted to choke out a spell but the bounty hunter's grip was too tight and she struggled for breath as several more dryads appeared, arrows nocked and pointed at Richard.

"They were right," Richard spat, his face red with rage. "The villagers. There was no reason to kill them. No reason at all. They were innocent. Only one thing kills innocent people without reason. A monster. You're monsters, all of you."

Calliope attempted to respond but couldn't, as Richard didn't have any intention to loosen his grip. She continued to struggle for breath as Richard pulled her away from the tree, lifting her higher into the air with one hand. The dryads who had come to her rescue loosed their arrows, but they never reached their target.

Richard clenched his free hand as they flew and each one stopped only inches from his head. He contorted the hand and the arrows rotated in mid-air, his eyes still locked with Calliope's. One final gesture and they flew back in the direction from which they had come. The encircling dryads collapsed in unison as the arrows crunched through their skulls and Calliope clawed desperately at Richard's wrists as her green face shifted to a deep blue.

She gasped as Richard flung her violently against the tree, her body falling limply to the ground as the green returned to her face. The bounty hunter continued to stand there for some time, acutely aware of the presence of more and more dryads in the surrounding thicket. And then he retrieved his sword from the tree and traced a portal, stepping through it without looking back.

The old stone fortress was as foreboding and uninviting as ever. It was silent—Richard's room had been left undisturbed and he saw no signs of activity in any of the other rooms lining the corridor. They, like his, had been left untouched. Even the illusions remained in place.

"Hello?" he shouted, walking in the direction of the atrium. "Kalahar?"

Kalahar didn't respond, and neither did anyone else. Richard eventually came upon a mangled body, sliced up and covered in red liquid. "Is anyone there?" he called, inspecting the body up close but unsure of what conclusions to draw. His voice echoed down the castle's empty passages and nobody ever appeared.

He reached the entrance to the atrium and broke into a sprint. In the centre of the room—levitating, shackled, her eyes closed—was the sorceress whose sister he had beheaded. The sorceress who newly populated Richard's resurfacing memories.

He stepped around the pentagram etched into the floor and quickly scanned the area above, the other passages into the bowels of the fortress. He again saw nobody, and the unending silence felt deafening. Richard carefully pulled the sorceress down from her levitation and broke the shackles with a spell, tossing them across the room. He shook her gently and she began to show signs of stirring as her eyelids fluttered open.

"Kal… Kalahar… please, I just want something to eat…" she murmured semiconsciously. Although her eyes were now open, Richard could tell she wasn't really there.

He left the sorceress on the floor and turned in the direction of the pantry. He had never been before but knew its exact location with the knowledge Kalahar had granted him. It was a peculiar feeling that he would never shake.

The pantry to which he arrived was a room comprising shelves upon shelves of various foodstuffs. Meats, fruits, vegetables, breads, desserts—all neatly organised, too. Richard's main concern revolved around the age of the room's contents, and how it hadn't spoiled when nobody who usually inhabited the castle ate. He pushed these questions to one side and grabbed a hunk of raw venison before leaving.

Lynn was still somewhat delirious when he returned, and he set about starting a fire to cook the meat. In the end he resorted to torching it with magical flame.

"Oh, that smells nice, Kalahar. It smells really nice. Better than the gruel, for sure," Lynn drawled, fondling Richard's arm. He shook her off and continued to roast the venison.

"Alright, wake up," Richard said, turning to the sorceress when he was confident the meat had been cooked through. He grabbed her face in both hands and looked into her eyes, which had glazed over. "Looks like I'm waiting," he sighed, resigning to one side of the room and sliding down against the wall where he sat and took a bite from the venison, keeping an eye on Lynn.

Some hours later she began to show signs of truly stirring. She stopped babbling to herself and looked around alarmedly at her surroundings, catching sight of Richard lying lazily against the wall. "Rich… Richard?" she said dazedly.

Richard tossed the stone-cold, half-eaten hunk of venison towards the sorceress, who grabbed it with both hands and devoured it in seconds.

"I need your help," Richard said, standing up as she wiped the grease from her face.

"And why is that?" she responded, looking for somewhere to wipe her hands and eventually resorting to her dress.

"I need to find Kalahar. I was hoping he would be here."

A contemptuous smile crossed Lynn's face as she let out a sharp exhale that sounded almost like a laugh. "He's been here. Keeping me prisoner for a while. But I haven't seen him in about a week. And I'm famished. That starter you brought me, as much as I appreciate it, I need more. Much more. Where did you find it?"

"We'll eat after we come to an agreement. Did he say where he was going?"

"Of course not... why did you kill my sister?"

"Lynn."

"I'm fucking starving, Richard, how do you expect me to focus? Please, can't we do this over a plate of roast pheasant?"

Richard sighed again, rolling his eyes and returning with the sorceress to the pantry. Her eyes lit up as they entered and Lynn scoured the many shelves, picking out enough items to feed a noble family of four.

Arms overflowing, Lynn looked expectantly at Richard, who decided to head in the direction of the dining room. They came across another mutilated body in much the same condition as the one Richard had found, Lynn nearly tripping and dropping the food that Richard hadn't offered to help carry. He stopped briefly to inspect it, but it was Lynn who drew a conclusion.

"It was me and my father," she declared as Richard peeled open one of the bloodless wounds. "When we came in search of Tregor. Who we found, in very much the same place you found me. But what did my father do, you're wondering? How did I end up there for the past two months? My father traded me, that's how. That self-serving, egotistic bastard left me here for dead so that he could save Tregor. Prioritising the life of his old master over that of his own remaining daughter."

Richard listened intently but silently as he continued on to the dining hall.

"And there was no chance of me saving myself, either, not without a crystal that I so neglectfully parted with. Why did I do that?" she rambled. "That vampire is more than he allows you to see. He's powerful—too powerful. He needs to die."

"He's not going to die," Richard said coolly. "I need him."

"For what? What can he possibly have that means leaving alive a threat to not just humanity, but the world?"

Richard didn't answer.

"We're alike, you and I, Richard." Lynn changed the subject. "I know we've had periods of disagreement, but I was only following orders. I am truly sorry for attempting to abduct you. Even though you killed my sister, I still believe we can work together—beyond finding Kalahar."

"We'll cross that bridge when we come to it."

They reached the dining hall and Richard uttered a spell to bring light to the room, the braziers, candles, and sconces flaring to life with real fire, rather than the artificial light preferred by the vampires. Lynn set straight to laying the food on the table, moaning something about her aching arms, and began to cook some of the meat with a spell. Richard grabbed an apple and took a seat, idly nibbling at it as he waited for her to finish.

"Oh, how I've longed for a proper meal," she said, organising various items of food onto a plate, having finished cooking the meat. "He fed me gruel, Richard. Gruel. Not even every day. I have never known such barbarism."

"That must have been really difficult for you," the bounty hunter replied with more than a hint of sarcasm.

"Oh, lighten up, for the gods' sakes. You weren't this icy with my sister, from what I heard."

Richard's expression hardened and he snatched a chicken drumstick, reclining dejectedly in his seat.

"I'm not my sister, Richard. I don't have this all-encompassing desire to please my father. Especially not after he left me in this forsaken dungeon."

"Is that why you attempted to convert me yourself?" Richard asked.

Lynn was physically taken aback. "How do you know about that?"

"Your father told me. Him and Tregor. I only just escaped them before coming here."

"Did they... did they tell you anything else?" she stammered, training her eyes on the plate below her.

"Yes, enough for me to begin to remember."

The sorceress blushed, seemingly struggling to eat the steak into which she had just cut. Richard tossed the bone of the drumstick across the room, and its rattling against the floor was the only sound in the hall for some time.

"So, as I was saying originally, I need your help," the bounty hunter finally said.

"I want to help Richard, I do. If only to make amends for my actions in the past. But I don't know where he is. And I don't know where he could be."

"Then you're going to help me look."

Richard's eyes were drawn to one of the entrances to the hall by what he thought was a flash of red. It was only brief, but he stood up slowly, casting an unsure gaze at the shadowy doorway.

"I think we're being watched," he said.

Lynn paused her meal and turned to the entrance indicated by Richard, who slowly drew his sword from its sheath.

The conjured blade sliced his torso as it materialised from the shadows. He cried out and ducked behind the wall to the left of the archway as a second blade crashed into the dining table. Lynn summoned her own magical blade and quickly joined Richard.

"Es tar an'dak'revvar," Richard whispered, his eyes brightening as he gained the ability to view the contents of the corridor in full detail. He saw their attacker—an elven woman, with pale skin and auburn hair.

"Faefion!" he snarled, dashing towards her as she loosed more conjurations, but Richard was now prepared to avoid them as they glanced off the walls with a series of clangs.

The elf turned and tried to flee, Richard giving immediate chase. He was faster than her but slowed by the magic daggers continuing to pepper the air. Another nicked his cheek, slicing it open and sending him stumbling to the side as Lynn caught up and continued the chase in his stead.

Faefion stopped running and summoned a cloud of daggers behind her, arms held out, fingers contorted. She cried one last command word and they flew forwards, forcing Lynn and Richard to fall to the ground. She then took the opportunity to flee, gaining considerable distance as they returned to their feet.

"Stop her Richard, damn it!" Lynn seethed. "One word and she's paralysed! What's stopping you?"

Richard ignored the sorceress's comment and sprinted ahead, sweat beading on his forehead as his adrenaline urged him faster and faster, the auburn-haired vampire lacking his biological limitations, but also his physical strengths. He dropped his sword and picked up the pace further still, the gap between him and the vampire narrowing as they careened around a corner, boisterously skipped a set of stairs, and nearly crashed into a stone banister, both vaulting it in the nick of time.

Richard was so close that he was almost stepping on the vampire's coattails. His breathing fast and heavy, a cramp rippling through his chest, he garnered all the energy he had left and dived.

He and Faefion crashed to the ground, disrupting an ancient carpet and rolling over each other. The vampire struggled against him as he grabbed her arms and pinned her to the ground. She squirmed like a worm, violently thrashing her legs and head, shouting indecipherable obscenities in a language Richard assumed to be her mother tongue.

"Just hold still, for Lanthanis's sake!" Richard hissed, swearing and struggling to control the writhing vampire. "Why did you even attack us?"

"The bodies," Faefion rasped, still not giving up on her struggle. "The bodies of my brethren. My friends. You think I haven't found them?"

"Where has Kalahar been keeping you, under a rock?" Lynn joined them. "Those bodies have been resting there for months."

"I was in hibernation until he awoke me," she claimed. "He entrusted me to watch over the fortress while he was away."

"Where's he gone?" Richard narrowed his eyes. "Not like him to vanish without a trace."

"What does it matter to you? You left here a long time ago, Richard Ordowyn."

"Is it a long time? You've been around for centuries, Faefion, what more is three months? Kalahar wants me to join him—he has already invited me. Now tell me where I can find him, or I'll be locking you away in another realm until the end of time like I have done to so many of your brethren already."

Faefion stopped struggling, lying flat and boring her eyes into the bounty hunter's. She scowled, looking between him and the sorceress.

"I'm not a threat. And neither is she," Richard reassured.

"Someone committed those murders," she nodded her head to the side. "And I want to know why."

"I did," Lynn confessed. "Myself and my father. We infiltrated the fortress in search of an ally of ours. A former ally of mine, now, as my father betrayed me to save him. We had been searching for this ally so he could help us kill Kalahar, in honesty. But that's not what I'm after anymore."

"Your lies might fool someone less rounded," Faefion spat. "But I see straight through them."

"Enough!" Richard snarled. "All it takes is a handful of words and you'll spend eternity in the void. Is that what you want?"

"I would happily tell you, Richard. I would tell you without hesitation where Kalahar has gone. But not her. Not someone whose thoughts are possessed by ways to kill him. You can't kill him, for Raeris's sake. He's immortal."

Richard growled through his teeth and lifted the vampire from the floor, grunting, before slamming her against the wall with a surge of strength fuelled by anger and adrenaline.

"Tell me where he is!" he shouted in her face.

He drew one of his hands back, contorting it, leaving only one to restrain her.

"Not while you align yourself with her," Faefion hissed. And then she ran.

She tore herself out of Richard's grasp and made it no more than five feet before the joints in her legs locked up and she fell to the ground with a crash.

"I don't like being forced to magic," Richard said, releasing the shape he had formed with his hand. "But you leave me no choice."

Faefion's eyes grew wide.

"Rez'kevar," Richard recited. "Dellessar. Tan'barath galar."

The rift sliced the air behind the vampire, expanding to the size of the average portal. It, like every such gateway to the dimensions Richard had fabricated in the past, showed only void. Endless, all-consuming void.

He stepped towards the vampire and picked her up without much care, hauling her towards the portal. Her eyes, already wide, managed to widen even further with each step.

"Wait, Richard!" she shrieked frantically. Richard did not wait.

He held her through the rift, not allowing her to fall into the void. Faefion was suddenly engulfed by emptiness, a realm devoid of substance, of sound. All she heard was white noise, and the faint ambiance of Letham Deregor.

"Tell me where he is," Richard enunciated, his voice resonating unnaturally through the corridor.

"The Heart of magic!" she squealed. "That's it! That's all I know!"

Richard pulled her back into Letham Deregor, shutting the rift with the other half of the spell. He then discarded her carelessly onto the floor. "El'kak ravir," he said, Faefion regaining the ability to use her limbs. The vampire darted her eyes between the various routes away from the situation, but was frozen by Richard's icy glare. "If you so much as think about running, I won't hesitate to reopen that portal and throw you through it for good. Now tell us. What is the 'Heart of magic'?"

"I-I-I don't know," she stammered. "He didn't tell me. He never tells me these things. He just said he needed to go there because of the Council. That's all, I swear."

"Because of the Council?"

"He said the Council were planning something with the Heart. He intends to put a stop to it, by the sounds of it."

Richard and Lynn shared a glance which was both knowing and confused. They understood the stakes at once.

"I've told you everything. Just don't try to kill him. For your own good."

"I've already told you." Richard turned to walk away. "I don't want to kill him. Come on, Lynn."

Lynn briefly hesitated as she looked between the vampire, visibly dishevelled by Richard's brutality, and Richard himself, free of hesitation as he marched back in the direction they had come. She opted to follow the bounty hunter, checking over her shoulder after some distance to see if Faefion was following. She wasn't—she had disappeared.

"You really don't know anything?" Richard asked as they returned to the dining hall.

"Actually, I think I might," Lynn said, a glint appearing in her eye as she settled back down into one of the cold seats around the table. "That elf girl—the one with the dragon. She mentioned it when she found me at the Retreat. And the dragon itself. They said that our crystals came from the Heart of magic."

"I take it they didn't say where that was," Richard sighed, grabbing and biting into a plum. It was perfectly ripe.

"But we do know where *she* is," Lynn said. "She was from one of the High Elven countries in Fenalia. Tyen... Tyen'Ael. Yes. And that she was some high-up in... oh, some acronym. But that's enough to find her. And if we can find her, surely we can find the dragon. And if we find the dragon—"

"We can find the Heart," Richard finished. "And we can stop Nendar and Tregor from doing whatever it is they're doing. Something nefarious, no doubt. And, hopefully, find Kalahar at the same time."

"I've never been to Tyen'Ael," Lynn said. "I don't suppose you have, either."

"You know I haven't."

"We're going to have to sail, then. Not many ships that travel from the lands of men to those of dwarves and elves."

"Astute observation." Richard tossed the stone of the plum across the table, aiming for the ceramic bowl next to the gem-inlaid throne. He hit it and it toppled over, spilling enough flawless gemstones onto the floor to pay for a hundred dowries in a wealthy village.

"I know Tyen'Ael is one of the northernmost countries on the continent," Lynn stated. "But we can access its southern ports by travelling through the Great Channel. It separates the continent in two."

"And how long will the journey take, you think?"

"A week, maybe, if we travel from a port I've visited in Canaris. Under optimal conditions. With magical enhancement. Which I cannot maintain without a crystal."

"You can teach me. But how are we meant to find her without knowing where to look?"

Lynn smiled, the same beautiful smile he had seen before on her sister's face. It filled him with resentment—resentment he quickly put aside.

"We'll have to ask around. But first, we'll have to find a ship."

"And some money…"

"Oh, I'm sure we can survive without that," a mischievous glint flashed in her eyes. "As long as we have our wits."

Richard looked at her and nodded. "Alright. Let's go, then."

Lynn polished off the plate she had in front of her before traversing to the other side of the table to stand with Richard. She traced a portal, grunting as she pressed forwards to open it.

Through the portal, Richard could see looming towers and mighty oaks in a colourful city where nature existed in harmony with the constructions of humans. Trees grew in the sparse empty spaces between the buildings, their architecture completely foreign to Richard. Standing on posts and lintels made from wood dyed white and red and yellow, with walls as thin as paper. Roofs curved down from pointed centres with eaves extending beyond the main structure to provide each building with a veranda. Some of these buildings extended multiple floors, each a mirror image of the one below, with one such building, taller and grander than the rest, standing over much of the city. Swathes of ivy stretched between the houses' wooden posts, painting bright splashes of green across already colourful façades.

Seabirds flying overhead were accompanied by what looked to be flying reptiles, but they weren't large enough to be wyverns. They had thinner, longer bodies, like snakes, as well as smaller wings which seemed utterly inadequate to allow the beasts to fly.

"Well, then?" Lynn interrupted Richard's awe. "Are you coming?"

Richard took one last look at the dingy table, the gemstones lining the throne and the floor, and the aftermath of their meal. He took a deep breath and then stepped through the portal.

CHAPTER 17

Elton drew his dagger and swung it at the portal behind him. Except he cut only air, because the portal was no longer there.

"He betrayed us," Elton hissed. "Two-faced bastard walked in here and lied to my face, took advantage of me. Took advantage of all of us."

"You were awful quick to trust him, boss," Felix said. "If anything though, we were lucky he was there. I don't see us getting out of that situation any other way."

"We've just made an enemy of Hortensio. Again," Elton looked down, rubbing hand on his forehead. "Oh, who am I kidding? He was always an enemy."

"If Villius poisoned the ale then Hortensio is on his way out. If he hasn't died from jumping into Jannis's sword, that is."

"The mage will heal him," Elton spoke with conviction, though he felt a strange sensation in his chest. A slight pang and tightening of his throat. It passed after a short period of silence, but he knew something was not as he was certain should have been the case.

"What was that journey he was witterin' on about?" Paul asked, breaking the tension. "Sounds like somethin' we ought to know about."

"I would have asked him about it had someone not poisoned the ale and with it probably the aristocracy of three powerful kingdoms. We have made enemies of more than just Hortensio by bringing him there."

"I don't know about that," Ferris spoke up. "I don't know how closely you were watching but I didn't see a single aristocrat—other than those wearing blue—drink ale. There was more going on than Villius let us know about."

"Well where is he now?" Elton waved his dagger in the air at the surroundings. "He was with us only moments before we crossed through that portal. Where is he?"

"Evidently still in the Blue Palace," Felix said. "It seems his plan had flaws."

Elton sheathed his dagger and looked contemplatively into the quiet streets, illuminated a soft white by the moon. There wasn't much activity outside of the resonating hollers of joy from distant taverns. A distinct change Elton had noticed since the dissolution of the Syndicate was the manner in which people traversed the streets at night—they no longer clung to the shadows, hands glued to pockets or bristling over the hilts of their weapons. Most people seemed not to carry a weapon anymore.

"Rosa," Elton said. "We need to check on Rosa."

"I doubt she'll have got much better in the hour we were away, boss," Paul said.

Elton ignored him and led the group into the Redhouse, where most of the staff had gone home for the night. Several people still milled around, but reception was empty, and it was primarily security guards patrolling the soulless hallways.

Rosa was found in her office alongside a servant who Elton dismissed for the night. He swore as he approached her body, still motionless apart from the gentle rising and falling of her chest.

"Alright, I need time to think," Elton announced, retrieving a cigar from his pocket and lighting it with a candle in the window. "The lot of you—go home. Ferris, here's some money for a room in a tavern. Don't let there be a repeat of last time."

"And how do you ask for a room in Santerosi?" Ferris asked, catching the jingling pouch of coin.

"Meni tonibri ponata, ny'laski," Elton said. "And then just give them the whole bag. Perhaps they'll give you an ale as well."

"I think I've been put off ale for a little while. Thank you."

Elton nodded as the trio left and went their separate ways. He looked over Rosa's wounds again, which he thought were showing improvement, before settling back into the chair at the desk and gazing into the night sky before falling into a slumber.

He awoke the next morning to find the sorceress still lengthways across the table at the side of the room. He sighed, checking her wounds once more before deciding to let time runs its course.

The morning was brisk and Elton decided to spend it at a nearby tavern. It happened to be the same one in which Ferris had spent the night, and the two came together for breakfast.

"We've the time, then, bard," Elton said, sipping a tankard of mead as Ferris lowered himself into the seat opposite him at one of the tavern's many empty tables. "Tell me who you are. And why you came here with Richard. And what Richard was doing, who he is. Last I spoke with him, it wasn't a very lengthy conversation and he kept to himself. That's excluding the time he tried to kill me on Kalahar's orders."

"He's a funny man," Ferris said, a plate of sausages, scrambled eggs, and slices of buttered bread arriving at their table. "He always was quiet. I journeyed halfway across the continent with him and this other woman. A witch, the daughter of the emperor I aim to kill. Let me tell you, Richard was never the one instigating the conversations.

"I joined him when myself and some guerrillas attacked the enemy-held fortress at the heart of my home town. It was after that when we set out on our journey, Richard and I sharing the same goal. A goal which was torn up when we discovered that the witch was spying on us the whole time.

"I managed to flee and eventually met Richard again in a city in Mirados. He told me everything that had happened. And he told me that he's looking for Kalahar because someone died that he wants to bring back to life. I don't know who, I don't know how. That's all he told me, and considering he attacked you without hesitation, I'd say he's certainly dead set on it."

Elton downed the rest of his mead, sucking out the dregs while Ferris devoured his breakfast.

"That's it!" Elton exclaimed, slamming his mug against the table and jostling Ferris's plate. "We've had mages right here, in the city, right under our noses, for months! The vampires! We can use them while Rosa recovers!" Elton rose from his chair, spurred on by a sudden jolt of excitement. "Be quick, bard, I'll be back at the Redhouse."

The Count hurried out of the tavern, almost jogging in the direction of Felix's and Paul's houses. He made sure to first seek out a pair of guards roaming the streets to act as his escort, but they weren't in that role for long with the speed at which he travelled.

"I'm amazed we haven't thought of that," Felix said, jumping from his patio onto the street after having heard Elton's plan.

"You've seen what Kalahar's capable of. Rosa said he's just a malevolent like all those we've been tracking down and trying to save from the mobs," Elton recounted. "And they're sentient—the question is, will they be as talkative as Kalahar?"

"I don't think anyone is..." Felix mused as they reached Paul's house and knocked on the door, knowing they would be waiting a while for an answer.

Paul eventually revealed himself, looking as if he had been dragged out of bed through both his expression and his clothing. He strapped a sword hanging by the door to his belt and then the four set off back to the Redhouse, Elton keen to meet with Ant and Fez.

They arrived at the intelligence office to find it thriving, Ant and Fez in their places as expected. They were typically some of the first to arrive, sometimes hours before the sun rose.

"Ah, Count," Fez greeted them as they entered. "We've got some progress on those explosives you wanted. Should have enough to reduce this fortress to rubble by the end of next week."

"Good work," Elton nodded. "But we're here to ask about something else. The vampire cells. You've still been tracking them?"

"Yes. Come with me."

Fez led the group into a side room occupied by several workers of the Dannosi Intelligence Service who saluted and left without being instructed to. Elton sighed as he took a seat alongside the others while Fez remained standing, bringing their attention to a detailed map of Dannos hanging on the wall.

"These green pins here are the last known positions of active vampire cells," Fez began, sweeping his hand over a dispersed array of pins on the map. "As you may notice, there are remarkably few of them. Many of the cells have been merging together with the increased number of attacks as of late. So instead of many smaller cells, we are now seeing fewer larger cells. And they're appearing to be getting a little bit bolder."

"What do you mean by that?" Elton leaned forwards on the table, clasping his hands.

"I mean they're no longer fleeing from the attacks. They're fighting back. Previously we've known these cells to let themselves be massacred when they are unable to flee. They would feebly fight off the attackers but with no real understanding of their abilities, they didn't do a very good job of it. It appears now that they're learning. There are reports from vampire hunters that they've been casting spells—fireballs, blades made out of shadows, bolts of lightning from their fingertips. This has made them much more dangerous. And in these large cells, the knowledge is spreading like wildfire."

"Are they attacking civilians?"

"There are no reports to indicate as much. They have solely been fighting back against their hunters. And can you blame them?"

Fez gestured back over the map, this time pointing to pins with red heads, of which there were far more than green. "These are all the cells which have been destroyed. The locations we have found their bodies. The vampire hunters have been efficient."

"These large cells," Elton said. "How many individuals are we talking?"

"Fifty, sixty in the largest. But most are no more than thirty."

"Which of these cells is nearest and has the fewest individuals?"

"Err..." Fez took a moment to inspect some of the scrawlings on various slips of paper tacked onto the pins. "There's a cell with only six individuals in an abandoned house near Megaross Square. Whether they're still there, we can't say for certain. They all move around a lot."

"I'll take that risk," Elton said, standing up. "Thank you, Fez."

"Might I ask as to what your plan is now, Count?"

"We need magical assistance while Rosa is out of action. If these vampires are learning to use magic as you say, then that will perhaps come to our advantage."

"Be careful," Fez warned. "They are very wary creatures. They do not trust easily."

Elton nodded and made his way with the others towards the Redhouse's exit, stopping briefly to check on Rosa. She was, as Elton had come to expect, still unconscious.

The streets had risen to their usual levels of activity by the time they joined the throng, people filing in and out of the Redhouse alongside them—just as had been the case before the dissolution of the Syndicate, except the characters Elton observed were an utter contrast to what he had known in the past. Nobles and aristocrats, those who had previously feared him, instead sought audiences with him while lowlifes were few and far between.

As expected, Megaross Square was bustling. Seemingly endless merchants organised themselves into neat rows to allow those with money to walk easily between them. Customers wore purses and bags with pride instead of clutching them with fear. The stage on which Hortensio had attempted to execute Elton was now occupied by buskers and other performers, and the scaffold was only a distant memory.

"That must be it," Elton said, wading through the crowd and extending a finger to point at a decrepit building visible at the edge of one of the back alleys leading away from the square. It was roughly the height of the adjacent buildings but its roof was caved in, its windows were boarded, and its door was missing.

The group made their way into the alley under the watchful eye of several shady individuals already present. Elton thought he recognised some of them, but he didn't stay long enough to be certain.

It was Felix who took the first step across the threshold. The wooden floorboards whined with each step and the sound from outside fell dramatically in volume. As did, as was immediately apparent, the temperature.

"Yeah, I reckon this is it," Paul said, slowly advancing towards the rickety stairs hanging loosely from the back wall.

"Why is it so cold?" Ferris asked, crossing and rubbing his arms. "I mean, this makes me feel at home!"

"The vampires," Elton explained. "It's their curse."

They proceeded one at a time up the stairs, none quite trusting them to bear their weight. It was Elton who felt most unsafe, a noisy creak resonating with each step as he clung desperately to the crumbling banister.

He successfully made it to the next floor, beads of sweat forming despite the permeating cold. It was just as abandoned as the floor below, the only remaining objects being wardrobes and cupboards ransacked and left to decay long ago. The stairs to the third floor were more forgiving, and they all carried on with no qualms. It was the third floor, comprising a series of closed doors along a narrow hallway, where the temperature dropped even further.

"This is it," Elton announced quietly, treading slowly across the creaky floorboards, which whined so loudly he felt he might fall through the floor at any moment. He approached the first door on their left and gently grasped the brass doorknob, looking to his companions for confirmation before twisting it open and pressing the door forwards.

The door swung with a creak much like that constantly provided by the floorboards, and Elton peered cautiously inside. There was a four-poster bed—or rather a three-poster bed, as one of its posters was missing—against the centre of the back wall, devoid of sheets or a mattress. A desk, half of its drawers open and basking in a square of sunlight, was coated in a layer of dust or sand or both. A chair accompanied it, but its backrest lay shattered beside it.

They moved onto the next room, leaving the first door ajar as Felix opened the first door on the right. A quick survey produced a similar result and they moved on once more to the second door on the left.

Elton retook the lead and thought he heard something move as he grabbed the door handle. Placing a hand gingerly on the hilt of his dagger, he opened the door.

The vampire flew at him with imperceptible speed, tackling him to the ground and wrapping her fingers around his neck. Elton's companions were quick to draw their weapons but the Count put up a hand to indicate them to stop.

"We are not being hunted today," the vampire hissed. "I'm not losing anyone else."

"We're... friendly..." Elton choked as he struggled for breath. As he said this, the vampire looked askance at the company, bristling with anticipation, and then back at Elton before loosening her grip just enough to allow him to breathe.

"What do you mean, friendly? Nobody in this damned city is friendly," she brushed her loose-flowing black hair behind her head.

"We came in search of your help. We need magical assistance, and you vampires are our only hope."

Her expression softened to betray a hint of curiosity, but she maintained her grip and position atop him. "Why can we trust you?"

"Because I'm Elton Redwinter," Elton said exasperatedly. "I'm the only person in this 'damned city' who has been protecting you. I'm the one that's been locking up and exiling the people who've hunted you. Without me, you wouldn't be here right now. And I hold complete power in this city, so nobody is going to veto my decision to protect you!"

The vampire hesitated but then slowly rose, a glint of trust appearing in her ruby eyes.

"What's your name?" Elton asked, pushing himself up from the floor.

"I don't have a name," she said sombrely. "None of us do."

"How did Kalahar—"

"You know of Kalahar?" she interrupted. "Where is he? Tell us!"

"Your guess is as good as mine. How about we settle down and discuss this calmly?"

The vampire timidly nodded her head and retreated through the doorway, beckoning Elton and the others to follow.

Inside, resting upon various destroyed items of furniture, were four other vampires, two men and two women. They all shared the same characteristic ruby eyes, stony grey skin, and jet-black hair, but their physical appearances otherwise differed.

"I thought there were six of you?" Elton queried.

"There were," the woman leading them in said. "Then one of us went out in search of a new hideaway. She didn't come back."

Any semblance of ferocity Elton had seen in the vampires on the day of the eclipse was non-existent in those who sat before him. They all stared at the group, eyes wide with only fear.

"Tell us about Kalahar," the first woman said. "He has killed more of us than any human has."

"That is why we have come in search of your help," Elton began. "Kalahar has been manipulating us ever since he introduced himself. He's very powerful, as I'm sure you're aware... how do you even know about him?"

"All malevolent vampires are linked," she explained. "We knew of his existence from the moment the curse took hold of us. We knew of his name, which he wove into the very threads of magic. He has cemented his iron grip and he knows of the existence of every last one of us. And he can feel us. He can find us if he only wishes. But we cannot find him—he has manipulated magic to prevent it. Just as he uses magic to protect himself from harm."

"We want to find him," Elton asserted. "And we think we know how to destroy this magical protection of his. But we need your help to get to him."

The vampire relaxed her tight body language, uncrossing her arms and instead clasping her hands together on her lap as she took a seat on a set of drawers. "Explain."

"There's a root which inhibits magical power—I don't know why, but apparently it does. If he protects himself with magic, as you say, then this root could prevent his magical shield from working. And then he would be vulnerable to oil and silver."

The vampire visibly recoiled as Elton finished the last sentence, the other vampires reacting similarly.

"Would you be able to help?" Elton pleaded.

"That depends," she said. "We need protection. Better protection than we have at the moment, because it's evidently not working. And it also depends on how exactly you need our help."

"As I said—we need help with magic. I've been told you vampires are starting to learn how to use your abilities. We could really do with that right now. Are you able to open portals?"

"He can," the vampire nodded to one of the men, sitting atop a wicker basket.

"And are you able to open portals with knowledge from other people?" Elton turned his attention to the vampire she had indicated.

"I.. I think so," he said unconfidently. "I've only done it once."

"That will have to do," Elton stated. "Do we have an agreement? Will you help us kill Kalahar?"

The vampires looked at each other apprehensively but then it was the original woman who finally gave an answer. "Yes," she said, with just a touch of pride. "We'll help you. As long as you keep us safe."

"I give you my word," Elton said.

The vampire and her brethren all stood up. "We can't travel the streets. Not during the day."

"It seems a perfect time to demonstrate your abilities, then." Elton looked expectantly at the vampire who had claimed a capacity for magic, physically characterised by his gaunt cheeks and sharp jawline. "And for the gods' sakes, we will need to give you all names. We'll start with you, spellcaster. In fact, what about just that? Spellcaster?"

"Spell for short," Paul chimed in. "Or Caster."

"I prefer Caster," Felix concurred.

The vampire sheepishly nodded, accepting the designation.

"And you," Elton turned to the first woman. "You remind me of someone I met a little while ago. What was her name? Elaine?"

"Somethin' like that."

"I like that," the vampire said. "I will accept this name."

"Wonderful," Elton said with diminishing patience. "Let's get a move on, shall we? Caster, I'll let you have knowledge of the Redhouse."

The vampire now going by Caster hesitantly approached Elton and placed his cold fingers upon the Count's forehead, whispering a spell under his breath while Elton conjured an image of the Redhouse's lobby in as much detail as he could.

"I've got it," Caster said. "I'll open the portal now."

Everyone stepped away to allow Caster a sizeable area of empty space in the room as he muttered the words of a spell clearly unfamiliar to him, based on the slowness with which he recited it. But he eventually began the familiar motion of drawing his hands up and tracing a circle, from which was born the familiar white rim of a portal and then, as he pressed forwards, a familiar image of the lobby of the Redhouse.

The group rejoiced as they returned to the dry heat to which they were accustomed. The vampires did not, but they didn't complain as they found themselves suddenly at the centre of a crowd of staring people. Some reacted with immediate fear, walking hastily away or even breaking into outright sprints. Others exhibited only apprehension, refusing to tear their eyes away from the grey-skinned creatures.

"We need to think of names for the rest of you, now," Elton started to say. "I was thinking—"

"Oi, Regi!" a booming voice sliced across the lobby.

Elton turned around to find the source of the voice—a burly man with bulging biceps begging to escape the confines of his dirty linen shirt. His hair, which fell halfway down his chest, was slick with grease. He held a sword, having already drawn it from the scabbard at his waist. And he wasn't alone.

With this man also stood a small army of people, none giving a particularly affluent impression judging purely by their physical appearance. They were all armed, some even with the silver swords still circulating the city in the wake of the eclipse. Elton had attempted to recover them all, but it was a task he knew would be impossible.

The guards in the Redhouse's lobby stood by, hands on the hilts of their own swords, but their faces bore uncertainty. They were severely outnumbered, even if the rest of the building's security was to reinforce them.

"That would be me," Elton said calmly. "And who would you be?"

"Doesn't fuckin' matter who I am," the man rasped, hawking and spitting onto the floor. "What matters is that we're here to finally do this city a favour."

Elton inspected the crowd closer and saw that many of the individuals had small glass vials affixed to their belts, inside which were varying amounts of thick red liquid.

"If you leave right now, I'll let the lot of you off this once. Otherwise, it will be the rest of your lives in the dungeon."

"You don't scare us, old man," the burly man said, to a chuckle of assent from the crowd. "Not you, not your witch whore, not your vampire slaves. You're a traitor to the people of Dannos! You punish our brothers and sisters who exterminate those vermin out of the goodness of their hearts and you let those killers walk free!"

"We were all misled, I have said it before and I will say it again," Elton raised his voice. "The entire plan was assembled with the help of one of their kind. He betrayed us. He tricked us into thinking they were brainless abominations. And on that day, they were. But the vampire who helped us, Kalahar Kefrein-Lazalar, lied. He never told us that they became docile at the day's end. Look at them now, for the gods' sakes!"

Elton swept his hands exasperatedly over the five vampires engaged in an intense stare-off with the crowd of intruders, but the crowd was still rocked by a murmur of dissent.

"We can't trust them!" someone shouted.

"Bloodsucking freaks of nature!" another added.

"I take it they're not happy about the vampires," Ferris said quietly to Felix, who stood at his side. Felix nodded and began to translate the man's words to him as they continued their standoff.

"We'll not stand by while a traitor lets monsters run amok!" the burly man said. "A traitor and a foreigner! We know the truth, Regi! We know you've got the same Salyrian blood as the bastard king! And we've had enough! Death to all monsters! Death to Elton Redwinter! Get 'im, boys!"

The crowd roared and stampeded through the limited space in the lobby, attacking everyone and everything associated with the Count. There were screams as a sea of swords screeched from their scabbards, the intruders indiscriminately cutting down courtiers, servants, guards, and anyone else unfortunate enough to have been in the vicinity. They advanced on Elton's company, vials and bottles of oil being unclipped from belts and retrieved from satchels.

A corked glass bottle flew from the crowd and shattered as it hit one of the unnamed vampires squarely in the face, the liquid inside splattering over him as he let out a monstrous howl and clawed viciously at the affected area. Elton did not wait any longer before taking off into the depths of the Redhouse, one location in his mind. Felix, Ferris, Paul, Elaine, Caster, and two of the nameless vampires followed. The only remaining vampire, the one falling into convulsions, was skewered by a stray silver sword as he attempted to join them in flight. He let out one last strained squeal before falling for the last time.

Elton took an extended route through the corridors of the Redhouse in an attempt to throw off their pursuers, who conveniently continued to update them on their position through excessive volume. The extended route also served the purpose of wrangling more guards into defending them, guards Elton knew would only fall in moments. But those moments bought him valuable time.

Another bottle of oil, this time its cork removed, flew over the heads of the guards and spattered the remaining two nameless vampires trailing the pack. They fell, crying out for help that would never arrive as they too became victims of the mob's silver swords.

"No!" Elaine screeched, turning and faltering for just a moment before she was forcefully grabbed by Felix and thrust back into flight.

Elton made a sudden turn into a stairwell leading underground, traversing the steps two at a time. He crashed to the landing with such force that it sent a sharp shooting pain through his leg, but he continued at speed, and with a slight limp.

The set of keys that Elton always kept on his person jingled furiously as he fished frantically through his pocket and found the correct one to open the bunker. He inserted it into the rightmost keyhole of the three on the door and twisted it until he heard the familiar clunk and began to turn the metal wheel, breathing so rapidly as if he had run a marathon and gesturing for the others to help him. Felix and Paul joined in, the wheel screeching under the speed of their entry. They then together thrust the thick steel door open and filed inside, charging against it and slamming it shut with a reverberating thud as the clamouring of their pursuers finally caught up with them. They then worked together to seal the entrance as the intruders banged their weapons feebly against the exterior.

The humans took a moment to catch their breath as they all listened to the incessant rattling of metal on metal permeating the door. The vampires' faces, usually expressionless, managed to bear melancholy as they hung their heads. But then Elaine's anguish turned to fury as she added to the cacophony of metallic clattering by grabbing the breathless Count and slamming him against the door.

"You said you would protect us!" she cried. "You said we would be safe!"

"I didn't know!" Elton shouted, pushing her away. "They're here for me, was that not evident?"

"I don't care if they were here for you, the fact is that we came here as five and now there are just two of us! We agreed to help you only minutes ago and now look!"

Elton looked regretfully over the pair of vampires, a pang of guilt lodging itself in his throat. But his eyes then widened with fear as he was struck with a sudden realisation as the banging against the door began to diminish.

"Rosa!" he exclaimed. "We forgot about Rosa! We need to go back! They'll kill her!"

CHAPTER 18

Elaeínn's first reaction as she stepped through the portal into the charred remains of the lobby was to drop the sword Flint had given her and fall to her knees.

The events of the battle for Fallía blitzed through her mind. She saw the white-haired woman stand up and lacerate the throat of her former leader. She saw Henna sacrifice herself to save her, flames engulfing the crowd of civilians as her strength gave way. She saw her own blade slice through the neck of the man she despised most.

She saw it all and more in the piles of blackened bones left as they had been three months prior.

"Come on," Flint urged, grasping her shoulder.

Elaeínn rose uneasily to her feet, clutching the sword tightly across her chest as she, Velrin, and Flint trudged towards the door. The mages appeared from the portal next, opting to delve deeper into the keep.

As they cautiously exited into the open, Elaeínn realised that the reminder of the destruction hadn't been limited to the lobby. Houses remained half-burnt, and more elven and dwarven bones littered the streets. Fallen weapons, loosed arrows and bolts, even a damaged ballista had been left in the thoroughfare where the battle had taken place.

"They're making an example of us," Elaeínn murmured, loosening her grip on her sword.

"Get yer heads down," Flint said, tugging her back into the lobby and pointing to the castle walls.

Despite the image of abandonment the Tyen'Aeli government had created, Elaeínn looked up to see several soldiers positioned atop the walls at regular intervals. They did not appear to be surveying the inside of the castle, but rather lazily scanning the lands nearby.

"How do we get up on those walls?" Flint asked.

"Follow me," Elaeínn ordered.

She crouched, keeping an eye on the soldiers as she dashed towards a tower forming part of the walls opposite the entrance to the lobby. She then gestured for Velrin and Flint to follow before ascending the spiral staircase.

The wind whipped the loose strands of hair that escaped her braid as she cautiously poked her head up through the exit at the top of the stairs. She could see two guards in the near vicinity—one on her left, one on her right. Neither were paying attention to her, and one appeared to be dozing, his legs hanging over the side of the walls.

She waited for Flint and Velrin to arrive before acting. Stepping carefully into the open, she trod silently across the walkway, the sound of her footsteps shrouded by the howling of the wind.

The dozing soldier didn't have time to react as Elaeínn placed her hands against his back and thrust him from the wall. His terrified scream cut through the air and she watched as he fell, the scream becoming quieter and quieter until it was brought to an abrupt halt as his body crashed into the moat. The only other guard who heard the scream turned as the axe buried itself in his chest. Flint withdrew the bloodied blade, kicking the body over the edge.

Their advantage of surprise was lost as the other soldiers dotted around the castle finally saw them, alarm spreading like wildfire as some ran in their direction while others dashed down into the castle.

The first soldier to approach charged at Elaeínn, swinging his sword wildly as he reached melee range. She parried the attack and used his momentum to guide his sword, and with it him, towards the edge. He reached out his spare arm to steady himself, but Elaeínn dashed quickly under his arm and pressed him forwards, bending her knees, and sent him over the edge with his other fallen comrades.

A second soldier approached from the other direction, coming face to face with Flint. The dwarf wasted no time,

throwing his axe in a lightning-quick motion. The elf had nowhere to go before it split his face in two, and his body fell
with a clatter to the stone walkway. Flint used his foot to then
shove him, too, over the wall.

The soldiers which had opted to travel into the castle made
their way through the wrecked streets towards the drawbridge, left open as the winches had never been repaired.
They exuded confidence as they reached it, shouting something to the pair of guards tasked with defending the entrance.
Then blades began to fall.

One by one, the soldiers of the Shadow Division cleaved
through the handful of soldiers, one appearing with each
blow. They were similar in appearance to Agria, wearing the
same dark leathers as well as masks on the lower halves of
their faces. And they were ruthlessly efficient. Elaeínn only
glanced at the drawbridge and watched the elven soldiers fall
in a matter of seconds.

The last of the soldiers on the wall was finished off by a
shot of lightning from Velrin, his convulsing body falling with
the rest to decorate the moat below. Flint wiped the blade of
his axe with a handkerchief and Elaeínn returned her largely
unused sword to its sheath.

"That was too easy," Flint mulled, furrowing his brow.
"Something's not right."

"I think they got cocky," Elaeínn said. "This is hardly a strategic position for them, considering they thought they knew
all of our movements. This is the first time an attack has taken
place that they didn't know about."

"I'm unsure," Flint said, uneasily stroking his beard.

They made their way back down to the keep where they
were greeted by the three mages. "We've been compromised,
General," Isak said with a hint of animosity. "A message got
out."

"A message?"

"It's best if ye see for yerself."

Isak led the group through the mess hall and up the stairs
towards the lord's quarters. Elaeínn saw the bed on which the
spy was sitting when they had found her. She saw the shattered table in the private dining room, turned into debris by

one of the brutish Ekkas. Where they were now, she didn't know.

They traversed the blue-carpeted corridor with the balcony at its end, the dried bloodstain from one of the Ekkas still present. Elaeínn gripped the hilt of her sword tightly, overcome by a deep sense of unease, looking around as if an officer of the State Security Service could appear at any moment.

"I was expecting this bloody castle to be fully manned," Flint said to himself as the mages opened the door to the war room. It, like everything else in the castle, looked as it had done on the day of the battle. Berri's bloodstained maps littered the floor. Delíen's bones rested in a corner. The trapdoor to the catacombs remained open.

Except one significant thing was different—a woman with typically High Elven characteristics and dress sat at the table, muttering something quietly to herself.

"Who is it?" Flint whispered.

"She wouldn't speak to us, but we found her here," Isak said at full volume. The woman didn't seem to react in any way.

Isak, Janria, and Tora stepped to the side to allow Flint to pass with Elaeínn and Velrin. The three apprehensively approached the woman, whose eyes they found to be closed.

"She's conversing with someone," Velrin said. "That's a communication spell. Do we have any hevula?"

The dwarven mages shook their heads.

"Oi! You there!" Flint shouted, slapping the woman in the face. She grunted, but continued the incantation. He raised his axe and drove it into the table, slicing clean through it with a crash. The woman still continued her incantation.

"Greetings, Elaeínn," she suddenly said. The voice had an unnaturally hollow sound to it, an overlaying echo. Elaeínn looked into her eyes, which had shot open, and found them to be glowing a bright white.

"Who are you?" she asked.

"I am Prime Minister Ferrilíen Vanad," the elven woman echoed. "It is my utmost pleasure to finally meet you. And may I commemorate you on your escape. It has brought my attention directly to failures in the backline."

"Where... where are you?"

"I speak to you from the safety of the walls of the Serenna Palace. I was of course disbelieving when Bellía told me that you were attacking your old fortress, but she turned out to be right. Who could have known?"

"What do you want?" Elaeínn's voice hardened. "This war is about to turn against you. I will rebuild the FTA from the ground up. Your own citizens will be the ones to lay siege to your chambers. You will lose, Prime Minister. You have taken the job at a very unfortunate time."

"On the contrary," Vanad's messenger said matter-of-factly. "While it is unfortunate that you have eliminated our source on the inside, it is only a minor setback. The dwarven forces at Molnor will be crushed in their pathetic attempt to retake the city. Those marching through the Darklight will not make it, either. You were a fool to think going to the dwarves would be your salvation, because you will be destroyed alongside them."

"You're bluffing," Elaeínn exclaimed. "You don't have a clue about any of our plans."

"Oh, your conviction is admirable. Admirably naïve. You really think I would just let you in to a formidable fortress so close to the old border without a fight?"

The elven woman then stood up and Flint raised his axe. She brought an arm down and pulled back her robe, revealing a device strapped around her torso before summoning a flame in the palm of her hand.

"Don't move," Isak said from the corner of the room. "That device is packed with explosives."

"Your friend is correct," Vanad said. "One wrong move and you all die. Put your weapons down."

Elaeínn looked to Flint, who nodded and placed his axe slowly on the table. She removed the sword from her belt and did the same.

"Very good. Officers, you may reveal yourselves. Apprehend them."

Four looming figures appeared from thin air, shackles in hand. One of them grabbed Elaeínn roughly by the scruff of her neck as a portal opened behind the woman wearing the suicide vest.

"I'm not going to prison again. I'm not doing it!" she cried.

Elaeínn shook herself free of the SSS officer's grasp and ducked under the extended reach of another. She grabbed her sword from the table and ran at full pace towards the portal behind the woman, closing her eyes with anticipation. The explosion didn't happen, and she passed through the portal to find herself in a location she happened to recognise.

She blew past the Regal Guards positioned at the table in the interrogation room, catching them entirely off guard. The door had been left unlocked and it was left swinging on its hinges as Elaeínn tore into the Regal Guard building, the guards having only just risen from their seats to pursue her.

The usual crowd of guests were present, but Elaeínn didn't have the fortune of a tour being held at that moment. She made the decision to ditch her sword, tossing it to one side as she squeezed between people amidst a growing murmur of alarm and shouts from the guards on her tail. She raced past the dozens of empty and occupied rooms, past the door labelled *Record Storage*, gaining a steady lead over her clunkier followers.

She reached the exit and slowed down as she entered the lobby, rapidly undoing her braid as she tucked herself behind a group of diplomats travelling towards the eastern wing of the palace. She shook her head to disperse the hair evenly across her back and then peeled away from the group, setting her sights upon the familiar corridor to the western wing of the palace.

The guard presence in the palace's lobby appeared to be much lower than she remembered, and she was able to slip into the west wing undetected, holding her head high and acting as noble as she could realistically pull off with the worn clothes she had stolen from the village.

The door to the Prime Minister's chambers was, as she had expected, locked. But unlike when she had last broken into it, this time, she lacked lockpicks. Instead, she had to rely on patience.

I left them all behind, she thought, standing flush against the wall next to the exit back to the lobby. *Just like I left Erría and Lysíen. I thought about saving myself and only myself. And now what am I going to do?*

She waited. A commotion reverberated down the corridor, but nobody ever arrived in search of her. Whether that was because they didn't think to search there or that they had called off the search, she didn't know. Each passing minute felt like an hour and she realised her options were slim, even if someone was to open to door as she was hoping.

What am I going to do, attack them? she thought. *With what weapon?*

She continued to doubt herself and repeatedly looked back down the corridor between increasingly regular intervals.

He was bluffing. Surely he was bluffing.

She turned and made the decision to walk back down the corridor as the doorknob twisted behind her. She turned 180 degrees to face the person in the doorway as the door drifted open.

"Miss Tinaíd," the man said. "You are bold."

He stood tall, much taller than his predecessor, nearly occupying the entire space of the doorway. His eyes were sharp, his posture impeccably straight, his grey hair in a braid on his back not unlike Elaeínn's usual style.

Her eyes darted between the corridor and the man she assumed to be Ferrilíen Vanad. He was strangely familiar—she must have seen him alongside Jaelaar in the past.

"The exit has been blocked so I do urge that you join me inside," Vanad said, smiling and gesturing her towards the entrance to his chambers. "No harm will come to you as long as you comply with a few basic expectations."

"What do you want?" she seethed, backing slowly into the corridor.

"I would like only to converse. You have knowledge about something very important to me. To us Aeli elves. Instrumental in securing our victory in this war and our superiority in the field of magic. And only you can help me, so don't think I will arbitrarily kill you as my predecessor attempted. I need you."

Vanad's promise that the corridor had been blocked was confirmed when Elaeínn turned to run but came face to face with two Regal Guards brandishing swords and looking sternly down upon the lone elf.

"There is nowhere to go so I truly implore you to listen to me. I am willing to offer you freedom in return for your co-operation."

"I've heard a very similar offer before," Elaeínn snarled.

"Jaelaar nearly threw away our only opportunity to harness the power of a creature known only in legends." Vanad's tone changed from one of soft kindness to one of harsh assertion. "I have a clear vision for the future of this country. The future of all high elves. It does not involve acting so brashly in the face of petty rebellion to the point where progress is discarded in the name of popular appeal. As long as that dragon lives, so will you, Elaeínn. But only if you agree to work with us. If you don't, then I'm afraid our only option will indeed be to exe-cute you."

Elaeínn walked slowly towards the Prime Minister, staring him in the eyes. They were grey and cold. She knew at once that those eyes had never borne the kindness he attempted to portray.

She turned and crossed into the Prime Minister's chambers, remembering the layout from the first time she had been there. The fireplace in the bedroom was her first objective, and she made her way there without bothering to look if the Prime Minister was behind her.

It was there. On the plaque, where she had first found it. And below it, the scabbard she had received from Aegard.

"That sword has been observed, experimented on, had spells cast on, poked, prodded... Jaelaar claimed to have tried to find out its secrets. We have tried a hundred times harder. Yet we find no results. Nothing at all. I've heard all the reports about its reaction to you, how it glowed such a magnificent gold in your hands. But we have been unable to replicate it. Damned near every citizen in Sanaíd has been made to hold that sword. And yet it was returned here, the only place where it's been of any use to us. As an ornament."

Elaeínn reached for the Dragonsteel Blade and caressed its moulded hilt. The runes lying dormant along its blade erupted with golden light the moment her fingers made con-tact.

She lowered it slowly, holding it flat to allow Vanad to ob-serve the runes more closely. His carefully crafted façade fell apart with awe as he ran a finger along them, before picking up the sword himself. As he did, the light faded.

"They've turned purple before, too," Elaeínn added. "When I killed someone with it."

She grabbed the sword from the Prime Minister's hands and held its tip to his throat.

"Sit down, Elaeínn," Vanad said, regaining control over his countenance. "You don't want to kill me just yet."

"And why's that? I missed the opportunity with Jaelaar in this very location. Explain to me why I would want to make the same mistake again?"

"You're very good at betraying your friends. I've come to understand that. Though I hope there is a scrap of compassion in your hearts when I say we have captured your little band of infiltrators and are willing to let them go if you comply. I die, though, and so do they. And so do you."

Elaeínn dropped her guard but kept hold of the sword, fetching the scabbard from above the hearth and affixing it to her belt.

Vanad led her to a table in the office adjacent to the bedroom, the same one she had rifled through during her last visit. He pulled the desk away from the wall and brushed the parchments and writing implements littering it into a drawer as he whispered a spell and dragged another chair from across the room.

"What spell was that?" Elaeínn asked apprehensively.

"I was asking the servant to bring us some tea," Vanad responded nonchalantly, taking a seat and gesturing for her to do the same.

She warily sat down, flitting her eyes around the room. Everything seemed to be the same as she had left it, apart from the mess, which had been cleaned up. Vanad was silent for some time as they waited for the servant to arrive, which he did after some minutes. He poured two cups of tea, and Elaeínn swapped the mugs before taking a sip.

"You don't trust easily, do you?" Vanad asked, contently accepting the other cup and.

"I'm sure you can understand why that is," she hissed.

"Really, what do you expect, though? You chose to turn to a life of insurrection. Near everything you do breaks some law

or another. You are an enemy of the people, Elaeínn, and for
what? What do you think you will achieve by aiding the dwarves in the war? It certainly won't achieve your political goals.
Sure, the National Party would be overthrown but who do you
think would then fill the gap? It wouldn't be your Liberal
Party. It would be the Hamatnarian king, whoever they choose
to replace Kagyan. If you continue as you are, a dwarven axe
will be the death knell to the Tyen'Aeli democracy you fight
so hard to protect."

Elaeínn drummed her fingers impatiently against the table.
"That's just propaganda."

"You know it isn't, though," Vanad said. "You have spent so
long blinded by your own ambitions that you haven't allowed
yourself to take in the reality of the situation. You have your
goals, yes, but what are the dwarves' goals? Have you considered that?"

She hadn't. Elaeínn found herself irritated by the rationality of the Prime Minister's words and although she did not
want to hear them, she couldn't help but reflect on her relationship with the dwarves.

"I'm not telling you to join us. We would never accept you,
anyways. I'm just saying be mindful. Mindful of when you're
being used to further the goals of another."

She scowled and stared at the surface of the desk, resting
her lips on the rim of her cup as she slowly sipped the tea.

"Now onto the matter at hand," Vanad said, retrieving one
of the pieces of parchment he had previously tucked away.
"I'm sure you recognise this?"

He slid the parchment across the table to reveal a detailed
illustration of Alazarioss in flight.

"I do recognise her," she nodded, sitting back in her chair.
"What of it?"

"Where is it?" Vanad asked bluntly.

"I wish I could tell you," Elaeínn said whimsically, finishing
her tea and setting the empty mug gently upon the table. "I've
been wondering that to myself for the past three months. She
disappeared to heal after Fallía. Raeris knows when she's going
to reappear."

"You have no way of contacting her?"

"I've tried. Usually she just reads my thoughts. Though I don't quite know the range on that one."

Vanad slowly drew the parchment back to his side of the desk. "How do you control such a beast?" he continued, his eyes focused on the drawing. "Jaelaar attempted to control it with magic on the island, so the report stated. But you—you're incompetent with magic."

"It's quite simple, really. I don't control her. I just understand her."

"If you understand it then you must know of a way to draw it into the open. To summon it."

Elaeínn considered her options carefully. "There is one thing that could work," she finally said. "Are you familiar with a Heart of magic?"

Vanad shook his head, inquisitively turning his eyes away from the parchment to focus on her.

"Alazarioss had one goal—to end the corruption of magic. She said that all magic flows through this Heart somewhere in our world, and that there are individuals who hack away at that Heart, taking shards of it so that they may enhance their own magical capacity. She wanted to return these shards to their rightful place. If this place was threatened, I am certain she would rise to protect it."

"These shards," Vanad said, opening a drawer and rustling around inside it. "Do they look like this?"

He placed his cusped hand on the table and allowed three purple crystals to clatter onto its surface.

"You took them!" she exclaimed, standing up.

"Of course I did. The interrogators at the prison had no idea what they were. They were examined at every level before being handed to me. And now you have told me what they are. Thank you."

He stood up, tucking the crystals back into the desk drawer, and placed his attention on a map of Fenalia pinned to the wall above where the desk had previously been situated.

"I will consult my mages, historians, everything. I will find out as much as I can about this Heart of magic. And then we will travel there, you included, if you ever want to see your freedom and your friends again."

He pointed to the empty space in the ocean west of the continent. "There was once someone who would probably have known the whereabouts of this Heart. But we lost contact with him."

He then bowed his head and returned to his seat. "You're free to go, Elaeínn. But know that you will be summoned when the time comes."

Elaeínn stayed where she was for a few moments as she processed her sudden liberation. She then quickly stood up, took one last doubtful look at the Prime Minister, and left.

CHAPTER 19

Nendar squinted, placing a hand over his eyes as he surveyed the white cliffs to their right.

"We're nearly there, I should think," Tregor said, appearing from below deck.

"Do you actually know where we're going?"

"A city I vaguely remember Ríyael telling me about when he was still alive. Telíana, if I recall correctly. The single largest port city in the entire country, as he described it."

"If that's the case, how are we expected to find the girl?"

"I'm sure fate will be on our side," Tregor said with conviction.

They had been at sea for nearly a week, having set out from the Vivian Isles west of mainland Valoria, the last obstacle to the open sea from the Redwater Passage in Sanskar.

As Tregor had predicted, they were nearly there. After another hour of sailing the cliffs levelled off towards sea level and a sprawling port city appeared along the shoreline continuing into and beyond the hills inland. The houses were all constructed from stone, the dockyard was heaving with ships of all shapes and sizes, as was the sea itself—galleons, cogs, barges all travelling between the city and into the distant fog where Nendar knew they would find the triracial countries of Folanta, Ferloris, and Junia on the geographically split continent's other half. Both sorcerers took notice of the heavy presence of military vessels, flying flags also seen hanging in the harbour which they recognised as belonging to Tyen'Ael.

They were fortunate enough to find a small gap between two merchant vessels into which Tregor expertly navigated their ship, dropping the anchor just as they were about to collide with the cobbled walkway. He leapt onto the jetty, securing the ship with a rope.

"Hurry then, Nendar," he called, Nendar opting to lower the gangplank to disembark.

As the two sorcerers made their way into the city, there was no amount of bustle that hid their abnormality from the prying eyes of the native elves and dwarves. Everywhere they went, they could feel the constant presence of inquisitive and suspicious gazes boring into their backsides, though it was Tregor who knew himself to be the primary subject of the locals' attention.

It didn't deter them from their objective as they forged towards one of the larger buildings in the city, resembling a barracks, or at least what Nendar would have described as resembling a barracks in the human nations with which he was familiar. His knowledge of elven and dwarven architecture was lacking, though it didn't seem outrageously different, judging by the residential buildings, warehouses, and dockyard structures populating their surroundings.

"Halt!" one of two guards, his chest emblazoned with a blue symbol unfamiliar to the sorcerers, said abruptly as Nendar and Tregor reached their destination. "You... you're—"

"Humans," Tregor finished, replying in perfect High Elven. "Is this the garrison of this city?"

"It... um... yes," the elf stuttered, still overcome with confusion. "Where are you—"

"That doesn't matter," Tregor interrupted again. "Would we be able to request a meeting with your commander?"

"I'll... I'll be a moment. Stay right there," the guard said, withdrawing into the garrison, a building constructed from the same stone blocks as everything else in the city but standing much taller and wider.

"What brings a couple of humans to Fenalia?" the remaining guard, significantly more composed than his counterpart, asked.

"We're looking for someone. An elf. Didn't think it likely to find them in the lands of men," Nendar supplied with a smile.

"S'pose that'd make sense." The guard shrugged.

"The commander says it's alright," the other guard said, re-emerging from the building. "Come on in, gentlemen. Oh, and I'll have to be taking your weapons, if that's alright."

Nendar removed his scimitar from its scabbard, handing it to the guard as Tregor revealed his silver dagger and placed it gently into the palm of the other guard. Both elves stood temporarily frozen, staring at the weapons with evident curiosity before they regained their composure. The first guard led them inside, stowing the ornate weapons in a cupboard with noticeable care.

"I think the commander is more interested than anything if she's given you two a meeting. She didn't even ask for a reason," the guard said, crossing an open stone-floored chamber with doors on all sides. "I just said there were some humans here and her eyes went wide as plates."

He twisted the ringed handle to a wooden door on the opposite side of the room to that from which they had entered, holding it open for the sorcerers. "After you. Don't get up to any trouble."

Nendar and Tregor nodded and continued into the room, the middle of which was occupied by a three-sided desk at which sat a woman, armoured in an azure gambeson with a rapier at her side. She watched them enter with obvious enthusiasm, not even pretending to look busy. Also in the room were two more guards, a man and a woman, who stood like statues holding swords with their tips against the ground.

"Welcome to Telíana," she greeted, extending a hand which the both of them shook in turn. "To what do I owe the pleasure? I have never seen a human in person before."

"We come in search of an individual. We know it is a stretch, but we are aware she is... infamous, shall we say. Perhaps her name will ring a bell," Nendar said.

"I mean... we elves have quite the assortment of infamous people, but... I might know them. Who is it?"

"One Elaeínn Tinaíd."

The commander's face dropped and she looked pensively at the scrap of parchment laying idly on her desk in front of her.

"You can bet I know her," she said, frowning. "Whole country knows her. Chief terrorist. Sliced off the head of the Prime

Minister in front of his own army. Captured and locked away, luckily."

"But I take it from your expression that she's not locked away anymore, is she?" Tregor prodded.

"I'm afraid I can't say any more," she tucked the sheet of parchment into a drawer. "Now, I must ask you to leave. This audience is finished."

Nendar and Tregor looked at one another, communicating their next action wordlessly.

They both stretched their arms out simultaneously, uttering the word 'sleep' in Archaeish. All three elves present in the room subsequently collapsed, the commander crashing noisily against the desk and the guards' swords producing a noisy metallic rattling as they fell to the ground.

"Ka'vak ga'kros," Nendar spoke, turning to the closed door as the guards hammered their fists against it from outside.

"Hello? Ma'am? What's going on in there?" they called, their words muffled by the thick wood of the door.

"Nothing to worry about, stay at your stations," Nendar said back, his voice imitating that of the commander.

"What was that ruckus?" they persisted, though ceasing to knock.

"One of the guards dropped their swords. Now return to your stations. That's an order."

"Y-yes, yes ma'am."

Tregor rustled the slip of parchment in the air with a smirk after retrieving it from the drawer. "She's coming here today, Nendar. How very convenient for us."

"Coming here for what?"

"The Prime Minister is loading her onto a ship. The details, however, are not provided. Except for those of the ship itself."

"So we just have to get onto that ship."

Tregor nodded affirmatively. "And then all that's left to do is wait."

CHAPTER 20

Richard's first impression of the city to which he and Lynn had teleported was that it was different—in so many ways.

Aside from the architectural differences he had already observed before crossing through the portal, it was also clear that there were vast cultural differences between this land, of which he had only heard stories, and his homeland, and even the much nearer territories of the Sanskari Empire.

For one, the language—utterly incomprehensible to Richard, and Lynn could only piece together small sentences—was incomparable to Miradosi. The people spoke with much more emotion, both in their voice and their body language, in what Richard assumed to be everyday conversations as they traversed the cobbled streets. The way they dressed, in long, decorative robes, the way they styled their hair, both men and women often seen sporting a bun, and the wicker cone-shaped hats seen commonplace across the heads of what seemed like every other person.

Richard felt out of place, and not just because of the crude way in which he was dressed, still wearing the bloodstained tunic gifted by the dryads. He and Lynn were on the receiving end of countless curious stares from the city's people, though never for long, as they all moved at remarkable speed and without pause.

"I can't steal from these people," Richard mused.

"Oh, Richard, you've done much worse, I'm sure."

They continued towards the harbour, passed by all manner of people from workers hauling wheelbarrows of fish to monks dressed in rags with shaved heads to people Richard could only describe as warriors, carrying enormous, slightly curved swords at their waists and armoured in only leathers over their white robes. Interestingly, they wore sandals, which Richard thought would have made footwork terribly difficult in the event of a confrontation.

Bards played melodies at the streetside, though not using instruments familiar to Richard. A flute-like instrument made from bamboo produced a soft lead, another busker playing the rhythm on a three-stringed lute with a significantly longer neck than that to which Richard was accustomed. He wanted to stop and listen for a while, but was dragged away by Lynn, who scolded him for bringing unnecessary attention to them.

Yet another noteworthy feature of the city was the abundance of cats—they were simply everywhere. Slinking between narrow alleys, running across high walls, sitting on shop fronts—there wasn't a direction in which Richard could look without seeing one. And as they reached the fish market adjacent to the harbour, the cat concentration only increased. Sellers chopped heads, tails, and fins from their product and tossed them to the innumerable hungry mouths clamouring around the ground by the stall, outnumbering the customers.

"I bet we could get away with that skiff." Lynn pointed to a small ship with a single sail tied to a post in the harbour as they reached the seaside from the bustling fish market.

"And travel across an entire ocean? We'd be devoured by the waves. I travelled across the Great Sea in a ship not much bigger and we were almost destroyed several times."

"What do you want to do? Take a crew hostage?"

"Or... we look for a ship providing genuine passage to our destination and pay for it."

"Richard, I don't know about you, but I personally don't carry any Canarian currency. So that puts a little bit of an obstacle in the way of your plan."

"We can find work. If we get ourselves aboard a bigger ship, not only will it be faster but we also won't end up as fish food."

Lynn sighed. "Alright. Let's find some work."

The variety of ships floating in and out of the harbour was grand, with the smallest fishing boats overshadowed by galleons and caravels with up to ten sails in rare instances. Some advertisements were posted on temporary notice boards adjacent to the ships' gangplanks, though Richard, like with the spoken language, could not decipher a word. The written language comprised symbols he would have described as runic, almost decorative, rather than a meaningful script with which to convey messages efficiently.

"That one..." Lynn hesitated, staring intensely at one of the inscribed pieces of wood next to a two-sailed cog. "Virilia, I think. And that one... Ashiyaga? Ashikaga? That's definitely not what we want..."

"What are the prices like?"

"Even if I did know how to pronounce this word which I'm assuming is their currency, I couldn't tell you the exchange rate... it's a fairly large number, though..."

"Merana? Myana? One of those... probably the former, Myana's on the other side of the continent... Endahar, Kalimar, Kel Ha Long... I'm surprised with the number of Sanskari cities, my father has imposed rather harsh tariffs on Canarian goods... this whole row here is just other Canarian ports... I don't even recognise whatever city that is..."

This continued for some time until they had traversed the entire harbour, even going so far as to double check. Some new signs had appeared in that time, but still none of them were destined for any cities outside of Valoria.

"I'm not really surprised," Lynn said nonchalantly as they resigned to a nearby bench to rest their feet, Richard gazing longingly at a steaming pan of food in a vendor across the road. "Our societies are completely segregated. Ríyael was the only elf I had ever known. Apart from the elven vampires I saw at Letham Deregor, but I'm not counting them."

They allowed themselves five minutes to relax before resuming their search for passage, but their way was blocked by two soldiers, similar in appearance to those they had seen earlier, who appeared from around the corner, hands on their hilts.

"Suki no anate! Anatudaharu?" one of them shouted, or at least it sounded like a shout as a result of the force with which they spoke.

"Translate?" Richard raised an eyebrow at the sorceress.

"Watashutachiha ryuko-shidesu," Lynn said slowly, struggling with the language. "Fenalia e ne tsu... tsuri o sagashi... ne... sagashimisu."

"Nuni ne fune de kitu ne?" the guard aggressively continued.

"Ue de... ue de..."

Lynn grabbed Richard's hand and tore him from the bench as she sprinted away along the harbour. He followed without much thought as the guards called after them, somehow shouting even louder than before.

Richard shoved his way through clusters of people, becoming the subject of numerous angry reprimands as he careened around a laden cart, jumped over a series of barrels being wheeled from a ship, and danced through a pile of fallen fish spread across the cobbles next to a wheelless wagon. Richard encountered the wheel shortly thereafter, it having fallen from the wagon and rolled a short distance away. He kicked it out of his path and continued his sprint away from the pursuing authorities.

"Koko ne madotte koi!" they cried, their voices splitting the crowds not already dispersed in Richard's wake as he finally caught up to the sorceress.

"They're gaining on us," Richard prompted, ducking beneath a wide basket filled with pots of various shapes and sizes atop a passer-by's head. "What did we even do?"

"I don't know, I hardly even know what I was saying in response," Lynn snapped. "Turn left."

"What?"

Lynn suddenly disappeared down a side alley, but Richard's momentum carried him onward. He faltered momentarily while deciding whether to pursue her but decided against it as the guards caught up with the passageway only seconds later. Both continued after the bounty hunter.

Richard continued down the harbour until a cart the size of a horse blocked his way. His eyes darted around frantically for another route, but there was only wall to his left and ocean to his right.

He ran up to the cart and leapt with all his might, extending his arms frantically to find a grip. His hand caught the wooden framework at the top, his fingers rubbing against the

linen canvas nailed over the wagon's roof. He pulled himself
up and held his arms out for balance, swaying on the narrow
strip of wood before jumping down to the other side. He then
ran on, the clamouring of the guards growing quieter and quieter as he finally found an opening back into the city from the
harbour.

The street into which he turned felt darker than the rest of
the city. It was completely encircled by tall buildings and
there was nobody around, the hustle in the harbour having
entirely disappeared. Richard stopped, bending over and placing his hands on his knees as he caught his breath.

"Koko ne wa daru ga imasu ke?" the first person, a man,
said as he emerged from one of the houses behind Richard.

The bounty hunter rose and turned to see the man, not a
guard, brandishing a dagger which resembled a miniature
sword similar in shape to those carried by the guards.

"Sutarogura," a second person, a woman, responded, appearing from an adjacent house and joining the man, idly fid-
dling with her long anthracite hair.

"I don't know you," Richard said, raising his arms. "But I'm
just going to be on my way."

"Gakoku hitu kazu! Kura wa supa kamu shirai!" the first exclaimed.

"Bakaguta wa ikanai! Kare ne mitu! Kare wa dare ne tame ni
supa o site inu nodaru ka? Sosute, nate watashutachi wa ki ne
suru nodeshu ka?" The second turned her attention from
Richard to her companion, her face plastered with ridicule.

"Enough of this..." Richard muttered. "Hablar Arcaea."

He subtly gestured towards the two individuals as they continued their argument.

"—was a spy, who would we give him to? The daimyo?"

"The daimyo would pay us well for a Sanskari spy!"

"The daimyo would have us interrogated for even being associated with one! And does he look Sanskari? His skin's paler
than fresh snow!"

"Sanskar's enormous, you brainless cretin. I don't know if
you know, but they control all the countries between us and
Mirados, which is thousands of miles away! I've known people
from Floria and Rendon, and they look by no means like a
typical Sanskari."

"Whatever! We're not bringing him in to the daimyo! But we will bring him in to the boss. He'll probably have some use for a foreigner."

The pair stopped their bickering and simultaneously turned their heads to look at Richard, who had by that point thoroughly regained his breath.

"You there! Do you speak any Canarian at all?" The man pointed his dagger at Richard, moving towards him.

"Yes," Richard lied. "What is it?"

"What was that foreign babble we just heard you yammering, then?"

"Miradosi, good sir. I'm from Mirados."

"I told you he wasn't Sanskari!" the woman said.

"He might be lying, you dumb ox!" the man retorted, turning his head.

"I've killed more Sanskari soldiers than I can count on my fingers," Richard coolly added.

"Still think he's a spy?"

"He might be a Miradosi spy!"

"We're not at war with Mirados! And why would you care?"

"Shut up!"

The man approached Richard, still holding his dagger towards him. The bounty hunter was unfazed, considering them both with only curiosity.

"Right," the man said. "I'm going to have to take your weapon off you. You're coming with us to the boss."

"That's not happening," Richard said calmly.

"Oh yeah?" The man moved so close to Richard that the bounty hunter could smell the anchovies on his breath. "What if I take it from you?"

Standing next to him, Richard now realised the man was remarkably short, only reaching his shoulders at full height. He was also by no means strong as was reflected by the ease with which Richard resisted his attempt to rip the sword from his belt.

"I'll... I'll cut you, if you're not careful!" the man threatened, taking a step back.

"My corpse wouldn't be worth much to your boss, I reckon."

"Oh, you've got a mouth on you, haven't you? Just a couple flesh wounds might shut you up."

Richard drew his sword and held its tip to the man's throat in one quick action. The man's eyes grew as wide as saucers as he dropped his dagger.

"I-I'm sorry! I wouldn't actually have cut you! Fuck, I've fucked it again…"

"You pathetic whelp," the woman hissed, joining them. The bounty hunter withdrew his sword, returning it to his sheath with a sigh.

"Who are you two?" Richard inquired.

"Hattori Akira and Makoto," the woman supplied, picking up the man's blade from the ground and handing it to him with a smirk.

"Mind explaining this… encounter?"

"We meant to threaten you and take you in to the boss but… you weren't particularly scared," the man, indicated to be Akira, said.

"Who's your boss?" Richard pressed.

"Can we tell him?"

"Everyone knows the boss."

"The daimyo doesn't."

"Of course he does, you halfwit! He just doesn't put a stop to him because they've got an arrangement in place!"

"Is that why the guards have never stopped us?"

"By the Flame, just tell him the boss's name!"

"Hada Jiro! His name is Hada Jiro! Why couldn't you just have said that if you were so offended by my reluctance?"

Richard glanced uneasily between the bickering pair and gingerly took a few steps back, scanning around him for a way out, but then he reconsidered. "Your boss, this… Jada Hiro, who—"

"Hada Jiro," Makoto corrected.

"Hada Jiro," Richard said through gritted teeth. "Who is he?"

"Weren't you listening? He's the boss," Akira said matter-of-factly.

"Lanthanis give me strength," Richard muttered. "Boss of what?"

"Boss of the Sakuru," Makoto said. "Biggest gang in Nakada. The daimyo turns a blind eye to us, long as we don't stir up too much trouble or cause him any personal problems."

"You mean to tell me you're gangsters?" Richard ridiculed, an amused smile forming on his face.

"Not very successful ones, admittedly," Akira said sheepishly. "I can't even bring myself to kill a man. But the boss helped us out, so we try to help him out to pay him back. And to make sure he doesn't punish us."

"Would he be offering any work for an outsider like me? I need enough to rent a ship and its crew."

"Boss has always got work, especially for outsiders," Makoto affirmed. "Clears him of any blame. Which is why he usually gets outsiders to do the work which upsets the daimyo."

"Right..." Richard trailed off. "And you've used the word more times than I can care to count, but I still don't know what it means. What's a daimyo and who is he?"

"He runs this city," Akira chimed in. "Think they call them barons or lords back where you're from. He's subordinate to Emperor Saburo."

"I was told Canaris had a king, not an emperor." Richard cast his mind back to Valerie's history lesson in the halls of the Old Keep in Limara.

"We may as well have a king, given that the entirety of our empire was taken by that bastard Emperor of Sanskar," Makoto clarified. "All the lands east of the Irena Mountains used to be Canarian vassals until the Vanquisher forced us out."

"That's enough history, I think," Akira asserted. "You want work, outsider? Come with us, then."

He opened the door to the house from which he had appeared and beckoned for Richard to follow. The trio slowly passed through what looked to be a living room. Richard thought the Canarian interior style felt warmer, more inviting than typical Miradosi housing. Akira then opened a door on the other side of the room and led them into the street, the thoroughfare once again present and in full strength.

"When you say, 'work which will upset the daimyo'," Richard said, looking at Makoto, "what exactly do you mean by that?"

"Oh, you know, just the things that are sort of technically not allowed," Makoto replied quickly, grunting as she forced her way through a group of pedestrians blocking the road. "Probably not any killing, though sometimes the boss orders people intimidated or maybe killed if they've really wronged him in some way, like if they've racked up a lot of debt they don't intend to pay back."

"I'm not killing anyone."

"I wouldn't worry about that. He'll probably send you to extort some businessmen, or maybe run a shipment."

"A shipment?"

"Yeah, he'll get you to run some cargo from one place to another. You are aware of the word's definition?"

"I'm perfectly aware. I want to know what kind of cargo."

"*Substances*. Usually. Sometimes people."

They continued through the city, Richard constantly on the lookout for Lynn. But she never appeared, or at least he never managed to spot her through the sheer mass of people.

They passed a number of guards who looked at them suspiciously, though they were never interrupted and many even seemed to recognise Akira and Makoto, greeting them as they passed before resuming their steely countenances.

"It's that building there. See it?" Akira pointed to one of the buildings Richard had seen when he had first entered the city, standing multiple stories high.

As they neared their destination, Akira took them along a detour through a number of back alleys filled with unsavoury types dressed in darker shades than the rest of the city's folk. Like the guards, these unsavoury types recognised Akira and Makoto, the corners of their lips forming into slight smiles as they passed through.

The last turn brought them to a dead end, the tall building towering above them with bare stone walls at their sides. In front was a lone door, guarded by two men with faces shrouded in shadow. They wore black cone-shaped hats and faced the floor, unmoving.

Akira approached the door and knocked three times, seeming to ignore the presence of the guards, as they ignored him. He stepped back, clasping his hands together as they waited in silence for a response. Though it wasn't total silence—the sounds of the city were still audible as faint background noise, and a louder metallic clashing could be heard from inside the building.

After some time, a mechanism in the door clicked and the door was pulled open from within, revealing a further hat-wearing guard who motioned the trio inside without a word.

The room beyond the door was a vast, open space, plain wooden floorboards beneath their feet, items of furniture few and far between. Windows lined the walls at regular intervals around the room's upper rim, far out of reach from the ground. At the back end of the room was a staircase, their view of which was blocked by the numerous dark-clothed individuals engaged in sparring practice. Not with training swords—they wielded wickedly sharp sabres. The guard who had let them in led them around the display and briskly ascended the stairs to the third level.

The resonating clash of steel subsided as they entered a floor even more open—the retractable walls remained open, providing a clear view of most of the city. In the room's centre was a man kneeling on a large white cushion, large enough to have been a mattress. He was alone, accompanied only by a sword which lay flat on the floor in front of him.

"Akira," the man said sharply, his voice a knife through the tranquillity. "Makoto."

"We've brought you an outsider, boss," Akira said, bowing to the man's turned back. "He's looking for work."

"Kare wa hoku no bugai-she to ishodeshitu ka?"

"We found him on his own, boss. No others."

"Hablar Arcaea," Richard barely opened his mouth to cast the spell, flicking his fingers in the direction of the kneeling man.

"Akira, Makoto—leave us," the kneeling man, who Richard then understood to be Jiro, abruptly announced. The two complied without hesitation, filing rapidly into the doorway and down the stairs.

"You're a spellcaster, outsider," Jiro declared, catching Richard off-guard.

"To an extent, sir," Richard responded cautiously. "My capacity is limited."

"But you speak the ancient tongue of the mages," he said. "Not something that can be said of many."

"I was taught by ancient people."

"Would their name happen to be Lopan?"

Jiro rose from the cushion and looked Richard dead in the eyes. The bounty hunter felt disarmed, struggling to maintain eye contact through a steadily heightening sense of discomfort.

"No," Richard said firmly. "But I know a Lopan. And I'm interested to know how you do, too."

"And I'm interested to know your connection to the Council if they are not your instructors. Tell me—if not them, then who? Who taught you?"

"I will tell you if you tell me how you know the Council."

A tense silence ensued, both men refusing to let their increasingly hostile gazes falter.

"What's your name?" Jiro finally asked.

"Richard Ordowyn. Bounty hunter," Richard said.

"You're more than a bounty hunter. You're a Child of Fate. I can sense that immediately. Did the Council send you here?"

"I don't know what you've perceived, but you've perceived it wrong. I'm not working for the Council. I never will. Hell, what's left of them is self-destructing as we speak."

"Interesting." The semblance of a smile crept onto Jiro's face for the first time since Richard had entered the room. "It's about time. Certainly wasn't that way when I left."

"You were on the Council?"

"Unfortunately. But that was a long time ago. This has been my life for nearly two hundred years. I'm surprised how peaceful it has been. I assume the same is not true for you, given your abilities?"

"What do you want from me?" Richard asked bluntly.

"Want from you? It was you who came to me in search of work. I was just curious about the state of affairs. And it's been a long time since I conversed with a fellow sorcerer. Do forgive me for my curiosity. Now, are you able to tell me who taught you? A question I ask out of pure, unadulterated interest? Or is it a secret?"

"I was taught by vampires. How's that?" Richard finally conceded.

"By Kalahar Kefrein-Lazalar?"

"You know him?"

"Of course I know him. Every mage on that Council knows him. At least, the ones who were around for the Siege of Pestion did. I can't speak for modern times, of course, because it was after the cursing of the land that I departed."

"Well... yes, it was Kalahar. In fact, I'm searching for him now. I need his help. But I need a ship to find him. A ship with a crew, because I'm not risking crossing the ocean without that again."

"That sounds expensive," Jiro said with a smirk. "But it just so happens that I have a ship with such a crew. And it can be yours for any use—on one condition."

Richard raised an eyebrow.

"Whatever it is, wherever you're going—take me with you."

"Absolutely not."

"You don't understand, Richard. I have no sympathies towards my old allies. I yearn for the adventure, the rush of it all, to stretch my atrophied magical muscles. Anything to finally move on from this life. Because it's either this or a noose around my neck—you have presented me with an opportunity I couldn't hesitate to accept. And besides, this city is mine. Without my approval, you're not getting out of that port on so much as a fishing boat."

A cat with pristine white fur clambered softly down the stairs behind Richard and padded across the room, settling next to Jiro and rubbing its face against his leg with fierce enthusiasm.

"Well, Richard? What do you say?"

"What will you get out of it?" Richard asked exasperatedly. "I'm not searching for the Council, I'm searching for Kalahar. For my own reasons. And once I have found him, I will be on my own way once again. Where would that leave you?"

"I would have to come back here, wouldn't I?" Jiro said as if it was obvious. "There's nothing else for me anywhere else. But to go on this adventure... I'm not looking to get anything tangible out of it, Richard. I just want the break. I just want to experience something in my old age. I'm nearly as old as Tregor Lopan, for the gods' sakes, and yet here I am. Running the same old show for more than a hundred years."

"And you don't have any grudges? Against the vampire?"

"I've spent no longer than a week in his company, Richard. Hardly long enough to form a grudge."

I wouldn't be so sure, Richard thought.

"Well? What of it?"

"I'm considering it," the bounty hunter said. "There is just one thing."

"Which is?"

"I came to this city with someone and we were separated after being chased by the guards. I don't know where she is. I need you to help me find her."

"I've got eyes all over the place." Jiro dismissed the difficulty of the task with a wave of his hand. "We'll find her in no time.

*

Lynn stopped running as she heard the guards thunder past the narrow entrance to the alleyway. In the rush of adrenaline, she hadn't taken any time to survey her new surroundings and took a seat on a nearby crate to regain her breath. And through her deep breaths, she didn't notice the group of individuals appearing to block both her paths.

"Kawai gaikoku hitu no anoko, doshitu koko ne tadoritsu no?" a gravelly voice rasped to her left.

Lynn looked at the man, who wore an eyepatch over his left eye and was covered in tattoos on every visible patch of skin.

"Stay back," she warned, standing up.

"Kanoji wa shoju ne chiganai," another tattooed man, this time to her right, said, cigar smoke billowing from his nostrils. "Kanoji no mite."

"Hablar Sanskarra," she uttered, directing the spell at the two men, who were then joined by a further trio on each side.

"What language was that?" the first asked, the question directed at his companions. They all shrugged.

"Pretty one, do you speak Canarian?" the smoke-billowing man prodded.

193

"It's fine if you don't, our clients don't particularly care. Flame, they don't even need you to speak at all," the first cackled, inciting a similar chuckle amongst his gang.

"Invectus," Lynn whispered, summoning the dark blade and assuming a defensive stance, holding it diagonally across her body.

"She's a fucking witch!" the smoke-billowing man proclaimed.

"She'll be worth double! Triple, even! Daimyos pay a shitload of money for a witch! Get her!"

The men revealed a diverse array of weapons—between the six of them, Lynn counted four daggers, a hatchet, two swords, a spiked mace, and a crossbow, the latter of which was pointed directly at her head.

"Don't move, pretty one, or you'll be getting a bolt between your eyes."

Lynn decided to try her chances.

The first thing she did was duck, the crossbow-wielder firing without hesitation as soon as she moved. The bolt sailed straight over her head and into the shoulder of a man wielding a mace behind her, who cried animalistically as the bolt embedded itself in his shoulder. She performed a half-turn, bringing her blade up to deflect an incoming blow from an opposing sword as the mechanism of the crossbow creaked with the sound of reloading.

The first hit she took was from the man wielding the hatchet, who brought his weapon down with such force that she could not parry the blow. The weapon's blade sliced open her hand as she growled and struck back in retaliation, finding the man's neck and severing one of his arteries. He dropped the axe and brought his hand up to the wound, and when he removed it, it had been painted red.

Lynn had just deflected another blow of the sword when the dagger caught her off guard. The bandit stabbed her leg, withdrawing the weapon and stabbing her once more in the same vicinity. She screamed, finding her assailant and plunging her sword through his chest and flinging his body through his comrades with a burst of magical energy.

The slight twang of the crossbow was mostly drowned out and the bolt crunched through her knee without warning. She fell to the ground in agony, howling as she looked back at the man using the weapon and sent her sword through the air. His eyes doubled in size as it buried itself in his neck and he died before he hit the ground.

"Invectus," she shrilled, dragging herself away from the remaining assailants, having recovered from the body knocking them down like pins. Another blade materialised in her right hand as the three remaining men converged on her, blades falling like rain.

She deflected three more strikes before one uppercut knocked her blade out of a defensive position and a subsequent hit sent it clattering to the floor where it dispersed into mist. Three swords were brought to her throat as tears swelled in her eyes.

"That was quite the effort, pretty one!" the original man snarled, crouching down to look her in the eyes. "Not many fight like you do!"

Lynn spat in his face. The man slapped her and disgustedly wiped the saliva off before one of his allies produced a cloth and held it over her mouth. Nobody could hear her muffled screams as the world turned to black.

*

"Looks like a healthy payday for us, eh?" the original man proclaimed, to a chorus of chuckles as they produced a grey sheet with which to cover the fallen sorceress.

Their elation was short-lived. Those who had survived Lynn's defence fell alongside her as a volley of throwing knives sailed noiselessly through the alley and into their necks, hearts, and temples.

Some died instantly, while others were left to drown in their own blood. Only one, the original man, was left in a condition where he could speak to the sudden assailants.

There were only two, both dressed plainly apart from the masks concealing their faces. One of them set about cleaning up the mess of corpses while the other leaned down over the original man, desperately clutching his chest.

"Are you the boss?" he said, placing a finger on the knife's protruding handle.

The man cried out and took deep, rapid breaths. "N-no," he stammered. "I'm just a grunt. A grunt!"

"You go back to your boss," the assailant said, pressing even harder against the handle. The man gritted his teeth and locked his head back as he fought the urge to scream. "You go back to your boss and remind him that this is Sakuru territory. You never come back. Do I make myself clear?"

"Yes," the man said without hesitation. "Yes, sir. Sakuru territory. You'll never see me again."

"Good," the assailant said.

He stood up and helped his comrade lift Lynn's body before the pair disappeared into the harbour.

CHAPTER 21

"Caster! We need to get out of here! Open a portal back to the lobby, we don't have the time to wait around!"

The spellcasting vampire looked to Elaine with an expression almost as if asking for permission. She scowled, eyes alight with sorrowful fury as she gestured for Caster to do as instructed.

Elton burst through the portal with a renewed course of adrenaline pumping through his veins. The lobby was surprisingly empty, the majority of the intruders still making their way back from the bunker. A shot of pain ran up his leg with each step, but he overpowered his limp, setting his focus on reaching the room in which he knew Rosa lay dormant.

His path was blocked by a pair of mace-wielding thugs, their weapons stained red with the blood of the innocents scattered across the room in varying states of mutilation. The first, a man missing at least half of his teeth, swung indiscriminately at Elton, who ducked the blow and swiftly drew his dagger. He planted the dagger in his assailant's unguarded chest before the other's mace fell, though not in attack, but because Felix's knife had found its way into his temple.

They retrieved their weapons and carried on, where they continued to observe further signs of looting and violence. Fallen guards littered the floor amongst civilians and servants, acting as obstacles in their unrelenting path. The little resistance they encountered was easily dispatched before they arrived at Rosa's office, the door hanging ajar. They stopped momentarily, Elton panting like a dog, as they listened to the arrhythmic pattern of grunts resonating from within the room.

Elton burst inside with a snarl to see two men hunched over Rosa's body while a woman distanced herself, instead opting to muse over the magical items cluttering the magician's desk. He saw only red as he charged through the room, crashing into one of the men bearing over Rosa. He was too busy to notice Elton's approach, and was not ready for it as he was slammed into the wall, breeches at his feet. The woman inspecting Rosa's desk fell quickly to one of Felix's knives, and the other man drew his weapon only to have his neck skewered by Ferris's rapier.

The remaining living man struggled to breathe as Elton clenched his fist around his neck, holding him against the dented wall with unanticipated strength. He released his grip with one hand to grab his dagger, using his other hand to clutch the thug's head and smash it into the wall.

The thug fell, whimpering pathetically as he crawled towards the exit. Elton stepped on his leg with brutal force, the thug crying with pain before being flipped over onto his back. He cut decisively, holding the man's severed member over him as he let out a gut-wrenching scream, before driving his dagger between his eyes.

What ensued was only silence as Elton calmed down, his companions unsure of what to say, if anything. He wiped his weapon on the slain man's tunic before returning it to its sheath, staring agitatedly at his bloodied palms.

"We need to get going, boss," Felix finally prompted. "There are still way more of them than there are us."

"Caster, can you open another portal?" Elton asked, pushing himself up with a grunt. "We need to get out of here, now. Leave until the situation calms down."

"Hey, he's not your pet, alright?" Elaine placed a grey finger against Elton's chest. "You can't just order him to do whatever bidding you want."

"Unless you know someone else here who can open a portal, one who isn't unconscious, I would love to meet them!" Elton retorted, raising his voice towards the end of his sentence. "Until then, I am going to have to result to Caster's abilities. I am not treating him like my pet. I am relying on him!"

Elaine grimaced and stepped back, while Caster sheepishly began to trace a portal. He completed the initial gesture just as the door flew open, producing Ant and Fez, both of their faces slick with sweat. They didn't spend long eyeing up each separate individual in the room, instead opting to blindly dive through the portal as Caster thrust his arms forwards, opening a rift to the decrepit house in the alley off Megaross square. It was then that Elton finally heard the racket of the approaching mob. He scooped Rosa up after ushering his companions through the portal before being the last to step through himself.

Caster uttered the spell to break the connection between them and the Redhouse, an expression Elton could only have described as fear somewhat semblant across the vampire's countenance. Though it remained that way only briefly before the usual absolute neutrality resumed its place.

"We may have an issue getting you those explosives by the time we had promised, Count," Fez said, scratching his head.

"Who are they?" Elaine seethed, darting her eyes suspiciously between Ant and Fez as they inspected the dilapidated furniture, struggling to decide whether it was safe to sit down.

"Friends. They're friends," Elton reassured. "Otherwise we would have killed them already. Just calm down for a second, would you?"

"Calm down?" Elaine's eyes flared. "Calm down? You expect me to calm down after leading me into what was effectively a trap? Sure, you may have been blind to it, but our friends were ruthlessly murdered as a result of your ineptitude! And now we've escaped, and for what? To end up exactly where we began! Do you have a plan, Elton? Do you? Do you have even the slightest idea as to how we are to escape this frankly insurmountable situation?"

"No! Because I haven't had time to think!" Elton set Rosa down carefully across a desk that wasn't quite wide enough for the entire length of her body, so her legs were left dangling over the edge. "I despise my lack of grip over the situation just as much as you do, and trust me, it is not a position I intend to maintain for long. But I've also been in this position plenty of times before and I have always, with careful planning and calculation, been able to rescue myself from it! So please, shut your mouth for one lousy second and allow me the space in my head to think!"

"You've rescued yourself before? What about the people around you? Have you always been able to rescue them? Or have you left them for dead, just as you left my friends?"

Elton didn't respond to the vampire's retort, instead pacing across the room as he racked his brain for ideas.

"If you fancy waking up any time now, that would be ideal..." he muttered as he settled his eyes upon the unconscious sorceress, her chest still rising and falling as softly as ever.

"They'll have a ringleader, won't they?" Felix suggested in an attempt to cut through the painful tension that had encompassed the room. "There's no way a force that size was able to just assemble organically from the peasantry. They will have a ringleader, someone in charge. Someone organising them. We just need to find out who. And then kill them."

"But who? Who would be in charge of that rabble? They seemed disorganised enough to me. And... utterly devoid of honour."

"And what was the Syndicate? In its early days, at least? And you remember Bloody Ramsey. This whole situation feels like a stark return to those days. I won't sit here and let that happen. You killed the old man. Surely you won't let his legacy be reborn?"

"He's right, bossman," Paul chimed in. "That lot right remind me of Ramsey's cronies."

"We won't be able to continue with our work while the Redhouse remains occupied," Ant added.

"They want to kill me. On sight. I hardly have the same leverage that I did once upon a time. Nor do I have the unassuming looks to hide in public."

"But you do have us. And we do have the unassuming looks," Felix said. "We go in there, pretend to be different people. Disguised, of course. We find out who's in charge. And we put a knife in their throat. It's simple, really."

"No, Felix, it's not simple. It's anything but simple. There is a much deeper issue this time than some coup by a great power. That mob, however unorganised they may be, comprised ordinary people. Ordinary Dannosi people who were genuinely angered. Who genuinely wanted to see me overthrown. This wasn't Hortensio, or the King of Santeros. This was local people. Local people who have lost their respect for me. Local people who will continue to undermine me regardless of who leads them. This isn't as simple as you say. Without respect, a leader is nothing. And I have no respect. That much was clear—abundantly."

Elaine and Caster had turned to quiet conversation during Elton's monologue, and they only turned their heads back after he fell silent in anticipation of a response. And naturally, it was Paul who first opened his mouth.

"Well, boss... you have a gone a bit... soft."

Elton scowled. "I went soft. I did go soft! I gave these people a chance to live a life free from persecution and unnecessary violence and bloodshed. And what do they do? They spat in my face. Well, thank you, Paul. You've made me realise it now. I can't be 'soft', anymore. It's time to reinstate a sense of discipline into these people. Let them know that in fact, I am in charge. And they're going to bloody well respect me. Because they'll have no other choice. They'll have no other choice."

This time, Elaine and Caster listened. And they seemed just as captivated as the rest of the room's occupants, over whom a blanket of trepidation had fallen, judging by the looks on their faces and the way their eyes fell upon the nearest stray objects.

"Well?" Elton questioned to nobody in particular. "What do you think? How about we show these people that we're not about to be bossed around?"

"I think that's a bloody brilliant idea," Paul happily replied.

"And how exactly do you intend to show the people that you're no longer 'soft', as you describe it?" Elaine inquired, standing up. "Because last I checked, they were dissatisfied with your acceptance of people like me. I haven't heard so much as a whisper of dissatisfaction with your general leniency. Are you to begin exterminating us as Kalahar has been?"

"For the gods' sakes, no! Do you take me for a fool? I have kept a stranglehold over this city for numerous years and I don't need you chewing me out over affairs you don't understand! You forget, vampire, you're three months old. Consider keeping your mouth shut when the adults are talking, because I'm not an idiot."

Elton looked at Rosa, who remained dead to the world. He didn't know what else to expect, but every time he checked there was some part of him hoping to find her awake.

"Well, then," Felix smirked. "Shall I go ahead with my plan... Regi?"

"No," Elton dismissed, a reply Felix took with shock, the previous excitement falling promptly from his face. "We'll do mine."

A touch of excited adrenaline coursed through Elton, a feeling he hadn't experienced since the day he had raided the Dawn Bank with the Syndicate. The smirk that had fallen from Felix's face returned just as quickly as it had departed, and it spread to Paul, too, as they eagerly awaited an explanation.

"Bard," Elton began. "You listen up, too. Because you've got a central role to play in this."

*

The bouncer the mob had installed outside the entrance to the Redhouse contorted his nose as Ferris approached, lute in hand. The bard wasn't carrying any weapons—that the bouncer could see.

"Greetings!" Ferris smiled, extending his arms into a gesture as if to say he was expecting something.

"What you want?" the bouncer spat, sucking smoke from a pipe.

Ferris didn't respond audibly, instead squinting and pointing to his lute, his face painted with ridicule. When this didn't incite a reaction, he dropped his head and stared directly at the bouncer, opening his mouth slightly.

"I'm a performer," he finally said, exasperated, the bouncer still having failed to respond to his implications. "Here for the boss. Would you mind taking me to him?"

The bouncer only snorted, drawing again from his pipe.

"I don't exactly see the humour of the situation." Ferris placed his hands on his hips, slinging the lute over his back before doing so.

"Boss ain't a man," the bouncer said. "It's a woman."

"And this is relevant... because?"

"You said he instead of she."

"Does that really matter? I was sent to see the person who took over the Redhouse. My... manager didn't disclose their gender. The point is, I'm here to see her. Are you going to take me or am I going to have to march myself in? Because I don't imagine she'd be very happy to hear that you've been stopping her performer from entering the building, the very performer she requested personally, mind you!"

The bouncer sighed, quenching the embers in his pipe and dropping it into his shirt pocket, riddled with holes and burn

202

marks. He turned and sauntered lazily away, Ferris left to assume he was meant to follow.

*

"I think the spell is working," Caster deduced, turning to face the others as they all watched Ferris disappear into the Redhouse.

"Judging by the fact that they... you know... had a conversation? I think it worked too," Felix patronised.

"In Santerosi? You really were able to teach him Santerosi so quickly?" Elton asked in disbelief.

"I didn't teach him Santerosi," Caster dismissed. "I just made it so all the words that he spoke or heard were Santerosi. Just like the equivalent spell for Archaeish."

"But how did you learn to do that so quickly?"

"I just... extracted your knowledge of the language and crafted a spell with it. It wasn't so difficult."

"So when do we go in?" Paul interjected, his attention still upon the Redhouse.

"I told you. When the bard gives us the signal," Elton stated impatiently.

"And what was the signal again?"

"For heavens' sakes..."

*

"You know, I frequented this place sometimes back when that grimy old Redwinter guy was in charge. I like what you folk have done with the place."

Ferris stifled a grimace as he was led through the messy corridors, still littered with evidence of the massacre in the form of bloodstains on the carpets and scattered debris nobody had bothered to tidy up.

"Boss's name is Enya. You might want to know that before you go in and insult her by not knowing her name," the bouncer said out of the blue as they approached a door at the top of some stairs.

Guarding the door were two more visibly dirty men, who looked down upon the bard with identical disapproving, but otherwise uncaring, gazes. They opened the door for the troubadour after feeling all over his torso for weapons and coming up empty.

203

Ferris hadn't spent long enough in the Redhouse to have learned its layout. But he had been inside the intelligence office and was able to recognise it as he stepped inside—but only just. The mob had destroyed the place—documents Elton had kept neatly filed were strewn across the floor, the tables, the seats, everywhere, all in different conditions, some torn into pieces, some shredded beyond repair. The label reading *Director's Office* on the next door through which Ferris was abruptly shoved hung freely on one nail, the other having been bent out of shape. The bard was confused more than anything. He usually thought he was quite talented at deciphering motivations, but at that point he was at a loss.

The table inside the director's office was found in surprisingly intact condition. Around it sat a few individuals, none too impressive. Two more men, one bald and preoccupied with a finger in the deepest recesses of his nose to notice the bard enter, and one with dark brown hair so unkempt it fell over his eyes and prevented him, too, from taking particular notice of Ferris.

The one person who took full notice was the woman at the head of the table, rising as the door behind Ferris was pulled shut. Her eyes were dark like the exquisite onyx hanging in a pendant from her neck, and intense, her penetrative gaze unfaltering as Ferris waited expectantly for implicit permission to take a seat. He never received it, and instead chose to just begin to speak.

"Enya, is it? It's an honour."

The woman, yet to confirm she actually was Enya, did not respond, and instead continued to bore her eyes into the bard for an uncomfortable length of silence.

"May we have the room? There is something I wish to discuss with you in private. It's an urgent matter. Of relation to Elton Redwinter."

Ferris caught a glint in the stone-faced woman's eyes, a brief glimpse of light in what he would otherwise have described as voids. She moved for the first time since Ferris had encountered her, in the form of a quick flick of her wrist to gesture the two men at her sides to leave. They did so without hesitation.

"My name is Ferris. I'm quite famous where I come from, actually," the bard explained after the guards had left the room. He slowly stepped around the table, progressing towards the end at which Enya remained standing.

"Dispense with the pleasantries." Her voice was cold and sharp. Ferris shivered, and not just with unease. It was as if the physical temperature inside the enclosed room had dropped. "Tell me about Elton Redwinter. What do you know?"

"Come, now, you've inherited a great fortune. I'm afraid that with it come the burdens of statesmanship. Which, at the most basic level, includes some degree of politeness and per-sonability."

Ferris had made it halfway across the room, at which point Enya traversed the other half in quick, long strides. She stood at the same height as him, and the bard felt increasingly un-comfortable as she stared coldly into the depths of his eyes.

"I don't care about statesmanship. I don't care about per-sonability. I don't care about politeness and I don't care about you. I care about Elton Redwinter. Finding him and killing him. So start talking."

"Alright, alright! Who even are you, anyways?" Ferris stepped back, but didn't make much progress with the wall behind him blocking his way. "It's not often that a nobody is able to muster such a loyal following so quickly. How did you do it? I'd like tips, honestly."

Enya furrowed her eyebrows into a vicious scowl. Ferris darted his eyes left and right as she reached the point of phys-ical contact with their closeness. He felt trapped, despite his usual confidence. And he felt cold.

"Can we sit down? Talk about this like adults? If we can't do statesmanship, can we at the very least do civility?"

She withdrew, still maintaining her paralytic glare, before turning around and pacing almost provocatively back to her seat.

Ferris bent down and drew the dagger from his boot in one fluid motion. He leapt elegantly across the room, grasping Enya's waist as he landed before embracing her and bringing the blade to her throat. She did not resist as he cut.

She collapsed with a thud and Ferris stood speechless over the body, unsure of his next action. It had been so easy, to the point where he almost felt remorse.

He went to return his dagger to his boot but stopped, something about the weapon catching his eye. It was clean—there wasn't a trace of blood along its blade. And when he looked at the corpse on the floor, he realised there was no blood anywhere.

Shivering, Ferris reached to touch Enya's neck where he had made the killing incision. He felt the severed tissue in his fingers, but as he brought his hand back into the light, he found it to be clean.

Enya turned around so quickly that if Ferris had blinked, he would have missed it. Not that it would have changed his fate, because she placed her inhumanely strong hands around his neck and squeezed beyond the point where he could breathe.

"Surprised? Good. That's what I hope for," she spat. "Where is Elton Redwinter?"

Ferris clawed futilely at his throat, the strength draining from his body as his face shifted through several shades of purple. He tried to speak, but no words could escape.

"How's this for statesmanship?" she asked. "Who did you think you were, coming in here and lecturing me? Was there not a single point at which you thought that might have been bold, to say the least? Now talk to me! Where is he?"

She loosened her grip enough to allow Ferris the slightest breath, and he coughed with such force that he worried he would rupture his throat.

"He's... I don't know..."

"You'd better think really carefully about your next words."

"He's outside... he's waiting outside... in the alley near the... the tavern..."

"What's he waiting for? How many are with him?"

"Just a handful..."

"Answer the first question."

"Remind me... what it was?"

Enya tightened her grip and the trickle of air Ferris had enjoyed was cut off. She held him firmly for no longer than a minute, but it felt to the troubadour like a lifetime.

"Answer," she enunciated, allowing Ferris to breathe even less comfortably than before, "the question."

"For you," he choked. "I was meant... to get you... to leave somehow. And that's... when... they were going... to ambush you."

Enya clenched his throat in her hands and this time, she did not let go. She began to monologue about something, but Ferris had stopped listening to her, and not voluntarily. Her words had become a blur as he squirmed violently, vigorously, in a doomed endeavour to capture just a single breath of air. He tried to raise his arms to claw at her hands once more but could not muster the strength. But then he had an idea.

He leaned suddenly forwards as much as Enya's grip allowed, which wasn't far. But it was far enough.

Ferris opened his mouth and snapped his teeth shut, tearing through the flesh of Enya's nose. She yelped, but she did not stumble. Releasing one of her hands from Ferris's neck, allowing him just a moment to draw a pained breath, she drove his head into the wall with a thunderous crack and allowed him to slump to the ground like a ragdoll.

Ferris didn't really feel the pain. It was a dull throbbing in the back of his head. He gingerly dabbed his fingers on the hair at its source and they came back red.

He had dropped the dagger at some point. When, he couldn't remember exactly. But Enya had found it. And she drove it through his chest so hard that it pinned him to the wall.

*

"He's takin' his time, isn't he?" Paul exclaimed.

"Too long. It's been too long," Elton said. He felt the urge to pace back and forth but forced himself to remain still and calm.

"Easy, boss, he knows what he's doing," Felix urged. "At least, that's what he tells us."

"What if he's betraying us? We hardly knew him. He could be telling her people where to find us right now."

"You, uh, you could be right, actually. Look."

Felix pointed to the entrance to the Redhouse, from which a veritable battalion of thugs had appeared. They all brandished weapons, and leading them was a single woman most distinguishable by her pale skin and the dark cavities in place of her eyes. She shouted orders across the various groups that had assembled, and they began to disperse into the city's myriad alleyways.

"The bard didn't say a word," Elton concluded. "He's dead."

CHAPTER 22

SANAÍD, TYEN'AEL

It had been a while since Elaeínn had felt a sense of calm. When she didn't feel the constant need to look over her shoulder, to be ready to flee at a moment's notice. But a few days after her encounter with Ferrilíen Vanad, walking casually through the streets of Sanaíd, among the thousands of others going about their daily lives, she finally felt she could relax and let down her guard. Not entirely, though.

Despite the immunity granted to her by the Prime Minister, she never felt accepted back into the society she once called her own. She remained the recipient of innumerable icy glares from people who recognised her—civilians, guards, even soldiers who marched through the streets. There were the occasional heckles, though they were few and far between.

She visited the forge previously belonging to her friend Aegard. He wasn't there anymore, and operating the forge instead was a much younger man. Elaeínn didn't approach, only watching him work from a distance, cursing Jaelaar's name under her breath.

She visited the School for Young Magicians, moving towards the entrance in an attempt to go inside. The guards outside would not allow it, citing her as a dangerous person. She didn't argue, instead trudging away while muttering a request for Caeran to forgive her.

Elaeínn considered visiting the university library, wanting some form of retribution for Saníya's betrayal. She decided against it, figuring she would just be turned away as she had been at the school. And she didn't want to be thrown in prison for the short duration of her freedom.

On one of these ordinary days, Elaeínn had taken a seat on a streetside bench when three people suddenly approached her from the crowd. She had been busy with a meat skewer she had purchased from a vendor on a nearby square when they surrounded her, forcing her to look up.

"Elaeínn?" one of them—a young woman, perhaps in her thirties—queried. Elaeínn hesitantly nodded, too preoccupied with chewing a charred chunk of beef to respond verbally.

"We know you. From Fallía," a second person, a stick-thin man younger than the first woman, claimed. "We fought in the battle against the army."

"And we were forced to flee," the third person, a slightly older woman, finished. "But we can't stand here and watch as Vanad destroys everything we fought so hard to protect."

"Keep your voices down," Elaeínn hissed, tossing the finished skewer into the bushes adjacent to the bench and wiping her mouth with her sleeve. "They've got eyes everywhere. Come, I'll take you somewhere safe."

Elaeínn stood up and quickly surveyed the surroundings, searching for anything that caught her eye as suspicious. She decided the coast was clear and gestured for her surprise companions to follow as she set off in the direction of Kíra's house. Although she had told them it would be safe, in truth, she was not sure what she would find.

It became immediately apparent as she trekked through the city with her new entourage that the suspicions focused on her were contagious to those with whom she associated. Even the guards began to glance at each other with expressions Elaeínn interpreted as suggesting action. She remedied this by instructing the three FTA fighters to fall behind, which seemed to allay the suspicions of passers-by.

Elaeínn's heart sank as she reached the former place of residence of her fallen comrade and lover. The building had crumbled into a state of disrepair—the door hung open, the windows were shattered, and as she ventured inside, she could see that all of Kíra's belongings had been thoroughly pilfered, every nook and cranny ransacked. On the bright side, she had expected the house to have been seized. The one thing that remained, and could not be pilfered, was privacy.

Elaeínn took one last observational glance at the surrounding street before signalling for the others to join her. They moved with the throng of civilians until directly in front of the decrepit house before dashing inside, Elaeínn having already slunk upstairs.

"I'm going to need to know your names," Elaeínn said as soon as they joined her. She had settled on the bed, its sheets missing and myriad unidentifiable stains scattered across the ragged mattress.

"I'm Relía," the younger woman introduced. "We fought as a unit. This is Tolnír"—she gestured to the stick-thin man, who smiled weakly—"and Zanvía"—she gestured to the older woman, who seemed unsure of how to introduce herself. In the end, she awkwardly extended her hand, which Elaeínn struggled to reach from the bed.

"Tolnír," Elaeínn commented, casting her gaze upon the stick-thin man. "That sounds awfully dwarven."

"It was originally just Tolnir," the man explained. "I was raised by dwarves. They had to flee when the war started and I haven't seen them since. I elvenised my name to avoid being ostracised. It's worked, a little bit."

"You're from the South, then?"

"Yes, Commander. Near Evekar."

"Don't call me Commander."

"Y-yes…"

"Elaeínn. Just Elaeínn. Elle for short."

"We're all from the South, Elle, sir," Relía said, Elaeínn rolling her eyes in resignation. "I know the situation seems bleak here, but you've got real support among the southerners. They hate the Nationals and they hate the war, especially given that they have lived alongside dwarves their whole lives. If the FTA is to rise again, that's where we need to start."

"A good suggestion," Elaeínn said. "But there is one small problem. I'm not actually free. The Prime Minister will be summoning me sometime soon to travel to the Heart of magic. Raeris knows where that is, but they want to go there to hurt Alazarioss. The dragon, which I'm sure you've seen. And quite frankly, I'm not going to let them do that."

"We could help," Zanvía suggested. "Wherever you're going, they'll probably travel by portal. My mother runs a shop selling magical trinkets—there's this pair of talismans which are linked and you can activate them to open a portal between the pair. I'm sure I can convince my mother to hand them over. Then it's as simple as you smuggling one of them along with you and activating it at the right time. We'll be waiting and ready."

Elaeínn's eyes lit up with the long-forgotten flame of ambition as she considered the feasibility of Zanvía's plan. And the more she considered it, the more she was confident it could work.

"You three will have to stay somewhere safe and prepared at all times," she said. "You'll have to be armed. And can any of you fight?"

"We're competent with a blade," Relía said, indicating herself and Zanvía. "Tolnír… is better in the back line."

"I didn't want to be the one to suggest it," Elaeínn teased. Tolnír cracked a slight smile.

"What will we do when you do activate the talisman?" Zanvía asked.

"What do you think?" Elaeínn smirked. "Parade on in and let all hell break loose. I've killed one prime minister already—what's another?"

"Surely he'll be guarded, though."

"We'll have the element of surprise. I'll make sure to position myself real close. Then we strike quickly, dealing as much damage as possible. If we can, engage the guards he'll inevitably have with him and take out the whole lot of them. If we lose the upper hand, we just retreat back through the portal."

"And then what?"

"And then…" Elaeínn trailed off. She hadn't thought of what came next.

"We can go south," Tolnír provided. "If we can find your dragon, she will become the figurehead the FTA so desperately needs. Something the people can rile behind. The government has convinced everyone that the organisation is dead, that there's nobody left to fight with. The dragon is just what we need to convince them otherwise."

"You really think we have that much support in the South?" Elaeínn's tone rang out with disbelief.

"We do! And I can tell that you don't believe me, which is just further evidence of the false conviction they've managed to sow. If they've managed to convince you that the FTA is broken, then why wouldn't they be able to convince the thousands of oppressed nobodies being drafted into a war they don't support? The thousands of nobodies whose democratic rights are being torn away from them? You've got a reputation for your stubbornness, if that's alright for me to say, Elle, sir. You can't let yourself believe their lies."

"If this is true," Elaeínn spoke, "then we might not even need to work with the dwarves. It embarrasses me greatly but something Vanad said really made sense. And it made me reconsider my options. If it really is possible that an organic elven population could be the driving force of the resistance, then... forget the dwarves! You're right, Tolnír, and I haven't been able to see it in my solitude. We'll go south and muster a new army for the FTA. And then we will fight back. And this time, we will win."

It was three days after her encounter with Relía, Tolnír, and Zanvía when Elaeínn finally felt the metal-clad fist on her shoulder meaning her time in the city was at an end.

She accompanied the two Regal Guards back to the Serenna Palace without resistance, comfortable with the knowledge that her new allies were waiting, prepared for action. They had decided to leave central Sanaíd, seeking refuge in one of the Raerist churches in the suburbs disguised as pilgrims. The priests had been kind enough to grant them a room, and it was from there that they would spring into action, having smuggled daggers and one of the talismans into the church under their clothes. The other talisman, a round object cast in silver and covered in archaic elven symbols, rested with Elaeínn, tucked into a pocket on the inside of her robe.

They bypassed the usual bureaucracy endured by the visiting crowds at the palace and were taken straight to the lobby, where the Prime Minister awaited with several other senior National politicians and Tyen'Aeli mages.

"Elaeínn, what a delight it is to see you," Vanad called across the open chamber, a smile stretching across his face.

His company didn't seem quite as interested in feigning approval of her, instead collectively grimacing and grumbling dissentingly amongst themselves.

"You found it, then?" Elaeínn asked. "The Heart?"

"We certainly think so," the Prime Minister said confidently. "I hope you're ready for another journey across the ocean. This time, we're going south."

"South? To the Eye?"

"Much further. Beyond the realms of elves and dwarves. An island in the middle of the Great Sea. That is where the Heart is described to be," he said. "We found a description in the loose documents left behind by the Ríyael, who served a more important role to us than you realise."

"I don't really care what role he served," Elaeínn scoffed.

"I'm certain," Vanad said dismissively. "But there is no point in dwelling on events of the past. We depart today from the southern port of Telíana, where a ship is being prepared for us as we speak. But wait! Before we leave, there is something I must show you. Come."

Vanad detached from the group and beckoned for Elaeínn and her escort to follow him. Elaeínn did not have much of a choice as she was marched away with the guards' firm grips ever present on her shoulders.

They stopped in the back of the lobby where Vanad brought his arms up and traced a large oval, pressing forwards to reveal a portal to a square full of people. Elaeínn recognised it as the Common Square at once. They crossed through it and were suddenly on the podium, in front of the clamouring crowd. It was unclear what was happening, but it was happening quickly—Elaeínn remembered passing through the Common Square before being taken to the palace, and it had been nearly empty. Now people were packed like sardines.

"Let my voice be heard by all," Vanad spoke, closing his eyes and contorting his hand. "Ladies and gentlemen of Sanaíd!" he then boomed, the volume-increasing spell taking immediate effect.

Elaeínn looked off to the left-hand side of the stage as she herself was removed from the podium and taken to stand with another pair of guards. Being hauled up the stairs was an individual, a black bag over their head concealing their identity.

The guards were not treating them with any care as they were tossed to the ground in the centre of the podium, in front of a rectangular block of wood and a wicker basket.

"Today marks the beginning of the end for the dwarves. For I have some excellent news. Kagyan the murderer is dead!"

The crowd erupted with cheers, applause, and whistles. Despite this, it wasn't hard for Elaeínn to find several faces among those celebrating which betrayed a different reaction to the Prime Minister's news.

"But you're not here for that, I'm quite aware," Vanad continued, the volume of the crowd immediately collapsing. "Oh, you're here for the entertainment. So what do you say we rid ourselves of some traitors?"

The crowd erupted into cheers once again, this time more enthusiastic than before. From her new position off-stage, it was more of a strain for Elaeínn to see the commotion in the middle of the podium but she thought she could see another figure tossed to lay beside the first.

"The first, a Liberal member of the House found to have been sending High Elven secrets to the intelligence services of Hamatnar and Sahloknir! One who would rather see this country overrun by dwarves! Today they receive their punishment for treason!"

Elaeínn's heart began to race as the bag was removed from the woman's head and she was dragged up from the floor, her head slammed against the wooden block. She squealed something inaudible as one of the Regal Guards drew their sword slowly, scraping the metal intentionally against the scabbard's innards. Her squeals were then cut abruptly short as the blade fell and sliced cleanly through her neck, much to the amusement of the lively crowd.

Her body was removed and the next brought up to the block as Elaeínn's heart fell to her stomach. She felt the urge to run, to flee, but she couldn't. The Prime Minister wanted her to watch.

"The next, a dwarf! And not just any old prisoner of war, no! This is a very important dwarf—may I introduce you to General Flint Korvald of the Hamatnarian Army, head of dwarven intelligence!"

The bag was ripped from Flint's head and his bright red
hair stood out like a beacon among the blonde, brown, and
black heads of High Elven hair. He looked around, face
stricken with animalistic ferocity and desperation, his eyes
widening as his face was shoved against the block.

"You heartless bastards!" Flint's voice, unlike the previous
captive's, was clearly audible from a significant distance away.
"You fearmongering cowards! You will never win! You may
have the upper hand now, but nothing is a match for dwarven
resolve! We will storm this city and plunder your armies! We
will—"

His shouting was cut short by the blade as it dropped his
head into the basket with the first. More cheers. More applause. More whistling. Elaeínn felt overcome with a wave of
guilt, and an even stronger wave of paralytic worry.

"And finally, someone you might have thought you could
trust. Someone you thought you could confide in. Someone
you may know yourself. He used to be a professor at our very
own University of Sanaíd. But he chose to betray his students
and his land, and now he pays the ultimate price!"

A third figure, who Elaeínn hadn't seen until then, was
placed onto the block, now stained with blood. The bag was
removed from his head and she saw Velrin, face frozen with
terror. Their eyes met, and the terror was then joined by a
subtle anger, disappointment. He mouthed something which
Elaeínn couldn't make out, and then he too was deprived of
his head.

The roaring of the crowd, Vanad's booming voice, the
clanking feet of the guards' and soldiers' metal boots as the execution drew to a close—it all became background noise.
Elaeínn felt as if she wasn't there, as if she was spectating the
events from outside her body. She moved with the guards as
Vanad stepped off the podium and opened a portal back to
the Serenna Palace, though she did so without conscious decision. Everything became a dull hum.

"And that, Elaeínn, is why you do not cross your own people," Vanad said nonchalantly. But she could hardly hear him.

I did it again, she thought. *I sentenced someone to death to save
myself.*

She slowly began to return to reality as one of the mages in Vanad's company in the lobby opened a portal to the harbour in a seaside city she thought must have been Telíana. There were high elves, light elves, and dwarves all bustling around without even a hint of tension. It was because of this that she knew they must have been in the South.

They stood next to an enormous ship comparable to the galleons on which she had travelled to the island of Ríyael with the previous prime minister. She felt a sense of déjà vu, images of their preparation in the northern port of Lae- thyvaerd flashing through her mind. Except Laethyvaerd was a small town, hardly a soul around—Telíana was as busy as Sanaíd, if not busier.

Unlike Jaelaar's journey to Ríyael, Vanad had no intention of making a spectacle out of the expedition, and that was re- flected in the crew. There were no random-picked mages, only a select few specifically chosen by the Prime Minister himself. There were Grandmasters, but only Tyen'Aeli high elves. And there was not an array of ships, but one, and it was more than enough to house them all.

Elaeínn felt her arm twitch anxiously as she was loaded onto the ship and taken below deck to a bedroom almost identical to that in which she had stayed during her previous voyage. The guards made it clear that she was not expected to leave, so she took the opportunity to get comfortable, placing the Dragonsteel Blade into a cupboard and changing into a clean white blouse and tight-fitting pair of leather trousers she found tucked under the bed. And then with nothing to do, she reclined back into the bed and let herself fall to sleep.

She didn't know how long she had been asleep when the knocking on her door woke her up, but the rocking of the ship encouraged her quickly from her room. She raced past Vanad, who stood somewhat dazed in her doorway, and incited mur- murs of confusion from the mages traipsing around below deck. They did not stop her, though, as she continued up onto the main deck and made a beeline for the ship's side, throwing herself against the railing and releasing the contents of her stomach into the churning waters.

"I wanted to let you know of the plan for when we arrive at the Heart, whatever it looks like," Vanad said, arriving around a minute after her rapid departure. Elaeínn did not turn to face him, wiping her mouth clean of stomach acid before swishing saliva around her mouth and spitting.

"You told me my friends would be let go if I complied," she said, her voice trembling. She felt herself reaching for the Dragonsteel Blade, but then remembered she had left it below deck.

"I had to convince you to join us somehow. They were going to die, regardless. There was nothing you could have done to save them."

"What's stopping me from jumping into the ocean right now? That would be a spanner in your plans, I should think?"

"Hopefully the inevitability of your death by drowning were you to pursue an action so brash and foolish."

"And what's stopping me from putting a sword through you and feeding you to the fish?"

"Don't be banal, Elaeínn. You're a criminal, a terrorist. You have seen plenty of your allies perish. In what world did you think we wouldn't be executing a couple more?"

Elaeínn hawked, acid burning her throat, and spit again. "You're a bastard."

"You're entitled to your opinion," Vanad dismissed calmly. "Now may we continue?"

"How long was I asleep?"

"Not very long." Vanad passed her a waterskin, which she used to finish expunging her mouth of the lingering contents of her stomach. She then guzzled what remained until it was empty. "Maybe a few hours at most."

The sun was nearing the horizon as clouds moved in overhead and the sky bathed in a dark shade of red.

"Go on, then," Elaeínn said curtly, tossing the empty waterskin aside. "Tell me this plan."

"We're going to attempt to damage the Heart with our cannons." Vanad reached down to pick up the waterskin with a disapproving frown. "Hopefully that will draw her out, but we really have no idea. You are the only one who has ever managed to summon her."

"Not on purpose..."

"You will then speak to her, tell her we mean no harm."

"Good luck getting her to believe that."

"And our mages will cast a restraining spell, stop her from breathing fire—"

"Jaelaar tried that, you said it yourself. It won't work."

"Jaelaar did not have these shards." Vanad revealed the three lirenium crystals again. "Alongside Ríyael's notes on the Heart were interesting memos about these shards, dubbed lirenium by him and his associates. And our Grandmasters have unlocked their use. This time, we will not fail to restrain the dragon."

"Fine," Elaeínn pretended to concede. "We'll try that. Don't be surprised when it does fail, because... you know... you're trying to wrestle control of a mythical creature which has the ability to turn this ship into ash at a moment's notice..."

"It was wounded by a few ballista bolts. It's hardly immortal," Vanad retorted. "Do not try to betray us, Elaeínn. The only reason you are still alive is to assist us on this mission. One wrong move and I will shut off your brain with a flick of my wrist."

One of the sailors approached the Prime Minister from below deck, moving at a pace that could almost have been described as a sprint.

"Prime Minister! We've got stowaways!"

"What?" Vanad ridiculed, furrowing his brow and leaving Elaeínn at the side of the ship, though she finally turned around to pay attention.

The door from which the sailor had arrived swung open to produce a further pair of sailors exiting backwards, swords drawn and pointed into the open doorway. They kept moving slowly onto the main deck as another pair of men arrived, one with pale white skin and dark hair wielding an ornate scimitar, the other with darker skin and a translucent black blade. And they both had rounded ears, though they were not dwarves.

"Would you be the Prime Minister?" the dark-skinned man asked, warding off a further pair of sailors approaching them through the doorway.

"I am, yes," Vanad said gruffly. "You ought to explain yourselves fast, humans, before I order you thrown overboard."

"A word in private, if we could," he responded. "I believe we share an objective here."

Vanad looked at the sailors and gestured them to lower their swords, and the two human men sheathed and dispelled their own blades respectively. The Prime Minister took them below deck and the sailors dispersed back to their duties, Elaeínn left alone to turn back around and stare over the endless open ocean. She reached a hand into her satchel, feeling the surface of the talisman, having transferred it from her robes.

Not yet, she told herself. *Not yet.*

Elaeínn did not see any more of the two human men for the next few days, despite her best efforts to find them. It was as if they had disappeared, and the Prime Minister with them—she only saw him at meal times, and even then he sometimes wasn't present.

She spent her vast free time practicing her swordsmanship on the main deck, though the runes decorating her sword never glowed. She imagined the masts were soldiers in the National army, and she received plenty of stern gazes from the working sailors by coming dangerously close to damaging the ship's woodwork. But she remained in control of her weapon.

They continued to sail without end, the landmasses of Fenalia long since having disappeared, and for the longest time all Elaeínn could see was boundless ocean. Until one day, a week after they had left the port city of Telíana, something finally came into view.

"Land ho!" one of the sailors shouted from the crow's nest, spyglass in hand.

A small rocky island rose from the mist ahead, characterised by sharp stone formations which looked almost like fortifications around the island's rim. The foliage was sparse, not a single tree in sight and the only greenery visible taking the form of patches of moss across the numerous rocks as well as low-lying patches of weeds and grasses.

Elaeínn sheathed her sword, steadying her breathing, and ran up the stairs to the front deck where she was soon joined by Vanad and an assortment of mages. Including, finally, the two human men.

"We've not been properly introduced," the pale man said, extending a hand to Elaeínn. "I'm Lorenzo Panam."

"And I'm Torellio Manz," the dark-skinned man added, also extending a hand.

She shook both apprehensively in turn before refocusing her eyes on the approaching island. And she once again tucked her hand into her satchel, caressing the shiny surface of the talisman, more and more certain that the time to use it was approaching.

CHAPTER 23

THE GREAT SEA

The little crew had sailed under Kasimir's command for nearly a week. Jannis had been unsure of the validity of the mage's promises, but he had had nothing else on which to rely. To relinquish control to him had not been a decision made without careful consideration, but staring at the lacerated, soulless body of his king had made it easier.

"We will meet some allies of mine at the Heart," Kasimir announced as Jannis arrived from below deck, threading his fingers through his curly locks, agitated at the damage inflicted by the salty air.

"You never told me this," he retorted.

"I never thought it necessary. You won't need to engage with them in any way. They will just be helping me breathe fresh life into your king. Is that not what you want?"

"Is he going to be the same when he comes back? He won't have changed?"

"Shouldn't have. That is very much dependent on whether we are able to complete the spell without disruption. That will be down to you."

"Disruption? From what?"

Kasimir only shrugged, and Jannis wasn't sure as to whether the vagueness was intentional. He chose not to prod any further.

"It's bloody warm up here. Either that or weirdly cold below deck," he mused. "How close are we?"

"Close. We'll be there by sundown. Thank goodness, because I don't feel like resorting to fish."

"I thought you said the island was barren."

221

"It is. But my allies will be travelling aboard a ship much larger than this one and certainly more well-stocked. With elven foods, too. Divine."

Jannis faltered momentarily as Kasimir turned towards the helm. "Did you say elves?"

"I did. You've never met any?"

"I didn't think they existed. You're being serious?"

"They are very much real, though reclusive. Them and the dwarves live isolated on a continent in the North. Beyond the reach of humans. Well, not really—you just choose never to go there. Quite rightly so, because you wouldn't be welcome."

"*You* choose never to go there? You're a human too, are you not?"

"I meant you in the social sense. I don't pledge belonging to any particular group or people. I have no political aims. I just watch the world go by."

A deckhand approached the pair with a wooden platter in his arms, presenting them with a selection of salted beef, cheeses, dried fruits, and two bottles of ale. Jannis took the platter from him and dismissed him back to his duties before prioritising the ale and swigging.

"I never got around to asking, but who is that woman for whom he so brazenly sacrificed himself?" Kasimir inquired, tenderly chewing a hunk of beef.

"Just some nobody maid the idiot has apparently fallen for. I should have seen it coming, really. They've spent the past few months doing nothing but making eyes at one another. But by the gods, I didn't think he would be so stupid as to let himself die for her."

"Are you sure he's the type of person you can trust to run your kingdom? Someone so easily wiled by a frankly plain girl? What if she's a spy for Elton Redwinter? Hortensio could have told her secrets. She could have been the one that let them poison the vats. It's become quite clear to me that he was careless as a result of blind infatuation. Can you trust that? Is it worth bringing him back to life only for him to further endanger all Salyria?"

"You watch your mouth," Jannis growled. "Hortensio is the strongest king our country could ever wish for. He is not careless, and your words are bordering on treasonous. He is not just the King of Salyria—he is Salyria. We are nothing without him."

Jannis turned and walked away, scowling. Kasimir did not follow him, instead keeping his eyes on the open sea ahead.

The sorcerer fished into his pocket and revealed a small mirror. A quick glance around confirmed the fact that Jannis had disappeared below deck, and he muttered the spell quietly enough that the deckhands and sailors wouldn't take much notice.

His face disappeared from the looking glass's surface as the usual pale blue sheen appeared, mist arising from its silver frame.

"Kasimir? Are you nearly there?" Tregor's distorted voice spoke, the image of his face appearing shortly thereafter.

"We'll be there in a couple hours. I told the Salyrians it would be by the evening."

"Hurry yourselves. We can just about see it. Your friend still expects you to perform a resurrection?"

"I captured the King's soul. He watched me do it. Please, Tregor, we must do it for the sake of maintaining my position in his council."

"At what point do you think we'll have the opportunity? The elf girl who killed Ríyael is on this ship and is chomping at the bit to get her hands on the throats of some of these other elves. There is going to be bloodshed, and a lot of it. Not to mention the fact that we are expecting to be able to mine lirenium without any fear of repercussion from unaccounted sources. The dragon said she was connected directly to it. We're expecting her to appear to defend it. Counting on it, even. So no, we will not have the opportunity to resurrect your king."

"And what am I meant to say to his general, then?" Kasimir lowered his voice to a hiss. "The two are practically conjoined. I tried to convince him just a moment ago that he wasn't worth resurrecting. He told me that was treason, and that I need to shut my mouth."

Tregor shrugged, a gesture hardly visible on the small surface of the looking glass. "Figure something out, Kasimir. This is your position, you chose it. It's now your job to deal with the politics of it. Es tar, closs."

CHAPTER 24

"What do you mean, you don't know where she is? It's your job to prowl! To snoop! I pay you to do it! A woman goes missing in broad daylight and you haven't heard about it? By the Flame, you must know at least something? Anything?"

The two men shook their heads sheepishly, avoiding eye contact with Jiro as he paced back and forth across the alley.

"What if she escaped?" one of them suggested. "You said she's a witch—can't witches make portals?"

"She hasn't escaped. I—we would know if she had. She is still in this city and for some reason neither of you have found out where. So get back to work and you'd best not show your faces again until somebody has found her."

They nodded and dashed away, pulling their hats back over their heads as they disappeared into the throng occupying the connecting street.

"Why don't we look for her?" Richard asked. "Can't you track her magical signature? That's supposed to be something you sorcerers can do."

"I can't pinpoint her. There's too much noise," Jiro curtly responded. "And it's too soon. If these people have managed to evade detection to this point then they're not amateurs. My reckoning is that they will be waiting precisely for another catch. They're being greedy. And if they're not amateurs, chances are that they know she was with you and are hoping for you to come looking for her. Makes sense?"

"How long exactly do you want us to wait? Lanthanis knows what they could be doing to her."

"Nothing. They're doing nothing to her. Calm yourself."

Jiro closed his eyes and fell to his knees, placing his arms on his legs and muttering under his breath. Richard watched, slowing his breathing in an attempt to quell his stress. It didn't work, instead leading to him only feeling more agitated over Jiro's calmness and refusal to act.

"I want to find her just as much as you do, Richard," Jiro interrupted his incantation just as the bounty hunter was about to open his mouth. "If only because of the fact that your original mission is time sensitive, and I don't want to miss out. Be patient."

Richard pursed his lips and tempered his breathing once more, leaving Jiro in peace to resume his incantation. He assumed the role of bodyguard, ensuring by various mediums of intimidation that the occasional passers-by didn't dawdle.

An uncomfortable length of time passed before Jiro finally fell silent. Even after that, he didn't rise to his feet for at least five minutes, when he finally spoke up. "They've found her."

"Who has?"

"Those two I told off earlier. They say she's been boarded onto a ship by independent people smugglers. At least, they claim to be independent. I can be certain they aren't."

"Are you speaking directly to them? They can use magic?"

"No. I can read their thoughts, and they know that. And then I can send a message to them. So actually, technically, yes. We're directly communicating."

"Well, then? Are we going to go now?" Richard turned and took a few steps towards the main street, looking over his shoulder for Jiro's affirmation.

"I'm not going. You can."

Richard stopped. "What do you mean you're not going?"

"I don't do the physical work myself. I send someone else. That's what being the boss is all about. In this instance, I'm sending you. You have no qualms about that, I'm sure?"

"One little qualm. I'm a stranger in your city. I don't speak the language. I don't know the layout."

Jiro shook his head and smirked. "I'm sure this is standard procedure for you by now. Give me your head."

Richard retracted his few steps away and proffered his head for Jiro, receiving his knowledge of the city's layout, a spell Richard recognised as sounding remarkably similar to that which Kalahar had cast back in Letham Deregor.

"And the language. Hablar Canaria."

At once, the foreign hubbub sounded clearer to the Miradosi bounty hunter. Even though the words individual people were saying were entirely indistinguishable, somehow the entire cacophony sounded more familiar.

"Down at the port. You were there today; you would've known where it was even without the spell. One of the larger ships, a merchant's galleon. Three masts, five sails, flying the Vivian flag. Hard to miss. Oh, and Richard. Don't travel by portal. It's too conspicuous."

"I was never going to," Richard shook his head. "I'm going to find Lynn."

"Good luck."

Richard nodded and virtually ran from the alley in a further attempt to quash the agitation which left him so high-strung. He continued at this pace for some time, navigating the city as if it was the familiar streets of Myana. It was only after he paid attention to his surroundings that he decided to slow his pace to more of a walk, noticing the quizzical gazes focused on him from every direction. He also assumed that the guards would have still been looking for him and decided to reroute through the back streets.

The looks he received while traversing the back streets turned out to be just as distasteful as those he had received on the main streets. He kept his head down and forged ahead, avoiding eye contact as he made his way closer to the port, the sound of it already audible.

Even though he was avoiding eye contact, Richard couldn't help but feel like he was being watched. He took notice of shady clusters of individuals around every corner and even though none of them moved to approach him, he couldn't shake the feeling that every single group had their eyes trained on him as he passed.

One last alley, so narrow that only one person could fit through it at a time, and Richard made his way into the harbour. He was nearly killed by a wagon full of fish, its driver not interested in slowing down or swerving to avoid him, and then had to slide through a group of patrolling guards who, like most others, gazed leisurely at the foreigner moving so urgently through their city.

It's a port city. Don't they see enough foreigners?

Looking for a ship with Lynn had been an impossible task, mainly because they had no idea what they were looking for. Jiro's description had made his objective significantly easier, and he spotted the ship described to him less than a minute after emerging into the harbour. Three masts, five sails. Flying the unmissable Vivian flag, its red stripes a stark contrast against the cloudless blue sky.

Annoyingly, it was guarded, and not by those he would have fingered as criminals. They weren't unsimilar in appearance to the guards he would see prowling the streets of a typical Miradosi town in the way they were armoured and the standardised swords that hung from their belts. Badges affixed to their pauldrons betrayed them to be hired mercenaries, though they didn't appear to be ethnically Canarian.

Richard stepped to the side, evading another high-speed wagon, and mulled his options. He could only see two guards blockading the gangplank onto the ship, but there were plenty of city guards making the rounds. He decided as he approached them that violence would be unwise.

"Gentlemen," he said, climbing the stairs onto the jetty and extending his arms in greeting as if to an old friend.

The guards shot each other a dubious glance and did not respond.

"Did he not tell you? The captain, he forgot, didn't he? He always forgets, the brainless imbecile," Richard continued, maintaining his pace and stopping only once any further steps became impossible.

"Who are you?" the guard on the right, substantially taller than his counterpart, asked.

"What do you mean, who am I? Has the captain not mentioned me at all? The whole purpose of your trip was to collect me. I've been waiting for two weeks!"

In the corner of his eye, Richard spotted a black-clothed individual appear in a doorway leading to the lower decks. He didn't leave the doorway, instead leaning against the doorframe and training his gaze upon the bounty hunter as he continued his performance.

"Alright, gentlemen, let me make something clear," Richard lowered his voice, still acutely aware of the shady individual's surveillance. "I don't know what they're paying you, but whatever it is, you let me on this ship after that guy behind you disappears and I'll double it. No, don't look at him! Do you want to make it any more obvious? I'm not interested in the money—these people have wronged me. And I assume—"

The fist crashed into his face with such force that Richard was nearly launched into the harbour. He stumbled backwards and managed to steady himself as the second fist met the other side of his face and sent him spiralling to the floor.

Richard's reluctance to resort to violence evaporated as he rolled backwards to evade another hit and drew his sword, wishing longingly for a bow. The guards, instead of continuing their onslaught, chose to retreat onto the ship and call for help.

A scowl creased Richard's face as he leapt across the gap occupied moments beforehand by the gangplank, swiftly withdrawn by the guards in their retreat. They were outwardly surprised by the bounty hunter's agility and their eyes reflected apprehension as they readied their spears in defence.

Their defence was meaningless, Richard falling between their weapons after feinting a movement to the side. The bounty hunter used this crucial moment of deception to thrust his sword through the unguarded underside of the shorter guard's neck before pirouetting and grabbing hold of the shaft of the taller guard's spear. They struggled for control of the weapon, though Richard had never intended to take it. He manoeuvred the guard to the ship's side where he subsequently let go of the weapon, dropped to his knees, and mustered all his adrenaline-boosted strength to send the guard into the murky port waters.

The ensuing splash was enough to alert not just the rest of the ship's crew but also people milling around the harbourside—and amongst them, city guards. Richard contemplated lifting the anchor as a pair of guards rushed down the jetty and shouted to him to lower the gangplank in exchange for his life. He ultimately decided that it would take too long and that the guards would find a ladder before the ship drifted far enough away from the shore.

As he turned around with the intent to delve below deck, he found his path blocked by several people. All were dressed in dark clothes, wielding a diverse array of weapons but sharing the same unyielding, critical gaze. The bounty hunter knew that in standard, fair combat, he was easily outmatched. Except it was never fair combat, and though he hated to, he knew he could always rely on his trump card.

"El'kak favor," he uttered, with a gesture addressing each of his targets as they rushed at him in unison. And it was in unison that they froze. They could move nothing but their eyes and mouths and the confident, even cocky expressions borne only moments ago were replaced by hopeless fear.

"What have you done, wizard?" one of them hissed. "You cheat!"

"Where is the sorceress?"

"The who?"

Richard met the response with an unrestrained strike to the face. The man fell unconscious and Richard rubbed his knuckle as it joined his face in throbbing with hot pain.

"You!" He turned to another of the frozen assailants. "I'll try again. Where is the sorceress?"

"He'll kill us if we tell you," she grunted.

"I'll kill you if you don't," Richard spat back. "Think quickly as to who you're more interested in impressing. Oh, and if you're working for someone, you can tell me where they are, too. Go on, speak."

"I don't—"

She was silenced by Richard's left fist, not delivered with as much force as his right, but still more than enough to render her unconscious.

"One more time! Roll up, roll up! Which of you wants to tell me where I can find the sorceress and your boss? You can stop stalling for time because the guards are not getting onto this ship!"

To make his point clear, Richard left his captives and stood at the side of the ship where the city guards had returned with a ladder, which fell at his feet just as he arrived. They were about to clamber aboard as they looked up and laid eyes upon the bounty hunter, who grabbed the ladder and attempted to pull it aboard. They scrambled to contest the action and one of them was able to loosely clutch one of the bottom rungs as its base left the jetty. At first, Richard attempted to win the contest only through pure strength. But when it became evident that this would fail, he once again resorted to magic.

The ladder slipped from the guard's grasp, sailing into the air and disappearing somewhere out of sight alongside a loud crash and splintering. The guards immediately barked something about sorcery and took off back down the jetty, Richard turning around with an unamused expression to face his captives.

"Last chance. I don't want to be made to look for them."

"They're below deck. Flame, where else would they be?" someone snapped.

Richard hadn't seen the person who had spoken and so punished the captives equally. By the end of his fit of rage, his fists were red and he was surrounded by unconscious bodies. He released the effect of the spell as he slunk downstairs.

The passageways between the various cargo holds of the merchant vessel were themselves rammed almost to capacity with crates and sacks. Richard inspected several as he traipsed the quiet corridors and squeezed through narrow space after narrow space. He found all assortments of illicit goods—high-grade weapons, unidentifiable substances—as well as goods he thought seemed remarkably legal—expensive spices, exotic foods, rare dyes, to name a few. There were barrels filled to the brim with money, though not all Canarian—in fact, most of the currency Richard found was in the form of Sanskari pestas. There was a sack of Vivian crowns and, disappointingly, an even smaller sack of Miradosi rions.

At the end of one corridor, he twisted a door handle and was agitated to find the door wouldn't open in its entirety. Further pushing and shoving proved to be futile, so he rolled his eyes and squeezed painstakingly through the available gap.

The room into which he finally passed was yet another cargo hold, crates and barrels stacked to the ceiling. He didn't think it worth his time to paw through their contents as he had been doing, instead narrowing his focus to finding Lynn.

Traversal of the cargo hold was akin to gymnastics with how densely packed it was. Richard found himself on his knees, crawling through tight spaces, more often than on his feet.

She was there. Richard finally found an opening in the maze of containers and practically fell out of it when he saw her crumpled figure, lying in an open space carved from the rest of the cargo, her arms bound above her head to a wooden pole.

"Lynn!" he whispered sharply, regaining his composure and drawing his sword quietly. He darted his eyes around the empty space as he cut her free, her unconscious body falling the rest of the way to the floor.

Richard looked around once again, overcome with suspicion at the lack of resistance. He saw nothing which made him think anything was amiss. However, in his observations, he had neglected to look up.

A trapdoor fell open with a slight creak and Hada Jiro dropped through, brandishing a katana sheathed in a scabbard coated in gold decorations. Two more people landed gracefully beside him, converging on the bounty hunter as he stood up with the sorceress's body over his shoulders. Richard recognised them through their disguises.

"Jiro?" Richard asked, stepping backwards as Makoto un-clipped a steel bola from her belt and swung it over her head. Woven through the chain interconnecting its twin steel weights was a familiar root.

It hit him like a horse as it wrapped around his legs and there was nothing he could do to prevent his fall. One of the weights crashed into his right kneecap, the other into the back of his left knee. Lynn became a cushion as his legs gave way and it was Akira who then leapt onto him and shackled his wrists, kneeling on his back to prevent him from getting back up. It was an unnecessary gesture—the excruciating pain rip-pling from his knee told Richard that he wouldn't be standing up unassisted for some time.

"I didn't think it would be true. And given the ease of your capture, I'm still not sure it is," Jiro exclaimed. "You're a Fateborn? Really? And you did not detect my presence? Sure, you used some banal little hex to freeze my men on the deck. But you did not stop me in the time between that trapdoor opening and these two restraining you? There was ample time! They should have been turned to ash! What gives? Are you a fraud? A charlatan?"

"Why are you doing this?" Richard asked through gritted teeth.

"Why am I doing this? Money, Richard. Money. I'm sure Tregor Lopan would pay a lot of money for you. You know, he's made it a lifelong objective of his to gain control of some-one like you. You believed that little story about wanting to explore? Gullible. You're gullible, Richard, and you trust with-out apprehension. You've been manipulated before, haven't you? And you allowed yourself to be manipulated again. Trained by Kalahar. Who did he think he was training? A fool. That's the bottom line, Richard. You're a fool. It's a miracle you haven't been killed yet. It's an even greater miracle that you haven't fallen into the hands of the Council. Oh, you will be so very valuable. You and Lynn. Nendar will pay hand-somely for her, I'm sure."

"I wouldn't be so confident," Richard muttered.

"Wouldn't you?" Jiro crouched so that he and Richard could make eye contact. "Would you care to elaborate?"

"No."

Jiro looked up at Akira and nodded.

Richard winced as the bola was gently removed from his legs. Akira then brought his knee down like a hammer to meet the back of Richard's right knee. The ensuing pain was blinding and Richard felt on the verge of passing out. But he maintained consciousness, and with it, his resolve.

"There's no amount of pain you can inflict that will change anything," he rasped. "I've suffered a lot worse. I continue to suffer. Torture me, please. You'll achieve nothing."

"He's bluffing. Since when does anyone ask to be tortured?" Akira said.

Jiro paid no heed to his accomplice's comment, instead scrutinising Richard with an apprehensive stare. The bounty hunter met his gaze and maintained eye contact for a lengthy period of silence. Though they did not use words, they managed to communicate.

"Every man exists for something," Jiro finally stated. "Otherwise, what is the purpose? You would just kill yourself. So tell me, Richard. For what purpose do you keep yourself in life? If not for yourself, your own betterment and fulfilment, then for what? Or who? For her?" He pointed at Lynn. "Surely not. So tell me! Tell me why you carry on!"

Jiro paced across the empty space and looked idly askance at Makoto, when he was struck by inspiration.

"It's a girl, isn't it?"

Despite Richard's efforts, nothing could clear the sudden image of Linelle from his mind. And the sheen that decorated his eyes gave Jiro all the information he needed to know.

"I see how it is," he said. "Who is she, then? Because I could find her, if I wanted. I have people who speak Miradosi. They could find her, whoever she is. Or you could just cooperate."

"You won't find her," Richard said softly.

"Really? And why is that?"

The bounty hunter finally averted his eyes.

"Oh," Jiro said. "Oh, I understand. But at the same time, I don't. If she's dead, then why do you continue to fight for her? Is there something I'm missing? Please, provide me with something here. Otherwise we will just be forced to resort to pain. Okay, back to square one. Why wouldn't Tregor Lopan be interested in you when he has dedicated his life to it?"

"Because he already found me," Richard rasped. "And he let me go."

Jiro snorted and a disbelieving grin crossed his face. "I find that very hard to believe. There's not a soul to have walked the land more dedicated than Tregor. You're telling me he gave you up?"

"That's what I'm telling you. Take it as you will. Are we finished here?"

"Ah, no. I'm afraid not. Because you see, I'm afraid the market for mages is not quite so limited as one person. Don't worry—I'll still find buyers for the two of you. The Canarian daimyos are very generous—especially when it comes to sorceresses."

As if on cue, Lynn groaned, but did not stir. Richard gritted his teeth, struggling against Akira's weight on his back. Akira simply embedded his knee further into the bounty hunter's spine.

"Let him stand, Akira. He's powerless," Jiro ordered, and although he was no longer weighed down, he could not stand up. His arms shackled behind his back meant he had no means to even prop himself up, let alone lead him to his feet. And his knee was in total disagreement with any and all movement.

"Here's what's going to happen, Richard. I'm going to attempt to contact Tregor, just in case he does happen to have any lingering interest in you. If he does—great. He'll teleport here and hand over a tidy sum and we'll all go our separate ways. If not, Akira and Makoto are going to sail you to the capital, where you will be sold. From then on, you're not my problem. I don't want to see you ever again. If I do, I'll kill you. Are we clear?"

"Very clear," Richard spat.

"Wonderful. I won't be a moment."

Jiro leapt from the hold, easily vaulting the distance between the floor and the hatch with the assistance of a spell.

"You're good actors," the bounty hunter said, wishing to say anything to break the remaining tension. Akira and Makoto both trained their eyes on him with intensity as if he would disappear at a moment's notice. "Had me completely fooled. Really, it was good."

They didn't respond and Richard sighed, turning his head and resting it as he waited for Jiro to return. Some time later, he did, the grin present on his face implying Richard had been wrong.

"They were more than interested, as it happens," Jiro confirmed the bounty hunter's suspicions. "And they'll be arriving shortly. He and Nendar must return to Sanskar to gather the necessary funds. Congratulations, Richard. You're the most expensive person I've ever sold."

"I'm thrilled. Can you repair my knees now?"

"Tregor has supple knowledge of restorative magic, don't worry. As I've understood it, they're paying for Lynn, too, though they weren't really focused on her. Ah, but Richard. I'm afraid there is a little procedure that must take place. You're not to be delivered here anymore, so you need to be transported. If you allow me to cast a spell to put you to sleep, it will save both of us so much pain. Wouldn't you agree?"

Richard sighed once more and accepted the mage's gesture as he uttered the command word. It didn't take long to black out.

CHAPTER 25

FREE CITY OF DANNOS, SANTEROS

The decision to flee was not one Elton enjoyed taking, particularly given the fact that the frequency of his flights was already at a record level in recent times. But he had managed to reign supreme over the free city for a long time for the very reason that he was able to take decisions he disdained.

They didn't run, comfortable in the knowledge that they had a head start on their pursuers, who themselves didn't know where to look. This was a practice to which Paul and Felix were well accustomed. Elaine, however, was not afraid to exhibit her frustration.

"They aren't going to be walking, looking for us," she said. "They're going to be running. Why aren't we running? Or teleporting?"

"Do you listen to anything I say?" Elton snapped. "Your arrogance is remarkable for a newborn. It takes most at least a few years to get to be so insufferable."

"My point stands. Why don't we teleport away?"

"Because the entire populace is on the lookout for magic-wielding vampires? Do you think at all of the consequences of your actions? Because I suggest you start, or you won't last much longer. There's a reason humanity has spread so far and it's because despite our flaws, we're really a capable lot. So don't put yourself on too high a pedestal, because you'll just be knocked off of it."

As they reached the end of an alley leading into a busy road, Elton held his hand out to instruct his companions to stop. He cautiously stepped out into the street, scanning in every direction for signs of the thugs dispersed to find him. He saw none.

"I have a theory," he exclaimed, turning back to face the others. "But we're going to have to split up."

"Do you care to share?" Elaine raised a scornful eyebrow.

"There was a woman who I'm assuming to be their leader stood outside the Redhouse. And I'm almost certain she's a vampire. I want to speak to her."

"Are you out of your mind? She's a homicidal maniac," Felix blurted out. "She isn't a negotiator. That much was proved when she murdered Ferris."

"It's a front," Elton claimed. "She has to put on a strong appearance, otherwise her rot-brained followers will catch on to the fact that they, the do-gooding vampire hunters, are being led by a vampire themselves. But I know something that will undoubtedly scare her."

"Kalahar," Elaine mouthed.

Elton gave a slight affirmative nod and briefly considered the likelihood of his plan's success before issuing orders. He was counting on the hope that the woman he suspected of being a vampire would not react irrationally. He also hoped that she actually did share the other malevolents' insurmountable fear of Kalahar.

As he was thinking about the ways in which the plan could fail, a less diplomatic solution entered his mind. It took far less consideration than his previous idea.

"Paul, Felix, and I will hand ourselves in," Elton finally decreed. "We will refuse to speak to anyone but her. You two—go back and look after Rosa. If she wakes up, send her to us. Ant, Fez—you go find enough people to take back over the Redhouse once we're through with our job."

"What's to say this new woman isn't crazy like Hortensio?" Felix scrutinised.

"It's irrelevant. She won't be in charge for long."

"An old-fashioned plan, eh, boss?" Paul's eyes flashed with excitement.

"Indeed. But we need a few things first."

"And we're being put on babysitting duty?" Elaine complained. "Let us come with you. We'll be more use there than being sat around doing nothing."

"Our agreement was that we would protect you if you helped us. What do you think this woman will do if they see you? A pair of vampires? She's evidently more developed than you and would detect you immediately. And then kill you. Does that sound like protection?"

Elaine sighed. "We'll go back to look over Rosa."

"Good. Felix, Paul, let's go. First port of call—the market."

The group split up, Elaine and Caster hurrying back in the direction of Megaross Square, Ant and Fez towards the Redhouse. Elton, Felix, and Paul continued into the street and began the trek to Silverstone Square. The market in Megaross Square would have been undoubtedly larger, but Elton was confident he would find what he needed in Silverstone. It had become a common commodity in recent times.

"So, from what I've gathered, we are doing my plan after all," Felix commented as they arrived at the Square.

"In a sense," Elton admitted. "But with extra steps. You really think this vampire would let us walk in with weapons?"

"What, are you going to strangle her?"

"Very funny. Aha, look."

Elton pointed to a particular stall already entertaining a set of three customers, who rapidly concluded their business as they noticed Elton's approach. The merchant sitting behind the pop-up counter was unfazed, taking a swig from a tankard before standing to greet the trio.

"Regi Redwinter, in the flesh," he said. "I've heard you're in a spot o' bad luck."

"A slight disturbance. Soon to be dealt with." Elton pointed at a corked beaker half-filled with crimson liquid on a shelf behind the merchant. "That had better be real oil."

"Oh, this?" The merchant retrieved the beaker and swirled it around to demonstrate its viscosity. "Most definitely. It'd be 'ard to sell fake stuff. Wouldn't make much sense, either. It's cheap enough to get your 'ands on real stuff."

"How much?"

"For you, Regi? Let's say five marks."

Elton raised his eyebrows in pleased surprise as he fished the necessary coins from his pocket to pay the merchant. They then exchanged a smile, the merchant's significantly larger than Elton's.

"And how are you expecting to sneak that in?"

"Painfully. You'll see."

Equally easy to find as the oil was a stall selling silvered weapons. A blacksmith, one Elton recognised, had established himself near the centre of the square and was being flocked by the types not unlike those who had stormed the Redhouse. They were equipped with all manner of stereotypical vampire-hunting paraphernalia from stakes to garlic necklaces, although they were found alongside genuinely useful silver chains and flasks of oil.

"I'd be careful, here, boss," Felix warned. "I'm not sure—"

Elton extended his hands and thrust two people out of his way as he forged a path to the front of the crowd. The recognition was instant, as was the subsequent furore.

"It's the vampire lover!"

"What's that bastard doin' here?"

"Oi! Wait in the queue!"

The Count presented himself to the blacksmith, who diverted his attention from two brawny customers so hairy that Elton thought they could have been distantly related to bears. The customers also pivoted to face him, furrowing their enormous eyebrows and squinting with scrutiny.

"Count Redwinter. It's been a while," the blacksmith stood up and proffered his leathery hand, which Elton shook firmly.

"Xavier," Elton acknowledged. "I was hoping you had something quite particular."

"Why the fuck are you servin' this traitor? We ought to bash his skull in!" one of the brawny men interjected, scrunching his fists into balls. He and his partner stepped forwards to encroach upon the Count and it was then that Elton drew his dagger and brought it precisely to one of their throats. The other's squinted eyes expanded in shock and his arm moved to draw a sword from his belt, but he couldn't. Felix's knife flew, penetrating the fabric of his shirt and pinning him to a wooden post supporting the structure of Xavier's stall.

"I'm about to kill a vampire. The very one you rally behind," Elton hissed. "You and the idiots you associate with have forgotten whose city this is. Let me remind you—it's mine. And let me give you a reason not to forget."

Elton withdrew his dagger from the man's neck before driving it into his thigh. He howled in pain and his partner rushed forwards, tearing his shirt and reaching once again for his sword but once again failing. This time, Felix didn't aim only to immobilise.

The rest of the crowd seemed to thin as Felix's target fell dead, his blood spilling into the silver cobbles. The man Elton had stabbed in the thigh seemed to forget about his own wound as he fell to his knees over his partner, removing the bloodied knife from his face. His mouth hung open as Felix joined them to recover his weapons, retrieving a handkerchief from his pocket and cleaning them nonchalantly.

"That's the Regi Redwinter I know," Xavier exclaimed with a devious grin. "Now, you said you wanted something particular?"

"I need something small. Really small."

"Smaller than that?" The blacksmith pointed at Elton's dagger.

"Much smaller."

"I think I'm with you. I might have just what you need."

Xavier ventured to the back of his stall, opening a chest and rummaging around inside it amidst a symphony of metallic clattering and curses. Eventually, he exclaimed with glee and fished out an implement so small Elton wasn't sure he could label it a weapon.

"I know it doesn't look like much." Xavier brought the object into the light, and it appeared to be a shiv of sorts, though only the length of Elton's little finger. It also didn't look particularly sharp. "But it will do the trick. If you've managed to trick a vampire into getting close enough, it doesn't take all that much. Most folks don't go the stealthy route as I'm gathering that you are."

"You could have tried at least a little bit harder to retain its sharpness," Elton sighed, plucking the shiv from the blacksmith's fingers and lightly poking his finger with its point.

"Have you ever silvered any weapons? It's not that easy. The Thornish may make it look easy, but be assured, it isn't."

"I believe you," Elton lied. "How much for... this?"

"Ah, just have it. I was never going to sell it to anyone else. Just remember me kindly when it comes to missing taxes."

Elton nodded and gestured to Paul and Felix that they were departing. The crowd—many still focused on the fallen man and his partner—practically split to allow them to pass.

"Gotta say, boss, I was not expectin' that," Paul declared as they exited the square, walking in the direction of the Redhouse.

"How's that for gone soft, then?" Elton raised his voice, attracting the unwanted attention of startled passers-by. "You think people will have respect for me now? You think I'll finally get this rabble under control, now that I've made a bloody example of someone? What a farce."

"People need to fear you if they're going to obey you, boss," Felix said calmly.

"And what a ridiculous concept that is! What is it that people reject about true liberty? Why do they feel such a need to be oppressed?"

"People are stupid, boss."

By the time the trio arrived at the Redhouse, having successfully evaded the patrols ineffectively scouring the city, daylight was retreating. Elton held the shiv up to his face and grimaced. He then uncorked the beaker of oil and recoiled at its scent before pouring some into his mouth.

He nearly vomited as the alchemical concoction singed his gums but he forced himself to maintain his composure. He then inserted the shiv blade-first until its tip nearly grazed the back of his throat. His mouth was capable of closing, but the shiv's base scraped against the back of his teeth.

Paul and Felix had been informed of the plan, and they had at first reacted with ridicule before realising that Elton was entirely serious. And they accepted their roles without even the notion of protest.

The thugs guarding the entrance to the Redhouse reacted mostly with uncertain shock when the ousted Count was presented to them, arms held behind his back. They raised their pikes warily, as if unsure as to the reality of the situation. It was clear from their expressions that they recognised not just Elton but Felix and Paul, too—and Elton recognised them, too, as former grunts from the Syndicate.

"We got bored of serving a traitor," Felix explained. "But he's not in the mood to talk to anyone except your boss."

"I bet," one of the guards spat. "We'll take 'im from 'ere. And we'll make him speak, 'cause as it happens, he's not in fuckin' charge."

"He's our prisoner," Felix protested. "We will accompany him to your boss. The lady in charge. What's her name?"

"I don't think you understand how this works. You lot ain't in charge anymore. Hand 'im over."

The guard took two steps towards the trio and Felix took two of his own, grasping the handle of the guard's pike just beneath its head. He fought against it, but their strengths were similar enough to lock them into stalemate. The second guard stepped in and thrust his own pike directly at the defenceless Felix. Paul was quick enough to react, drawing his sword and parrying the blow before performing a half-turn and bringing his sword up to the guard's undefended neck.

"What's the meaning of this?" a woman's voice called from within the Redhouse. The source of this voice then made itself visible moments later, and Elton was face-to-face with the stone-faced figure of the presumed vampire.

"Ah, the boss," Felix exclaimed. "Our prisoner wants to speak with you. Privately."

"Elton Redwinter," the woman said, an unsettling smile adorning her face. "My name is Enya. It is most exciting to meet you at last."

Enya ignored her guards' plight and strode between them to greet Elton, extending a hand. Through the nausea endangering his consciousness, Elton somehow managed to meet her handshake, though any idea of firmness was fantasy.

Felix seemed to recognise the Count's weakness and let go of the pike, hopping out of range and moving to support him. Yet at the same time, he looked at Elton with an expression as if to implore him to strike. But Elton was not about to act so prematurely.

"Let them go, you two. Come inside, I insist. What exactly was it you wanted? Handing in your boss?"

"A reward would be nice," Paul said.

"Oh, you'll get a reward. A most generous one."

"What are you going to do with him?" Felix asked, flicking his eyes at Elton.

"I've devised quite the plan for Mr Redwinter here. Something spectacular. You won't want to miss it. Now, let's be heading inside, and I'll find you your reward. Oh—you'll need to leave your weapons, of course. Guards—pat them down."

The guards split themselves between Paul and Felix, confiscating their weapons and receiving stern warnings about their fates if any of Felix's knives were to go missing. Enya herself took Elton's dagger, exhaling a noise of approval as she cast her eyes over it in admiration.

The news of Elton's arrival had apparently taken no time to spread, as the lobby was swarming with thugs eager to catch a glimpse of the disgraced Count. Like the first guards they had encountered, Elton recognised many as having served in the Syndicate. It was they who shouted the loudest when the insults rained down.

"Traitor!"

"Kill the vampire-loving prick!"

The insults were then accompanied by various objects and Elton had to be very careful not to impale himself with the

shiv balanced so precariously across his tongue. That was no
easy task, as the nausea brought on by the oil's continued
presence in his mouth was only intensifying. And to make
him regret his plan further still, his head had begun to throb.

But he remained in control. Of the objects thrown, none
were particularly dangerous, rather they seemed to be items
the thugs had found around the Redhouse and saw no use for.
Enya was leading them away quickly enough that most
missed, and Felix and Paul were at the receiving end of the
few that did hit, forming a human shield at Elton's sides.

They eventually lost the crowd as Enya brought them
through the mostly empty intelligence office and then into
the director's office, where she twisted the handle to the door
and lightly pressed it open, seemingly for dramatic effect.

If Ferris's emaciated corpse had been an attempt to shock
them, it had failed. Elton didn't so much as blink, and only
Paul reacted with any kind of surprise, his jaw falling briefly
open. She had placed a chair on the table and hauled the
bard's body up onto it, contorting his hands to grip the dagger
protruding from his bloodied chest. Elton was certain he saw a
flicker of pride in Enya's expression as they laid eyes upon
him.

"I very much appreciated your friend's visit," she said. "He
was unfortunately smart enough not to rat you out, knowing
full well that he was going to die either way. Do you know
how embarrassing that is? That I sent out half of my followers
and yet not a single one found you? It took two of your own
yes-men to hand you in? I need to find new grunts..."

"So, about that reward..." Felix interjected. "I take it that's
coming out of the coffers you've just plundered?"

"But where else? Mr Redwinter left us such a fortune that it
would be wasteful not to use it."

"And what's stopping us from killing you now and retaking
control? You may have taken our weapons, but there are three
of us and only one of you. I feel as if the odds aren't in your
favour."

Enya smirked. "I can tell you categorically that they aren't.
You can't hurt me. Nobody can."

"Is that so? How, exactly?"

"That's our little secret. Now, Mr Redwinter, I truly was
hoping to speak with you and you've yet to utter a single
word. Please, indulge me. How do you want to die?"

Her question went in one ear and out of the other as all Elton could think of was the pounding in his head and the burning in his mouth. Felix was saying something to distract Enya, but Elton couldn't make out a single word. His grip on reality was faltering and there was no scenario in which he saw himself continuing to hold the liquid in his mouth. Part of him was disappointed that his plan hadn't taken place exactly as he had imagined. But the relief he felt as he sprayed oil over Enya's face after removing the shiv immeasurably counteracted any faint regret.

The effect was immediate, and the vampire screamed, her human façade crumbling as she clawed ferociously at her singed face. Two guards rushed into the room, swords at the ready, but they did not attack. They looked at the quivering vampire, understanding what had occurred, and then back off to allow Elton to pepper Enya's chest with stab wounds. The adrenaline rush had temporarily cleared his mind of nausea and all he saw was vengeance as he stabbed again and again and again. He didn't stop until the vampire's monstrous cries had been silenced and even after she had stopped moving, he stabbed her a few more times for good measure.

As the adrenaline cleared, he rose to his knees and looked at the mess of a body he had created before dropping the shiv and then rising further to his feet.

"You two," he growled at the two guards. "Let it be known that I am no traitor. And that anyone who accuses me of such will not be exiled but hanged publicly. This city belongs to me, and don't any of you forget it."

Their only response was a submissive bobbing of their heads as they dashed away. Paul and Felix gazed upon Elton with a sense of awe as he brought his breathing under control and was reminded of the vile tang of oil still permeating his mouth.

"One of you," he barked. "Get me a drink. A strong one."

*

Several shots of strong spirits had finally cleared the taste of oil from Elton's mouth, but a burning sensation remained. It was bearable, and as the Count assisted in the tidying of the former Syndicate headquarters, looking proudly over his returned employees, he knew without doubt that it was worth it.

"Back in business, then?" Fez said, appearing from a side corridor. "I've got something that'll probably make your day even better, boss. Those explosives? Turns out the supplier we found is able to provide them earlier than expected. They'll be delivered early next week, rather than at the end of it."

Elton stopped brushing and took a moment to process the news. Rosa remained out of action, but Caster was also capable of creating portals. Which meant that if Kalahar had been somehow aware of their plan, the explosives' expedited delivery gave them an element of surprise.

"Don't let anybody know about that," he said gravely, walking with Fez to the intelligence office. "The moment they arrive, we set off. We can waste no time and allow the information to leak."

"She's dead, then?" the familiar voice of Elaine rang out. "That's it? No struggle?"

"No, because I know what I'm doing." Elton looked expectantly between her and Caster, as it was clear from their expressions that they had something more to say.

"I heard it was rather ruthless. How many times did you stab her?" Elaine continued.

"Enough to make sure she didn't come back. I've fought a lot of vampires before. I'm not about to take any risks."

"I've heard that you're cracking down on vampires. Is that true?"

Elton narrowed his eyes as he held open the door to the intelligence office. "I'm cracking down on meaningless dissent. Now be quiet or you'll make people suspicious. You are safe. Our agreement still stands. As long as you continue to help me."

Elaine nodded contently and led Caster away, while Elton beckoned Fez to follow him into the director's office where they could converse in private.

"Shall I let our suppliers know to keep things on the down low?" Fez suggested.

"Yes. And get the guard on high alert. Even so much as a whiff of disruption to our plans and I want it snuffed. By any means necessary. Vampire-hunting vigilantes? Rounded up and put down. Vampires themselves? Likewise. Nothing is getting in my way this time. I'm going to kill Kalahar. And then I'm going to return and live out the rest of my days without having to deal with endless futile quarrels. Dannos will understand the meaning of order, now that they've brought it upon

themselves. No more exiles. I want at least five criminals publicly hanged. Daily. Guards are to randomly search anyone
who looks suspicious. Any large groupings are to be questioned. I want agents placed into known opposition groups to
gather intelligence, and then I want every member of said
groups to be killed, discreetly. Perhaps then—then we will see
order. Then I will be able to go even one day without having
to defend myself against something new."

"Right on, boss. I'll spread the word."

Fez left Elton to mull in silence, accompanied only by the
bloodstains the cleaners had been unable to completely erase.
His mind was preoccupied only by his desire to put an end to
Kalahar, and that remained the case for the following few agonisingly long days.

Rosa still slept as Ant and Fez arrived at the weekly meeting of the Dannosi Intelligence Service where Elton and Felix
were already present alongside several other officers. The
Count was brimming with excitement at the news he expected
to hear. But Ant and Fez had an entirely different message to
announce.

"The shipment has been intercepted," Ant said, uneasily
combing his hand through his hair and staring at the table.
"And diverted."

"What?" Elton slammed his fists against the table and rose
from his seat faster than he had ever risen from any seat. "By
who? Bandits? There was ample protection!"

"Not bandits, Count. Salyrian knights. Not only did they
confiscate the shipment, but they're on their way here."

"Again? Hortensio is dead, for fuck's sake! What grudge do
they still hold? This is finished!"

"That's the thing," Fez chimed in. "Hortensio should be
dead. But he's not. He's leading the charge."

CHAPTER 26

It had taken immense willpower to resist activating the talisman, but Elaeínn had persisted. Through the time they had spent finding somewhere clear to lower the anchor, unloading reams of cargo, and surveying the island, not a single moment had felt right. Though the urge remained stronger than ever.

"Well, then," Vanad began, overlooking the erection of a set of tents in the small area of flat stone they had managed to find some distance away from the ship. "Summon her. Do whatever it is you need to do."

"Oh, right, I forgot I could just 'summon' her. How easy do you think this is?" Elaeínn retorted. "She's an intelligent creature. As I said, I do not control her. I simply had the idea that she might appear to defend the Heart should it be threatened. It was a theory that might well be incorrect."

"Okay, then how do you suggest we threaten the Heart?"

"It would help to know where it is."

As if on cue, the pair were joined by the two men that had introduced themselves as Lorenzo Panam and Torellio Manz. There was something suspicious about them, and Elaeínn didn't trust them. Not least because of the fact that they were human.

"Torellio and Lorenzo know exactly where the Heart is," Vanad said. "They knew Ríyael. Are you two aware that the murderer of your friend is this young lady?"

Lorenzo looked concernedly at Elaeínn, who maintained a defiant composure, crossing her arms and straightening her posture. Though the Prime Minister's words about their connection to Kíra's killer had triggered alarm bells in her head, and she began to think very quickly about her next move.

"I was close with Rí. We both were. What would drive you to kill him? What could he have done to you?"

"As if you don't know," she seethed.

"She says she needs to know where the Heart is if we're to have any chance of summoning the dragon," Vanad interjected. "Would you be able to lead us to it?"

"But of course," Torellio said. "It's in plain sight."

He began to walk away, gesturing for the group to follow. They left the flat outcropping where the camp was coming together and precariously clambered down several sheer rock faces until they were almost at sea level, where the stone evened out once again and they came to face an arrangement of sharp boulders blocking their way. Torellio paced around the crevice in which they waited, casting a prospective gaze upon their obstacle, before ultimately deciding to close his eyes and mutter a spell, warding the others away.

The stone exploded from beneath the sorcerer's soft hands and he grunted as shards whizzed past his face, some making contact and leaving messy trails of blood in their wakes. He brought his hand to his face, smudging the seeping wounds, as Lorenzo pressed ahead through the open space. Elaeínn tailed him closely, keeping ample distance between herself and the Prime Minister while ensuring that she remained close to the front of the group.

The ground sank even further as they continued inwards, to the point where Elaeínn was certain they must have been standing beneath sea level. Their foray through the barrier of boulders had revealed a circular formation, seemingly unnatural in the fact that the ground was almost structured like sets of steep steps. At the bottom of the steps was an opening, water lapping over its edges. It couldn't have led to the open ocean.

"Is this it, humans?" Vanad increased his pace to stand next to the two human sorcerers as they peered eagerly into the watery abyss. Elaeínn did the same, but she could see nothing apart from impenetrable darkness and the occasional glimmer of light.

"It is," Lorenzo confirmed. "Now we require your men to dive in there and mine the crystal. Keep hacking away at it until the dragon has no choice but to appear."

"My men? You never told me my men were implicated in this plan of yours. I was under the impression you were going to be the ones mining the crystal."

"Look at us. Do we look like the types to be doing deep dives and manual labour? We're sorcerers. Not particularly athletic ones. This is a job for your deckhands."

"We don't have any pickaxes."

"Do you have any tools?"

"Weapons, mainly, but..."

"That will do. Bring all of your men and all of your tools. The Heart is some ways down."

Vanad furrowed his brow before issuing a curt command to one of the Grandmasters that had followed them to the opening. He departed and the group waited patiently, listening only to the gentle lapping of water from the hole and the squawking of seabirds overhead.

"Tell me about Ríyael," Elaeínn blurted out, approaching Torellio and Lorenzo as they stood apart from the elves. "I take it you're both on the Council? That's how you know him?"

"I'm sorry, girl, I don't know what you're talking about," Lorenzo said patronisingly.

"Bullshit!" Elaeínn retorted, feeling warmth flood into her face. "You let him keep my friend hostage in that hideaway of yours! You let him torture her until she couldn't go on!"

Torellio and Lorenzo feigned ignorance in their expressions, and Elaeínn became acutely aware of the attention focused on her at that moment as she stepped even closer to the two humans, bristling with fury.

"We knew Ríyael because he taught us the ways of magic. That is all he was—a teacher. One with whom we developed a close bond. If he was involved in something else, something more sinister, then he never told us."

"You're lying," Elaeínn hissed, lowering her voice and narrowing her eyes. "But so be it. If you refuse to tell me the truth, I'll found out another way."

She turned away and marched to stand on her own as the Grandmasters congregated around the humans and began to bombard them with questions of their own, though of an inquisitive nature rather than interrogatory.

When Vanad reappeared, this time accompanied by an entourage of uncertain sailors and deckhands, he himself bore an expression Elaeínn could only have described as angry confusion. He gestured for the workers to wait before dispersing the mages still crowding around the humans and engaging in hushed conversation. Judging by the look on his face and his body language, he wasn't content. About what, Elaeínn couldn't discern.

Before their conversation had concluded, a ginger-haired man dressed in black emerged from the opening in the boulder wall, trailed closely by a man with curly hickory hair and clad in a full suit of armour. Both were human, and they were also accompanied by a crew of their own.

Elaeínn stared with fierce curiosity at the ginger man and thought that she saw him nod subtly to Lorenzo and Torellio. She followed his gaze and caught the pair returning the same nod.

The talisman in her satchel felt extraordinarily heavy.

"So tu tzieje?" the armoured man huffed to his counterpart, more than loudly enough for everyone in the vicinity to hear. Not that it mattered, given the linguistic barriers between those present.

The response given by the ginger-haired man was much quieter, and although Elaeínn tried to read his lips, she could make out nothing. The armoured man backed away, evidently disgruntled as he found a position against the boulder wall where he could comfortably lean back and fold his arms. A scowl was the final accoutrement to his moody façade.

Shifting her focus back to the Prime Minister, it was clear that he himself was unsure of how to react to the sudden arrival. He maintained in his stance an aura of authority, but his eyes betrayed uncertainty as he wrapped up his conversation with Lorenzo and Torellio and began to order the workers into the water.

"It's freezing!" one shouted, withdrawing their foot from the still surface.

"And how long do you think we can hold our breath for? I can't even see what we're looking for!" another added.

Vanad said nothing, only looking to Lorenzo and Torellio with an expectant glower.

"You're elves, are you not? You surely can cast a spell so simple as insulation against the cold?" Lorenzo spoke, addressing the workers.

"If you want us jumping into the ocean, human, you can cast the spells yourself!"

"Cast the spells, gentlemen. That is our condition," Vanad affirmed.

Lorenzo sighed and stepped forwards, muttering words under his breath and gesticulating, going through each individual worker in turn. It did not go unnoticed by Elaeínn or any of the elven mages that he was able to cast these spells without tiring. Even the workers, many of whom—despite Lorenzo's reservations—were not experienced spellcasters, made idle comments about the fact.

"Any more complaints?" Lorenzo bellowed as he cast the final spell.

"Prime Minister, I must protest." One of the older members of the crew stepped away from the rest, ignoring Lorenzo's glare as he came to stand before Vanad. "We did not agree to this when we volunteered ourselves for this mission. We are not divers. We are not magicians. We're sailors. We aren't made for this and respectfully, you are sending us to our deaths."

Elaeínn wanted to break into applause but she stayed silent, as did everyone else. The workers seemed taken aback by their colleague's objection, many sharing worried glances between each other, as if expecting punishment.

Vanad looked at the ground as he stepped past the protestor before stopping and looking to those gathered around the cavity.

"You signed up to come on this expedition," he enunciated, spinning rapidly to face the protestor's back. "You signed up to serve your country and your people. The exact terms of that agreement were never something for you to decide. We have made an arrangement. Our guests have exerted themselves so that you will not freeze to death. Now get in that hole and start mining. Otherwise you'll not be coming back when we depart."

The protestor clenched his fists, inhaling sharply as the uncomfortable silence resumed. But his shoulders fell, his chest withdrew. And he joined his counterparts in resigning to their orders.

From all the mixed emotions spread across the workers' faces, one was clearly predominant—anger. Anger born of confusion over Vanad's perceived defence of the humans. There was no further protest, but the workers did not plunge into the watery void with grace. The water's surface briefly writhed as they made their way into the depths before settling back into a quiet stillness.

"You're the humans' dog now, Vanad?" Elaeínn provoked. "You make such a show of strength and you bow to their command? These people you've never met? What kind of leader are you?"

"You be careful, Elaeínn," Vanad rasped, settling his eyes upon her with ferocious intensity. "You're quite aware of how tenuous your position is."

"I'm quite aware of how essential I am, really. Don't pretend you don't need me to speak to Alazarioss. I'm your only hope to have any chance of wrestling control of her."

"The dragon is fallible. She has demonstrated that already. If you really cannot contain yourself, we will have to resort to force."

"It took you an army to take her down last time! What good would a misfit bunch of mages be? You'd be incinerated in moments!"

"I wouldn't be so certain," the Prime Minister said conclusively.

What's that supposed to mean?

It had been about three minutes since the sailors and deckhands had dived into the flooded cavity before the first of them returned for air. They clambered out of the hole to make room for others to escape before collapsing to the ground, splayed out as they fought for breath.

"Well?" Vanad asked, standing over them. "Did you find anything?"

One of the first workers to have returned slammed a hand against the ground and then raised it to reveal a large shard of purple crystal. The Prime Minister picked it up, eyes brimming with curiosity as he was joined by Lorenzo and Torellio.

"Mam tego dos che!" someone suddenly exclaimed, ripping the group's attention from the discovery. It was the curly-haired man who had arrived late, and his outburst was focused on his red-haired companion, who attempted to calm him with words spoken too quietly to be heard by Elaeínn. Whatever those words were, it became evident they hadn't worked when the man unsheathed his sword.

"What's going on?" Vanad demanded. "You! Get him under control, whoever he is! Whoever you are!"

"Kasimir!" Lorenzo called. "Deal with him! If you could not come to an arrangement then kill him!"

"Kasimir?" Elaeínn mused quietly. "That makes—"

She raced across the uneven terrain, closing the distance between her and the pair of human mages in a few leap-like strides. She drew her sword with grace, its blade shining a vibrant gold, and brought its tip to Lorenzo's throat. The elven mages retreated towards the back of the open circle, gasping and muttering with profuse uncertainty amongst themselves.

"Elaeínn!" Vanad roared. "What in Raeris's name are you doing? I knew you were uncontrollable but this is... have you no sense?"

"Don't move any closer!" Elaeínn screeched.

It only took the moment of distraction for Lorenzo to clench his fist and mutter a spell. Elaeínn's grip on her sword loosened involuntarily and the weapon clattered to the ground, the runes fading back to silver upon contact.

"Let me go!" She kicked her feet in the air indiscreetly, but the mage had already levitated her far enough that she could cause no harm.

"Can you feel that, Tregor?" Lorenzo said to Torellio. "I feel a great magical presence approaching our position. It looks as if we no longer need the girl to lure her here."

"What? You need me! She won't talk to any of you!"

"It would appear that way, Nendar. Would you like the honours, or should I? Or you, Mr Vanad? She's *your* public enemy number one."

Elaeínn stopped flailing and craned her neck to look down upon the Prime Minister, who looked very small from where she was floating.

"Drajza!" the armoured man cried, and Elaeínn had a bird's eye view as he was backed into a wall by Kasimir, who held a translucent black blade in his hands.

"Bring her down," Vanad said, having never taken his eyes from her. "I have wanted to do this for a long time."

Elaeínn squirmed against the magical force as it lowered her, slowly, dramatically, until she was freed. It was at that point that she reached her hand into her satchel and drew out the talisman, holding it in the air and calling the activation word she had been taught by Zanvía.

Nothing happened.

Elaeínn looked at the silver device with sickening realisation.

It's magical, she thought. *It was never going to work.*

A thunderous roar rocked the island as Alazarioss's shadow cloaked the pit in darkness.

"Kill her, elf!" Tregor barked. "If you want to capture this dragon, kill her!"

Vanad picked up the Dragonsteel Blade, admiring its runes despite the urgency of the situation.

"Hurry yourself!"

Alazaríoss! Elaeínn thought. *Help me!*

The Prime Minister drew his arm back and Elaeínn tried to run. Tregor flicked his wrist and she fell, her chin smashing against the ground. Pain rippled through her skull and she twisted to see Vanad as he launched his arm forwards to finish her.

The blade never found its intended target. Instead, it clanged feebly off the ice-white scales of the dragon.

Vanad froze. Alazaríoss was not concerned with the efforts of the three human mages as they abandoned him, regrouping and beginning to chant a spell.

"This isn't how it was supposed to go," he mused, Alazaríoss having lowered her head to be level with him. "We've been—"

Alazaríoss opted for a more brutal method than her usual torrent of flame. Her claw reduced the Prime Minister to a bloody pulp in one stroke, splattering his fragmented body across the boulder wall.

Elaeínn felt triumphant. She and the dragon both turned their attention to Tregor, Nendar, and Kasimir, still entrenched in an incantation. The elven mages had disappeared within moments of Vanad's death, as had the man who had accompanied Kasimir.

You. You all wield corrupted magic, Alazaríoss spoke telepathically, narrowing her reptilian pupils. The mages were not broken from their trance.

A rumbling resonated from the dragon's stomach through the air and the stone as she prepared to engulf the trio in flame.

Tregor's eyes opened, and they glowed the same purple as the crystals from which he drew his power.

"Your mind is my mind, dragon!" he cried, his voice echoed by a ghostly whispering. He then pulled the shard of lirenium, still resting at the edge of the water, to him. "Magic cannot be created, but it can be destroyed!"

Alazaríoss's mouth opened as he finished the incantation.

"Hri'tash keh'lak grev'az! Vil tak po'lash mri'ake! Danakh kri'gash! Akhlak!"

Through the stream of flame, scorching the stone on which they stood, charring the boulder wall a deep black, there was a light. A light which shined brightly enough that it penetrated the torrent. A light so bright that Elaeínn was forced to avert her eyes.

The light then disappeared as the crater was rocked by a sound like an explosion. Alazarioss reared her head back, roaring, and the trio reappeared amongst the ashes, unscathed.

"Alazarioss?" Elaeínn stepped back, her triumph shattered. She looked around for shelter as the dragon thrashed wildly, heavy limbs flailing. Tregor, however, was more confident than ever. He took precise steps towards the dragon, dodging each of her blows before they arrived. She wasn't defending herself—she couldn't.

"Succumb to my command, dragon!" he cried, though his voice was hardly audible over Alazarioss's pained screams.

Elaeínn's eyes searched the barren crater for the Dragonsteel Blade. She found it still in Vanad's grip, or rather in the grip of his severed arm. Pressing herself against the wall, she edged closer and closer, keeping her eyes trained on the dragon as well as the sorcerers. When she reached the sword, she crouched down slowly to pick it up, the runes lighting up just as she caressed its golden hilt.

"Tarimaji! Ale zosta rudejo pri zatya!"

The armoured man reappeared from the gap in the boulder wall, this time accompanied by an entirely separate crew of human sailors and deckhands. His face burned with fury and in his arms he carried a long crate which he set down before drawing his sword.

Elaeínn and the human crew converged on the sorcerers as one, an alliance formed without words. She led the group as they charged, her focus falling upon Tregor.

"Tregor!" Nendar shouted. "Finish it!"

Elaeínn burst through Nendar and Kasimir, uninterested. She left them for the humans.

"Tregor!" Kasimir echoed.

Tregor's hand finally touched Alazarioss's neck and the flailing stopped.

The air fell silent—or at least, that's how it felt when the incessant roaring came to a halt. Elaínn's blade swung to slice the lead sorcerer in two, but he materialised a blade of his own with just enough time to deflect. He then pirouetted, planted his heels and attacked Elaeínn with all the pent-up energy he had left from channelling into his assault on the dragon. His blows came fast and hard and without the unnatural dexterity Elaeínn found with the Dragonsteel Blade in her grip, she would have been reduced to pieces in moments. But her sword moved almost without thought.

Alazarioss crashed into the crater, her eyes falling shut, as Elaeínn and Tregor fell into performance. She saw nobody but him as light clashed with shadow. As their weapons met they did not clang, they sang. For Elaeínn it was a song of un-yielding duty against motives she could not understand, but she knew were wrong. She had fought people she knew to be wrong in the past, but this felt different. It felt sinister.

Despite her efforts and her courage, it had never been an even fight. Tregor still pulsed with magical energy and he did not seem to tire. Elaeínn, however, was steadily succumbing to biology. Her chest was sore from panting and each time she raised her sword to block Tregor's strikes her muscles pulsed with pain. Parrying was out of the question, as was counterat-tacking. It was now just a desperate struggle for survival—one that she knew she was losing.

Tregor seemed to understand this and his already rapid at-tacks came faster and faster. Elaeínn fell to the ground, hold-ing her sword across her body with the little energy she had left. The runes which had glowed so vibrantly faded to a dull brass.

Her sword was knocked from her grip and she exhaled a sigh of defeat, but for the second time that day a killing blow was blocked in the nick of time.

One of the human deckhands extended their sword to cross paths with Tregor's conjuration. Elaeínn did not move, immobilised by a combination of exhaustion and shock. Tregor looked at the man with clear contempt and lashed out at him, expecting to fell him quickly. That was not the case.

Instead, the man moved his sword as if it was weightless. As they began to duel, the sailor met, and even exceeded, the speed of Tregor's movements. Elaeínn sat up, for the first time taking in the chaos that had been inflicted around her. Many of the humans had been slaughtered, their bodies lacer-ated, blood streaming down into the flooded cavern. Nendar and Kasimir were not standing. Instead, they lay flat on the ground, not dead, but seemingly restrained. The same was the case for the armoured man.

The duel continued and, just as there had been while Elaeínn was fighting, there was a clear power imbalance. But this time, it was Tregor who was weaker.

"Bastard vampire!" Tregor roared. "Why must you always ruin everything?"

Elaeínn blinked and the sailor's eyes shifted from an unremarkable green to a deep ruby-red.

"Ruin everything?" the sailor spoke. "No, Tregor, you're terribly mistaken. It is you and your Council who always ruin everything. I aim only to improve. Come, you surely did not think I would ignore this plan of yours? Take control of a dragon? Does that really sound like something that can be glossed over?"

"How did you find out?" Tregor seethed.

Through the constant clashing of steel and the inhumanely quick motions, Kalahar managed to find the time to perceptibly shrug. All the while, his skin shifted from tan to a stony grey, his hair to jet-black.

"I will not let you have this! I have worked for far too long to let this opportunity slip away!" Tregor panted.

"Tregor, you know I have the power to end this fight at a moment's notice. I'm giving you the chance to escape before I kill you. I suggest you take it."

The fighting stopped and the vampire held his sword across his body defensively. Tregor hunched forwards, drawing in deep, sharp breaths. But then he looked up and muttered a spell, dispersing his conjured blade.

"You aren't going to kill me, Kalahar," he said confidently. "If you were, you would have done it already. What's stopping you?"

He raised his arms to his sides, nodding at his own chest.

"Do it. Kill me. I'm not resisting."

Kalahar strode past the sorcerer, making sure to collide with him as he did so. He stopped as he came to stand between Kasimir and Nendar, suggestively flitting his eyes back and forth, before looking at his sword and plunging it into Kasimir's chest.

Whatever spell the vampire had cast on the helpless sorcerer prevented him from even gasping as the blade penetrated his heart. Kalahar did not immediately withdraw it, instead maintaining a firm grip on its hilt and craning his neck slowly to peer down at Nendar, before finally refocusing his sights on Tregor.

"Get out of here, Tregor," Kalahar seethed, and his voice was ethereal. Elaeínn heard it in her head, all around her.

Tregor stood still, motionless apart from the agitated rising and falling of his shoulders. He refused to quench the vampire's thirst for dialogue.

"Release Nendar," he rasped.

"But of course," Kalahar agreed. "I still need him, after all."

Kalahar flicked his wrist and whispered a command which allowed Nendar to stand. The sorcerer did not wait before making use of his regained capacity for movement, making an immediate dash towards the still-restrained Kasimir.

"Leave him, Nendar."

Nendar looked up and was surprised to see it wasn't Kalahar, but Tregor who had issued the command. He glanced scathingly at the vampire who in his limited expression was perfectly able to appear smug.

Kasimir's eyes, the only part of his body not completely frozen, were beset with sadness and betrayal as Nendar sheepishly walked away to join his ally. But they soon glazed over as Kalahar finally retracted the blade and allowed him to bleed out.

"Elaeínn. That is how you pronounce it, isn't it? Oh, of course it is, I haven't forgotten," the vampire droned cheerily, not caring to watch as Tregor and Nendar disappeared through a portal. Instead, he released the armoured man from his magical restraint and cast his eyes up and down his body as he pressed himself up from the floor.

"What do you want?" Elaeínn glowered. The vampire had not attacked her or even shown so much as a hint of aggression, but still she could not shake the deep sense of unease she felt every time they spoke.

"Oh, it's good to see you again, too! Such hostility, such hostility!" Kalahar reached out an arm to encompass her shoulder, a gesture she fiercely rejected. "Such hostility. And for what?"

"What do you want?" Elaeínn repeated, enunciating each syllable.

"A chat, my dear, only a chat. A chat about what I intend to do with your dragon. But before that, how would you like to witness a resurrection?"

The armoured man had nearly escaped the boulder wall but he stopped upon hearing Kalahar, having raised his voice at the end of the sentence.

"What's your plan this time, vampire?" he called. "You've clearly begun your spellcasting nonsense. Can they understand me?" He gestured to the human and elven workers peering through the break in the boulder wall.

"No. I'm not interested in them," Kalahar answered. "But I am interested in you, Sir Jannis. Or rather, General Jannis. Although, both are technically correct, aren't they? But you prefer General?"

"You can call me General," General Jannis growled.

"That's beside the point. What's more to the point is that you came to this island for a reason. Do you happen to have that reason with you?"

"You just executed the man who was supposed to resurrect my king. How am I meant to trust you? Not to mention the fact that you're a bastard monster. You think I've forgotten your affiliation with Elton Redwinter?"

"It would appear to me your mage is indisposed. If you want Hortensio brought back to life, you'll need me. I do have a condition, but I'm sure it's one you'll appreciate."

"A condition," Jannis repeated sarcastically.

"You appear to have given up on Elton. My condition is as such—you stop giving up. You will go back to Dannos and this time you will not fail as you have already done. You will kill him. And all his associates."

Elaeínn saw the flicker of a smirk cross Jannis's face.

"No funny business, vampire," he said. "You lot—go back to the ship. Stay there."

The humans saluted and withdrew while Jannis removed the lid of the long crate left miraculously unscathed over the course of the battle.

"Very well," Kalahar said. "We shall begin."

The vampire reached into Kasimir's bloodied robes and drew out a single lirenium crystal, inspecting it between his thumb and index finger.

"He's a resilient soul, your king," he mused, still focused on the crystal. "I mean that quite literally. I can feel his urge to escape this terrible prison. He wishes for nothing more."

"Do you want me to unwrap him?"

"Please."

Jannis kneeled, bowing his head as he carefully removed the cloth wrapped tightly around Hortensio's emaciated corpse. He was in very much the same condition as when he had died, complete with the same black streaks running through his veins.

"Vile, reprehensible magic," Kalahar commented. "I will make this quick, for he will feel great pain. Terrible pain."

Elaeínn shivered as Kalahar lowered himself to his knees, a breeze sweeping over the boulder wall and toying with her hair. She moved to stand next to Jannis, and they shared an apprehensive glance as the vampire began to whisper an incantation.

"Fil'kazash il'drakh'dar ka'vosh... pri'gath tor'kash ka'vosh... vos vakh dal'krakh..."

The crystal laying at Kalahar's knees, equidistant between him and Hortensio, began to glow a vibrant white.

"Fi'kak valakh ti'raz... grev'az ri'takh..."

Hortensio's corpse lifted into the air, stopping to hover about a metre above the ground.

"Salakk pa'rosh! Ri'gash va'laz!"

Light poured from the lirenium into the corpse, taking the form of animated threads as they shot through the air and wrapped around it. A dull humming emanated from the crystal as its light diminished and then Kalahar placed his hands on the King's body. Elaeínn watched the blackness clear slowly as it battled against the light, meandering effortlessly through his veins. He rose higher, now above Elaeínn's head, and Kalahar had to levitate himself to maintain physical contact.

"Maranakk val'gash! Kan'dakh'revaz!"

Hortensio's eyelids opened not with the gradual pace at which his veins had cleared but immediately, like an animal in flight. He sucked in a deep breath, and then he fell.

"My king!" Jannis exclaimed, rushing forwards as the crystal erupted into what must have been millions of microscopic pieces. It didn't sound much louder than the cracking of a window and so went unheard by the General, obsessing over the King as he found his footing on his own.

"Yes, it's beautiful. I expect you to fulfil the condition promptly, of course," Kalahar said.

The blond-haired man, dressed as if attending a ball, blinked and raised a hand over his eyes as if staring into the sun. He scrutinised the vampire before standing up with a groan and took several weary steps backwards, practically carried by Jannis.

"So sie tutaj vidzylo" he mused. "Gdjest Penelope?"

"Mind you, his memories obviously stopped at the time of death," Kalahar explained. "You will have to tell him everything that's happened. There will be some... hmm... growing pains as he eases himself back into the world of the living. But now, lady and gentlemen! For the final act! Please turn your collective attention to this magnificent beast we have slumbering over here!"

Kalahar walked with such dramatic strides to stand in front of the dragon's face that it could almost have been described as goose-stepping. He slicked back his hair and straightened his clothes as if preparing to give a speech for an important audience.

The wind picked up and Elaeínn shivered once again, grey clouds rolling in overhead to accentuate the loss of warmth. She stood bewildered, numb, paying more attention to the resurrected human than Kalahar as he returned his hands to Alazarioss's scales.

"Please, this really requires your full attention! What I'm about to do here is not a spectacle to be missed."

Finally, Elaeínn shook herself out of her stupor in time to watch the first of Alazarioss's muscles twitch as Kalahar muttered another incantation, too quietly for anyone to hear. It was only subtle, a leg muscle, and then it was a wing, her nostrils flared, her tail jolted. And then she opened her eyes.

What had always been a vibrant turquoise instead glowed red. The exact same hue as those of the vampire which stood before them, the vampire which looked at the dragon and chuckled. A chuckle which turned into light laughter before progressing into an outright guffaw. He cackled maniacally, unrestrictedly, as Alazarioss rediscovered the use of her limbs and soared into the air. Tendrils of lightning lit up the clouds behind her, followed shortly thereafter by the accompanying crack of thunder. She roared, and it sounded deeper than usual, ominously so.

"What have you done?" Elaeínn asked. She wasn't sure what to think. She was so cold and exhausted and confused and she could focus on nothing other than the vampire as he began to calm down. "What have you done?"

"The beginning of a new era, Elaeínn," he said. "With the might of the dragon on my side, finally I will be able to achieve my goals without being thwarted by pitiful, meaningless humans. I will finally be able to prove my power. He will have no doubts about joining me. And then I will shape this domain into my image."

"Who will have no doubts?"

"I used to be careful about my words. But I don't care anymore. I have control over one of the most ancient beasts this world has ever seen. A very piece of the magic which flows through anything and everything. With magic on my side, nobody will be able to stand in my way. Nobody."

"Alazarioss! What has he done to you?"

The dragon did not respond. She only fell from the sky, gracefully, landing back behind the vampire and narrowing her pupils as she laid eyes upon her former rider.

"What I've done, Elaeínn, is turned her to my side. I've bent her will. Hijacked the spell that Tregor and Nendar so carefully crafted so that she now serves me. A snap of my fingers and I could have you turned to ash," Kalahar answered in her stead.

"You're evil," Elaeínn hissed. "Free her."

"Evil?" Kalahar's jaw dropped, though Elaeínn recognised his sarcasm. "What exactly about my behaviour is evil, Elaeínn? Evil is acting with a complete lack of direction. It's having no goal, nothing for which to strive. It's acting without reason. Me, Elaeínn? I am not acting without reason. I have very clearly defined goals. And I am taking the necessary steps to achieve them. I am not evil, Elaeínn. We simply hold differing points of view."

The vampire evaporated into a mist and travelled against the wind to land upon Alazarioss's back, where he transformed back into his usual form.

"Go back and fight your little war, Elaeínn. These affairs in which I'm involved? They don't concern you. I suggest you resign yourself back to lands of the elves and dwarves and don't even think about interfering. Because if you do then I won't hesitate to make your own dragon kill you.

"Now, I must be leaving. There's someone who needs my help. Goodbye, Elaeínn. Hortensio, Jannis. The sooner Elton dies, the better."

Kalahar uttered a command word to Alazarioss and they lifted into the air, the gales generated by the dragon's wings nearly sending the three left on the ground to their feet. And then they soared into the clouds, Alazarioss letting out one last roar as they disappeared.

"Come with us, elf."

Jannis's words shook Elaeínn from a trance into which she didn't realise she had fallen. She once again felt the wind as it lashed her bare face, felt the rain as it began to fall.

"Come with us. Your comrades will have long sailed off without you. And unless you can open a portal like our dearly departed friend over here"—he gestured meekly to Kasimir's mutilated corpse—"you've not got much in the way of choice."

Elaeínn walked across the crater and stopped at the mangled remains of Vanad's body. She kneeled down and fished through his robes, ignoring the blood as it painted her hands red, and found what she was looking for.

"Well, elf? My offer is not going to stand indefinitely. My king needs to see a medic."

The crystal was uninspiring. It didn't glow like that which had penetrated the dragon's flame only minutes before. It remained a dull purple. Elaeínn felt no great sense of relief when she tossed it into the water. Neither for it, nor any of the others she found in the fallen elf's possession. She felt no pride in looting the dead, especially those she had not defeated herself.

What she did feel was a renewed sense of urgency. To finish the mission that she had promised the dragon months ago. To find Tregor and Nendar, and bring an end to the Council. As well as a new objective.

"Last chance, elf. Either come with us or you'll be stuck on this rock until the gulls pick your bones clean."

Elaeínn found her sword teetering on the edge of the water. She picked it up, looking dejectedly at the runes. They did not glow gold. They glowed red.

CHAPTER 27

"You know what we have to do, Tregor. We have to kill him. Before the vampire gets to him."

"The vampire has a dragon now. We would be better off going into hiding. It's just us now, Nendar. We are all that's left of the Council. If we have any hope to rebuild, we must bide our time."

"And watch the world burn? I can't. And let's not forget the fact that I am still the sovereign of the largest empire in the known world. We're too important to disappear. We just can't."

"And if we're hunted down and exterminated? Then what? Then your precious empire will collapse anyways, because you won't even be able to orchestrate it from the shadows. Kalahar, whatever his indiscernible goals may be, will have free reign to do whatever he pleases, with the Fateborn at his command. He has outwitted us all. Not just us on the Council. He has seduced and tricked the Fateborn. He's destabilised the politics of an entire continent. The current order is fragile. The only way we are to survive it is by hiding."

"Or by killing the Fateborn. He is still naïve, foolhardy, headstrong. His pride still holds him back. Which is why we must put an end to him now, while he is still vulnerable. Before Kalahar corrupts him beyond return."

"He's lost in the largest forest in all Valoria. We wouldn't be able to find him, even if we wanted to."

Tregor suddenly furrowed his brow and fished into his pocket, revealing a decorated silver looking glass no larger than his hand.

"Es tar, galar," he said confusedly.

The mirror's reflective surface faded, mist pouring from its centre and revolving around its edge as the image of a man began to assemble.

"Hada Jiro?" Tregor gasped.

"Greetings, old friend. I'm impressed I was able to actually make contact with you. How are things?"

"There must be a rather important reason for you to be reaching out to me after all this time, Jiro," Tregor said sharply. "Let's not obsess with formalities. What do you want?"

"I have an offer for you. Are you still looking for a Child of Fate?"

Tregor looked up at Nendar, both of them struck with alarm.

"I happen to have come across one. As well as another sorceress who came with him. I'm looking to sell. Are you looking to buy?"

"Where are you, Jiro? How did you find him?"

"Wandering around my territory. The details really don't matter, do they? I have him. At least, I'm almost certain it's him. Lean build, longish brown hair? Reclusively quiet, seemingly miserable? I haven't got the wrong person, have I?"

"Are you in Nakada?" The alarm initially inflicted upon the pair quickly developed into paranoia. "We will be there shortly. How much money do you want?"

"No haggling? Fine by me. Do you want to pay in rin or pestas? I would prefer pestas, actually."

"Pestas, Jiro! How much?"

"Fifty thousand."

Tregor and Nendar glanced at each other and Nendar nodded without hesitation.

"We'll do it. Where in Nakada?"

"My men will be on the lookout for you. They'll take you there, so don't be alarmed when you're approached. I'll be seeing you. Es tar, closs."

CHAPTER 28

When Richard awoke, he was back in the open-air room with the retractable walls where he had first met Hada Jiro. Except it wasn't very open to him, as he was chained to the one wall which hadn't been retracted.

"Ah, you're awake," Jiro commented without turning around. Richard hadn't noticed he was there—the sorcerer was kneeling on the cushion at the centre of the room, completely still. "You'll be glad to know your buyers are on their way. My men are just collecting them. And then you'll be out of my hair."

"Oh, I can't wait," Richard muttered.

He heard Lynn stir next to him and awkwardly shuffled to face her, fighting fiercely against his shackles. The struggle only reminded him of the pain emanating from his knees, or rather his right knee, and he attempted to lay it still, gritting his teeth. Lynn looked up and glanced dazedly around the room before pulling on her own shackles and swearing.

"Where are we, Richard?" she whispered angrily.

"At your father's mercy."

"Father? That would make you Nendar's daughter?" Jiro interrupted. "Fascinating. Now keep it down, if you would. I'm trying to meditate."

"How do we get out of this?" Lynn continued through pursed lips. "You're the Fateborn. Where's your limitless power when we need it?"

"I detest that title and I'd rather you didn't address me with it."

"Cry me a river. Can you get us out of here or not?"

Richard used his eyes to bring her attention to the hevula-laced shackles attaching them to the wall and then shot her a glance as if to say, "You're joking."

"They use this for normal magicians. You're not normal, Richard. Surely you can transcend it?"

"In all aspects, I feel like a 'normal magician'. The only time I've ever performed anything spectacular was my little incident a few months back. And that was unintentional. If I ever think about trying to do anything like that, I can't. It's not that easy."

"Normal magician... I saw you tear open rifts through space and time without breaking a sweat. You saw me and Val attempting the same and failing. Richard, you're anything but a normal magician, and that's why my father and Tregor are so afraid of you. They're terrified of what will happen if you side with Kalahar, because they know that you have the potential to destroy the world at the snap of your fingers."

"I'm not going to be doing that, though, am I," Richard muttered.

Creaks echoing up the stairs indicated that their buyers had arrived, and moments later, they were there. Led by Akira and trailed by Makoto, a disarmed Tregor Lopan and Nendar Varanus between them. As they came onto the open floor, both stared like snakes at Richard, and Lynn snorted in amusement.

"Was the payment correct?" Jiro said, rising from the cushion and turning to face the newcomers.

"Yes, boss," Akira confirmed. "Everything was there. A little bit extra, even."

"And that's for you to keep, Jiro. As a gesture of our goodwill," Tregor declared. "Now, we really must make haste. We need to take him as soon as possible."

"And her, yes? Of course, you can leave her with me if you'd prefer. I'm curious, as well—what's the rush?"

"We're racing against Kalahar. He wants to take the Fateborn for himself."

"It's a race you'll never win," Richard droned. "And whatever it is you want to do with me, you know I'll never succumb."

"You'll succumb or you'll die," Tregor snarled. "We won't allow you to fall into the vampire's clutches, Fateborn. You will let us convert you, or we will kill you. You have no other choice."

The shiver that ran down Richard's spine was not natural. Nor was it a result of Tregor's attempted intimidation, which the bounty hunter largely ignored. It heralded to him that he was finally nearing the end of his long journey.

A deep rumbling rocked the atmosphere, creaks rippling through the wooden panels of Jiro's temple. The sorcerers looked out towards the ocean, where a bright white spot stood out against the dreary grey backdrop. Another rumbling, this time with an accompanying roar, and the sorcerers shot each other worried glances. Richard grinned with anticipation.

"It's surely not the dragon," Tregor murmured. "Why would the elf come here?"

"I'm sorry—dragon?" Jiro interjected.

"It's not the elf," Richard spoke softly.

The dragon had flown close enough that its features were visually distinguishable, and as it let out one last screeching roar, it turned to look at Jiro's temple—specifically, the open-air floor on which the sorcerers and prisoners were situated. Its eyes, as red and vibrant as sparkling rubies, were beacons against the cloudy backdrop.

"Jiro! Unlatch him from the wall!" Tregor shouted, his face ripe with raw anger.

Jiro gestured to Akira and Makoto, who fumbled with a set of keys and released first Lynn, and then Richard. Both still had their hands bound behind their backs, but they were finally free to stand up, though Richard opted not to, and Lynn couldn't. Nendar traced a portal and thrust his palms forwards as the dragon drew closer and closer, though its rider was still too far away for their identity to be confirmed.

"It's really a dragon," Jiro mused, before raising his voice. "You've brought a bloody dragon to my city!"

Richard chuckled as Nendar attempted to drag him towards the portal, an image of the room from the tower in the dryad forest visible. He resisted the Emperor's movements, who responded by attempting to use magic to force him through the portal. Richard found a purchase on one of the floorboards and managed to resist this, too, until Tregor stepped in to help Nendar by stamping on the bounty hunter's fingers. Sharp pain coerced him to instinctually draw his fingers back, and he had to grit his teeth to prevent himself from crying out.

He kicked his legs in a fierce final attempt to stop the sorcerers from abducting him once again, an action which made his knee feel as if it had been set aflame, and Nendar brought his boot down on Richard's left ankle before abruptly kicking his right. He felt a snap at some point, accompanied by the expected eruption of pain.

Nendar roared with the effort of dragging the unwilling bounty hunter through the portal and pulled one last time. Richard moved far enough to have gone through, except for one inhibitory fact. The portal had closed.

As the dragon reached the tower, she performed a sharp ninety-degree turn upwards, sending a gale-force gust through the room and knocking those still standing to their knees. As she disappeared, so did the portal with her, and standing behind what had previously been the opening to the tower in the forest was instead the familiar figure of Kalahar Kefrein-Lazalar.

The vampire waited for the sorcerers to stand before speaking. Richard, convinced he had broken several bones, laughed through the excruciation.

"Hada Jiro. I have business with these two," Kalahar said modestly. "I offer you the opportunity to vacate the premises—actually, just this floor—with your associates there. I won't make a mess, be assured."

"You stay right there, Jiro," Tregor snarled. "You're a part of this now, whether you like it or not."

"I don't know, Tregor, it doesn't sound like I am," Jiro responded, holding his hands behind his back. "It sounds like the vampire is offering me a route out. Out of curiosity, vampire—what do you plan for them?"

"I'll leave that up to your imagination. But you will be safe. My dragon won't touch your city."

Jiro crouched down to retrieve the sword which had blown from its position in front of the cushion across the room.

"I'm afraid it seems an easy decision for me, Tregor. Akira, Makoto—we're leaving."

Akira and Makoto could not have predicted the projectiles which launched at impervious speeds from Tregor's hands, conjurations in the forms of dark knives. They struck Jiro's associates in their respective temples with pinpoint accuracy and enough force to continue travelling through, where they struck the room's only wall and dispersed into clouds of purple-grey mist. Jiro himself was not so inexperienced as to allow the third to strike him, and he fell out of the way as it sailed past, into the air outside, and disappeared.

"You bastard," Jiro mouthed, regaining his footing. "You evil, reprehensible man."

"Don't lecture me about morality, Jiro. If you leave, this vampire will use his dragon to take over the world and rebuild it in his image. Is that what you want? The empire you've built will be meaningless in Kalahar's creation. And you still want to choose neutrality? Or is it just apathy?"

"Take over the world?" Kalahar repeated incredulously. "That is a terrible stretch."

"What do you think he wants the Fateborn for if not to dominate the world?" Tregor insisted, refusing to acknowledge the vampire. "For what else would you require such uninhibited power?"

"A lot of things," Kalahar continued to respond in place of Jiro. "I do have a plan, of course, but world domination certainly isn't it. What value would come of that?"

"Tell us, then," Tregor snapped, finally turning to face him. "Tell us what it is you plan and why you need the Fateborn."

"That would really ruin the mystery, wouldn't it? It's nothing you need to worry about, dear Tregor. After all, what do you have to lose? Your Council is dead. Assuming your daughter over there, Nendar, would still side with you—which it doesn't look like she would—there would be three of you left. Three of you to exert influence over… nobody. Your entire reason for being is to influence the use of magic in Valoria, and you've lost that influence. What else is there for you still to lose?"

"As long as Nendar remains Emperor of Sanskar then our influence lives on. You wouldn't understand it, vampire. You've always tunnel-visioned on your own goals that you never stopped to consider how others' worked."

"As I remember it, you always upheld vehement opposition to Nendar's position. Now you use it as justification? This whole discussion is futile, Tregor, and we are delaying the inevitable. The inevitable being that I free Richard and take him away from here, away from you. And you're not going to stop me, because I will kill you if you try. I will give you one detail about my plan – it doesn't involve you. Which means as a gesture of goodwill I am letting you go. But even a hint of involvement in my affairs and I will not be so generous again."

"Do you ever think, vampire, that sometimes people do things simply because it's the right thing to do? That perhaps we want to stop you because we know whatever it is you're planning, it's not going to be for the greater good? Not everyone is so driven by personal gain as you are. I know when I'm defeated, so I won't try to stop you now. But know that in the future, we will meet again. And I will be ready to defeat you. We both will." He looked to Nendar.

"I'm sorry, this is hilarious to me." Richard pressed himself up, grimacing. "You do things because it's the right thing to do? You just killed two innocent people in cold blood for no reason other than that they were in the wrong place at the wrong time! You're a murderer! You—you, and your Council, you're responsible for more deaths than perhaps anyone else in this world! Think of the good that could be harnessed by people if they were allowed to access magic. If you hadn't worked so hard over time to prevent it from being learned by the common folk. Not to mention the Corrupted—how many people do you think are torn asunder every day by those monstrosities *you* created? You cursed an entire continent to keep it in check! If anyone deserves to be stopped, it's you! If you both die, there's no scenario I see where the world ends up worse! I'd put a sword through you both right now if I could stand!"

"Don't worry, Richard, I'll happily do it for you," Jiro growled.

"No," the vampire transported himself across the room to stand before Jiro, who had begun to walk towards Tregor, brandishing his sword. "Killing them would be too kind. I won't allow it. They escape today."

"Why?" Richard cried. "Why let them go? We could do so much good putting an end to them right now. Why drag this out any longer?"

"He likes a good show," Nendar concluded. "Except we're not going to let him have it."

"I'm leaving now," Kalahar declared, striding through the scattered array of people to Richard. He traced an anonymised portal and reached down, gently picking up the bounty hunter in both arms. He winced as the vampire brought one of his arms to support his shattered right knee.

"What about you, Lynn Varanus?" Kalahar then abruptly said. Lynn had remained at the wall, only a few steps from the exit to the stairwell. "You're free to join us. The tension between you and your father, my, you could break it with a finger."

"I'm going my own way," Lynn responded coldly. "Apologies, vampire, but I don't hold the same high regard for you as Richard does."

"Fine. Goodbye, everyone. We'll be seeing you. All of you."

Nobody stepped forwards to attempt to stop Kalahar as he carried Richard through the anonymised portal. Nor did anyone follow them as they finally left Nakada and were overcome by a stuffy yet comfortable warmth.

Richard craned his neck to observe a roaring fire in a cobbled hearth, the centrepiece of a timber wall adorned by shelves housing a miscellany of ornaments, books, and trinkets. There was a bed in one corner of the room, the wool-stuffed duvet draped across it thicker than any Richard had ever seen. It was accompanied by two feather-stuffed pillows which almost enveloped his head as Kalahar laid him down.

"Where are we?" he asked.

"Southeast Mirados. About as far from civilisation as you can get," the vampire said softly. "It is here that you will rest and heal. I will do everything I can to accelerate the process, but nature must take its course. And after that, we can return to Letham Deregor, where there are things I would like to teach you."

"When... when can you help me bring Lin back?"

"When the time is right. There are many things you must learn, first. Now, I will cast a spell to numb your pain and then recite a more complicated regenerative incantation. If you'd like, I can send you straight to sleep."

Richard didn't think he would need the vampire's spell to send him to sleep, because despite the pain still fiercely occupying his knee and leg, he felt himself drifting away in the comfort of the bed.

"Yes..." he muttered anyway, and he felt the vampire's cold fingers caress his forehead before a vignette engulfed his vision and severed his connection to the conscious world.

*

"Good morning, Richard. You must be hungry."

The bounty hunter lurched forwards before remembering where he was, his vision focusing on the platter Kalahar held above him. It was then that the scent of assorted meats, herbs, eggs, and nuts wafted up his nostrils and he began to salivate

271

uncontrollably as the vampire lowered the platter onto his lap, still covered by the duvet.

"I didn't know you could cook," Richard commented before tearing voraciously into the meal.

"Oh, don't be ridiculous. I've never cooked a meal in my life. Magic did that." He gestured to the food, nearly a quarter of it already gone. "Cooked it, that is. How is your leg? Your knee?"

Until the vampire's reminder, Richard hadn't felt even the semblance of pain. When he thought about it, a dull throbbing still resonated from his shattered knee, but it was rapid progress from outright agony.

"How long was I asleep?"

"A good while. Fourteen hours, perhaps?"

"And since when did you own a cabin?"

"I built it. For you. When you're finished that, you can come outside and wash. You won't have healed enough to walk unassisted, but there are crutches under the bed. The chest in the corner has a new set of clothes, so you can get rid of that distasteful amalgamation you picked up in the forest. And I've also another surprise for you, but we'll leave that until you're healed, I think."

Richard finished his meal, wiping his mouth with his sweat-sodden tunic and pulling himself out from under the covers. As he set foot on the hardwood floor, the dull throbbing in his knee turned sharp and he winced as Kalahar retrieved the crutches from beneath the bed. He begrudgingly accepted them and found that his left leg, though also subject to acute pain, was not so unusable as his right, and he managed to make his way to the door.

Further north, the landscape would have been embraced by spring. Southern Mirados was a different story, and it was as if the region only had two seasons as opposed to the usual four. The blast of cold air and the tender touch of falling snow was a shock, but not one to which Richard couldn't quickly acclimatise.

"This path leads to a lake, perhaps a five-minute walk away," Kalahar said, emerging from the cabin behind him. "If you'd like, I can simply teleport you there."

"No," Richard said curtly. "I'd like to walk."

"And of course be wary, Richard, it is freezing. You might be the Fateborn but you are still susceptible to cold shock as any mortal is. I would recommend heating the water before bathing in it."

"No. I can take it. I want to."

Richard hobbled inefficiently along the path to which Kalahar had gestured. It was almost indiscernible, the falling snow constantly working to mask it. And it was deceivingly dangerous, as Richard discovered when his foot found a patch of ice. He fell, the crutches giving way and his whole body meeting the cold-hardened ground without resistance.

His knee throbbed with pain akin to the day before and he gritted his teeth to suppress a moan. He had made it perhaps twenty feet, the warmth of the cabin almost tangible, and the vampire's critical gaze very much tangible. He glided towards the bounty hunter and reached down to help him up, but Richard fiercely combatted his attempts at support. The bounty hunter found his footing with his left foot and used the crutch in his right hand to stand up, and then he continued on his way.

It became clear that the vampire's estimation of a five-minute walk was based on an able-bodied person, but Richard did eventually make it to the lake without any further accidents. It was, by his judgement, about twice the size of the lake in the dryad forest, much of its boundary encircled by stone ridges. Atop the largest was an immense willow, its leafless branches drooping down over the ridge and coming to rest just above the water's surface. Other various deciduous trees surrounded the lake and formed a sparse forest beyond.

Richard's dirty tunic was inadequate against the cold and he was shivering by the time he arrived, but he set down his crutches and stripped himself naked before diving without hesitation into the dark blue water.

The moment he made contact he knew he had made a mistake. He gasped as his head fell beneath the surface and his lungs flooded with freezing water and he began to sink, hyperventilating as his body reacted involuntarily to the change in temperature. His heart started to race and he fought to return to the surface.

He then found himself back in the cabin, violently coughing up the water in his lungs before vomiting up his breakfast from the morning. He continued to hyperventilate as his body slowly warmed and the vampire muttered a spell to dry him before draping the duvet around his shoulders. His teeth chattered, but he was beginning to regain control of his breathing and his heartrate was returning to its normal pace.

"Rest for the remainder of today," Kalahar said, gently moving him to lay on the bed. "I will find some reading material for you to learn from. We will begin more practical lessons when you are able to walk."

With assistance from Kalahar's magic, Richard made a swift recovery from the cold shock and spent the rest of the day reading a specific book written in Archaeish. Titled *The Origin of Everything*, it was about the sun and moon, the greater powers which created the world, the history of magic, its known limits. Much, Richard noted, was marked as being speculation.

He came upon a paragraph about Children of Fate, which stated that only three had ever been discovered and attempts made to raise them. It went on to say that all three ended up dead within a year of the discovery of their powers—one by assassination, one by overexertion, and the last as collateral damage in a pogrom. The book was not dated, but Kalahar told him it was a thousand years old, and the information within it still very much up to date, apart from the number of discovered Children of Fate.

"Doesn't bode well for me, then, does it?"

"You won't die, Richard. I won't let you."

"Who wrote this book, anyways? The history is... broad."

"I did."

The book then described the prior attempts of the Children of Fate to manipulate what it constantly called 'constructions of the greater powers'. This sounded familiar, and Richard recalled Kalahar using the same sequence of words to convince him not to manipulate the sun and moon to prevent the eclipse. It stated that they, also during total solar eclipses, had attempted exactly that, and that was the way in which the second Child of Fate had died. The other two were simply unsuccessful, and they had met their fate later.

"You're different to the others, Richard." It was some time in the evening when Kalahar appeared through the front door.

"What do you mean by that?" Richard was secretly relieved to rest his eyes, if only momentarily.

"They were weak. Children of Fate are, in theory, meant to be limitless. Their power should know no restraint. It should be impossible for them to reach a ceiling. But as you've read, that wasn't the case.

"I knew all three of them. The first was a king's son, in a country which ceased to exist some two-and-a-half thousand years ago. I discovered him. I taught him. We were to put a stop to an eclipse, as you suggested at Letham Deregor. And then on the day of the eclipse, just as the sun and the moon were about to cross, just as he was preparing to teleport to the place we had agreed to meet, his own brother walked into his chambers and placed a dagger in his heart."

"Rivalry for the throne."

"It was. But that's not the point. The Fateborn should have felt his brother's approach. He should have predicted his strike. He should have repaired his wound. But he didn't. He was too weak. He fell too easily, in a way that he shouldn't have."

"Maybe he wasn't a Fateborn."

"He most definitely was. But he was weak. Just as the second Child was. I discovered her when she was only young, seventeen. A peasant child, already married off to a squire from a wealthier family and pregnant with his child. Approaching her was more difficult, but she was a quick learner. Unfortunately, she was also terribly weak, and made weaker every day by the child sapping her of every spare droplet of energy. That didn't stop her, though, and she was terribly ambitious. She tried spells she had never practised before. She would draw too much power from herself instead of from the environment and the flow of magic. It led to her miscarriage, and it led to her death."

"And that shouldn't be possible."

"Yes. There should have been no scenario in which she suffered because she drew upon herself. She had boundaries far beyond that of any normal human, of course, but not the limitless boundaries thought to be possible—no, standard—in a Fateborn."

The vampire looked wistfully at the ground and then stood up to adjust the venison.

"The third was a dwarven miner, a four-hundred-year-old man who had shunned the prospect of magic use as elven nonsense. When I approached him, he threatened to report me to the guard. And he did, because I persisted. When I was not found, his whole village labelled him a lunatic. A madman. And yet he refused to cooperate with me. It was just my luck, too, that he happened to live in a dwarven community in an elven country. And when they were all put to the stake, there was nothing he could do to save himself. I was taken by surprise myself. It was an unprovoked attack. And I was too late to save him."

He returned to his seat in the corner. "I didn't go into much detail about them in the book. But the bottom line is that they all failed when they shouldn't have been able to. You, though, Richard, you're different. You're stronger. You're more resilient. Your boundaries have been tested and you've blown past them every time. Every time you have clashed with anyone magically you have come out on top without breaking a sweat. And, most importantly, your head is on straight. That's why I have faith that we will achieve great things together. Great things that the others could never have. I was sceptical when you suggested it months ago, when we were only scratching the surface of your potential. But now? After everything I've seen, everything you've learned, everything you've demonstrated? That cataclysm you caused, it was the single greatest surge of magical energy I have ever experienced. I felt it halfway across the continent. That was when I knew you were the one to finally complete this project that I have made the purpose of my life."

"I'm sorry, I don't follow. You've got an awful habit of saying a lot without saying much at all."

"We're going to best the constructions of the greater powers, Richard. You and I, together. With my guidance, my knowledge, and your power, we can do it."

"What about... what about Lin?"

The vampire sighed, and Richard was sure it was for dramatic effect.

"I haven't been entirely truthful with you," he admitted. "We will still be able to resurrect her. But it will not be easy. You see, in order to resurrect someone, you must still be in control of their soul. That can be done in one of two ways— ensnare it as it is released from the body upon its death and perform the resurrection immediately, or capture it and store it in a crystal of lirenium, where it can then be used for a later resurrection. In the case of your Linelle, her soul was not captured, and it escaped."

Richard's head shot up to look the vampire in the eyes.

"But," Kalahar spoke quickly. "Not all hope is lost. There is a third, untried method."

"If you're tricking me," Richard seethed, "then I will tear you limb from limb. Your immortality will be nothing. I will leave your bones for the wolves."

"I am loyal to you. I am only working to help you to achieve your potential. And I want the best for you. How many times have I saved you from the clutches of the Council? The Council, who—if I hadn't intervened—would have turned you into their brainless drone to unleash their bidding across not just the continent but the world?"

"I was able to resist them every time they tried to convert me. That wasn't you."

"Every time? No, that isn't entirely true. Do you remember being strapped to the operating table in the Virilian Palace?"

Richard nodded slowly.

"You really think that in your untrained state that you resisted two lirenium-fuelled Varanuses? I was protecting you. The whole time. I stood and watched as they attempted to convert you. I allowed it to happen, to give you an idea of your powers. I know I needed to convince you that you weren't normal. And then when Tregor arrived with the rest of his lackeys, I knew that was when I needed to step in. You saw me when I arrived, and I did not arrive from the frame of a portal. I was always there. Always protecting you. And I will continue to always protect you."

"Why?" Richard asked plainly. "What do you gain from protecting me?"

"I need your help. I have—"

Kalahar looked idly at the fire, finally breaking eye contact and falling silent.

"What is it?" Richard probed.

"I have never admitted this to anyone before," Kalahar said in a voice completely foreign to the bounty hunter, his tone almost resembling regret. "I am not infallible. I have a weakness. And it is why I ask for your help. I wish to alter the path of the moon so that a total solar eclipse may never occur again. Not only does it bring so many vicious malevolents into the world but it also, for its duration, deprives me of my sanity. It is a curse, one that cannot be lifted. So instead I must create a prevention. For that, I need your help."

The fire crackled and the pair fell into silence for some time. Richard's stomach churned with hunger, which Kalahar seemed to detect. He wordlessly rose and exited the cabin, returning some time later with a skinned hare which he set about roasting over the fire.

"You don't want to use magic?" Richard commented.

"I thought you would prefer something more authentic."

The bounty hunter sat back and smiled, returning his attention to Kalahar's book as the vampire continued about cooking his dinner. When it was ready, he had it delivered to him on a platter.

"You're a shit cook," Richard exclaimed as he peeled the last chunk of charred flesh from the hare's bones.

"It's not something I've ever done before, as I said."

Richard lifted the duvet and swung himself around to let his feet fall to the floor. He tested standing on both legs, which only resulted in a sharp—but improved—pain in his knee. Sighing, he picked up the crutches and hobbled to the chest Kalahar had said contained clothes, opening it and retrieving a pair of undergarments, sepia trousers, an off-white linen tunic, a girdle, a pair of sturdy leather boots, and a heavy fur mantle. He dressed himself with difficulty, constantly ready to fend off the vampire's offers of assistance. He was thoroughly surprised when they never came. Dressed, he then retrieved his crutches and manoeuvred over to the door before submitting himself to the mercy of the Miradosi tundra.

The snow shone in the light of the full moon under a cloudless night sky. It wasn't snowing, but it was still unyieldingly cold. Richard continued along the path away from the cabin, this time not heading towards the lake, but into the hills in the other direction.

He walked, warm in the embrace of his cloak, until he reached the precipice of the first hill. It hadn't been an easy task, burdened with the crutches, and several times he had fallen and had to break his fall with his arms.

He carefully lowered himself to the ground and lay in the snow, watching the stars. There wasn't even a glimmer of civilisation in the surroundings and in the brief observation he had carried out before setting himself down he hadn't seen so much as a road.

His eyes then fell upon the moon, which he watched for some time as it meandered through the sky. Closing his eyes, he focused on the moon as he would any object he moved with the use of magic.

As he pulled, he felt a familiar resistance, though much stronger than what he would feel for an everyday object, or in fact a much larger object. He channelled more energy into the spell and began to feel physical strain, tempering his breathing as beads of sweat formed on his forehead. Continuing to pull, he inhaled, and then exhaled. Pull. Inhale. Exhale. Grunting with exertion. He did not give up and instead only tried harder. His body burned and the beads of sweat turned to streams and then rivers. From his forehead, his neck, his armpits. Grunts turned to cries. Inhale. Exhale.

Without his knowledge, he lifted into the air, his eyes still closed. He pulled harder, but there was still resistance. His cries became one, continuous. A spherical veil, weak, shimmering, and ice-blue, formed around him. His eyes, though they were closed, turned blue, too. And when he finally opened them, rocking his head back with the effort, they glowed with the intensity of bonfires. He illuminated the snow beneath him and continued to rise, continued to sweat, continued to scream.

And then he fell. Not with an explosion, but with a lapse. He had let his focus fall only momentarily, and it had been enough to knock him unconscious.

The veil disappeared and Richard's eyes returned to normal as he plummeted back to the snow-cushioned ground. But what cushioned his fall even more was the spell Kalahar cast to slow his descent to a speed at which a feather might travel, before catching him in his arms. He walked back to the cabin and set Richard onto the bed, touching his knee and uttering another spell.

"Not yet, Richard," he murmured. "Not yet."

He exited the cabin once again and set out along the path leading to the lake and the woodland beyond. Not thirty seconds later he gave up on walking and traced a portal instead.

Dragon, he thought, spotting a deer. He used a spell to snap its neck and then traced a portal beneath it to allow it to fall straight into the clearing outside the cabin.

Yes, master, Alazarioss responded.

I'm going to need your assistance. How high can you fly?

As high as you need, master.

Excellent. Would that include beyond the restraints of this world?

Yes, master. At great magical cost.

And can spells be channelled through you?

Yes, master. Also at great magical cost.

The vampire conjured a blade and hacked amateurly at the deer's neck.

But would that all be possible through use of the Fateborn?

The dragon's response, as it had been every for each of the vampire's prior questions, was instantaneous.

Yes, master.

CHAPTER 29

Elaeínn's decision to abstain from participation in the blood-bath was not a choice made with difficulty. She held no moral objection to the killings themselves, but it was the fact that she had met the man they were travelling to kill that prevented her from stepping in to aid. That, and the fear of persecution.

It soon became evident that she wouldn't be needed, anyways. The knights comprising the majority of the convoy didn't waste so much as a single swing of their swords. The guards surrounding the caravan they had encountered along the road were killed efficiently and ruthlessly, none left alive.

"Would you mind explaining what's going on here?" Elaeínn hopped out of the caravan reserved for her and approached Jannis as he dislodged his sword from a fallen guard's lacerated chest.

"These wagons are full to the brim with bombs," Jannis said, sheathing his sword and setting about clearing the bodies from the road. "Headed to none other than Dannos, home of Elton Redwinter. Now I don't know what Elton Redwinter could possibly want with enough bombs to reduce the Blue Palace to rubble, but it can't possibly be good. We're parking them here and bringing them back with us when we finish our business in Dannos."

"Why do you hate him so much?"

"I'm not the one you want to ask about that. I hate him because he's a fat bastard criminal who disrespects my king. If you want a more descriptive reason, that's who you should ask."

"I'm sure you know enough to tell me."

"It's a family issue," Jannis conceded. "There are some deeper complications to it, but that's the gist of it."

"I hope you know I won't be killing anyone without justification for it."

"That's fine. Kalahar didn't ask you. He asked us. And we have no issue with that."

Jannis tossed a final body into a ditch at the side of the hardened desert road and then tore back the sand-stained sheet draped over the contents of one of the caravans. As he had claimed, it was overflowing with bombs crafted from cast iron, their designs less elegant than those to which Elaeínn was accustomed in Tyen'Ael. Some fell with a metallic clattering to the floor and she jumped back with fright. They didn't explode, and Jannis snorted in amusement.

"Didn't you say Elton controls this city now? What makes you think you'll be able to get close to him?" she continued to ask, brushing off her moment of embarrassment.

"How about you just sit there in your little chamber and let the world go by while we do our job?"

"Chego ona terasce?" They were joined by Hortensio, his own blade wet with so much blood that it was more red than silver.

"She's being nosy about why we hate Elton."

"Powied je, zey trymala shibska buzie na klodke."

"What's he saying?" Elaeínn prodded.

"He says you should keep your nosy mouth shut. Now get back in your caravan. We're moving on."

She hesitantly did as she was told, if only because she had no other option. The convoy trundled along for days, Elaeínn peeking constantly through the gap in the curtains separating her from the outside world. Although she didn't see much, the culture that she did periodically witness was a shock. The people, the buildings, the fashion—it was unrecognisable, utterly foreign. As was the language, which, over the course of their journey, had shifted from that spoken by Hortensio and Jannis to something mellower, smoother. And the temperature had steadily risen, felt by Elaeínn in the form of her skin becoming irritably dry.

She had lost count of the days since they had returned from the Heart and had long since given up trying to glean information about their strategy from Jannis. One thing that worried her was the spell enabling them to communicate—she had no idea when it would run out.

Her free time had mostly been occupied by study of her sword, attempting to recreate the red glow that had engulfed its runes on the island. In every attempt she had failed, not just to make it glow red but to make it glow at all. Though it hadn't particularly discouraged her.

Somebody bellowed a command and the convoy drew to an abrupt halt. Elaeínn abandoned an attempt to communicate with Alazarioss and poked her head through the gap in the curtain, craning her neck to try to see as much of the oncoming path as she could.

What lay ahead was not more path but a city of sandstone. Through her prior concentration Elaeínn had failed to take notice of the volume generated by the passers-by that had been so rare in the days before. That was no longer the case, a constant noisy stream of people travelling into and out of the city gates—mostly traders, judging by the wagons many hauled behind them.

"You're up, elf." Jannis appeared without warning and Elaeínn instinctively retreated into the caravan and grabbed her sword. "Don't stab me with that, but you're going to need it," he continued nonchalantly.

"What do you mean by that?"

"We're not welcome here, as I'm sure you've come to understand. But Elton knows you. He'll surely let you in."

"I already told you, I'm not killing him," Elaeínn said coldly.

"We thought you might say that," Jannis sighed. "Let me make this clear to you, elf. We saved you from that island. We fed you and transported you halfway across the continent. Why do you think we did that?"

"I'm coming to understand it's not out of the kindness of your hearts."

"Correct. We need someone who that fat old bastard trusts. Or at the very least doesn't distrust. My king isn't stupid—he knows we couldn't stroll into Dannos with a few cavalrymen and expect not to be slaughtered. We need to send one person. An assassin."

"Perhaps you should have confirmed your assassin before travelling all that way, then. Because I'm not doing it. You should have believed me the first time I said it."

"If you don't do it, we'll kill you. How does that sound?"

Elaeínn felt nothing. And that was not what she expected. She didn't feel fear, she didn't feel adrenaline. His threat, one she knew was very real, did not instil the terror it had intended. She smirked, and then she laughed.

"Do it," she said. "I've got nothing to lose."

Jannis reached into the caravan and grabbed Elaeínn by the collar, dragging her into the open. She kicked and screamed, an outburst met swiftly by a metal-clad fist. Stars danced across her vision and she fell limp.

*

"Too hard," Hortensio chided.

"I barely touched her, the pathetic thing," Jannis spat, dropping the elf's unconscious body to the trodden road. "She's not going to do it. Why would she? We don't have any leverage."

"Apart from, oh, death?"

"I tried that. She told me to 'do it'. I don't know what she's scared of, but it's not that. What are we meant to do now?"

The pair stood in silence for a time as they traversed their thoughts for ideas. Passing travellers took notice of the stopped convoy with its trademark white horses and gleaming sets of armour. But at no point were they challenged, despite their proximity to the gates.

"I've got it." Hortensio raised a confident finger. "She doesn't want to help us by choice. Fine. She can help us by accident."

Hortensio kicked her body gently to the side of the road and placed a hood over her head to conceal her ears.

"We leave her here. Not here, but somewhere public, like here. One of us will pose as some drifter related to her and ask some passer-by to go get help. They'll call the guards—we'll go with them, and her. When we're inside the walls, we'll reveal her identity and say she knows Elton. They'll never have seen an elf before, so they'll believe us—we then take her, still unconscious, to him. And then—"

"We get him while his soppy heart weeps for the poor, injured thing," Jannis finished. "It's brilliant, my king."

"You'll have to be our stooge. You look the most local. And you speak the language more convincingly than the rest of us," Hortensio continued.

"They'll recognise me, surely."

"I doubt it. They know what you look like in that getup." Hortensio gestured up and down to Jannis's suit of armour. "Put on some commoner's rags and you'll be unrecognisable. Maybe rub some sand through your hair."

284

Jannis took a deep breath. "Alright," he agreed. "Strip me down."

Behind the cover of the caravans, Hortensio and the other knights spent the next half hour removing Jannis's armour before dressing him in the some of the plain clothes they had brought with them for the journey's nights. Jannis then proceeded to roll around in the sand off the path until he was adequately dirty.

"I suppose I'll take her somewhere, then," he said. "You all stay out of sight. Fat bastard will have heard about us being here by now. I'm surprised he hasn't sent anyone to inspect."

"Good luck, General." Hortensio saluted, and all the other knights followed suit.

Jannis picked up Elaeínn's motionless body, securing her sword in its sheath, and left the path in search of a suitable spot for his ambush. He turned briefly at the thunderous trundling of the caravans' wheels as they turned around and retreated into the distance before returning his focus solely to the mission.

It didn't take long to find somewhere satisfactory to set her down. He ducked under a small wooden bridge crossing a fissure in the road and waited for the hum of traffic to die down. Once it had grown quiet, he glanced into the open, confirmed there were no nearby bystanders, and hauled Elaeínn onto the bridge.

"Help!" he cried. "Somebody, please help me!"

CHAPTER 30

FREE CITY OF DANNOS, SANTEROS

"Oh, thank goodness! Thank goodness!" the wailing man said with joyful tears in his eyes as Elliot and his partner, Jacob, returned from the guardhouse with a wagon. "Please, allow me to go with you! She's a friend of the Count—she cannot just go to any old hospital!"

Elliot glanced scathingly at Jacob, and both rolled their eyes as they loaded the woman's motionless body roughly onto the cart. The drifter continued to babble as they headed back into the city, though neither felt much like listening to anything he had to say.

The man eventually ran around to stand in front of the cart and the guards were forced to bring it to a halt against the momentum from walking down the hill.

"What the fuck are you doin'?" Elliot exclaimed, grabbing the man and thrusting him against a sandstone pillar holding up the roof between the inner and outer city walls.

"You haven't been acknowledging a thing I've been saying, sirs! This is no ordinary woman! She's a close acquaintance of Count Redwinter himself! We must be delivered to him!"

"We? Why not just 'er? She's the one who knows 'im. Or do you know 'im too?"

"Does she look in any condition to speak? The Count will want a thorough explanation as to how she has ended up like this!"

"The Count can suck my massive schlong. I ain't taking her there," Jacob muttered.

"She's goin' to the infirmary," Elliot asserted. "If she's that important, the Count can come find her."

The man began to argue back and then faltered, nodding and looking away.

They traversed the city in relative silence from that point on, interrupted only by the man's occasional questions.

"Will it cost much to have her treated here?"

"Is the Count not going to be too preoccupied to make time for a visit all the way out to the infirmary?"

"You will tell the Count, will you not? You won't leave us here without letting him know?"

"Who even is she?" Elliot broke at the last question, stopping the wagon and marching to the other end of the wagon, where the woman's head rested on a pillow of straw.

"She's a friend," the man said frantically, rushing to stand between Elliot and the woman. "That's the only thing that matters."

Elliot pushed past him and lifted the hood concealing the woman's head.

"What in divine's name?"

Enticed by Elliot's surprise, Jacob also joined them from the other side of the wagon and prodded the woman's visible ear with a gloved finger. "I've never seen anything like that."

"Where'd you find 'er?" Elliot turned to the drifter, eyes alight with curiosity.

"She's not from here," the man explained calmly. "Please do not tell anyone about it except the Count. We cannot risk making a scene when she is unwell."

Jacob placed his hand on the woman's head and turned it to reveal a vibrant purple bruise adorning her cheek. He glanced apprehensively at Elliot, who transferred the glance to the drifter.

"We were attacked during our journey," he quickly explained.

"And that's why she's knocked out?" Elliot inquired.

"Possibly? I don't know—I'm not a doctor. We managed to continue for a while afterward, but then she collapsed. We were lucky enough to be in the vicinity of the city by then."

"Very lucky," Jacob mused, running his finger along the scabbard attached to the woman's belt and eyeing the drifter up and down. "I take it she was the one doing the defending, eh?"

"She—please don't touch that—"

Jacob's hand found the ornate handle protruding from the top of the scabbard and raised an inquisitive eyebrow. He rolled her body to a position from which he could safely draw the sword and then looked to Elliot for his opinion. Elliot simply shrugged.

He drew the weapon and his face was enchanted with a smile as a series of delighted gasps escaped his mouth. Elliot forgot about both the drifter and the injured woman and joined his partner in admiration, his mouth falling similarly ajar.

"How much do you reckon this is worth?" Jacob enunciated.

"More than we get paid in a month. A year," Elliot responded.

"I almost don't want to sell it."

Jacob died with his mouth still ajar as the drifter's dagger penetrated his temple and then Elliot's throat. Elliot fell to his knees, clutching meaninglessly at the river of blood flowing from his neck, and then entirely to the ground as he joined his counterpart in death.

*

"I don't think it's a good idea for you to go meet him, bossman. Nothing about this sounds right."

"I'm not meeting him myself. I'll have this lot"—Elton gestured to the array of guards clearing a path through the street leading to the North Gate—"protecting me. And you four, of course."

Elton marched with Felix and Ant on his left, Paul and Fez on his right. They were then flanked by a further set of six guards, three armed with crossbows.

"The report said he's just standing there. With Jannis and all the others. Why would he do that?" Felix persisted.

"I don't know. That's why we're going to find out."

"Don't worry, boss. He ain't gonna touch you," Paul said, slapping Elton on the shoulder enthusiastically.

The company filtered uninterruptedly through the set of pillars dissecting the exit to the desert and marched onward. The commotion attracted a loud, prying entourage to follow, though the guards at the back of the group efficiently dispersed anyone who made their way too close.

"Is this the spot?"

They arrived at an uninspiring patch of road that had been described in a report by the messenger at the group's helm.

The only people there were a pair of robed pilgrims who passed by promptly.

Elton pushed through the guards until he stood before the messenger, his face contorted with worry.

"Where are they?" he asked gruffly.

"T-they were right here, Regi—Count. I promise. Weren't just me who saw 'em, either. Ask anyone."

"I believe him, boss," Fez said, crouching and seemingly pinching the air on the ground. As Elton stepped closer to inspect, he could see what Fez had picked up.

"Ain't a single horse for a hundred miles with hair that white," Paul said as they crowded around to gaze upon the single horsehair.

"Where the bloody hell have they gone?" Elton muttered.

"Mr Redwinter! Mr Redwinter, sir!"

A messenger boy snaked between the legs of the people in the crowd that had formed and was allowed to pass by the guards creating a buffer to reach the Count. From his waist hung the silver dagger Elton had gifted him after the eclipse.

"A man stabbed a pair of guards, Mr Redwinter, sir!" The boy said breathlessly. "He says they were trying to rob his mistress!"

"How is this relevant to me? Are the guards inside the city incapable?"

"He also says his mistress knows you, sir! Says her name is… El… Elaine?"

Elton looked warily to his allies and mouthed, "Vampire?"

"Surely not," Ant replied. "She's nobody's mistress."

"Oh! Mr Redwinter, sir!" the boy added. "They're saying the mistress has got weird ears, sir! Pointy!"

The decision to abandon the investigation was made instantly and Elton ordered the guards to clear the crowd as they moved back towards the city with haste.

"Where is he? Did he run?" Elton asked the boy.

"They're both at the hospital, sir. Some guards have blocked him in but he refuses to go anywhere without his mistress."

"Does this man have pointy ears, too?"

"No, sir. He looks pretty normal."

"She's not his mistress, then," Elton murmured to himself. "Who is he? And what's the elf doing *here*?"

Elton opted for the company to take a quicker route to the infirmary through the back alleys, despite the risk. They arrived to find a crowd blocking the entrance and the guards once again had to forcibly disperse people to allow the Count to make his way through.

"Where are they?" Elton asked fervently, his hand twitching over his sheath.

"Guards are surrounding them inside, sir."

Forgoing the protection of the company, Elton shoved his way through the guards warding off the bystanders. There, lying on a bed, unconscious, was the figure of Elaeínn Tinaíd, whom Elton had only met once before. The fact that she was in his city was significant—he just didn't know why.

Standing beside her was a hooded man in peasant's garb, his only visible features being several strands of hickory hair escaping the confines of his cowl. He looked down upon the woman's motionless body with worry, but he was not an elf. At least, he didn't seem to be.

"You!" Elton barked. "Who are you? Why is she here?"

The man didn't respond, instead fidgeting with something below his waist, invisible to Elton from where he stood.

"Well?" Elton stepped closer, brushing aside the nearest guard. "Answer me!"

*

Vampire, you had better be able to hear me. Because you are my only way out. I'm doing what you asked.

The noise of the crowd had disappeared with Elton's arrival, replaced by a dulled droning and the incessant rapid beating of Jannis's heart. His fingers sweated as they caressed the dagger already dirty with the blood of the guards he had killed. There was truly no escape—the bystanders had made sure of that. And he was not about to give up.

"Well? Answer me!"

Jannis drew a breath and exhaled, closing his eyes and muttering a prayer.

*

Elton's reactions were usually fast for a man of his age. But they weren't fast enough. Luckily, Felix's were.

290

Jannis's dagger penetrated Elton's tunic and the ringlets of the chainmail underneath. He grunted with pain and reached for his own dagger to defend himself but Felix's throwing knives were faster.

The first embedded itself squarely within Jannis's shoulder. The second lacerated his thigh, and the third pinned him to the wall.

Jannis had left his dagger in Elton's chest and the Count fought the sudden urge to vomit as he stumbled into the guards behind him, who surged around and fell upon Jannis like rabid hounds. His cries cut through the air like the knives that had thwarted his assassination attempt.

"Regi!" Paul said, appearing above Elton. At some point he had fallen to the ground and his fingers gripped the blade of the dagger which felt like an extension of his body. "We're in a hospital, for fuck's sake! You lot—you've killed 'im! Leave it, now, and turf out these nosy urchins! We need a surgeon and we can't fuckin' move in this mess!"

The guards assaulting Jannis, now a butchered, bloodied corpse, followed Paul's command and set about clearing the many pedestrians that had gathered to catch a glimpse of the affair. Ant and Fez ran to find the nearest doctor, the majority of which had fled in the commotion. Felix recovered his knives and hoisted Jannis's corpse onto his shoulders, walking to the exit and unceremoniously tossing it into the street.

"No," Elton coughed. "We need to… keep… the body. For—"

He devolved into a coughing fit and covered his mouth with his hand. When he recovered, he found it to be spattered with hot, sticky blood.

"We don't all need to be here! Ant, Fez—go find Hortensio and put an end to him. Permanently, this time!"

"He needs treatment, fast. If we don't find a doctor—"

"They've all run off! What about the vam—"

"Watch your mouth! Do you want to incite another rebellion? And forget it—he won't be able to do what we need."

"It's better than nothing!"

Elton couldn't tell who was saying what as he felt the waning beat of his own heart pulsing through the knife in his chest. He felt himself losing balance and grabbed hold of the bed in which Elaeínn still lay unconscious as he fell. Paul and Felix were quick to help him up as his chest tightened and his breathing grew pained.

"What do we do?" someone cried as Elton was lifted onto a vacant bed. "What do we do?"

*

"How long has the old man been waiting for her to wake up, do you think? I've never seen her conscious."

Elaine and Caster stood guard over Rosa, having transported her carefully back from the ruined house off of Megaross Square. Caster was preoccupied with practice of a spell, which meant that Elaine's guard duties were mainly focused on preventing discovery of his activity. But that was as simple as closing the door and placing her chair in front of it.

"She appears to be in a coma of sorts. But I believe it's magically induced," Caster said. "To force her body to focus on healing."

"You mean to say she did that to herself? They seem to think she might die any day now."

"Oh, definitely not. She probably predetermined a length of time to remain in that state and will wake from it when it's elapsed. She's definitely erred on the side of caution, because her body is entirely recovered. As should be expected, really— I suspect she cast a regenerative spell before sending herself to sleep."

"Is there a way to... I don't know, check?"

Caster shook his head. "If there is, I don't know how."

The pair of vampires were suddenly startled as Rosa inhaled a breath far sharper than was typical in her unconscious state. They rushed to her side but did not act as her eyelids fluttered open and the glaze faded from her eyes.

The first emotion to adorn her face was alarm. She shot out of the bed that had been assembled and subsequently collapsed to the floor under her weakened legs.

"Careful," Caster said, helping her return to her feet and assisting her back into the bed. "You haven't walked in a while. Your body will need to readapt."

"Where's... where's Regi?" she asked, darting her eyes around the room like a trapped animal. "Who are you?"

"Elton isn't here," Elaine said. "I'm Elaine. And this is Caster."

"You're... vampires?"

"How could you tell?"

"Your auras. You haven't masked them."

292

Elaine looked at Caster alarmedly. "If she can detect us—"

"The only people who can sense it are those trained to do so. Don't worry," Rosa cautioned. "I need to find Regi."

"Like I said. He's not here." Elaine crossed her arms defiantly.

"Well, where is he? Not often he forays out on his own free will."

"We don't know. We were put in charge of babysitting you. Don't tend to leave this room."

Rosa cursed and attempted to stand once more, this time with more success, and she managed to walk across the room to the door, where Elaine allowed her to pass.

"You!" She grabbed a passing guard in the corridor outside and ended up using him to stabilise herself as she lost balance again.

"Miss Rosa!" he exclaimed. "I—"

"Where's Regi?"

"He... um... went out. Apparently the Salyrians are here."

"Hortensio?"

"Yes, except... he's supposed to be dead. He was killed while you were asleep. But he's back? I don't understand what's going on..."

"Where was he spotted?" Rosa gripped the man with both arms and stared into his eyes, slowly enunciating her words.

"Outside the walls, by the North Gate... but some of the boys came back and said he's not there anymore."

"Where did he go?" she said slowly.

"I... I'm sorry, mistress, I don't know."

Another guard rounded the corner and walked at speed towards Rosa and the first guard. "Oi! Laz! Did you hear what's happening at the hospital? Oh! Miss Rosa!"

"What's happening at the hospital?" Rosa let go of Laz and turned her attention to the new guard.

"Some pointy-eared freak has turned up. Ain't never seen nothin' like it. And the man she's with murdered two of our boys."

"Pointy-eared?"

"Um... yeah! Like... her ears end in points! They ain't round!"

Rosa stumbled her way out of the Redhouse and proceeded in the direction of the hospital as fast as her legs would allow.

*

The voices faded as Elton felt himself drifting into darkness. Paul and Felix fervently continued to try to find a doctor among the bystanders who had not yet dispersed.

Not even killed by the little rat himself, Elton thought. *He would make a good successor.*

Though the sound was a blur, Elton could still discern variations in volume. He felt his eyelids flutter as there was a surge in activity and he was suddenly overshadowed by three faces.

"Sorry, boss, this is gonna hurt."

He was almost shocked out of consciousness by the stabbing pain as the knife was ripped from his chest. The only thing that kept him conscious was the rush of willpower fuelled by Rosa's arrival.

The pain quickly dulled as Rosa set about issuing a series of spells. One incantation after another, Elton could feel his body's repair as it took place.

"I'm... I'm out of practice," Rosa huffed. "And I don't know enough spells. I can't... can't do any more."

"You saved 'im, Rosa," Paul said.

"He needs more help. We need to get him to someone who knows what they're doing."

"No," Elton coughed. The world around him roared to life and he found the strength to sit up in his bed. Rosa placed cautious hands on his shoulders but he shrugged them off amid a sharp pang in his chest. He fought through it and found his feet, taking in a deep breath and walking slowly to view Jannis's mangled corpse. He had been stabbed too many times to count and his face was mostly unrecognisable. Elton smiled.

"We are going to go out there and find that shipment," he stated, clutching his chest. "And we're going to destroy Kalahar with no... no distractions!"

"Boss, I think you should sit down—"

"Sit down? Sit down after this victory? We have hit Hortensio where it hurts. Wherever he is, he is nothing. We have the upper hand now and with it we are going to strike. Send people out. Find Hortensio and put him down—he can't have gone far. After that, we march. We march as far as it takes to find someone who knows something about our explosives. And then our plan gets executed and Kalahar goes down. Once and for all."

Another pang sliced through Elton's chest and a rush of blood to his head forced him to take a seat back on the bed. He slowed his breathing and forced himself to be calm.

"We want this as much as you, boss," Felix said. "But you've just been stabbed in the heart. You can't expect to get on the move straight away."

"I... I..."

"We'll find Hortensio, boss," Rosa added. "We'll find your explosives. But you need to rest. I just did for a couple weeks. You can manage a few days while I work on healing you in your entirety."

"Meanwhile"—Felix turned and looked at Elaeínn, who was yet to show signs of stirring—"we need to figure out what to do with her."

CHAPTER 31

Dragon riding was a task much more difficult than Richard had anticipated. It was hard enough to mount its back in the first place, but to then maintain balance as it thrust into the air and soared through the sky, always at the mercy of a passing current—it was another ordeal entirely. And what was more, Kalahar wanted him to do it without the use of his hands.

He fell to the ground for the twelfth time that day, his muscles sore from the previous days of training that had already taken place. He had mastered riding with his hands to assist balance by the end of day two, but he was still some ways off being able to cast spells while up in the air.

"Your refusal to harness your full potential is grating, Richard," Kalahar said as the bounty hunter raised himself slowly from the snowy ground.

"I don't see why we have to spend my time learning this when we could be learning something I actually need. Something I want."

"You know our arrangement. We are helping each other. Help me best my curse, and I will teach you to bring your lover back from the dead. Speaking of which... what have you done with the body?"

"She's safe. I'm keeping her hidden, preserved in ice until I can finally bring her back."

"How safe? Is it protected from the elements? Nature? Wanderers?"

"She's safe," Richard repeated curtly, mounting the dragon as it landed gently beside him. "It's my duty to take care of her. Not yours."

Clutching tightly onto one of the dragon's spines, Richard instructed it to take off and they launched into the air, travelling almost perpendicular to the ground. Higher and higher they flew, the atmosphere thinning and the temperature falling rapidly as Kalahar faded to become but a speck on the ground far below.

Channel your focus into balance. Use the words I taught you. You must let go of your reservations, the vampire spoke telepathically. *The dragon needs you, too. It cannot cast spells for itself. It is relying on you for that.*

As they continued to rise, their rapid velocity fell dramatically and Richard let go of the dragon's spine. He felt himself losing balance and cursed before uttering the spell he had learned earlier that day.

"Hel ti bazal," he chanted. "Hel ti re'naz."

It made an immediate difference and as the dragon struggled to continue its ascent, Richard suddenly felt attached to it, as if their bodies were one. Its wings felt like an expansion of his own limbs and he channelled energy into continuing their ascent. The magical strength which came so naturally to him flowed into the dragon and they soared once more, passing the barriers they had until that point consistently failed to reach.

Exhilaration. That was the feeling dominating the bounty hunter as he and the dragon surpassed the boundaries that nature had put in place to restrict them. It was the rush he felt as he looked down and saw not a snowy landscape but an entire landmass. He saw ocean to east and west, land stretching beyond the horizon to the north. He saw the Vivian Isles in the bay, encompassed by the deserts and savannas of the Empire, the snowy mountains and lush valleys of Canaris. Beneath him, the white sheet of Mirados.

The next spell, Richard! Now!

In his wonder, he had forgotten there was a necessary next stage. He opened his mouth to speak the required spell but found himself unable to articulate any words at all. Not only speaking, but breathing had become impossible and he was overcome by panic as he instructed the dragon to bring them back down.

Their rapid ascent flipped into a nosedive and they re-entered the atmosphere with a boom and an onslaught of flame, caressing the dragon like a shield and passing harmlessly over

Richard. Had he not protected himself with a spell before their ascent, he would have been seared to a crisp.

With the return of oxygen Richard drew a grateful breath and finished their descent in a controlled manner. And although he then proceeded to practically fall from the dragon's back, it was still the most elegant end to an attempt yet.

"What were you thinking?" Kalahar scolded. "You could have died that high up!"

"Well," Richard wheezed, relaxing on the ground while he recovered his energy. "I didn't."

"We're going to leave it there for today. Tomorrow we will try again. And you will not put yourself in danger like that."

"It's still the afternoon. We have plenty of time left. I can go again now."

"No. I will not have you overexert yourself. You did well, Richard. Terribly well. We cannot make a mistake by acting with haste."

"I'm not making a mistake. I'm doing what I know I can do. And I don't need your approval or your help. The faster I get this done with, the faster I get to see Lin again and frankly, that's the only thing I'm worried about."

He pushed himself to his feet with a strained grunt and attempted to climb onto the dragon, but it backed away. He walked towards it and was nearly knocked off his feet when it suddenly beat its wings and rose into the air, flying to rest atop a nearby hill.

"I see. I don't have a say. Naturally," Richard spat. "You need me, vampire. I can stop my cooperation at any time."

"Don't be banal, Richard. You need me more, much more."

Richard scowled and cast his eyes to the dragon, considering the use of magic to wrangle it under his control. It wasn't a consideration long-lived, though, and he instead just sighed and walked resignedly back to the cabin.

He retrieved his bow and arrows from a weapon rack Kalahar had somehow constructed during one of the nights and set back out in the direction of the forest. Throughout the course of an hour, he took down a deer, several squirrels, hares, ducks, and grouse. He even was able to sit idly by and observe a lynx catch one of the very animals he was about to kill himself. It was easier than he was used to—it felt almost like the animals were letting themselves be hunted.

Of all his kills, he brought back only a pair of ducks. He then proceeded to cook them himself as the sun disappeared.

Kalahar was nowhere to be seen, and he had no problem with that.

*

Kalahar counted Richard's snores after he fell asleep and only once he reached a hundred did he materialise from his invisibility.

"Sleep, dear Richard," he said, crossing the threshold silently and waving a hand gently over the bounty hunter's forehead. "El'platan vanos."

Richard's snores grew louder as the spell took immediate hold and the vampire fell to his knees, weaving his fingers through the bounty hunter's knotted hair.

"I don't suppose you'll wake from this... lak mil an dakh manar."

*

Richard didn't often remember his dreams. He was almost certain he didn't have them. But that night, he dreamed so vividly that he wasn't sure if he was dreaming.

An image of Linelle materialised before him, just as he remembered her from the day of the eclipse. At first, she stood alone on an empty canvas, but then he watched in horror as the surroundings generated around her. Snowy hills, muddy roads, army tents, bonfires, notice boards. It was all joined by people, soldiers rushing in every direction, panicking, and then she was where he remembered first seeing her, atop a broken cart. The details came so quickly and so accurately, and he felt a sick feeling of dread for what was yet to come.

He heard himself cry out to her and wanted to scream for them to run. He wanted to open a portal and drag her through it, no matter how she would resist. But that wasn't what happened. Instead they conversed, aimlessly, as he futilely attempted to convince her to run away. And, as he knew she would, she refused.

He wanted to cry, to sob, and above all to wake up as she died. But he continued to dream, reliving the cataclysm, the destruction and simultaneous preservation as he fell to rest next to her untouched body in the decimated landscape. And then he relived the steps he took thereafter.

299

As he awoke from the unconsciousness into which he had fallen after the cataclysm, he looked around frenziedly, apprehensive that he had been taken somewhere without his knowledge. All around him was ruin—the ground was scorched black, thousands of bodies reduced to ash, the trees that hadn't been vaporised in the explosion burning like torches.

And yet, Linelle's body remained intact, and he was keen to keep it that way. With the utmost care, he leaned down, scooped her from the charred ground, and began to walk.

The expanse of the damage was incomprehensible. He walked for miles and miles and still saw no end to the destruction. He walked and he walked and night fell and still he walked. He walked through the ruins of a village and the remains of several fields of crops. He walked until finally the hellscape gave way back to the tundra for which he was looking.

He managed to find a village perhaps fifteen minutes after reaching the edge of the destroyed area, dead silent in the grip of night. The only person around was a woman, middle-aged, sitting alone on a bench and smoking a pipe.

"Excuse... excuse me," Richard approached the woman, who glared at him with wary contempt. Her eyes softened as they fell upon Linelle's bloodied corpse. "Do you have a shovel?"

"I'm so sorry," the woman croaked. "Do you need help with the burning?"

"Burning?" Richard queried, confused. "No, not a burning. I... I need to preserve the body."

"She'll fall foul of the Corrupted, will she not? I know it's hard, love, but you must let her go."

"I... I just need a shovel. Please. She won't corrupt, I promise you."

"And how do you promise me that? There's a reason we don't bury folk in this land and it's 'cause of that blasted curse. I'm sorry, love, I can't let you—"

"She won't corrupt," Richard repeated, his voice suddenly cold.

The hostility in the woman's eyes that was present when Richard had first approached returned, but she did not argue. Instead, she extinguished her pipe and tucked it into a pocket before hobbling away and gesturing uneasily for the bounty hunter to follow.

The woman led Richard to a rickety old shed on the outskirts of the village and inside it she found a rusty, chipped shovel which she presented disdainfully.

"You're lucky I have the respect not to wake folk to deal with you," she hissed. "Now you keep the damned shovel. But take her far away from here. I've seen your face. I'll not hesitate to go the garrison if a Corrupted woman pops up and wreaks havoc upon the place."

"Don't worry," Richard enunciated. "She won't corrupt."

He looked at the shovel in the woman's arms and slung Linelle's body over his shoulder to make space in his hands for it. He then uttered a quick word of gratitude and departed back into the wilds.

The sun was beginning to rise when he found a location with which he was content. It was the base of a hill some ways away from the nearest road, deep enough into a patch of trees that he was confident nobody would find it easily. And so he began to dig.

Between short rests and hunts for food, over the course of several days, Richard excavated a chamber in the side of the hill. It was no larger than a bedroom in a respectable tavern, but it was what he believed to be sufficient.

The excavation was only the first part of his plan. He proceeded to spend another week searching for bounties in nearby villages and using the money to pay for timber which he used to conceal the chamber. When his work was finished, an hour's snowfall would conceal the entrance so that it looked natural against the side of the hill. Finally, he set about filling the inside the of chamber with snow, packed so tight to the point where it felt solid. He inserted Linelle's body into the area that was left before covering it with the timber and collapsing with exhaustion.

*

Kalahar retracted his fingers from Richard's head and the bounty hunter soon fell still.

The vampire stepped back and exited the cabin, tracing a portal and thrusting forwards to open a gateway to the hill he had seen in Richard's dream. He found it completely invisible amongst the snow and cast a flame in his hand to melt his way to the sheets of wood he knew he would find.

301

He levitated the wooden cover out of the way and found the packed snow inside the tomb to be intact. And inside it was Linelle's body, preserved in the same state it had been since the day of the eclipse.

"It hasn't corrupted," Kalahar mused, drawing the body out of the icy crevice. He muttered a spell and raised his eyebrows in amusement. "Because he protected it. Clever boy... but I never taught him that... should have watched more of the dream..."

The vampire set about tracing another portal, this time leading to the roof of Letham Deregor. He lugged the body carelessly through before following suit.

As he raised his hands to direct another spell, he caught himself with a thought and transformed into a mist to travel into the vampiric fortress. The room he sought was his own quarters, though he did not frequent it particularly often.

Tucked into a drawer on his desk, a grand masterpiece of carpentry left to gather dust over the centuries, was a pile of yellowed paper from which he grabbed a single sheet. He cast a spell to remoisturise the dried pot of ink that had sat unused for what must have been years and in it dipped the tip of a quill. He then set it to the paper and began to write.

Several minutes later, after allowing the ink to dry, he bundled the letter into a scroll and tied it with a loose piece of thread before tucking it back into the desk and flying back up to the roof.

"Id va'dar kvetan," Kalahar muttered, coming to stand over the lifeless, bloodied corpse. A flame appeared in each of his hands, and he drew his arms back. "Yl'dekkar, farez!"

As he extended his arms, he brought his hands together, and the gentle flames combined and erupted into infernos. It burned with the intensity of a lighthouse fire, a lonely beacon in the forest shrouded by night. It continued to burn and even caught the attention of several of the vampires sheltering in the keep as they came out to investigate. They knew better than to question Kalahar's intentions, and instead just watched.

The fire raged for almost a minute before Kalahar clenched his hands to snuff it out. Where Linelle's body had laid remained only a pile of blackened ashes and bones atop the charred stone, and the vampire completed the spectacle by summoning a gust which scattered these remains to the winds.

And then without even acknowledging the crowd that had assembled, he traced a portal and returned to the cabin.

CHAPTER 32

FREE CITY OF DANNOS, SANTEROS

Elaeínn awoke with a throbbing headache and residual soreness where she had been struck. She didn't know where she was, but she lay flat, and above her were several faces—some of which she was glad to recognise.

"Pori allabra ketana, ela pori di tenara, iy deflani."

The person speaking wasn't one of those standing over her, but it was a voice she recognised, even through the language barrier. Her encounter with him had only been brief, but it was not one she would easily forget.

She sat up in the bed, whole body beset by aches, and laid eyes upon the man about whom she knew so little, but now seemed to be her only hope.

"You're going to need to repeat that in a way I can understand," she said.

One of those standing over her, who she remembered as Rosa, uttered a spell and the chatter in the background ceased to be a foreign racket and became comprehensible. As was Elton's question when he repeated it.

"We've got some questions that we hope you can answer."

"How long have I been out?"

"Not long," the bald man she remembered as Paul said. "You'll have plenty of time to rest before any more action, 'cause boss himself needs to rest, too."

"Why were you with Hortensio? Where is Hortensio?" Elton sat up and came to stand beside the others around the bed, but they quickly guided him back to sit on his own bed. "Where has he sent our bombs?"

"What happened to you?" Elaeínn asked.

"Your protector stabbed me in the heart. It's irrelevant—I need you to answer my questions. What is going on?"

Elaeínn huffed. "I can give you the short explanation and miss out a lot of the details, or you can hear the long one—and I wouldn't worry about the bombs, they aren't going anywhere."

She proceeded to tell the story of her expedition to the Heart of magic and the appearance of Jannis alongside a deceased Hortensio. She recounted the appearance of the vampire and the way he had brought Hortensio back to life, the way he had hijacked the sorcerers' attempt to take control of the dragon, and her defeated journey back across the ocean with the Salyrians.

"Your bombs? Stopped just off the road maybe a day's ride from here. That's at a slow pace. I think they left a few guards, but not many. They're entirely expecting the rest of the knights to come back for them."

"And you can visualise this location?" Rosa inquired.

"There was nothing special about it, but... yes." Elaeínn leaned forwards, gesturing sarcastically to her face. "Here's my forehead. Do what you will with it."

Rosa dismissed Elaeínn's scorn and muttered the words to a spell as her fingers caressed her forehead.

"If we can teleport there and bring our shipment straight back, we can forget all about Hortensio, because we'll be in Letham Deregor preparing to turn it to rubble," Elton said.

"You've got two options, boss." This time it was the last of those present she recognised, Felix, speaking. "You can let yourself heal and we will wait to strike. A little bit of extra preparation never hurt anybody. Or we could go without you, but I didn't think you would like that."

"Or we do neither," Elton growled. "I'm healed. Rosa healed me. We can—"

As if on cue, he fell into a coughing fit lasting what felt like much longer than it really was. When he finally recovered, he found himself at the receiving end of three sceptical gazes.

"Go get the bombs without me," he conceded. "But I'm resting at home. Rosa—"

The magician cut him off with a nod and assisted him onto his feet before the pair hobbled out of the room. Elaeínn was yet to register where exactly she had ended up, and she took a quick survey of the surroundings in an attempt to remedy that. She saw lots of beds, but not so many occupants, and along the walls were cabinets and shelves on which she could see various surgical implements and vials of solution.

"It's, uh, nice to see you again," Paul said, breaking the silence that had fallen since Elton and Rosa's departure.

"It would be nicer if it had been of my own accord. Hortensio and Jannis betrayed me without a second thought."

"Well, one of them's dead. That's the blood on the floor there. It's pretty weird, actually, how easy it was."

"Weird?" Felix echoed. "It's downright shocking. He pretty much handed himself over, the way he trapped himself in. What was he expecting?"

"I don't know if it's what he was expecting, but rather what he wasn't expecting," Elaeínn said. "Elton said he was stabbed in the heart?"

"By Jannis, yes," Felix answered. "Would've killed him if Rosa hadn't turned up."

"Even with that luck, it doesn't seem a very smart move to trap himself in. I think he must have been banking on help of some kind. Kalahar was the one who set them off on the assassination mission. Do you think he could have been expecting Kalahar's help?"

"Doesn't really matter, does it? It never came. That vampire doesn't care for anyone, and if he managed to trick Jannis... well, that's Jannis's fault. We made the mistake of trusting him once and nobody should ever repeat that." Felix sighed and rubbed his forehead. "And now he has a dragon. What in hell is he planning to do with a dragon?"

"He doesn't have a dragon. He has trapped Alazarioss," Elaeínn growled. "And we're going to free her."

"Let's take things one step at a time—we need our bombs, first. I'm sure the boss will happily have you tag along."

"Come on, let's go out of here," Paul suggested. "Place reeks of death and sick."

Elaeínn hauled herself out of the bed to protests from her body. She ignored the discomfort and exited alongside Felix and Paul, and she allowed herself to be led through the foreign desert city.

Of the many observations she had made about the human culture, that which stood out was the volume. Everything was so loud, the people so expressive over the most menial of happenings. Everywhere they went, there was some variety of melodrama, some argument or squabble taking place, and it was grating, especially in concatenation with her pounding headache. She found herself longing for the quiet of elves.

"Welcome to the Redhouse," Paul announced as they came to a building immediately distinct from its rundown surroundings, with ornamental pillars and a wide entryway, guards stationed outside, even workers with brushes tidying the adjacent road. It was the only part of the city that Elaeínn wouldn't have marked down immediately as looking like a slum.

"This is where your organisation works, then?" she asked as they passed through into the lobby, a chamber pleasantly organised and welcoming.

"Not really an organisation anymore. Boss made it into a government," Paul supplied. "But it's the same building it used to be when it was the Syndicate." He then spotted a pair of individuals in the corridor ahead and jogged over to meet them.

"I really hope we can kill him and be done with it, done with it all," Felix suddenly mused. "He's gone mad, elf. That bloody vampire is the only thing he thinks about. It's harming his work here, it's harming his health, it's no good for anybody. And it's even worse that we don't understand the vampire's motives at all. Not once has he stated his goals."

"His goals won't matter when we're done with him," Elaeínn said confidently.

"El... Elaine, this is Elaine," Paul rejoined the pair and gestured to a grey-skinned woman with vampiric features, a physiologically similar man at her side. "She's actually named after you."

"Me? What do you mean, named after me?"

"Boss said she reminded 'im of you. I don't really know what he meant by that. And the other one is Caster. We call 'im that 'cause he can cast spells."

"Imaginative," Elaeínn commented mutedly. "You look like—"

"Vampires?" the female vampire, Elaine, finished for her. "That would be because we are. But don't fret, we want to kill Kalahar as much as everyone else. If only because of the fact that he takes great pleasure in the frequent massacre of our kind, without explanation. We won't be hunted down any longer."

The group grew again when they were joined by two more men, both similar in stature and appearance.

"Where's the boss?" the first of them, his hair wavier than the second, asked as they appeared.

"Rosa took him somewhere to rest," Felix answered. "Did you find Hortensio?"

"Someone spotted them banded together around a convoy of carriages and wagons. They're camped out underneath the ridge off the northern road. If we were to round up as many guards as we can find, we would be able to overwhelm him—he hasn't even brought an army. Our scout counted maybe thirty carts, a hundred knights."

"We can wait. Keep an eye on them. They don't know Jannis is dead—we need to keep it that way. And we need to get those explosives back. As soon as possible."

The discussion continued for some time, the two newcomers introduced to Elaeínn at some point as Ant and Fez, and she increasingly felt the need to interject with every mention of their mission. "I've been meaning to ask. What exactly are the bombs for?"

"We want to kill Kalahar. You're following that far, yes?" Felix said, his tone laced with patronisation. "Except we need to track him down first. Track him down or trap him. We're going to threaten to destroy Letham Deregor, plant enough explosives to turn it to a mound of debris, should we light any fuses. Hopefully, in whatever magical way he works, he will realise and teleport straight there, springing the trap."

As Felix finished his explanation, the group was then made complete with the arrival of Rosa.

"And now we can finally get working. How does a little bit of combat sound, elf?"

The apprehensions Elaeínn had had the last time she was asked to partake in a skirmish were entirely absent. She responded with a smile and an enthusiastic nod.

"I've set him off to sleep," Rosa reported impatiently. "But he wants us to get those bombs now. Will the group of us be enough, Elaeínn? Or do we need backup?"

"A few knights? Provided you're skilled fighters, we won't need anyone else."

"Alright. Here's what's going to happen—I'm going to stay on this side, keep the portal open. Guards are going to block the road to make sure nobody interferes. You seven will go through and dispatch the knights—we're not interested in taking prisoners. And then the cargo is ours. Real simple."

"Real simple," Ant echoed. "Salyrian knights are no foot soldiers."

"We've fought 'em before," Paul asserted, waving a hand. "And if these are the ones Hortensio left behind on guard duty, I don't reckon they're the best fighters."

"We'll be fine," Felix agreed, fishing a knife from his jerkin and twirling it in his fingers. "The sooner this is done, the better. Let's get a move on."

They group filed hastily out of the Redhouse and into the street outside, alive with activity. Rosa set about ordering the guards to clear the area—a task which, Elaeínn noticed, they seemed to accept with glee.

"You're sure you're in a state to fight?" Felix asked Elaeínn as Rosa brought her hands together and began to mutter an incantation.

"I can take a beating," she replied assuredly, drawing her sword. Felix's eyes expanded as they found the blade's intricate runed surface and he let out a whistle of admiration.

Rosa brought one of her hands up and placed the other on the ground before stepping carefully across the street until she had crossed about the width of a carriage and then some. She brought her hands back together, stepped into the middle point of the invisible portal frame, and thrust forwards with a grunt. A portal opened, revealing the barren landscape where the Salyrian knights awaited with the diverted shipment.

"This is where the fun begins," Felix chuckled.

The knights had seen the portal open from the other side but were slow to react as Elaeínn and the Dannosi charged through, weapons at the ready. A small encampment had been assembled and the rest of the guarding force was quick to appear from their tents, unarmoured and utterly unready for the onslaught that had so suddenly appeared. Those that had been ready were the first to fall.

Felix led the group and unleashed two knives the moment he set foot on the dusty track. One of them found their mark with expert precision, sinking into the neck of the nearest guard and felling him before he could draw his sword. The second clanged ineffectively off the breastplate of another, further away.

The remaining armoured guards numbered three, while those readying themselves in the centre of the camp brought the total up to ten.

"That's more than a few, elf," Paul said.

"We'd best be quick, then."

Elaeínn vaulted the rudimentary fence that had been erected to mark the boundary of the camp and sprinted to catch up with the retreating guards. She reached them as they reached their compatriots, who had found swords and shields, but no armour. But just as they rallied together as one, so did the Dannosi as they formed around Elaeínn.

The first strike was made by Elaine as she turned into a blur, dashing into the guards and lashing out with claws extended. They were taken completely aback and scattered in every direction as jets of blood shot into the air. Paul peeled to the left and cut down one knight before falling into a duel with another. Ant and Fez took to the right and clashed with another pair while Elaeínn and Felix dashed into the centre of the fray.

Elaine's speed made her impervious and any hope the knights had had of surviving the attack was shattered. Though they were skilled fighters, their morale failed to materialise as the vampire reduced them to shreds before the others cut down the stragglers.

Elaeínn came to face an armoured guard who had managed to escape Elaine's flurry and their swords came together with a clang. She retracted her arm and swung wide, opening him up to Felix's knife as it sailed over their blades and struck him between the eyes. The clattering of his armour as he rocked against the ground was the last sound before the dust settled and they could rest.

"And that is the reason people are so terrified of your lot," Fez said as Elaine retracted her claws. "You're lucky we moved out of sight of the portal before you did that."

"I was doing my part!" she snapped, though Fez had already moved on to the carts stationed at the back of the camp.

"Is it all there?" Felix called, collecting his knives.

Ant and Fez set about inspecting the wagons, peeling the sheets back and returning gestures of affirmation. The entire group then joined them, working together to wrangle the carts out of the sand and through the portal. The knights' bodies—in the case of those slain by Elaine, the remnants thereof—were shoved aside and discarded with no notion of burial, mere obstacles in the path of the mission. The fence was knocked down and the wagons, successfully unstuck, were wheeled up onto the road and through the portal back into the street outside the Redhouse.

As had become custom, a crowd had formed to watch the affair, amazed gasps rippling through swathes of people who had never seen a portal in their lives. And yet there were exclamations linking the use of magic to vampirism, conspiracies that went ignored by the majority as the last of the carriages were hauled through the portal. Rosa, tempering her breathing, her clothes drenched with sweat, was finally able to issue a command to close it.

The task of storing the bombs was delegated to labourers in the Redhouse and the group reconvened in the intelligence office. Ant and Fez, who had through everything still been working on the tracking of the malevolent vampires, presented an update in which they demonstrated that no more killings had taken place.

"Kalahar, whatever he's doing, is more preoccupied with that than Dannos," Ant said. "I'm not all too sure that's a good thing."

"It's not," Felix stated assuredly. "Which is why we need to deal with him. Sooner, rather than later, because who knows what he's going to do? He has control of a dragon. He has... divine knows what else. I hate to suggest it, but I think we should go without the boss."

Several pairs of incredulous eyes fell upon the young head of the intelligence service as if he had suggested they all walk barefoot across hot coals.

"You're jokin', right, Felix?" Paul was the first person to react verbally.

"Not in the slightest. This is a serious task. I know it's the boss's personal vendetta, but perhaps it's for the best."

"I agree with you," Elaeínn chimed in.

"This isn't your fight. Pipe down," Rosa scolded. "We're not doing it without Regi."

"The longer we wait, the longer it gives Kalahar to find out about our plans and kill us all," Felix argued. "We know he's capable of it. He just—for reasons none of us can understand—hasn't. It's now or never."

"This is Regi's project! We're not doing it without him!"

"Regi will forgive us for not giving him the glory! He wants Kalahar dead at any cost and I don't know if you've noticed, but the city is suffering for it! The man is going mad! We would be doing him a favour to act now!"

"Why don't we just ask him?" Elaine suggested.

311

"Because he knows what the answer will be." Rosa glared at Felix.

"Some things have to be done for the greater good. Isn't that part of the whole philosophy behind moving past the Syndicate? Killing Kalahar is in everybody's interest, even if it is the boss's vendetta. I don't want to cut him out of it either, Rosa, but it's the best option."

Rosa's gaze flicked from Felix to Ant and Fez. "Well? Where do you stand on this?"

Before either of them could answer, she then turned her attention to Paul. "And you disagree with this too, right?"

Ant and Fez moved to stand behind Felix. "It's the right thing, Rosa. It's the smart thing. It's what the boss would want if he could see through the emotion clouding his judgement."

Her brow furrowed in heightened frustration. "Paul?"

"I... I can see both sides."

The vampires followed Ant and Fez in drifting to Felix's side. "I just want to kill him. I don't really care about what Elton thinks."

"One word and I could have the pair of you lynched," Rosa hissed.

Elaine backed away, her hands twitching as they had done in the moments before she had lunged at the Salyrian knights in the desert. "That isn't a wise idea."

"I have more authority than you, Rosa," Felix said firmly. "I'm making the decision to go without him. And without telling him, too. I would really like you to come with us."

Rosa pursed her lips and then hung her head resignedly as Paul became the last to wander to Felix's side. "I'm not happy about it."

"I don't need you to be happy about it. I just need you on our side. Now let's kill that fucking vampire."

Redhouse workers were tasked with searching the city for the longest lengths of rope they could find, and others spent the afternoon preparing a set of heavy silver chains with hevula. Elaeínn was taught, she thought arbitrarily, how to brew the oil that unlocked the vampires' vulnerability to silver, but she found it interesting enough to be worth her time. Additionally, she was given a silver sword and spent the evening acclimating to its heavier weight.

The following morning was an early start. Elaeínn spent the night in a nearby tavern where she gorged on the fullest meal she had eaten for some time. It was Rosa who woke her just as the sun was rising, and the group assembled downstairs in the tavern where Elaeínn had stayed.

An uneasy sensation hung over the table as they ate breakfast in eerie silence. During their preparation for the operation, the only emotion anyone had exhibited was raw confidence. Something had changed, and it was overwhelmingly evident to Elaeínn that she wasn't the only one having doubts. But nobody said anything, and they proceeded after breakfast to the Redhouse, as per the plan.

Elton remained in the dark as they once again blocked off the street outside the Redhouse and carts with all the necessary supplies were wheeled into the open.

"This is it," Felix proclaimed, twirling a knife on his finger, though in a manner more nervous than usual. "Are we ready?"

His question was directed at Ant and Fez, in charge of logistics. They watched as the last cart, laden with flasks of oil, rolled to a stop, and nodded in unison.

"Rosa? You're rested enough to hold the connection?"

"I'll be fine," she stated curtly.

"And you two." He turned his attention then to the vampire duo and lowered his voice. "It's likely we will scuffle with other vampires. Can I trust you to fight them?"

"We don't align ourselves with those who fight in Kalahar's name," Elaine said defiantly.

"Good. Then, uh, yes. Let's get it done."

He looked at Rosa and nodded. The sorceress drew her hands up and traced a portal of similar size to that from the day before, and the labourers standing by in the street set straight to work hauling the supplies into the dreary vampire fortress.

From a state of agonising anticipation, everything then happened very quickly. Elaeínn followed Felix and Paul into the portal and they dragged a line of rope, bombs attached, through the winding labyrinth until they ran out of slack. They repeated this over and over with the many prepared lines of rope until every corridor leading away from the central point of the operation, the atrium, was laced with explosives.

Through their adrenaline they didn't take any time to stop and consider the strange lack of opposition. Not a single vampire had appeared to stop them, nor Elaine and Caster as they carried out the same task on the floor above. It was only when they ran out of bombs that they finally slowed down and took a moment to think.

"Something isn't right," Felix declared. Sweat glistened on his forehead despite the biting cold as he returned to the atrium alongside Elaeínn and Paul, having laid the last of the lines of rope. The labourers, their job finished, had returned through the portal to Dannos. Elaine and Caster were also present in the atrium, their arms full with the silver chains.

"Are we ready to set the trap?" Elaine asked impatiently.

"Where are all the others? This place should be crawling with vampires and we've not seen a single one. Where are they?"

His voice echoed off the walls of the open room, the only sound in the heavy silence.

"Hello? I don't really care. The less opposition, the better. Can we do this?" Elaine rattled the chains and raised her eyebrows.

"It... it could only mean one thing." Elaeínn saw in Felix's eyes a deathly fear. "He already knows we're here."

He jolted his head around, darting his eyes in every direction as if they were surrounded. A sickening dread crept through Elaeínn like she had been submerged in icy water.

"He already knows we're here!" Felix repeated. "Get back through the portal! Abort!"

The portal's position in the centre of the room meant that it should have been simple to quickly jump back through. Felix ran for it as if his life depended on it, an urgency which spread naturally to the others as they, too, accepted his order to retreat.

But when they reached the portal it closed in front of their eyes. Elaeínn swore and drew her silver sword as the silence that had enveloped them for so long was finally split by a monstrous shrieking from what sounded like every direction all at once.

CHAPTER 33

Elton could think of nothing he wanted to do less than rest. Though his body offered him no choice, and neither did Rosa as she led him up the stairs to his bedroom and forced him to lay down.

The rest of the day passed extraordinarily slowly. His servant brought him something to eat as the light began to die and he spent much of his time thinking through various plans for the assault on Letham Deregor. He played out several scenarios in his head, covered numerous sheets of paper in strategies, and drank half a bottle of wine to cope with the overbearing stress he felt as a result of his self-perceived uselessness. And eventually, overcome by fatigue, he went to sleep.

His slumber was interrupted later that night by a faint knocking on his front door. It was enough to wake him, as he had been yet to fall into a deep enough sleep to escape the grip of his anxiety. He crept out of bed, picking up his dagger and placing his ear to the door to listen to his servant greet the midnight visitor.

The front door closed and the servant proceeded to climb the stairs, though Elton thought he could discern two sets of footsteps. His fingers twitched nervously around the hilt of his blade and he double-checked the latches to make sure they were secure.

"Aldran?" Elton called through the door as the footsteps reached his floor. "Who is it?"

"Just me, Count," a muffled voice responded. "Someone is at the door for you. They say Kalahar is back."

"Who is it?" Elton repeated, slower.

There was a delay, only slight, but noticeable enough for Elton, before Aldran's response. "It's Rosa, Count."

"Tell her to teleport in here then. I'm not unlocking the door."

A forceful banging sounded three times from the door before a being reinforced by a recognisable voice. "Open the door, Elton! Open the door or he dies!"

Elton gritted his teeth and clenched his dagger tighter.

"I'll do it, Elton! I'll cover your walls in his blood!"

Elton relaxed the grip on his dagger and walked over to the barricaded window.

"Where is Jannis?" Hortensio cried, his tone rife with real anguish. "What have you done to him?"

Hortensio began to kick the door, vigorously, powerfully, again and again. Wood splintered with each hit, but Elton knew he wouldn't be able to bring down the door by himself. It was the sturdiest in all Dannos.

"You killed him, you bastard! You evil man! In fact, to call you a man is an insult to men! You're nothing! You're a bug beneath my shoe! You ruin the lives of everyone around you! And it makes me sick to my core that I have the displeasure of knowing that you're my father!"

"The louder you shout, the more likely it is that somebody will hear you," Elton said, loudly enough that it would be audible through the door.

The banging stopped and there was a faint thud which Elton could only imagine was Aldran.

"How's that, old man? Someone else just died because of you! I might have been set on this mission by Kalahar but he is far from the reason I am pursuing it. I'm pursuing it because it's the best thing for all the world. Everybody will be better off when there's no more Elton Redwinter!"

His foot collided with the door once again and tremors translated through the walls and adjacent furniture within Elton's bedroom. Ornaments and miscellaneous objects rocked in place, some shifting dangerously close to falling. Elton disarmed the bell and removed the grate from the window before opening it and looking down into the square below.

He had expected to see other knights in plain clothes, as Jannis had dressed to slip past detection. But the square was empty, apart from the usual lowlifes. A pair of guards walked through on patrol and pricked up their ears as they heard the distant rhythmic bashing of Hortensio's foot against the door. They looked at each other and then shrugged and walked on.

"Give up," Elton said, walking back to the door and sheathing his dagger. "No matter how much you try, you're never going to succeed. All it takes to have you killed is one word out my window."

Hortensio finally capitulated in his attempt to break down the door and could be heard sliding down the wall outside. Elton placed his ear back against the door and thought he heard a gentle sobbing.

"Throw your sword down the stairs," he said softly.

A prolonged metallic clattering rang through the air to confirm that Hortensio had complied. Elton fished a ring of keys from a drawer in his desk and unlocked each of the many locks on his door, followed by the latches. He then grasped the door's handle tightly, took a deep breath, and pressed with enough force that the door fell open just a crack.

He jumped back in anticipation of an attack but none came. Instead, Hortensio remained slumped on the ground. Beside him, his chest gently rising and falling, was the unconscious servant.

"I don't suppose you're proud of me," Hortensio mused. "I'm not a murderer."

"What are you doing?"

"I don't know. I came here to do what the vampire said. But it's not what I wanted. I wanted... I just wanted to stay home."

"How very childlike of you. What happened to your great, ambitious dreams of conquest? The whole continent, was it not? And now you don't even want me?"

"You don't understand, alright?" Hortensio stood up and Elton's hand fell instinctively to his dagger once more as the young King entered his bedroom. "I died, Elton. I died. I saw my life flash before me. I saw the future. The world. *Everything*. I saw the threads of existence. I saw things so much more important than control and conquest and ideology. I actually experienced death and I was brought back. I'm not about to waste that. I want to go home and I want to experience joy. I want to be with Penelope until the day I die—the day I truly die. The way I'm meant to, not with a sword in my gut."

Elton had spent the entire duration of Hortensio's monologue staring into his eyes, searching them. He found nothing but distraught sincerity.

"You can still make the choice to turn around and leave," Elton said.

Hortensio turned around a took a step out the door.

"I... but then I don't know if it would be right." His voice trembled. "My... my conscience says it's the right thing. To not leave."

Hortensio pivoted in place and leapt onto Elton with a sudden ferocity at a speed that caught him completely unaware. He drew his dagger but Hortensio grappled with him and managed to knock it to the floor before wrestling him into the wall. His hands found Elton's neck and he pressed hard.

"What are they doing, Elton?" Hortensio rasped. "What are they doing with those bombs?"

Elton's arms flailed as Hortensio's eyes flashed red and his hand found a half-full bottle of wine. He drove it into his assailant's temple and it shattered, red liquid and shards of glass scattering over the room as Hortensio lost his grip and allowed Elton to pick up his dagger.

"Are they for me, Elton? Wait, I don't need to ask you." Hortensio backed away, towards the door, holding a hand to the side of his head. "I can just go find out myself."

"What's happened to you?" Elton's voice was cold as he pointed his dagger at Hortensio's unguarded chest.

The young King's eyes flashed red again, more intensely than before. "Kalahar resurrected me. I am paying him back for it. I am wiping your stain from the face of this world!"

Hortensio barrelled recklessly towards Elton and crashed into the cabinet behind him, the Count stepping out of the way at the last second. He roared and changed direction without stopping and Elton once again stepped out of the way as he crashed this time into the bed.

"Snap out of it!" Elton shouted. "This isn't you!"

"I'll kill you! If it's the last thing I do!"

Hortensio leapt from the bed and dodged Elton's dagger, aiming for his legs and bringing him tumbling to the ground. He once again wrapped his hands around Elton's neck and this time, there was no bottle of wine on standby.

"He's... making... you... do this..." Elton choked. Hortensio's eyes no longer flashed red. They remained red.

"I'm fighting him, Elton! I'm fighting him! I don't want to kill you!" the King pressed harder and the colour began to drain from Elton's face. "Yes I do! I am doing what is right!"

"Think... Pen... Penelope..."

Through the unwavering red in Hortensio's eyes, Elton saw a glint. And the grip on his throat relaxed, just slightly, enough for him to draw a breath, and enough for him to reach, grab his dagger, and plunge it into Hortensio's side.

The King cried out and Elton took the opportunity to bring his foot back and drive it into his son's ribs, launching him into the bedframe. Elton struggled to his feet while Hortensio continued to wail.

"I don't want to do this," Elton said mutedly. "But I'm doing what is right."

"I tried to fight," Hortensio sobbed. "I tried to. But he controlled me. He knew my every thought. I was his slave."

Elton wrenched the dagger from his son's ribs, blood spurting over the floor as Hortensio futilely tried to stem the wound.

"He's still trying to control me now. Whatever you're doing... with the bombs... he—"

His speech cut off abruptly and his head rocked back, bashing loudly against the corner of the bedframe.

"He... he's taking over... kill me, Elton! Kill me! Please!"

His whole body contorted and he buried his head in his hands, howling like a rabid animal.

"Kill me! Kill me! Kill me!"

Elton's hands trembled and he took three uneasy steps to stand above the young King. When Hortensio again lashed out, this time, Elton was quick enough.

CHAPTER 34

The tension between the sorcerers in Jiro's tower felt so tangible that it was as if it could have been cut with a knife.

"The vampire isn't here anymore," Jiro seethed. "What's stopping me from killing the pair of you?"

"I'm not going to answer a rhetorical question," Tregor replied. "We apologise for our actions in the killings of your associates. It was perhaps unnecessary."

"Unnecessary?" Jiro roared. "It was murder!"

"You run a criminal enterprise, for the gods' sakes!" Nendar chimed in. "Don't act as if you're not accustomed to it!"

"We want to stop Kalahar, Jiro. That is our only goal. For the good of everybody. I know that we have acted in our own self-interest in the past, but for once, I can say with complete and utter honesty that we are doing this for the good of mankind. And elf- and dwarfkind. In fact, everybody in our world. Nobody is safe while Kalahar corrupts the Fateborn."

Jiro crossed his arms and cocked his head. "Enlighten me, then. Do you have a plan for this? Because I do believe it involved the Fateborn, and we know good and well that the vampire has made off with him. I will be keeping the payment, by the way."

"They don't have a plan." It was Lynn, her voice scathing, who spoke up. "They don't know what they're doing. They have chased Richard for months. They've caught him multiple times. And it always ends the same, because they're greedy and stupid. If they really wanted to stop Kalahar, they would've killed him back in Virilia, but no, here we are once again. A naïve inability to accept the Council's demise and a selfish desire to cling onto the semblance of power means that our world is doomed, because there's nobody with a genuine interest in the greater good willing to act to stop him."

The sorceress hobbled determinedly to her father and reached a hand into the inner pocket of his robe, deftly stealing a lirenium crystal.

"You three can squabble here until the end of time, for all I care. I'm going to go and stop Kalahar. Not that you're interested."

She stepped back and muttered a spell to cloak her magical signal and then traced a portal, anonymised. None of the three sorcerers said a word as she looked expectantly at each of them before shaking her head and departing.

*

Silvered daggers and vampire oil were in strong supply in the armoury at the Virilian Palace. Lynn took several of the daggers and loaded a satchel with vials of oil until she couldn't fit any more. Then, after a day spent regenerating her wounds, she moved on to Letham Deregor.

She shivered, not just because of the cold. A quick spell revealed to her the presence of numerous vampires, spread throughout the fortress. She muttered a prayer to a god she didn't believe in and began her search for something, anything that could have been used to put an end to Kalahar's plans. A dagger remained permanently in her hand, an uncorked vial of oil in the other.

She stopped midway through a corridor leading to a stairwell as she sensed the presence of someone walking towards her. A room to her left seemed to be her only escape from detection, and she ducked into it just as the vampire reached the bottom of the stairs.

Her plans changed in that moment and she stood, breathing rapid but hushed, against the wall in the darkness. She glanced out of the doorway and waited for the vampire to pass, and as it did, she leapt out, showered it in oil, covered its mouth with her hand, and then planted her dagger in its skull.

Three more vampires met the same fate as she continued her search before she was finally detected. A screech echoing through the fortress signalled to her that one of the bodies had been found, which she had expected, as they hadn't been hidden with much care.

Her progress slowed significantly as more of her time was spent hiding than searching. One advantage of the stronghold being so large, its layout so illogical, was that she did not struggle to evade her pursuers. But the hours passed and still she failed to find anything of use.

Hunger and fatigue set in which she forced herself to ignore. Under normal circumstances she would have suppressed such sensations with a spell, but to do so in that moment would have been akin to ringing a bell.

She carried on. In one isolated corridor she came upon a set of what seemed to be bedrooms, lavishly furnished but containing nothing of substance. Another opening led to a balcony facing the ocean, the red setting sun reflecting off the waves. It was a beautiful scene, but she didn't allow herself long to rest and admire.

With the fall of night, the temperature only descended further, to the point where her breath became visible. Yet she fought on, undeterred by the perfect storm of conditions working in unison to batter her morale. And eventually, several hours and another slain vampire later, her patience and determination paid off.

On the fringe of giving up, having lost track of which routes she had traversed and which she hadn't, Lynn opened a heavy oak door leading to a spiral staircase. She climbed it, up and up, until she came upon a single door at its peak. Pressing through, she came upon another living chamber, even larger and more opulent than the others, though showing signs of abandonment in the dust gathered on the furniture. Though one particular item stood out in its lack thereof—a desk, expansive, masterfully constructed. It was to this that Lynn was drawn immediately.

The objects on the desk's surface didn't offer much in the way of information or use, and she turned desperately to its drawers. And it was in the very first drawer that she found exactly what she was looking for.

Dear Richard, the letter began. The handwriting was almost illegible, and it was written in Archaeish. *We don't like that this is the option we have to pursue, but you leave us with no other choice.*

All other attempts at motivation thus far have failed. So we must resort to extremities. We have taken the body of your beloved and hidden her somewhere only we know. We can only hope that it is with her permanent removal from your access that you will finally realise your potential and apply it for the greater good. Stop inhibiting yourself and obsessing over this wasteful pursuit of meaningless emotion. You are meant for greater things—don't squander it.

You know how to find us if you decide, hopefully, to accept your fate.

Yours truly,
Nendar Varanus.

"Devious, Kalahar," Lynn muttered distastefully. "Truly despicable."

She read the letter again, then a third time and a fourth before rebinding it into a scroll and returning it to exactly the same position in which she had found it.

CHAPTER 35

MIRADOSI WILDERNESS

Very good, Richard. Very good.

Richard could not feel his skin as it was leached of all its warmth. He could not feel much of anything. He channelled himself into the dragon as they soared, defying the restrictions of nature, an unbridled force of magic.

His eyes opened and he saw the moon. It was by no means close, yet it did not feel far. As he manipulated the strings of magic, attempting to pull on the celestial mass, he found the resistance manageable. And that was the end of the test.

They descended in a controlled manner, wrapped as usual in a cocoon of fire, but, also as usual, unharmed.

"I had a dream last night," Richard said, climbing down from the dragon's back. "But it didn't feel like a dream. It was a memory. Everything that happened in the dream... happened exactly like what happened in reality."

"Well? What was it about?" The vampire summoned a fire in his hands with which to warm the rosy-cheeked bounty hunter.

"I buried Lin. I just... completely relived the entire process. And I didn't have any control, either. I was just watching everything happen through my own eyes. Does it mean anything?"

"I doubt it. Dreams are strange, and entirely disconnected from the real world. They are largely random constructs of your own mind."

Richard sighed and shook his head, retreating to the cabin and finishing the remains of a breakfast he hadn't been in the mood to eat earlier that day.

"I could move the moon now," he declared nonchalantly, sitting in front of the fire. "When were we going to stop testing and actually do whatever it is you wanted? Because the sooner we get it done with, the better. Well? Did you have any idea at all? Kalahar?"

He craned his neck to look behind him and could not see the vampire. Grunting, he stood up and peered outside, spotting him frozen in place some ways along the path leading towards the hills in which they had trained.

"Vampire?" Richard stepped quizzically towards him, unsure what to make of the vampire's glazed expression.

"This plan has not worked, you useless imbecile. It was never going to work," Kalahar murmured almost inaudibly. "I should never have trusted you!"

"Kalahar!" Richard shouted louder. "What's going on?"

The vampire snapped out of his trance and glared sternly at the bounty hunter. "Not now, Richard. I'm preoccupied."

"With what?"

"Not now! Leave me in peace!"

He muttered a spell and returned to his trance, continuing to mutter as if in conversation with someone. Richard turned away, scowling, and trudged a few paces back to the cabin but then turned around and retraced his steps.

"No," he said. "I want to know what's going on."

When the vampire didn't respond, Richard resorted to shaking him. But still he achieved nothing.

"Stop resisting! You are mine!" Kalahar's muttering turned to shouting as his trance grew more active. He began to wander around, though not consciously.

"Kalahar! I demand an explanation!"

"No, no, no! You are not strong enough for this! You cannot possibly break free!"

"Kalahar!"

The vampire cried out and trained his eyes, entirely present, on Richard. "When I say to leave me in peace, I do not expect to be interrupted again!"

He tried to re-enter the trance once more and Richard didn't hesitate to interrupt him, grabbing him by the shoulders and being launched into the snow in response.

"What do you think you're doing?" Kalahar restrained himself from further physical affront. "I'm going to lose him!"

"Who? Lose who? Explain!" Richard pushed himself up and stood defiantly close to the vampire.

"I'm mentally connected to another person. You don't know him, and it doesn't involve you. Allow me now to finish!"

Kalahar uttered the words to the spell, and then again, cursing in Archaeish as he tried a third time. His hands clenched into fists and he stormed away with heavy steps. Richard followed.

"He's been killed. I've lost him."

"Mentally connected?"

"It doesn't matter. We have a big problem."

Kalahar walked determinedly and without consideration back to the dragon, undeterred by Richard's incessant protests. "Get on. This mission will resume once we have dealt with this."

"I'm not moving one step until you tell me what's going on," Richard argued, maintaining his defiance. "You can't keep leaving me in the dark, Kalahar. I'm your apprentice. Not your servant."

"You'll be whatever I want you to be," Kalahar, until then so tender and measured with his speech, snapped. "I'm the only way you'll ever see your lover again. So you will do as I say. Elton Redwinter is about to destroy Letham Deregor. We aren't going to let him do that."

The vampire turned into a mist and drifted onto the dragon's back before materialising.

"Get on," he growled.

With a scowl so severe it cast shadows over his eyes, Richard obeyed.

Not a word was spoken, verbally or telepathically, during the hours-long journey around the continent. To avoid detection, Kalahar instructed the dragon to fly east, beyond the coast and over the ocean, before turning north. They were sighted by the occasional trading vessel and warship, primarily in the waters near the front line, but within seconds they had moved on. Nobody would believe the sailors when they returned home to share their stories.

The sun was setting by the time they arrived and nothing seemed amiss. The dragon landed gracefully on the fortress's roof and both riders climbed down with unnecessary haste, proceeding to vault onto a balcony and tear into the atrium.

"Excellent. We have time to spare," Kalahar mused. He clapped his hands twice, sharply, the sound echoing throughout the barren chamber and connected hallways. "Everyone! Gather here at once!"

Several figures appeared almost immediately, while others took their time in arriving. Regardless, it wasn't long before they found themselves surrounded by the entire population of Letham Deregor. They numbered remarkably few, and Kalahar seemed to notice that himself, though he didn't say anything.

"Elton Redwinter is going to arrive soon," Kalahar spoke emphatically. "He and his goons intend to rig this fortress with explosives. We are going to let him."

He paused for long enough to allow the ripple of confusion amongst the spectators to take place, but not for any of them to ask why.

"Let them believe they have the element of surprise. Let them set whatever contrived trap they have planned. And when it is complete, that is when we will strike. Together. Let their morale climb, and then let us shatter it. Let them believe they are succeeding. And then destroy them. This is it, my friends. I have fantasised this moment for a long time. Now, it finally becomes a reality. This is the end of Elton Redwinter. And the beginning of a new era. Our new era."

There was no applause, but there was a muted understanding. The crowd dispersed, save for Faefion, who approached Kalahar while glaring scornfully at Richard.

"We've suffered an attack already," she admitted curtly. "Someone snuck in about a week ago and killed five of us. Nobody wanted to admit it to you."

"Not even you?" Kalahar snarled, his ruby eyes flaring.

"I knew you were busy, Kalahar, I know what you're like. I couldn't be asked with the fuss. But I thought it sensible to tell you now that you've returned."

"Well, where are they? You pacified them, I assume? Who were they?"

Faefion shook her head. "We don't know. They masked their presence. And they hid well. And they were well equipped. And after all the killings they committed, they then... just... disappeared. I don't know what their objective was, but it was no ordinary vampire hunter. It was a skilled magician."

"We don't have time for this right now." Kalahar clenched his fists and pursed his lips. "After we have dealt with Elton, you will discover the identity of this intruder, Faefion. You will not fail again."

Faefion knew better than to respond and she joined her compatriots in hiding. Letham Deregor fell silent, and it felt entirely empty.

"What about us?" Richard's fingers bristled uneasily over the hilt of his sheathed sword.

"We aren't going to fight," Kalahar chuckled. "We aren't going to shed a drop of blood. But we are going to have front-row seats. Saka los."

The vampire brushed Richard's shoulder as he cast the spell and their physical appearances fell away. The two found a stairway leading to the first level above the atrium floor, proceeding to lean on the balustrade as they watched and waited.

Hours passed with nothing to experience but the deafening silence and the gentle breeze as it filtered in from outside. Richard grew impatient, but Kalahar refused to allow either of them to lose focus. The bounty hunter wanted to ask him what they were focusing on but knew it would have been a pointless endeavour.

Their wait came to an end with the opening of a portal, in the centre of the atrium, several hours after they had arrived. An array of unimpressive workers hauling carts full of supplies brought noise to the soundless fortress with the trundling of wheels, the squeaking of rusted axles, the clinking of half-full glasses, and the rattling of chains. Richard recognised those who followed them. It was not Elton, but his companions who he had first met in that very stronghold.

Alongside them was a pair of new faces, a man and a woman, and it wasn't immediately clear to Richard who they were. Kalahar, however, radiated anger through his invisibility and it was as a result of this that Richard was able to discern the new arrivals to be vampires.

Another unexpected face was one Richard recognised, though he had only seen her once before, and to try to recall her name was futile. The only thing he could remember about it was the impossibility of its pronunciation.

Their presence went unnoticed by the arrivals, who were too caught up in a predetermined routine to spend time searching for opposition. But in the little search they did carry out, they found nothing.

"When do we act?" Richard whispered aggressively. "It looks like they've rigged enough bombs to destroy the whole bloody fortress!"

"Not yet," Kalahar whispered calmly. "You must understand, Richard. It's not just about the end result. It's about execution. It's theatre."

More time passed and they listened in to the conversations taking place below them. Uncertainty was spreading, and Richard could imagine with perfect clarity the mischievous expression that would have been occupying Kalahar's face at that very moment had it been visible.

The two vampires who had arrived with Elton's crew came within dangerous proximity to Richard and Kalahar as they laid explosives around the floor on which they stood watch. But Kalahar remained calm. The anger that had initially flowed through him was no longer present.

"Something isn't right." The man speaking, Felix, if Richard remembered correctly, was easily audible in the echoey chamber. His voice was accompanied by an insistent rattling from a lengthy set of chains in the arms of the vampires.

"Are we ready to set the trap?" It was one of the two vampires, the woman, holding the chains.

"Where are all the others? This place should be crawling with vampires and we've not seen a single one. Where are they?"

"Hello? I don't really care. The less opposition, the better. Can we do this?"

"It... it could only mean one thing." Richard saw in Felix's eyes a deathly fear. "He already knows we're here."

Okay, my friends, Kalahar said telepathically.

"He already knows we're here!" Felix repeated. "Get back through the portal! Abort!"

It's showtime.

CHAPTER 36

LETHAM DEREGOR

The vampires emerged from every opening on every floor, falling from great heights through the atrium and approaching with reckless speed. But once the fighting began, instinct taking over, Elaeínn realised they weren't that outmatched at all.

There was no deliberation, no sense of attacking in waves. Everything happened at once. Elaeínn found her blade clanging noisily against the extended claws of a supernaturally quick blur of a vampire, one instance of sound in a veritable orchestra of violence. She deftly uncorked a vial of oil hanging from her waist and coated her assailant in it before skewering them through the skull. Her next attacker fell upon her before she had withdrawn her blade and raked their claws across her midriff, spiralling past without care for precision.

She gritted her teeth and turned to face them but nearly fell victim to Paul's sword as he split the skull of another vampire behind her. She gave him a brief nod of thanks and pirouetted to deflect a strike from above, her opponent falling from the ledge above with a translucent black blade in its clutches. They landed with miraculous grace and the two clashed, Elaeínn barely managing to keep up with the vampire's speed. Though she had practiced with the silver sword, something about it felt unnatural. The elegance with which she usually duelled was absent, and she had an innate understanding of the reason for it.

"Someone cover me!" she yelled, a request fulfilled by Felix as he tossed a flask of oil at her assailant. It shattered and the contents forced the vampire into a fit, leaving Elaeínn with a moment to finally land the necessary blow.

In the precious seconds between downing one opponent and dealing with the onslaught of another, Elaeínn dropped her sword and drew the Dragonsteel Blade. It felt light. It felt familiar. And it glowed a brilliant gold.

"Keep fighting!" Felix called. The panic that had defined him moments ago was non-existent. He radiated only confidence, absolute surety.

"Where is Kalahar?" Elaine hissed, parrying the blows of two attackers at once. She and Caster were unable to deliver any killing blows themselves, so they made themselves useful by corralling the aggressors into situations where someone else could.

"If we kill them all then he'll have no option but to appear! He can't stay away forever!"

As the battle raged on, the feasibility of triumph became realer and realer. It was a scene that reminded the Dannosi of the day of the eclipse, a mess of lacerated grey bodies making movement around the room difficult. But unlike the day of the eclipse, the enemies didn't spawn without end. Each felled vampire was a tangible step towards victory.

A shadowy blade whizzed through the air and caught Felix's shoulder, a jet of blood spurting onto a floor already slick with crimson. It was followed by another, and then another, the latter of which catching Caster in the midst of an attempt to cast a spell. He doubled over as the blade dispersed from within him, but was not permanently harmed.

"There!" Elaeínn gestured with her sword in the direction of the source of the conjurations, her eyes falling upon an auburn-haired vampire hiding in the mouth of one of the corridors feeding into the atrium. Their gazes met and she narrowed her eyes before launching yet another conjured blade aimed at Elaeínn.

The elf dodged the attack and bounded across the chamber to come to face the magic-wielding opponent, twisting and turning to avoid each further projectile that came sailing her way. She brought her sword upwards to deflect a final blade as she closed the gap between them and unclipped a vial of oil from her belt.

"Wait!" the vampire squealed.

Elaeínn did not wait.

The vampire screamed, clawing at her face as it was coated in solution, and then fell silent as one of Felix's silver daggers implanted itself in her forehead. Her body fell lamely to the ground and once again the group was engulfed by silence.

It wasn't a lasting silence. No more than thirty seconds passed as they regrouped to assess the situation before the air was rocked by a soft chuckling, progressing into a maniacal cackling. Elaine went straight for the chains, tossing half to Caster as everyone looked anxiously around for the source of the noise. There was no doubt as to who was laughing. It was just a matter of where he was.

Without even making an appearance, the confidence that had invigorated the group all but disappeared. The runes lighting Elaeínn's blade faded as she returned it to its sheath. Felix kicked one of the fallen bodies and cursed.

"Get us out of here," he said. "Caster. Make a portal and get us back to Dannos."

"I'm not leaving until we've lit the fuse," Elaine protested.

"He'll kill us, alright? Don't you see what he's doing? He's toying with us! That whole battle, we thought we were fighting for our lives but no! It was a charade! If we light those fuses then we are done!"

"Then at least we'll go down for a good cause."

"He wouldn't even let us light the fuses! Everything we have achieved, he has let us do it! He let us arrange to come here! He let us rig the whole place with bombs! Why do you think we were only attacked after we finished setting them up? He planned it all!"

"You're cutting him too much slack," Ant chimed in. "We can't give up now."

"We give up or we die!" Felix grabbed his counterpart by the shoulders. "Don't you see? Everything that has happened here has been part of an agenda. One written by Kalahar!"

"And don't you think that you leaving would only be another item on said agenda?" Fez suggested calmly. "One spark, Felix. One spark is all we need. And the whole place goes down."

"With us in it!" Felix was shouting. His eyes betrayed raw panic and his breathing was rapid. "Caster! Open a fucking portal!"

The submissive vampire followed the order with a concerned nod and without hesitation. Or rather, he tried to follow the order. The portal frame he traced and activated revealed the street outside the Redhouse for a moment before immediately falling closed. Caster, horrified, attempted the spell again. He achieved the same result.

"It's good to see you all again!" Kalahar's voice sounded deeper than usual as it echoed through the hall. He materialised in the pentagram at the room's centre, hands placed formally behind his back.

All attention fell upon the vampire in the instant of his appearance. Said attention mostly took the form of fear, in the way that nobody responded to his greeting, all their seven pairs of eyes locked unfalteringly upon him.

"It's good to see you too, Kalahar!" the vampire mused sarcastically, taking a step out of the pentagram. He looked curiously over each person in turn before settling his gaze on Elaine and Caster. "You two. Do you feel no regret in the murder of your brethren?"

Elaine didn't mince her words. "Fuck you."

Kalahar sighed and sauntered to stand before the pair. "Silver chains? Is this supposed to be how you finish with me? You already know I'm invulnerable to it."

The vampire turned and walked through the group to Elaeínn, whose hand fell instinctively to her sword's pommel. "And you. What are you doing here? This isn't your fight."

"It is now," Elaeínn growled.

"Well, don't bother drawing that sword. It's useless against even a lesser vampire, as I'm sure you're well aware."

He then turned his attention to Felix, who clutched an uncorked flask of oil in one hand and a silver dagger in the other.

"You're quite right in your theory, might I say," Kalahar said matter-of-factly. "It's... almost uncanny how right. In fact, I'm curious. What do you expect me to do next?"

Felix's shoulders rose and fell with his shallow breaths. "You're... you're going to kill us all."

"Wrong."

Kalahar flicked his wrist and from his fingers extended dark tendrils at imperceptible speed. They punctured Felix's face, blood and brain exploding from the back of his head as he immediately fell limp and the anxious quiet fell apart. Paul roared and smashed a full flask of solution over Kalahar's head, the vampire responding with a roar of his own as he fought through the pain. His silver sword was ineffective as it pierced his opponent's stomach and exited the other side, leaving Paul defenceless. Kalahar did not waste the opportunity.

"I was only going to kill the one of you, but if you all wish to perish, then so be it!" the vampire gargled. He pulled the blade from his torso with a strained grimace as he uttered a spell, a magical burst of energy sending Ant, Fez, and Elaeínn flying across the room.

Caster and Elaine stood their ground, having been standing further away, and ran towards the vampire with the chains. Kalahar extended his arms, contorting his hands and muttering, almost grunting a spell, stopping the pair in their tracks as they rose into the air. The chains fell from their grasp as Kalahar continued to contort and raise his hands, Caster and Elaine rising higher and higher into the air as he did so.

Of the three who had been flung backwards, Elaeínn was the first to regain her feet. She charged at Kalahar, scooping up the fallen chains and lunging before he could react.

His hands dropped, and with them, Caster and Elaine, but he was too slow. Elaeínn crashed into him and the pair tumbled to the ground, the elf wrestling furiously with the chains, the vampire screeching and squirming to escape.

"I will not fall like this. This is not how it ends!" Kalahar growled. He thrashed like a caged animal as Ant and Fez arrived to reinforce Elaeínn, joined further by Elaine and Caster. "Invectus. *Invectus!*"

The vampire's hand twitched and he looked at it expectantly, but nothing appeared. He repeated the spell again and again as his assailants tightened their hold on him before letting his head fall back in resignation. His attempt to escape ceased and he allowed himself to be restrained.

"Woven through these chains is a root I'm sure you're familiar with," Elaeínn stated. "Hevula. Or jägar. Either name is used depending on where you're from."

"I know what it is." Kalahar, though he spoke to her, was not focused on her. His gaze fell somewhere behind them all, seemingly into space, zoned out.

"You protect yourself from your weaknesses with magic. Is that right?"

Kalahar didn't answer her this time. Instead, he smirked, and then chuckled. Only softly, before bursting into laughter as he had done before they defeated him.

"What's so funny?"

"It's just amusing," he droned, slurring his words as if drunk before laughing again. "I have managed to keep that a secret for so long. And then Nendar and Tregor, they came so close to unveiling it themselves. In the sewer… of course, none of you were there except for… that one." He pointed at Felix's corpse. "And now you discover it. Well done. I am not, in fact, immortal. But I am so terribly sorry to inform you that despite this, I will not die today. Or ever. This secret dies with you."

The drawn-out hissing of a sword being pulled from its sheath stole Elaeínn's attention from the immobile vampire. Standing in the centre of the atrium, amongst the piles of grey carcasses, was a lone, at first glance ordinary man, his face shrouded in shadow and a bow slung over his back.

"Release him," the man said calmly. Elaeínn recognised him, though she had met him only briefly. Judging by the expressions on Ant and Fez's faces, so did they. Only Elaine and Caster were left clueless.

A portal opened behind Richard and he raised a hand, closing it without so much as turning to look. He looked up from the floor, his eyes meeting each of those standing over Kalahar in turn.

"Let him go," he repeated, and his voice reflected cold confidence.

"Who is this? Who is he to stop us now?" Elaine hissed.

Richard lifted his sword ever so slightly. "Step away."

Elaine was stopped before she had even started to attack. Richard reached out his hand and brought her to a halt as she turned with an expression betraying her intent. He contracted his arm and she flew towards him, stopping only inches away, arms locked to her sides and neck snapped back.

"One move," he continued, speaking through Elaine to the entire group. "One wrong move and you all die. You all die, as does everyone in Dannos. Every last vampire, lesser or malevolent." For the last sentence, he did shift his focus to Elaine.

He relaxed his arm and the vampire fell, crumpling to the ground but promptly recovering and valiantly returning to her feet.

"We can work together, Richard," Elaeínn cautiously negotiated. "I don't know what he's done to make you work for him, but we can do it too."

Kalahar laughed. "No, you can't. It is something only I can provide."

Richard was unreadable. "Step away from him. Or I will have to force you to."

"They aren't here to negotiate, Richard. They're here to destroy us. A band of thieves, monsters, and terrorists. I couldn't imagine a less noble bunch. That is the reality of who stands before you. Remember that before you make any naïve decisions."

"We aren't monsters," Elaeínn argued. "We aren't thieves or terrorists. We're people. Just like you."

"And if they kill me, you know what happens, Richard."

The bounty hunter didn't waver. "Step away."

Elaeínn caressed the pommel of her sword and drew it slowly, its runes emanating a soft gold. "If this is how it must be, at least be honourable about it."

It was difficult to discern from his stony countenance, but Elaeínn thought she saw him smile, if only slightly.

They came together with elegance. Richard's blade, though basic and uninspiring in the face of Elaeínn's luminant artifact, was wielded with the prowess of a master swordsman. The magical enhancement to her ability granted by the Dragonsteel Blade was rendered no advantage in the matchup. They fought as equals.

Each clash resonated like the twang of an instrument as they danced through the atrium. Richard strode definitively with each strike, Elaeínn nimbly dodging and parrying as she looked for an opening.

"It's a trick, Richard!" Kalahar called. "Use your magic, for the hells' sakes! She has no concept of what it means to be honourable!"

Elaeínn's opponent paid the vampire no heed as he continued his resolute onslaught. She parried a strike from the left but he pirouetted to deflect her counterattack, using the momentum to strike again and again.

A third sword joined the fray, followed shortly thereafter by a fourth. Ant and Fez's assistance meant that suddenly, Elaeínn wasn't bound to defence.

Until that point, Richard had acted without so much as a hint of struggle. It wasn't much, but Elaeínn noticed him furrow his brow as he stepped backwards to avoid the tips of her allies' blades as they were thrust forwards.

Ant and Fez were skilled, but not in comparison to their adversary. Richard quickly realised this and in a series of deft movements disarmed Fez, bringing his foot up and kicking him squarely in the ribs. Fez crashed to the ground and crawled to retrieve his sword as the battle waged on.

"I don't want to kill you," Richard said as he deflected Ant's blade. "I just can't let you kill the vampire. You can live, go home, carry on with your lives. But I need him."

Elaeínn was not deterred, attempting a jab which was parried with ease. "He took control of Alazarioss. Bent her to his will. He's evil, and he will continue to be evil even if we leave! We can't stand idly by! It's not the right thing to do!"

"I have no choice!" Richard was now shouting. "If you are going to stand in my way then you leave me no option but to destroy you!"

A fireball similar in size to a clenched fist blazed across the hall, missing Richard's head by a hair's length. He leapt backwards in anticipation of a second, which materialised and was subsequently quenched mid-flight with the extension of his hand and the uttering of a spell.

Ant was too hasty in an attempt to exploit the distraction and moved forwards without Elaeínn. He swung his weapon too wide, leaving Richard an opportunity to strike at his chest. He took it.

Elaeínn was running out of options, but Caster's spells gave her an idea. While Richard spent precious seconds removing his sword from Ant's body, Elaeínn found the talisman she had kept since its failure to activate on the island. She ran over to Caster as he summoned and launched another fireball.

This left Richard briefly magically defenceless as he focused on quenching it. It was enough for him to fail to notice the portal as it opened beside Caster, Elaine, and Elaeínn, and though Kalahar tried to warn him, he could not react fast enough.

Fez knew better than to spend time mourning the loss of Ant and he made his way swiftly to join what remained of his allies. They stepped through the portal one by one—first Elaine, then Fez, then Elaeínn. Caster stayed behind and summoned one last fireball, though his target was not Richard. He launched it at the section of intertwined rope where all the fuses had been tied together, and it burst into flame.

The world shook as he joined the others in escape.

CHAPTER 37

For almost a week Relía, Tolnír, and Zanvía had clung onto the hope that eventually, at last, a portal would take shape before their eyes and they would spring into action.

It didn't happen. They agreed to go their separate ways, leaving their cover and carrying on with their lives as usual, assuming the worst. Yet hope persisted, and Zanvía held on to the talisman and intended to do so until she found closure.

Closure didn't arrive all at once. Part of it arrived in the form of rumours. A crew of sailors and mages had travelled out to sea alongside the Prime Minister, and the Prime Minister had failed to return. This news was quick to circulate, and speculation about his death was rampant.

To Zanvía, it sounded like good news. She was glad Vanad was dead, but it was incomplete. Of the gossip which transpired, none of it could claim to be rooted in a reliable source. Nobody could claim with complete surety the cause of Vanad's death. And nothing was ever said about Elaeínn's fate, or the fact that she had ever been part of the crew at all.

"We need to move on," Relía said. Zanvía had met her and Tolnír at an inn on the outskirts of Sanaíd, away from the prying eyes of the Regal Guard. Still, they spoke in hushed tones, acutely paranoid of the possible presence of informants.

"She's the face of the resistance. Her and the dragon. What chance do we have without her?" Zanvía argued.

"The government is leaderless. The dwarves are without a king. The current state of affairs is unstable. Now is the perfect time to act—people will rise up, regardless of whether or not it's to rally behind Elaeínn and her dragon."

"They'll find a replacement for Vanad just as he was the replacement for Jaelaar. And the dwarves, if anything, gained the upper hand by losing their 'king'. Now that the elves have lost their direct line to the top of the dwarven chain of command, I see this war going in a very different direction."

"Why don't we just go south? To Telíana? Or any of the port cities? They hate the Nationals down there for reasons both ideological and economic. We would be safe to build on her legacy. She will be a martyr. People always fight for a martyr."

Zanvía felt a vibration in her pocket and knew at once its cause. She reached eagerly to grasp the talisman and presented it to the table, the symbols decorating its surface aglow with golden light. All doubts as to Elaeínn's survival were dispelled in that moment as a portal carved itself out of the air beside them.

It wasn't Elaeínn who appeared through the portal. It was a grey-skinned woman, and then a man, both with rounded ears but the statures of elves. Finally, Elaeínn made her appearance. She made no acknowledgement of the trio and their attempts at communication, wholly focused on the portal through which they could still see one adjacent individual, softly illuminated against a background of darkness. A fire lit in his hands and they watched as it burned through the air on the other side before he, too, stepped into the rundown Sanaían tavern.

From the portal then resonated an explosion with the volume and force of a thousand simultaneous cracks of thunder. And then, just as abruptly, the portal fell closed and with it came a smothering silence.

It was only at this moment that Elaeínn, bloodied and bedraggled, gave heed to the existence of Relía, Tolnír, and Zanvía.

"Hello again," she said with stoic calmness. "How would you like to accompany us in saving the world?"

CHAPTER 38

To be ripped from his sleep for a second time that night was not something Elton expected or appreciated. He appreciated it even less when the person banging against his front door gave up on knocking and, instead of leaving, forced their way in.

He picked up his dagger and slid into his chainmail before standing tensely by the door, confident it would hold, as it had for Hortensio, but ever paranoid of the slim possibility that it wouldn't. And then he heard Rosa's voice.

"Boss?" From one word, Elton picked up on a sense of distress. "I'm sorry. I'm so sorry."

He unlocked the door and opened it to see Rosa in a completely foreign state. Her cheeks were wet with tears, white in the moonlight streaming through Elton's window. She fell into Elton's arms like a child and he confusedly embraced her as she sobbed into his shoulder.

"I told them we shouldn't have gone without you! And I was stupid enough to go along with it anyways!"

"Slow down." Elton pressed her gently away, keeping his hands firmly on her shoulders. "What are you talking about?"

"We went to Letham Deregor. Without you," she explained. "I stayed here and kept the portal open, and everything was going fine, perfectly, too perfectly! And then it all went wrong and my portal was shut off and every time I tried to open another one it just wouldn't work and now..."

She trailed off and broke down into another round of sobs, falling back against Elton's shoulder.

Elton felt suddenly hollow. His skin was numb and he became acutely aware of his breathing, intensifying and quivering.

"Who went through the portal?" he enunciated, hardly aware of his own voice.

"All of them... Felix, Paul, Ant, Fez, the vampires, the elf..."

"And have any of them returned?"

Rosa provided her response without words as she withdrew from Elton's wet shoulder.

"You know what this means, Rosa?" Elton turned around and sauntered to the window. "He's going to destroy us. He's going to raze this city to the ground and then he's going to take the rest of the world with him. He's been playing until this point, but now we're a threat. We have actively attempted to kill him. To destroy his home. He won't stand for that."

He turned back around and barged out of the door, practically falling down the stairs with urgency. Rosa fell in pursuit, asking questions all the way, but Elton was not focused on her. He found two sturdy leather bags and began to fill them with essentials—food, water, wine, tobacco, clothes, money. He urged Rosa to do the same, and the pair had soon amassed enough resources to survive for weeks without human contact.

"We're leaving," Elton finally stated. "And we're going on horseback. You're not to utter a single spell, no matter how insignificant. That vampire will tear the world apart looking for us, and we won't give him any help."

The Count filed out of the front door and didn't bother to lock it. After locating the nearest stable, picking the lock to open its gates, he chose two of the healthiest-looking horses and equipped them with saddles and saddlebags, loading them up with the supplies he and Rosa had just gathered.

The city was silent as they left through the East Gate. Several individuals spotted and recognised them, but Elton paid them no attention, and received none in return.

They travelled through the night, for hours and hours without pause. The sun rose and still they continued, through the morning and into the afternoon. Neither Elton nor Rosa had an appetite.

It was only later that evening, as the horses began to exhibit signs of exhaustion, that they finally took a break. They had arrived at a little hamlet comprising no more than ten houses, with an inn and adjacent stable. The money they had brought was ample, and they paid for a place in the stables for the night before settling down for a meal and a drink.

Elton still didn't feel hungry but forced himself to pick at his meal when it arrived. He stared down at the table, moving his fork subconsciously between his plate and his mouth.

"Hello? Are you there?"

The bartender was standing next to the table, his head cocked and face dressed with scrutiny. Rosa stared idly into space as Elton realised the bartender had been trying to speak to him for some time.

"We're... we're fine, thank you," he muttered, taking an unenthused sip from his mug.

"Did you want a room for the night?" the bartender pressed. "It's near midnight."

"Um... yes. Thank you."

The bartender raised his eyebrows. "That'll be six marks, then."

Elton fished a coin of unknown denomination from his pocket, not thinking to check it, and handed it over. The bartender accepted it wordlessly and wandered away, returning briefly to hand over a key before disappearing again.

"What are we going to do, boss?" Rosa spoke for the first time since they had left Dannos. Her idle gaze remained uninterrupted.

"What are we going to do?" Elton echoed. A lengthy pause ensued as he mulled over how to continue. His eventual response was concise.

"I don't know."

CHAPTER 39

LETHAM DEREGOR

As the dust settled, Richard was finally able to open his eyes as his concentration fell from the spell protecting himself from the explosion. Beneath his feet stood the rubble of the atrium, a smouldering pile of refuse, the bodies of the vampires which once inhabited the ruined fortress buried beneath tonnes upon tonnes of stone.

He began his search without delay. In the milliseconds between the fireball's launch and the subsequent explosion, he had been unable to protect Kalahar with the spell he had used for himself. And so he worked through the day, turning over every last body.

Mounds of debris were lifted and discarded with great feats of telekinesis, great feats repeated time and time again as the day went on and drew to a close. Richard did not tire, neither physically nor mentally. He persevered through the night, assisted all the way by the dragon, though working without much in the way of active thought. His actions were not conscious, but he knew of no other option.

As he lifted a crippled pillar, tossing it with great velocity and toppling a section of nearby trees, he laid eyes upon a single silver link, glimmering in the moonlight. Like a frantic animal he dug away the surrounding rubble, forgoing the use of magic, and unveiled Kalahar's body. Without turning him over, Richard could see that his arms and legs were broken in several places, and he wasn't moving.

The bounty hunter wrestled the vampire from beneath a slab of what used to be the mezzanine and turned him over. His heart fell and he felt suddenly weak.

Kalahar was unrecognisable. In the collapse, his face had caved in under the weight of the falling stone. He was unmoving, even after Richard pulled him into the open.

"Kalahar?" his voice trembled. "Wake up. Wake up! This can't kill you, I know it can't kill you! Nothing can kill you!"

Tears welled in Richard's eyes and he fell to his knees. His eyes fell to his sword in its sheath.

I'm here.

"Kalahar!" The sorrow was replaced in an instant by joy and Richard looked back to the mangled body, expecting to see the vampire in his former state. That was not the case.

I have been wounded. But it is nothing time won't heal, Kalahar said, speaking only telepathically. *I need your help. It is now up to you to exact revenge on those who tried to kill us. Do you understand what I'm asking you to do?*

Richard nodded, and then, when Kalahar didn't respond, audibly said, "Yes."

And not just those who tried to kill us here. All who have stood in our way. Tregor Lopan. Nendar and Lynn Varanus. Every single person who ever served Elton Redwinter. And every fighter in the Free Tyen'Ael Army. Everyone associated with our enemies must perish alongside them. Only then will we be able to build a new world, Richard. A world where we can thrive, together. A world without bitter, endless conflict and strife. A world without suffering. A world without loss.

"I know what I have to do." Richard had never felt so assured in his life.

Take the dragon. Strike fear into their hearts. Let them know before they die that they made a mistake following the paths they did. Let the world know that a new era is beginning. And that you are its harbinger.

"What are you going to do? I need to get you somewhere safe!"

I will be safe as long as you are out there defeating our enemies. No harm will come to me, I promise. Now go.

The dragon seemed to understand what was happening and flattened itself as much as was possible against the uneven wreckage. Richard climbed onto its back and instructed it to lift into the air, its monstrous wings disturbing the settled dust as they soared into the sky.

Richard removed his hands from the dragon's spine and uttered the words to create a portal. Except he traced it with his mind, instead of with his hands.

The air tore open before them, a rift more than wide enough to fit the entire dragon. The bright sands of Dannos shone like a beacon in the night. The dragon knew not to hesitate and glided unhesitatingly through the portal.

A great shadow fell over the unsuspecting population as they descended. And then, upon Richard's command, the great shadow was lit up by the torrent of flame dispensed from the dragon's mouth.

The city burned and the people cried. And they continued to do so until there was nothing left.

End of book two